A *New York Times* Notable Book of the Year

P9-DVQ-641

"The speculative spin on a locked-room mystery would be enough to make it readable, but its setting gets it singing. Watts creates a meticulously solid environment into which he shanghais his dysfunctional heroes. . . . A satisfying, complex first outing."
>—*The Georgia Straight* (Choice of the Week)

"A gritty deep-sea tale . . . a restrained yet chilling sub-plot . . . Watts's evocation of the nightmarish claustro-phobia of Beebe Station is good, and he writes well and with authority about the weird beauty of the vents and their strange inhabitants. He's clearly in for the long haul."
>—Paul J. McAuley, *Interzone*

"Peter Watts bathes a gonzo hopeless-pessimism reminiscent of Philip K. Dick or Joanna Russ in the cold, edgy light of hard science fiction à la Benford, Bear, or Tiptree. It is a tribute to the brilliance of his writing and his intense evocation of character that the reader is willing to see the end of life on Earth as we know it as a satisfactory resolution to almost any of his stories, of which *Starfish* is the best to date. In *Starfish,* Watts creates in his protagonist a poetry of dysfunction which is angry and eerily redemptive, and which makes compelling, almost compulsive reading."
>—Candas Jane Dorsey

"I read *Starfish* in several large gulps. The story drives like a futuristic locomotive. It's a hypnotic read, somber and compelling. Best thing I've read in a long time. Peter Watts is an author to watch for."
>—Robert Sheckley

STARFISH

PETER WATTS

TOR®

A TOM DOHERTY ASSOCIATES BOOK
NEW YORK

This is a work of fiction. All the characters and events portrayed in this book are either products of the author's imagination or are used fictitiously.

STARFISH

Copyright © 1999 by Peter Watts

Edited by David G. Hartwell

A Tor Book
Published by Tom Doherty Associates, LLC
175 Fifth Avenue
New York, NY 10010

www.tor.com

Tor® is a registered trademark of Tom Doherty Associates, LLC.

ISBN: 0-812-57585-7
Library of Congress Catalog Card Number: 99-22967

First edition: July 1999
First mass market edition: February 2000

Printed in the United States of America

0 9 8 7 6 5 4 3 2 1

For Susan Oshanek,
on the off chance that she's still alive.

And for Laurie Channer—
who, to my unexpectedly good fortune, definitely is.

CONTENTS

PRELUDE

CERATIUS

THE abyss should shut you up.

Sunlight hasn't touched these waters for a million years. Atmospheres accumulate by the hundreds here, the trenches could swallow a dozen Everests without burping. They say life itself got started in the deep sea. Maybe. It can't have been an easy birth, judging by the life that remains—monstrous things, twisted into nightmare shapes by lightless pressure and sheer chronic starvation.

Even here, inside the hull, the abyss weighs on you like the vault of a cathedral. It's no place for trivial loud-mouth bullshit. If you speak at all, you keep it down. But these tourists just don't seem to give a shit.

Joel Kita's used to hearing a 'scaphe breathe around him, hearing it talk in clicks and hisses. He relies on those sounds; the readouts only confirm what the beast has already told him by the grumbling of its stomach. But *Ceratius* is a leisure craft, fully insulated, packed with excess headroom and reclining couches and little drink'n'drug dispensers set into the back of each seat. All he can hear today is the cargo, babbling.

He glances back over his shoulder. The tour guide, a mid-twenties Hindian with a zebra cut—Preteela someone—flashes him a brief, rueful smile. She's a relict, and she knows it. She can't compete with the onboard library, she doesn't come with 3-D animations or wrap-around soundtrack. She's just a prop, really. These people pay her salary not because she does anything useful, but because she doesn't. What's the point of being rich if you only buy the essentials?

There are eight of them. One old guy in a codpiece, still closing on his first century, fiddles with his camera controls. The others are plugged into headsets, running a program carefully designed to occupy them through the descent without being so impressive that the actual destination is an anticlimax. It's a thin line, these days.

Joel wishes this particular program was a bit better at holding the cargo's interest; they might shut up if they were paying more attention. They probably don't care whether Channer's sea monsters live up to the hype anyway. These people aren't down here because the abyss is impressive; they're here because it costs so much.

He runs his eyes across the control board. Even that seems excessive: climate control and in-dive entertainment take up a good half of the panel. Bored, he picks one of the headset feeds at random and taps in, sending the signal to a window on his main display.

An eighteenth-century woodcut of a kraken comes to life through the miracle of modern animation. Crudely rendered tentacles wrap around the masts of a galleon, pull it beneath chunky carved waves. A female voice, designed to maximize attention from both sexes: "We have always peopled the sea with monsters—"

Joel tunes out.

Mr. Codpiece comes up behind him, lays a familiar hand on his shoulder. Joel resists the urge to shrug it off. That's another problem with these tour subs: no real cockpit, just a set of controls at the front end of the passenger lounge. You can't shut yourself away from the cargo.

"Quite a layout," Mr. Codpiece says.

Joel reminds himself of his professional duties, and smiles.

"Been doing this run for long?" The whitecap's skin glows with a golden tan of cultured xanthophylls. Joel's smile grows a little more brittle. He's heard all about the benefits, of course: UV protection, higher blood oxygen, more energy—they say it even cuts down on your food requirements, not that any of these people have to worry about grocery money. Still, it's too bloody freakish for Joel's tastes. Implants should be made out of meat, or at least plastic. If people were meant to photosynthesize, they'd have leaves.

"I said—"

Joel nods. "Couple of years."

A grunt. "Didn't know Seabed Safaris was around that long."

"I don't work for Seabed Safaris," Joel says, as politely as possible. "I freelance." The whitecap probably doesn't know any better; comes from a generation when everyone pledged allegiance to the same master year after year. Nobody thought it was such a bad thing back then.

"Good for you." Mr. Codpiece gives him a fatherly pat on the shoulder.

Joel nudges the rudders a bit to port. They've been cruising just off the southeastern shoulder of the Ridge, floodlights doused; sonar shows a featureless landscape of mud and boulders. The rift itself is another five or ten minutes away. On the screen, the tourist program talks about giant squids attacking lifeboats during the Second World War, offers up a parade of archival photos as evidence: human legs, puckered with fist-sized conical wounds where horn-rimmed suckers cored out gobbets of flesh.

"Nasty. We going to be seeing any giant squids?"

Joel shakes his head. "Different tour."

The program launches into a litany of deepwater nasties: A piece of flesh washed up onto a Florida beach, hinting at the existence of octopus thirty meters across. Giant eel larvae. Hypothesized monsters that might once have fed on the great whales, anonymously dying out for lack of food.

Joel figures that ninety percent of this is bullshit, and the rest doesn't really count. Even giant squids don't go down into the *really* deep sea; hardly anything does. No food. Joel's been rooting around down here for years, and he's never seen any *real* monsters.

Except right here, of course. He touches a control; outside, a high-frequency speaker begins whining at the abyss.

"Hydrothermal vents bubble and boil along spreading zones in all of the world's oceans," the program chatters, "feeding crowds of giant clams and tubeworms over three meters long." Stock footage of a vent community. "And yet, even at the spreading zones, it is only the filter-feeders and muckrakers that become giants. The fish, vertebrates like ourselves, are few and far between—and only a few centimeters long." An eelpout wriggles feebly across the display, looking more like a dismembered finger than a fish.

"Except here," the program adds after a dramatic pause. "For there is something special about this tiny part of the Juan de Fuca Ridge, something unexplained. Here there be dragons."

Joel hits another control. External bait lights flash to life across the bioluminescent spectrum; the cabin lights dim. To the denizens of the rift, drawn in by the sonics, a veritable school of food fish has suddenly appeared in their midst.

"We don't know the secret of the Channer Vent. We don't know how it creates its strange and fascinating giants." The program's visual display goes dark. "We only know that here, on the shoulder of the Axial Volcano, we have finally tracked the monsters to their lair."

Something thumps against the outer hull. The acoustics of the passenger compartment make the sound seem unnaturally loud.

At last, the passengers shut up. Mr. Codpiece mutters something and heads back to his seat, a giant chloroplast in a hurry.

"This concludes our introduction. The external cameras are linked to your headsets and can be aimed using normal head movements. Focus and record using the joystick on your right armrest. You may also wish to enjoy the view directly, through any of the cabin viewports. If you require assistance, our guide and pilot are at your service. Seabed Safaris welcomes you to the Channer Vent, and hopes that you enjoy the remainder of your tour."

Two more thumps. A gray flash out the forward port; a sinuous belly caught for a moment in the headlight, a swirl of fin. On Joel's systems board, icons representing the outside cams dip and wiggle.

Superfluous Preteela slides into the copilot's seat. "Regular feeding frenzy out there."

Joel lowers his voice. "In here. Out there. What's the difference?"

She smiles; a safe, silent gesture of agreement. She's got a great smile. Almost makes up for the striped hair. Joel catches sight of something on the back of her left hand; looks like a ref tattoo, but somehow he doubts that it's authentic. Fashion statement, more likely.

"You sure they can spare you?" he asks wryly.

She looks back. The cargo's starting up again. *Look at that. Hey, it broke its tooth on us. Christ, aren't they ugly—*

"They'll manage," Preteela says.

Something looms up on the other side of the viewport: mouth like a sackful of needles, a tendril hanging from the lower jaw with a glowing bulb on the end. The jaw gapes wide enough to dislocate, snaps shut. Its teeth slide harmlessly across the viewport. A flat black eye glares in at them.

"What's that?" Preteela wants to know.

"You're the tour guide."

"Never seen anything like it before."

"Me neither." He sends a trickle of electricity out through the hull. The monster, startled, flashes off into the darkness. Intermittent impacts resonate through *Ceratius*, drawing renewed gasps from the cargo.

"How long until we're actually at Channer?"

Joel glances at tactical. "We're pretty much there already. Medium-sized hot fissure about fifty meters to the left."

"What's that?" A row of bright dots, evenly spaced, has just moved onto the screen.

"Surveyor's stakes." Another row marches into range behind the first. "For the geothermal program, you know?"

"How about a quick drive-by? I bet those generators are pretty impressive."

"I don't think the generators are in yet. They're just laying the foundations."

"It'd still make a nice addition to the tour."

"We're supposed to steer clear. We'd catch royal shit if anyone's out there."

"Well?" That smile again, more calculated this time. "Is there?"

"Probably not," Joel admits. Construction's been on hold for a couple of weeks, a fact which he finds particularly irritating; he's up for some fairly hefty contracts if the Grid Authority ever gets off its corporate ass and finishes what they started.

Preteela looks at him expectantly. Joel shrugs. "It's pretty unstable in there. Could get bumped around a bit."

"Dangerous?"

"Depends on your definition. Probably not."

"So let's do it." Preteela lays a conspiratorial hand briefly on his shoulder.

Ceratius noses around to a new heading. Joel kills the bait lights and cranks the sonics up for one screeching, farewell burst. The monsters outside—those that haven't already retired gracefully, their tiny fish brains having figured out that metal is inedible—run screaming into the night, lateral lines burning. There's a moment of surprised silence from the cargo. Preteela Someone steps smoothly into the gap. "Folks, we're taking a small detour to check out a new arrival on the rift. If you tap into the sonar feed you'll see that we're approaching a checkerboard of acoustic beacons. The Grid Authority has laid these out in the course of constructing one of the new geothermal stations we've been hearing so much about. As you may know, similar projects are under way at spreading zones all the way from the Galápagos to the Aleutians. When these go online, people will actually be living full-time here on the rift—"

Joel can't believe it. Preteela's big chance to scoop the library and she ends up talking exactly like it does. A fantasy gestating in his midbrain vanishes in a puff of smoke. Try to get into fantasy-Preteela's jumpsuit now, and she'd probably start reciting a cheery blow-by-blow.

He switches on the external floods. Mud. More mud. On sonar the grid crawls toward them, a monotonous constellation.

Something catches *Ceratius*, slews it around. The hull thermistor spikes briefly.

"Thermal, folks," Joel calls back over his shoulder. "Nothing to worry about."

A dim coppery sun resolves to starboard. It's a torch on a pole, basically, a territorial marker beating back the abyss with a sodium bulb and a VLF heartbeat. It's the Grid Authority, pissing on a rock for all and sundry: *This is* our *hellhole.*

The line of towers stretches away to port, each crowned by a floodlight. Intersecting it, another line recedes directly ahead like streetlights on a smoggy night. They shine down on a strange unfinished landscape of plastic and metal. Great metal casings lie against the bottom like derailed boxcars. Teardrop ROVs sit dormant on flat plastic puddles frozen harder than basalt. Sharp-edged conduits protrude from those congealed surfaces like hollow bones sawn off below the joint.

Way up on one of the port towers, something dark and fleshy assaults the light.

Joel checks the camera icons: all zoomed, pointing up and left. Preteela, conserving O_2, has retired her patter while the whitecaps gape. Fine. They want more mindless piscine violence, give 'em more mindless piscine violence. *Ceratius* angles up and to port.

It's an anglerfish. She bashes herself repeatedly against the floodlight, oblivious to *Ceratius*' approach. Her dorsal spine lashes; the lure at its end, a glowing worm-shaped thing, luminesces furiously.

Preteela's back at his shoulder. "It's really doing a number on that light, isn't it?"

She's right. The top of the transponder is shaking under the impact of the big fish's blows, which is odd; these beasts are big, but they aren't very strong. And come to think of it, the tower's moving back and forth even when the angler isn't touching it—

"Oh, *shit*." Joel grabs the controls. *Ceratius* rears up like something living. Transponder glow drops off the bottom of the viewport; total darkness drops in from above, swallowing the view. Startled shouts from the cargo. Joel ignores them.

On all sides, the dull distant sound of something roaring.

Joel hits the throttle. *Ceratius* climbs. Something slaps from behind; the stern slides to port, pulling the bow back after it. The blackness beyond the viewport boils sudden muddy brown against the cabin lights.

The hull thermistor spikes twice, three times. Ambient temperature flips from 4°C to 280, then back again. At lesser pressures *Ceratius* would be dropping through live steam. Here it only spins, skidding for traction against the superheated water.

Finally, it finds some. *Ceratius* ascends into welcome icewater. A fish skeleton pirouettes past the viewport, all teeth and spines, every vestige of flesh boiled away.

Joel looks back over his shoulder. Preteela's fingers are locked around the back of his seat, her knuckles the same color as the dancing bones outside. The cargo are dead quiet.

"Another thermal?" Preteela says in a shaky voice.

Joel shakes his head. "Seabed cracked open. It's really thin around here." He manages a brief laugh. "Told you things could get a bit unstable."

"Uh-huh." She releases her grip on Joel's chair. Fingernail imprints linger in the foam. She leans over, whispers, "Bring the cabin lights up a bit, will you? Sort of a nice living-room level. . . ." And then she's headed aft, tending the cargo: "Well, *that* was exciting. But Joel assures us that little blowups like this happen all the time. Nothing to be worried about, although they can catch you off guard."

Joel raises the cabin lights. The cargo sit quietly, still ostriched into their headsets. Preteela bustles among them, smoothing feathers. "And of course we still have the rest of our tour to look forward to. . . ."

He ups the gain on sonar, focuses aft. A luminous storm swirls across the tactical display. Beneath it, a fresh ridge of oozing rock disfigures the GA's construction grid.

Preteela is back at his elbow. "Joel?"

"Yeah."

"They say people are going to be *living* down there?"

"Uh-huh."

"Wow. Who?"

He looks at her. "Haven't you seen the PR threads? Only the best and the brightest. Holding back the everlasting night to stoke the fires of civilization."

"Seriously, Joel. Who?"

He shrugs. "Fucked if I know."

BENTHOS

DUET

Constrictor

WHEN the lights go out in Beebe Station, you can hear the metal groan.

Lenie Clarke lies on her bunk, listening. Overhead, past pipes and wires and eggshell plating, three kilometers of black ocean try to crush her. She feels the rift underneath, tearing open the seabed with strength enough to move a continent. She lies there in that fragile refuge and she hears Beebe's armor shifting by microns, hears its seams creak not quite below the threshold of human hearing. God is a sadist on the Juan de Fuca Ridge, and His name is Physics.

How did they talk me into this? she wonders. *Why did I come down here?* But she already knows the answer.

She hears Ballard moving out in the corridor. Clarke envies Ballard. Ballard never screws up, always seems to have her life under control. She almost seems *happy* down here.

Clarke rolls off her bunk and fumbles for a switch. The cubby floods with dismal light. Pipes and access panels crowd the wall beside her; aesthetics run a distant second to functionality when you're three thousand meters down. She turns and catches sight of a slick black amphibian in the bulkhead mirror.

It still happens, occasionally. She can sometimes forget what they've done to her.

It takes a conscious effort to feel the machines lurking where her left lung used to be. She's so acclimated to the chronic ache in her chest, to that subtle inertia of plastic and metal as she moves, that she's scarcely aware of them anymore. She can still feel the memory of what it was to be fully human, and mistake that ghost for honest sensation.

Such respites never last. There are mirrors everywhere in Beebe; they're supposed to increase the apparent size of one's personal space. Sometimes Clarke shuts her eyes to hide from the reflections forever being thrown back at her. It doesn't help. She clenches her lids and feels the corneal caps beneath them, covering her eyes like smooth white cataracts.

She climbs out of her cubby and moves along the corridor to the lounge. Ballard is waiting there, dressed in a diveskin and the usual air of confidence.

Ballard stands up. "Ready to go?"

"You're in charge," Clarke says.

"Only on paper." Ballard smiles. "No pecking order down here, Lenie. As far as I'm concerned, we're equals." After two days on the rift, Clarke is still surprised by the frequency with which Ballard smiles. Ballard smiles at the slightest provocation. It doesn't always seem real.

Something hits Beebe from the outside.

Ballard's smile falters. They hear it again; a wet, muffled thud through the station's titanium skin.

"It takes awhile to get used to," Ballard says, "doesn't it?"

And again.

"I mean, that sounds *big.* . . ."

"Maybe we should turn the lights off," Clarke suggests. She knows they won't. Beebe's exterior floodlights burn around the clock, an electric campfire pushing back the darkness. They can't see it from inside—Beebe has no windows—but somehow they draw comfort from the knowledge of that unseen fire—

Thud!

—Most of the time.

"Remember back in training?" Ballard says over the

sound. "When they told us that the fish were usually so—small. . . ."

Her voice trails off. Beebe creaks slightly. They listen for a while. There's no other sound.

"It must've gotten tired," Ballard says. "You'd think they'd figure it out." She moves to the ladder and climbs downstairs.

Clarke follows her, a bit impatiently. There are sounds in Beebe that worry her far more than the futile attack of some misguided fish. Clarke can hear tired alloys negotiating surrender. She can feel the ocean looking for a way in. What if it finds one? The whole weight of the Pacific could drop down and turn her into jelly. Any time.

Better to face it outside, where she knows what's coming. All she can do in here is wait for it to happen.

Going outside is like drowning, once a day.

Clarke stands facing Ballard, diveskin sealed, in an airlock that barely holds both of them. She has learned to tolerate the forced proximity; the glassy armor on her eyes helps a bit. *Fuse seals, check headlamp, test injector . . .* The ritual takes her, step by reflexive step, to that horrible moment when she awakens the machines sleeping within her, and *changes*.

When she catches her breath, and loses it.

When a vacuum opens, somewhere in her chest, that swallows the air she holds. When her remaining lung shrivels in its cage, and her guts collapse; when myoelectric demons flood her sinuses and middle ears with isotonic saline. When every pocket of internal gas disappears in the time it takes to draw a breath.

It always feels the same. The sudden, overwhelming nausea; the narrow confines of the airlock holding her erect when she tries to fall; seawater churning on all sides. Her face goes under; vision blurs, then clears as her corneal caps adjust.

She collapses against the walls and wishes she could scream. The floor of the airlock drops away like a gallows. Lenie Clarke falls writhing into the abyss.

They come out of the freezing darkness, headlights blazing, into an oasis of sodium luminosity. Machines grow everywhere at the Throat, like metal weeds. Cables and conduits spiderweb across the seabed in a dozen directions. The main pumps stand over twenty meters high, a regiment of submarine monoliths fading from sight on either side. Overhead floodlights bathe the jumbled structures in perpetual twilight.

They stop for a moment, hands resting on the line that guided them here.

"I'll never get used to it," Ballard grates in a caricature of her usual voice.

Clarke glances at her wrist thermistor. "Thirty-four Centigrade." The words buzz, metallic, from her larynx. It feels so *wrong* to talk without breathing.

Ballard lets go of the rope and launches herself into the light. After a moment, breathless, Clarke follows.

There's so much power here, so much wasted strength. Here the continents themselves do ponderous battle. Magma freezes; seawater boils; the very floor of the ocean is born by painful centimeters each year. Human machinery does not *make* energy, here at the Throat—it merely hangs on and steals some insignificant fraction of it back to the mainland.

Clarke flies through canyons of metal and rock, and knows what it is to be a parasite. She looks down. Shellfish the size of boulders, crimson worms three meters long crowd the seabed between the machines. Legions of bacteria, hungry for sulfur, lace the water with milky veils.

The water fills with a sudden terrible cry.

It doesn't sound like a scream. It sounds as though a great harp-string is vibrating in slow motion. But Ballard is screaming, through some reluctant interface of flesh and metal:

"LENIE—"

Clarke turns in time to see her own arm disappear into a mouth that seems impossibly huge.

Teeth like scimitars clamp down on her shoulder. Clarke stares into a scaly black face half a meter across. Some tiny, dispassionate part of her searches for eyes in that monstrous fusion of spines and teeth and gnarled flesh, and fails. *How can it see me?* she wonders.

Then the pain reaches her.

She feels her arm being wrenched from its socket. The creature thrashes, shaking its head back and forth, trying to tear her into chunks. Every tug sets her nerves screaming.

She goes limp. *Please get it over with if you're going to kill me just please God make it quick—* She feels the urge to vomit, but the 'skin over her mouth and her own collapsed insides won't let her.

She shuts out the pain. She's had plenty of practice. She pulls inside, abandoning her body to ravenous vivisection; and from far away she feels the twisting of her attacker grow suddenly erratic. There's another creature at her side, with arms and legs and a knife—*you know, a knife, like the one you've got strapped to your leg and completely forgot about*—and suddenly the monster is gone, its grip broken.

Clarke tells her neck muscles to work. It's like operating a marionette. Her head turns. She sees Ballard locked in combat with something as big as she is. Only—Ballard is tearing it to pieces, with her bare hands. Its icicle teeth splinter and snap. Dark icewater courses from its wounds, tracing mortal convulsions with smoke-trails of suspended gore.

The creature spasms weakly. Ballard pushes it away. A dozen smaller fish dart into the light and begin tearing at the carcass. Photophores along their sides flash like frantic rainbows.

Clarke watches from the other side of the world. The pain in her side keeps its distance, a steady, pulsing ache. She looks; her arm is still there. She can even move her fingers without any trouble. *I've had worse,* she thinks.

Then: *Why am I still alive?*

Ballard appears at her side; her lens-covered eyes shine like photophores themselves.

"Jesus Christ," Ballard says in a distorted whisper. "Lenie? You okay?"

Clarke dwells on the inanity of the question for a moment. But surprisingly, she feels intact. "Yeah."

And if not, she knows, it's her own damn fault. She just laid there. She just waited to die. She was asking for it.

She's always asking for it.

Back in the airlock, the water recedes around them. And within them: Clarke's stolen breath, released at last, races back along visceral channels, reinflating lung and gut and spirit.

Ballard splits the face seal on her 'skin and her words tumble into the wetroom. "Jesus. Jesus! I don't believe it! My God, did you see that thing? They get so huge around here!" She passes her hands across her face; her corneal caps come off, milky hemispheres dropping from enormous hazel eyes. "And to think they're usually just a few centimeters long . . ."

She starts to strip down, splitting her 'skin along the forearms, talking the whole time. "And yet it was almost fragile, you know? Hit it hard enough, and it just came apart! Jesus!" Ballard always removes her uniform indoors. Clarke suspects she'd rip the recycler out of her own thorax if she could, throw it in a corner with the 'skin and the eyecaps until the next time it was needed.

Maybe she's got her other lung in her cabin, Clarke muses. *Maybe she keeps it in a jar, and she stuffs it back into her chest at night . . .*

She feels a bit dopey; probably just an aftereffect of the neuroinhibitors her implants put out whenever she's outside. *Small price to pay to keep my brain from shorting out—I really shouldn't mind. . . .*

Ballard peels her 'skin down to the waist. Just under her left breast, the electrolyzer intake pokes out through her rib cage.

Clarke stares vaguely at that perforated disk in Ballard's flesh. *The ocean goes into us there,* she thinks. The old knowledge seems newly significant, somehow. *We suck it into us and steal its oxygen and spit it out again.*

Prickly numbness is spreading, leaking through her shoulder into her chest and neck. Clarke shakes her head, once, to clear it.

She sags suddenly, against the hatchway.

Am I in shock? Am I fainting?

"I mean—" Ballard stops, looks at Clarke with an expression of sudden concern. "Jesus, Lenie. You look terrible. You shouldn't have told me you were okay if you weren't."

The tingling reaches the base of Clarke's skull. "I'm . . . fine," she says. "Nothing broke. I'm just bruised."

"Garbage. Take off your 'skin."

Clarke straightens, with effort. The numbness recedes a bit. "It's nothing I can't take care of myself."

Don't touch me. Please don't touch me.

Ballard steps forward without a word and unseals the 'skin around Clarke's forearm. She peels back the material and exposes an ugly purple bruise. She looks at Clarke with one raised eyebrow.

"Just a bruise," Clarke says. "I'll take care of it, really. Thanks anyway." She pulls her hand away from Ballard's ministrations.

Ballard looks at her for a moment. She smiles ever so slightly.

"Lenie," she says, "there's no need to feel embarrassed."

"About what?"

"You know. Me having to rescue you. You going to pieces when that thing attacked. It was perfectly understandable. Most people have a rough time adjusting. I'm just one of the lucky ones."

Right. You've always been one of the lucky ones, haven't you? I know your kind, Ballard, you've never failed at anything.

"You don't have to feel ashamed about it," Ballard reassures her.

"I don't," Clarke says honestly. She doesn't feel much of anything anymore. Just the tingling. And the tension. And a vague sort of wonder that she's even alive.

The bulkhead is sweating.

The deep sea lays icy hands on the metal and, inside, Clarke watches the humid atmosphere bead and run down the wall. She sits rigid on her bunk under dim fluorescent light, every wall of the cubby within easy reach. The ceiling is too low. The room is too narrow. She feels the ocean compressing the station around her.

And all I can do is wait. . . .

The anabolic salve on her injuries is warm and soothing. Clarke probes the purple flesh of her arm with prac-

ticed fingers. The diagnostic tools in the Med cubby
have vindicated her. She's lucky, this time: bones intact,
epidermis unbroken. She seals up her 'skin, hiding the
damage.

She shifts on the pallet, turns to face the inside wall.
Her reflection stares back at her through eyes like frosted
glass. She watches the image, admires its perfect mimicry of each movement. Flesh and phantom move together, bodies masked, faces neutral.

That's me, she thinks. *That's what I look like now.*
She tries to read what lies behind that glacial facade. *Am
I bored, horny, upset?* How to tell, with her eyes hidden
behind those corneal opacities? She sees no trace of the
tension she always feels. *I could be terrified. I could be
pissing in my 'skin, and no one would know.*

She leans forward. The reflection comes to meet her.
They stare at each other, white to white, ice to ice. For
a moment, they almost forget Beebe's ongoing war
against pressure. For a moment, they don't mind the
claustrophobic solitude that grips them.

How many times, Clarke wonders, *have I wanted eyes
as dead as these?*

Beebe's metal viscera crowd the corridor beyond
Clarke's cubby. She can barely stand erect. A few steps
bring her into the lounge.

Ballard, back in shirtsleeves, is at one of the library
terminals. "Rickets," she says.

"What?"

"Fish down here don't get enough trace elements.
They're rotten with deficiency diseases. Doesn't matter
how fierce they are. They bite too hard, they break their
teeth on us."

Clarke stabs buttons on the food processor; the machine grumbles at her touch. "I thought there was all

sorts of food at the rift. That's why things got so big."

"There's a lot of food. Just not very good quality."

A vaguely edible lozenge of sludge oozes from the processor onto Clarke's plate. She eyes it for a moment. *I can relate.*

"You're going to eat in your gear?" Ballard asks, as Clarke sits down at the lounge table.

Clarke blinks at her. "Yeah. Why?"

"Oh, nothing. It would just be nice to talk to someone with pupils in their eyes, you know?"

"Sorry. I can take them off if you—"

"No, it's no big thing. I can live with it." Ballard turns off the library and sits down across from Clarke. "So, how do you like the place so far?"

Clarke shrugs and keeps eating.

"I'm glad we're only down here for a year," Ballard says. "This place could get to you after a while."

"It could be worse."

"Oh, I'm not complaining. I was looking for a challenge, after all. What about you?"

"Me?"

"What brings you down here? What are you looking for?"

Clarke doesn't answer for a moment. "I don't know, really," she says at last. "Privacy, I guess."

Ballard looks up. Clarke stares back, her face neutral.

"Well, I'll leave you to it, then," Ballard says pleasantly.

Clarke watches her disappear down the corridor. She hears the sound of a cubby hatch hissing shut.

Give it up, Ballard, she thinks. *I'm not the sort of person you really want to know.*

Almost start of the morning shift. The food processor disgorges Clarke's breakfast with its usual reluctance.

Ballard, in Communications, is just getting off the phone. A moment later she appears in the hatchway.

"Management says—" She stops. "You've got blue eyes."

Clarke smiles faintly. "You've seen them before."

"I know. It's just kind of surprising, it's been awhile since I've seen you without your caps in."

Clarke sits down with her breakfast. "So, what does Management say?"

"We're on schedule. Rest of the crew comes down in three weeks, we go online in four." Ballard sits down across from Clarke. "I wonder sometimes why we're not online right now."

"I guess they just want to be sure everything works."

"Still, it seems like a long time for a dry run. And you'd think that . . . well, that they'd want to get the geo-thermal program up and running as fast as possible, after all that's happened."

After Lepreau and Winshire melted down, you mean.

"And there's something else," Ballard says. "I can't get through to Piccard."

Clarke looks up. Piccard Station is anchored on the Galápagos Rift; it is not a particularly stable mooring.

"You ever meet the couple there?" Ballard asks. "Ken Lubin, Lana Cheung?"

Clarke shakes her head. "They went through before me. I never met any of the other rifters except you."

"Nice people. I thought I'd call them up, see how things were going at Piccard, but nobody can get through."

"Line down?"

"They say it's probably something like that. Nothing serious. They're sending a 'scaphe down to check it out."

Maybe the seabed opened up and swallowed them

whole, Clarke thinks. *Maybe the hull had a weak plate; one's all it would take—*

Something creaks, deep in Beebe's superstructure. Clarke looks around. The walls seem to have moved closer while she wasn't looking.

"Sometimes," she says, "I wish we didn't keep Beebe at surface pressure. Sometimes I wish we were pumped up to ambient. To take the strain off the hull." She knows it's an impossible dream; most gases kill outright when breathed at three hundred atmospheres. Even oxygen would do you in if it got above a fraction of a percent.

Ballard shivers dramatically. "If *you* want to risk breathing ninety-nine-percent hydrogen, you're welcome to it. I'm happy the way things are." She smiles. "Besides, you have any idea how long it would take to decompress afterward?"

In the Systems cubby, something bleats for attention.

"Seismic. Wonderful." Ballard disappears into Comm. Clarke follows.

An amber line is writhing across one of the displays. It looks like the EEG of someone caught in a nightmare.

"Get your eyes back in," Ballard says. "The Throat's acting up."

They can hear it all the way to Beebe; a malign, almost electrical hiss from the direction of the Throat. Clarke follows Ballard toward it, one hand running lightly along the guide rope. The distant smudge of light that marks their destination seems wrong somehow. The color is off. It *ripples*.

They swim into its glowing nimbus and see why. The Throat is on fire.

Sapphire auroras slide flickering across the generators. At the far end of the array, almost invisible with distance, a pillar of smoke swirls up into the darkness like a great tornado.

The sound it makes fills the abyss. Clarke closes her eyes for a moment, and hears rattlesnakes.

"Jesus!" Ballard shouts over the noise. "It's not supposed to *do* that!"

Clarke checks her thermistor. It won't settle; water temperature goes from four degrees to thirty-eight and back again, within seconds. Myriad ephemeral currents tug at them as they watch.

"Why the light show?" Clarke calls back.

"I don't know!" Ballard answers. "Bioluminescence, I guess! Heat-sensitive bacteria!"

Without warning, the tumult dies.

The ocean empties of sound. Phosphorescent spiderwebs wriggle dimly on the metal, and vanish. In the distance, the tornado sighs and fragments into a few transient dust devils.

A gentle rain of black soot begins to fall in the copper light.

"Smoker," Ballard says into the sudden stillness. "A *big* one."

They swim to the place where the geyser erupted. There's a fresh wound in the seabed, a gash several meters long, between two of the generators.

"This wasn't supposed to happen," Ballard says. "That's why they built here, for crying out loud! It was supposed to be stable!"

"The rift's never stable," Clarke replies. *Not much point in being here if it* was.

Ballard swims up through the fallout and pops an access plate on one of the generators. "Well, according to this, there's no damage," she calls down, after looking inside. "Hang on, let me switch channels here—"

Clarke touches one of the cylindrical sensors strapped

to her waist, and stares into the fissure. *I should be able to fit through there,* she decides.

And does.

"We were lucky," Ballard is saying above her. "The other generators are okay, too. Oh, wait a second; number two has a clogged cooling duct, but it's not serious. Backups can handle it until—*Get out of there!*"

Clarke looks up, one hand on the sensor she's planting. Ballard stares down at her through a chimney of fresh rock.

"Are you *crazy*?" Ballard shouts. "That's an active smoker!"

Clarke looks down again, deeper into the shaft. It twists out of sight in the mineral haze. "We need temperature readings," she says, "from inside the mouth."

"Get out of there! It could go off again and fry you!"

I suppose it could at that, Clarke thinks. "It already blew," she calls back. "It'll take awhile to build up a fresh head." She twists a knob on the sensor; tiny explosive bolts blast into the rock, anchoring the device.

"Get out of there, *now!*"

"Just a second." Clarke turns the sensor on and kicks up out of the seabed. Ballard grabs Clarke's arm as she emerges, starts to drag her away from the smoker.

Clarke stiffens and pulls free. *"Don't—" touch me!* She catches herself. "I'm out, okay? You don't have to—"

"Farther." Ballard keeps swimming. "Over here."

They're near the edge of the light now, the floodlit Throat on one side, blackness on the other. Ballard faces Clarke. "Are you out of your *mind*? We could have gone back to Beebe for a drone! We could have planted it on remote!"

Clarke doesn't answer. She sees something moving in the distance behind Ballard. "Watch your back," she says.

Ballard turns. The gulper undulates through the water like brown smoke, silent and endless; Clarke can't see the creature's tail, although several meters of serpentine flesh have come out of the darkness.

Ballard goes for her knife. After a moment, Clarke does too.

The gulper's jaw drops open like a great jagged scoop.

Ballard begins to launch herself at the thing, knife upraised.

Clarke puts her hand out. "Wait a minute. It's not coming at us."

The front end of the gulper is about ten meters distant now. Its tail pulls free of the murk.

"Are you crazy?" Ballard moves clear of Clarke's hand, still watching the monster.

"Maybe it isn't hungry," Clarke says. She can see its eyes, two tiny unwinking spots glaring at them from the tip of the snout.

"They're *always* hungry. Did you sleep through the briefings?"

The gulper closes its mouth and passes. It extends around them now, in a wide meandering arc. The head turns back to look at them. It opens its mouth.

"Fuck this," Ballard says, and charges.

Her first stroke opens a meter-long gash in the creature's side. The gulper stares at Ballard for a moment, as if astonished. Then, ponderously, it thrashes.

Clarke watches without moving. *Why can't she just let it go? Why does she always have to prove she's better than everything?*

Ballard strikes again; this time she slashes into a big tumorous swelling that has to be the stomach.

She frees the things inside.

They spill out through the wound: two giganturids and some misshapen creature Clarke doesn't recognize. One of the giganturids is still alive, and in a foul mood. It locks its teeth around the first thing it encounters.

Ballard. From behind.

"Lenie!" Ballard's knife hand is swinging in staccato arcs. The giganturid begins to come apart. Its jaws remain locked. The convulsing gulper crashes into Ballard and sends her spinning to the bottom.

Finally, Clarke begins to move.

The gulper collides with Ballard again. Clarke moves in low, hugging the bottom, and pulls the other woman clear.

Ballard's knife continues to dip and twist. The giganturid is a mutilated wreck behind the gills, but its grip remains unbroken. Ballard can't twist around far enough to reach the skull. Clarke comes in from behind and takes the creature's head in her hands.

It stares at her, malevolent and unthinking.

"Kill it!" Ballard shouts. "Jesus, what are you waiting for?"

Clarke closes her eyes, and clenches. The skull in her hand splinters like cheap plastic.

There is a silence.

After a while, she opens her eyes. The gulper is gone, fled back into darkness to heal or die. But Ballard's still there, and Ballard is angry.

"What's *wrong* with you?" she says.

Clarke unclenches her fists. Bits of bone and jellied flesh float about her fingers.

"You're supposed to back me up! Why are you so damned—*passive* all the time?"

"Sorry." *Sometimes it works.*

Ballard reaches behind her back. "I'm cold. I think it punctured my diveskin—"

Clarke swims behind her and looks. "A couple of holes. How are you otherwise? Anything feel broken?"

"It broke through the diveskin," Ballard says, as if to herself. "And when that gulper hit me, it could have—" She turns to Clarke and her voice, even distorted, carries a shocked uncertainty. "I could have been killed. I could have been *killed!*"

For an instant, it's as though Ballard's 'skin and eyes and self-assurance have all been stripped away. For the first time Clarke can see through to the weakness beneath, growing like a delicate tracery of hairline cracks.

You can screw up, too, Ballard. It isn't all fun and games. You know that now.

It hurts, doesn't it?

Somewhere inside, the slightest touch of sympathy. "It's okay," Clarke says. "Jeanette, it's—"

"You *idiot!*" Ballard hisses. She stares at Clarke like some malign and sightless old woman. "You just floated there! You just let it happen to me!"

Clarke feels her guard snap up again, just in time. *This isn't just anger,* she realizes. *This isn't just the heat of the moment. She doesn't like me. She doesn't like me at all.*

And then, dully surprised that she hasn't seen it before:

She never did.

A Niche

Beebe Station floats tethered above the seabed, a gunmetal-gray planet ringed by a belt of equatorial floodlights. There's an airlock for divers at the south pole and a docking hatch for 'scaphes at the north. In between there are girders and anchor lines, conduits and cables, metal armor and Lenie Clarke.

She's doing a routine visual check on the hull: standard procedure, once a week. Ballard is inside, testing some equipment in the Communications cubby. This is not entirely within the spirit of the buddy system. Clarke prefers it this way. Relations have been civil over the past couple of days—Ballard even resurrects her patented chumminess on occasion—but the more time they spend together, the more forced things get. Eventually, Clarke knows, something is going to break.

Besides, out here it seems only natural to be alone.

She's examining a cable clamp when a razormouth charges into the light. It's about two meters long, and hungry. It rams directly into the nearest of Beebe's floodlamps, mouth agape. Several teeth shatter against the crystal lens. The razormouth twists to one side, knocking the hull with its tail, and swims off until barely visible against the dark.

Clarke watches, fascinated. The razormouth swims back and forth, back and forth, then charges again.

The flood weathers the impact easily, doing more damage to its attacker. Over and over again the fish batters itself against the light. Finally, exhausted, it sinks twitching down to the muddy bottom.

"Lenie? Are you okay?"

Clarke feels the words buzzing in her lower jaw. She trips the sender in her diveskin: "I'm okay."

"I heard something out there," Ballard says. "I just wanted to make sure you were—"

"I'm fine," Clarke says. "Just a fish."

"They never learn, do they?"

"No. I guess not. See you later."

"See—"

Clarke switches off her receiver.

Poor stupid fish. How many millennia did it take for them to learn that bioluminescence equals food? How long will Beebe have to sit here before they learn that electric light doesn't?

We could keep our headlights off. Maybe they'd leave us alone—

She stares out past Beebe's electric halo. There is so

much blackness there. It almost hurts to look at it. Without lights, without sonar, how far could she go into that viscous shroud and still return?

Clarke kills her headlight. Night edges a bit closer, but Beebe's lights keep it at bay. Clarke turns until she's face-to-face with the darkness. She crouches like a spider against Beebe's hull.

She pushes off.

The darkness embraces her. She swims, not looking back, until her legs grow tired. She doesn't know how far she's come.

But it must be light-years. The ocean is full of stars.

Behind her, the station shines brightest, with coarse yellow rays. In the opposite direction, she can barely make out the Throat, an insignificant sunrise on the horizon.

Everywhere else, living constellations punctuate the dark. Here, a string of pearls blink sexual advertisements at two-second intervals. Here, a sudden flash leaves diversionary afterimages swarming across Clarke's field of view; something flees under cover of her momentary blindness. There, a counterfeit worm twists lazily in the current, invisibly tied to the roof of some predatory mouth.

There are so many of them.

She feels a sudden surge in the water, as if something big has just passed very close. A delicious thrill dances through her body.

It nearly touched me, she thinks. *I wonder what it was.* The rift is full of monsters who don't know when to quit. It doesn't matter how much they eat. Their voracity is as much a part of them as their elastic bellies, their unhingeable jaws. Ravenous dwarves attack giants twice their own size, and sometimes win. The abyss is a desert; no one can afford the luxury of waiting for better odds.

But even a desert has oases, and sometimes the deep

hunters find them. They come upon the malnourishing abundance of the rift and gorge themselves; their descendants grow huge and bloated over such delicate bones—

My light was off, and it left me alone. I wonder—

She turns it back on. Her vision clouds in the sudden glare, then clears. The ocean reverts to unrelieved black. No nightmares accost her. The beam lights empty water wherever she points it.

She switches it off. There's a moment of absolute darkness while her eyecaps adjust to the reduced light. Then the stars come out again.

They are so beautiful. Lenie Clarke rests on the bottom of the ocean and watches the abyss sparkle around her. And she almost laughs as she realizes, three thousand meters from the nearest sunlight, that it's only dark when the lights are on.

"What the hell is wrong with you? You've been gone for over three hours, did you know that? Why didn't you answer me?"

Clarke bends over and removes her fins. "I guess I turned my receiver off," she says. "I was—Wait a second, did you say—"

"You *guess*? Have you forgotten every safety reg they drilled into us? You're supposed to have your receiver on from the moment you leave Beebe until you get back!"

"Did you say *three hours*?"

"I couldn't even come out after you, I couldn't find you on sonar! I just had to sit here and hope you'd show up!"

It only seems a few minutes since she pushed off into the darkness. Clarke climbs up into the lounge, suddenly chilled.

"Where *were* you, Lenie?" Ballard demands, coming up behind her. Clarke hears the slightest plaintive tone in her voice.

"I—I must've been on the bottom," Clarke says. "That's why sonar didn't get me. I didn't go far."

Was I asleep? What was I doing for three hours?

"I was just—wandering around. I lost track of the time. I'm sorry."

"Not good enough. Don't do it again."

There's a brief silence. It's ended by the sudden, familiar impact of flesh on metal.

"Christ!" Ballard snaps. "I'm turning the externals off right now!"

Whatever it is gets in two more hits by the time Ballard reaches Comm. Clarke hears her punch a couple of buttons.

Ballard comes back into the lounge. "There. Now we're invisible."

Something hits them again. And again.

"Or maybe not," Clarke says.

Ballard stands in the lounge, listening to the rhythm of the assault. "They don't show up on sonar," she says, almost whispering. "Sometimes, when I hear them coming at us, I tune it down to extreme close range. But it looks right through them."

"No gas bladders. Nothing to bounce an echo off of."

"We show up just fine out there, most of the time. But not those things. You can't find them, no matter how high you turn the gain. They're like ghosts."

"They're not ghosts." Almost unconsciously, Clarke has been counting the beats: *eight—nine—*

Ballard turns to face her. "They've shut down Piccard," she says, and her voice is small and tight.

"What?"

"The Grid Authority says it's just some technical problem. But I've got a friend in Personnel. I phoned him when you were outside. He says Lana's in the hospital. And I get the feeling . . ." Ballard shakes her head. "It sounded like Ken Lubin did something down there. I think maybe he attacked her."

Three thumps from outside, in rapid succession. Clarke can feel Ballard's eyes on her. The silence stretches.

"Or maybe not," Ballard says. "We got all those personality tests. If he was violent, they would've picked it up before they sent him down."

Clarke watches her, listens to the pounding of an intermittent fist.

"Or maybe—maybe the rift *changed* him somehow. Maybe they misjudged the pressure we'd all be under. So to speak." Ballard musters a feeble smile. "Not the physical danger so much as the emotional stress, you know? Everyday things. Just being outside could get to you after a while. Seawater sluicing through your chest. Not breathing for hours at a time. It's like—living without a heartbeat."

She looks up at the ceiling; the sounds from outside are a bit more erratic now.

"Outside's not so bad," Clarke says. *At least you're incompressible. At least you don't have to worry about the plates giving in.*

"I don't think you'd change suddenly. It would just sort of sneak up on you, little by little. And then one day you'd just wake up changed, you'd be different somehow, only you'd never have noticed the transition. Like Ken Lubin."

She looks at Clarke, and her voice drops a bit.

"And you."

"Me." Clarke turns Ballard's words over in her mind, waits for the onset of some reaction. She feels nothing but her own indifference. "I don't think you have much to worry about. I'm not the violent type."

"I know. I'm not worried about my own safety, Lenie. I'm worried about yours."

Clarke looks at her from behind the impervious safety of her lenses, and doesn't answer.

"You've changed since you came down here," Ballard says. "You're withdrawing from me, you're exposing yourself to unnecessary risks. I don't know exactly what's happening to you. It's almost like you're trying to kill yourself."

"I'm not," Clarke says. She tries to change the subject. "Is Lana Cheung all right?"

Ballard studies her for a moment. She takes the hint. "I don't know. I couldn't get any details."

Clarke feels something knotting up inside her. "I wonder what she did to set him off?" she murmurs.

Ballard stares at her, openmouthed. "What *she* did? I can't believe you said that!"

"I only meant—"

"I know what you meant."

The outside pounding has stopped. Ballard does not relax. She stands hunched over in those strange, loose-fitting clothes that drybacks wear, and stares at the ceiling as though she doesn't believe in the silence. She looks back at Clarke.

"Lenie, you know I don't like to pull rank, but your attitude is putting both of us at risk. I think this place is really getting to you. I hope you can get back online here, I really do. Otherwise I may have to recommend you for a transfer."

Clarke watches Ballard leave the lounge. *You're lying,* she realizes. *You're scared to death, and it's not just because I'm changing.*

It's because you are.

———

Clarke finds out five hours after the fact: Something has changed on the ocean floor.

We sleep and the earth moves, she thinks, studying the topographic display. *And next time, or the time after, maybe it'll move right out from under us.*

I wonder if I'll have time to feel anything.

She turns at a sound behind her. Ballard is standing in the lounge, swaying slightly. Her face seems somehow disfigured by the concentric rings in her eyes, by the dark hollows around them. Naked eyes are beginning to look alien to Clarke.

"The seabed shifted," Clarke says. "There's a new outcropping about two hundred meters west of us."

"That's odd. I didn't feel anything."

"It happened about five hours ago. You were asleep."

Ballard glances up sharply. Clarke studies the haggard lines of her face. *On second thought . . .*

"I would've woken up," Ballard says. She squeezes past Clarke into the cubby and checks the topographic display.

"Two meters high, twelve long," Clarke recites.

Ballard doesn't answer. She punches commands into a key-board; the topographic image dissolves, reforms into a column of numbers.

"Just as I thought," she says. "No heavy seismic activity for over forty-two hours."

"Sonar doesn't lie," Clarke says calmly.

"Neither does seismo," Ballard answers.

There's a brief silence. There's a standard procedure for such things, and they both know what it is.

"We have to check it out," Clarke says.

But Ballard only nods. "Give me a moment to change."

———

They call it a squid: a jet-propelled cylinder about a meter long, with a headlight at the front end and a towbar at the back. Clarke, floating between Beebe and the seabed, checks it over with one hand. Her other hand grips a sonar pistol. She points the pistol into blackness; ultrasonic clicks sweep the night, give her a bearing.

"That way," she says, pointing.

Ballard squeezes down on her own squid's towbar. The machine pulls her away. After a moment Clarke follows. Bringing up the rear, a third squid carries an assortment of sensors in a nylon bag.

Ballard's traveling at nearly full throttle. The lamps on her helmet and squid stab the water like twin lighthouse beacons. Clarke, her own lights doused, catches up about halfway to their destination. They cruise along a couple of meters over the muddy substrate.

"Your lights," Ballard says.

"We don't need them. Sonar works in the dark."

"Are you breaking regs for the sheer thrill of it now?"

"The fish down here, they key on things that glow—"

"Turn your lights on. That's an order."

Clarke doesn't answer. She watches the beams beside her, Ballard's squid shining steady and unwavering, Ballard's headlamp slicing the water in erratic arcs as she moves her head—

"I told you," Ballard says, "turn your—*Christ!*"

It was just a glimpse, caught for a moment in the sweep of Ballard's headlight. She jerks her head around and it slides back out of sight. Then it looms up in the squid's beam, huge and terrible.

The abyss is grinning at them, teeth bared.

A mouth stretches across the width of the beam, extends into darkness on either side. It is crammed with conical teeth the size of human hands, and they do not look the least bit fragile.

Ballard makes a strangled sound and dives into the

mud. The benthic ooze boils up around her in a seething cloud; she disappears in a torrent of planktonic corpses.

Lenie Clarke stops and waits, unmoving. She stares transfixed at that threatening smile. Her whole body feels electrified, she's never been so explicitly aware of herself. Every nerve fires and freezes at the same time. She is terrified.

But she's also, somehow, completely in control of herself. She reflects on this paradox as Ballard's abandoned squid slows and stops itself, scant meters from that endless row of teeth. She wonders at her own analytical clarity as the third squid, with its burden of sensors, decelerates past and takes up position beside Ballard's.

There in the light, the grin does not change.

Clarke raises her sonar pistol and fires. *We're here,* she realizes, checking the readout. *That's the outcropping.*

She swims closer. The smile hangs there, enigmatic and enticing. Now she can see bits of bone at the roots of the teeth, and tatters of decomposed flesh trailing from the gums.

She turns and backtracks. The cloud on the seabed is starting to settle.

"Ballard," she says in her synthetic voice.

Nobody answers.

Clarke reaches down through the mud, feeling blind, until she touches something warm and trembling.

The seabed explodes in her face.

Ballard erupts from the substrate, trailing a muddy comet's tail. Her hand rises from that sudden cloud, clasped around something glinting in the transient light. Clarke sees the knife, twists almost too late; the blade glances off her 'skin, igniting nerves along her rib cage. Ballard lashes out again. This time Clarke catches the knife-hand as it shoots past, twists it, pushes. Ballard tumbles away.

"It's me!" Clarke shouts; the vocoder turns her voice into a tinny vibrato.

Ballard rises up again, white eyes unseeing, knife still in hand.

Clarke holds up her hands. "It's okay! There's nothing here! It's dead!"

Ballard stops. She stares at Clarke. She looks over to the squids, to the smile they illuminate. She stiffens.

"It's some kind of whale," Clarke says. "It's been dead a long time."

"A—a whale?" Ballard rasps. She begins to shake.

There's no need to feel embarrassed, Clarke almost says, but doesn't. Instead, she reaches out and touches Ballard lightly on the arm. *Is this how you do it?* she wonders.

Ballard jerks back as if scalded.

I guess not—

"Um, Jeanette—" Clarke begins.

Ballard raises a trembling hand, cutting Clarke off. "I'm okay. I want to g—I think we should get back now, don't you?"

"Okay," Clarke says. But she doesn't really mean it. She could stay out here all day.

Ballard is at the library again. She turns, passing a casual hand over the brightness control as Clarke comes up behind her; the display darkens before Clarke can see what it is. Clarke glances at the eyephones hanging from the terminal, puzzled. If Ballard doesn't want her to see what she's reading, she could just use those.

But then she wouldn't see me coming . . .

"I think maybe it was a Ziphiid," Ballard's saying. "A beaked whale. Except it had too many teeth. Very rare. They don't dive this deep."

Clarke listens, not really interested.

"It must have died and rotted farther up, and then sank." Ballard's voice is slightly raised. She looks almost furtively at something on the other side of the lounge. "I wonder what the chances are of that happening."

"What?"

"I mean, in all the ocean, something that big just happening to drop out of the sky a few hundred meters away. The odds of that must be pretty low."

"Yeah. I guess so." Clarke reaches over and brightens the display. One half of the screen glows softly with luminous text. The other holds the rotating image of a complex molecule.

"What's this?" Clarke asks.

Ballard steals another glance across the lounge. "Just an old biopsych text the library had on file. I was browsing through it. Used to be an interest of mine."

Clarke looks at her. "Uh-huh." She bends over and studies the display. Some sort of technical chemistry. The only thing she really understands is the caption beneath the graphic.

She reads it aloud: "True Happiness."

"Yeah. A tricyclic with four side chains." Ballard points at the screen. "Whenever you're happy, really happy, that's what does it to you."

"When did they find *that* out?"

"I don't know. It's an old book."

Clarke stares at the revolving simulacrum. It disturbs her somehow. It floats there over that smug stupid caption, and it says something she doesn't want to hear.

You've been solved, it says. *You're mechanical. Chemicals and electricity. Everything you are, every dream, every action, it all comes down to a change of voltage somewhere, or a—what did she say?—a tricyclic with four side chains—*

"It's wrong," Clarke murmurs. *Or they'd be able to fix us, when we broke down—*

"Sorry?" Ballard says.

"It's saying we're just these—soft computers. With faces."

Ballard shuts off the terminal.

"That's right," she says. "And some of us may even be losing those."

The gibe registers, but it doesn't hurt. Clarke straightens and moves toward the ladder.

"Where you going? You going outside again?" Ballard asks.

"The shift isn't over. I thought I'd clean out the duct on number two."

"It's a bit late to start on that, Lenie. The shift will be over before we're even half done." Ballard's eyes dart away again. This time Clarke follows the glance to the full-length mirror on the far wall.

She sees nothing of particular interest there.

"I'll work late." Clarke grabs the railing, swings her foot onto the top rung.

"Lenie," Ballard says, and Clarke swears she hears a tremor in that voice. She looks back, but the other woman is moving to Comm. "Well, I'm afraid I can't go with you," she's saying. "I'm in the middle of debugging one of the telemetry routines."

"Fine," Clarke says. She feels the tension starting to rise. Beebe's shrinking again. She starts down the ladder.

"Are you sure you're okay going out alone? Maybe you should wait until tomorrow."

"No. I'm okay."

"Well, remember to keep your receiver open. I don't want you getting lost on me again—"

Clarke is in the wetroom. She climbs into the airlock and runs through the ritual. It no longer feels like drowning. It feels like being born again.

———

She awakens into darkness, and the sound of weeping.

She lies there for a few minutes, confused and uncertain. The sobs come from all sides, soft but omnipresent in Beebe's resonant shell. She hears nothing else except her own heartbeat.

She's afraid. She's not sure why. She wishes the sounds would go away.

Clarke rolls off her bunk and fumbles at the hatch. It opens into a semi-darkened corridor; meager light escapes from the lounge at one end. The sounds come from the other direction, from deepening darkness. She follows them through an infestation of pipes and conduits.

Ballard's quarters. The hatch is open. An emerald readout sparkles in the darkness, bestowing no detail upon the hunched figure on the pallet.

"Ballard," Clarke says softly. She doesn't want to go in.

The shadow moves, seems to look up at her. "Why won't you show it?" it says, its voice pleading.

Clarke frowns in the darkness. "Show what?"

"You know what! How—afraid you are!"

"Afraid?"

"Of being here, of being stuck at the bottom of this horrible dark ocean—"

"I don't understand," Clarke whispers. Claustrophobia begins to stir in her, restless again.

Ballard snorts, but the derision seems forced. "Oh, you understand all right. You think this is some sort of competition, you think if you can just keep it all inside you'll win somehow—but it isn't like that at all, Lenie, it isn't helping to keep it hidden like this, we've got to be able to trust each other down here or we're lost—"

She shifts slightly on the bunk. Clarke's eyes, enhanced by the caps, can pick out some details now;

rough edges embroider Ballard's silhouette, the folds and creases of normal clothing, unbuttoned to the waist. She thinks of a cadaver, half-dissected, rising on the table to mourn its own mutilation.

"I don't know what you mean," Clarke says.

"I've tried to be friendly," Ballard says. "I've tried to get along with you, but you're so *cold*, you won't even admit—I mean, you *couldn't* like it down here, nobody could, why can't you just admit—"

"But I don't. I—I *hate* it in here. It's like Beebe's going to—to clench around me. And all I can do is wait for it to happen."

Ballard nods in the darkness. "Yes, yes, I know what you mean." She seems somehow encouraged by Clarke's admission. "And no matter how much you tell yourself—" She stops. "You hate it *in here*?"

Did I say something wrong? Clarke wonders.

"Outside is hardly any better, you know," Ballard says. "Outside is even worse! There's mudslides and smokers and giant fish trying to eat you all the time, you can't possibly—but—you don't mind all that, do you?"

Somehow, her tone has turned accusing. Clarke shrugs.

"No, you don't." Ballard is speaking slowly now. Her voice drops to a whisper: "You actually *like* it out there. Don't you?"

Reluctantly Clarke nods. "Yeah. I guess so."

"But it's so—The rift can kill you, Lenie. It can kill *us*. A hundred different ways. Doesn't that scare you?"

"I don't know. I don't think about it much. I guess it does, sort of."

"Then why are you so happy out there?" Ballard cries. "It doesn't make any sense. . . ."

I'm not exactly "happy," Clarke thinks. "I don't know. It's not that weird, lots of people do dangerous things. What about free-fallers? What about mountain-climbers?"

But Ballard doesn't answer. Her silhouette has grown rigid on the bed. Suddenly she reaches over and turns on the cubby light.

Lenie Clarke blinks against the sudden brightness. Then the room dims as her eyecaps darken.

"Jesus Christ!" Ballard shouts at her. "You *sleep* in that fucking costume now?"

It's something else Clarke hasn't thought about. It just seems easier.

"All this time I've been pouring my heart out to you and you've been wearing that *machine's* face! You don't even have the decency to show me your goddamned *eyes*!"

Clarke steps back, startled. Ballard rises from the bed and takes a single step forward. "To think you could actually pass for human before they gave you that suit! Why don't you go find something to play with out in your fucking ocean!"

And slams the hatch in Clarke's face.

Lenie Clarke stares at the sealed bulkhead for a few moments. Her face, she knows, is calm. Her face is usually calm. But she stands there, unmoving, until the cringing thing inside of her unfolds a little.

"Okay," she says at last, very softly. "I guess I will."

Ballard is waiting for her as she emerges from the airlock. "Lenie," she says quietly, "we have to talk. It's important."

Clarke bends over and removes her fins. "Go ahead."

"Not here. In my cubby."

Clarke looks at her.

"Please."

Clarke starts up the ladder.

"Aren't you going to take—" Ballard stops as Clarke looks down. "Never mind. It's okay."

They ascend into the lounge. Ballard takes the lead. Clarke follows her down the corridor and into her cabin. Ballard dogs the hatch and sits on her bunk, leaving room for Clarke.

Clarke looks around the cramped space. Ballard has curtained over the mirrored bulkhead with a spare sheet.

Ballard pats the bed beside her. "Come on, Lenie. Sit down."

Reluctantly, Clarke sits. Ballard's sudden kindness confuses her. Ballard hasn't acted this way since . . .

Since she had the upper hand.

"—might not be easy for you to hear," Ballard is saying, "but we have to get you off the rift. They shouldn't have put you down here in the first place."

Clarke doesn't reply.

"Remember the tests they gave us?" Ballard continues. "They measured our tolerance to stress: confinement, prolonged isolation, chronic physical danger, that sort of thing."

Clarke nods slightly. "So?"

"So," says Ballard, "did you think for a moment they'd test for those qualities without knowing what sort of person would have them? Or how they got to be that way?"

Inside, Clarke goes very still. Outside, nothing changes.

Ballard leans forward a bit. "Remember what you said? About mountain-climbers, and free-fallers, and why people deliberately do dangerous things? I've been reading up, Lenie. Ever since I got to know you I've been reading up—"

Got to know me?

"—and do you know what thrill-seekers have in common? They all say that you haven't lived until you've nearly died. They need the danger. It gives them a rush."

You don't know me at all—

"Some of them are combat veterans, some were hostages for long periods, some just spent a lot of time in dead zones for one reason or another. And a lot of the really compulsive ones—"

Nobody knows me.

"—the ones who can't be happy unless they're on the edge, all the time—a lot of them got started early, Lenie. When they were just children. And you, I bet . . . you don't even like being touched—"

Go away. Go away.

Ballard puts her hand on Clarke's shoulder. "How long were you abused, Lenie?" she asks gently. "How many years?"

Clarke shrugs off the hand and does not answer. *He didn't mean any harm.* She shifts on the bunk, turning away slightly.

"That's it, isn't it? You don't just have a tolerance to trauma, Lenie. You've got an *addiction* to it. Don't you?"

It only takes Clarke a moment to recover. The 'skin, the eyecaps make it easier. She turns calmly back to Ballard. She even smiles a little.

" 'Abused,' " she says. "Now *there's* a quaint term. Thought it died out after the Florida witch-hunts. You some sort of history buff, Jeanette?"

"There's a mechanism," Ballard tells her. "I've been reading about it. Do you know how the brain handles stress, Lenie? It dumps all sorts of addictive stimulants into the bloodstream. Beta-endorphins, opioids. If it happens often enough, for long enough, you get hooked. You can't help it."

Clarke feels a sound in her throat, a jagged coughing noise a bit like tearing metal. After a moment, she recognizes it as laughter.

"I'm not making it up!" Ballard insists. "You can look it up yourself if you don't believe me! Don't you know how many abused children spend their whole lives hooked on wife-beaters or self-mutilation or free-fall—"

"And it makes them happy, is that it?" Clarke says, still smiling. "They *enjoy* getting raped, or punched out, or—"

"No, of course you're not happy! But what *you* feel, that's probably the closest you've ever come. So you confuse the two, you look for stress anywhere you can find it. It's physiological addiction, Lenie. You ask for it. You always asked for it."

I ask for it. Ballard's been reading, and Ballard knows: Life is pure electrochemistry. No use explaining how it *feels.* No use explaining that there are far worse things than being beaten up. There are even worse things than being held down and raped by your own father. There are the times between, when nothing happens at all. When he leaves you alone, and you don't know for how long. You sit across the table from him, forcing yourself to eat while your bruised insides try to knit themselves back together; and he pats you on the head and smiles at you, and you know the reprieve's already lasted too long, he's going to come for you tonight, or tomorrow, or maybe the next day.

Of course I asked for it. How else could I get it over with?

"Listen." Clarke shakes her head. "I—" But it's hard to talk, suddenly. She knows what she wants to say; Ballard's not the only one who reads. Ballard can't see it through a lifetime of fulfilled expectations, but there's nothing special about what happened to Lenie Clarke. Baboons and lions kill their own young. Male stickle-backs beat up their mates. Even *insects* rape. It's not abuse, really, it's just—biology.

But she can't say it aloud, for some reason. She tries, and she tries, but in the end all that comes out is a challenge that sounds almost childish:

"Don't you know *anything*?"

"Sure I do, Lenie. I know you're hooked on your own pain, and so you go out there and keep daring the rift to kill you, and eventually it will, don't you see? That's why you shouldn't be here. That's why we have to get you back."

Clarke stands up. "I'm not going back." She turns to the hatch.

Ballard reaches out toward her. "Listen, you've got to stay and hear me out. There's more."

Clarke looks down at her with complete indifference. "Thanks for your concern. But I don't have to stay. I can leave anytime I want to."

"You go out there now and you'll give everything away—they're watching us! Haven't you figured it out *yet*?" Ballard's voice is rising. "Listen, they *knew* about you! They were *looking* for someone like you! They've been testing us, they don't know yet what kind of person works out better down here, so they're watching and waiting to see who cracks first! This whole program is still experimental, can't you see that? Everyone they've sent down—you, me, Ken Lubin, and Lana Cheung, it's all part of some cold-blooded test—"

"And you're failing it," Clarke says softly. "I see."

"They're *using* us, Lenie—*don't go out there!*"

Ballard's fingers grasp at Clarke like the suckers of an octopus. Clarke pushes them away. She undogs the hatch and pushes it open. She hears Ballard rising behind her.

"You're sick!" Ballard screams. Something smashes into the back of Clarke's head. She goes sprawling out into the corridor. One arm smacks painfully against a cluster of pipes as she falls.

She rolls to one side and raises her arms to protect herself. But Ballard just steps over her and stalks into the lounge.

I'm not afraid, Clarke notes, getting to her feet. *She hit me, and I'm not afraid. Isn't that odd—*

From somewhere nearby, the sound of shattering glass.

Ballard's shouting in the lounge. "The experiment's over! Come on out, you fucking ghouls!"

Clarke follows the corridor, steps out of it. Pieces of the lounge mirror hang like great jagged stalactites in their frame. Splashes of glass litter the floor.

On the wall, behind the broken mirror, a fisheye lens takes in every corner of the room.

Ballard is staring into it. "Did you hear me? I'm not playing your stupid games anymore! I'm through performing!"

The quartzite lens stares back impassively.

So you were right, Clarke muses. She remembers the sheet in Ballard's cubby. *You figured it out, you found the pickups in your own cubby, and Ballard, my dear friend, you didn't tell me.*

How long have you known?

Ballard looks around, sees Clarke. "You've got *her* fooled, all right," she snarls at the fisheye, "but *she's* a goddamned basket case! She's not even sane! Your little tests don't impress *me* one fucking bit!"

Clarke steps toward her.

"Don't call me a basket case," she says, her voice absolutely level.

"That's what you *are!*" Ballard shouts. "You're sick! That's why you're down here! They *need* you sick, they depend on it, and you're so far gone you can't see it! You hide everything behind that—that *mask* of yours, and you sit there like some masochistic jellyfish and just take anything anyone dishes out—you *ask* for it—"

That used to be true, Clarke realizes as her hands ball into fists. *That's the strange thing.* Ballard begins to back away; Clarke advances, step by step. *It wasn't until I came down here that I learned that I could fight back. That I could win. The rift taught me that, and now Ballard has, too—*

"Thank you," Clarke whispers, and hits Ballard hard in the face.

Ballard goes over backward, collides with a table. Clarke calmly steps forward. She catches a glimpse of herself in a glass icicle; her capped eyes seem almost luminous.

"Oh Jesus," Ballard whimpers. "Lenie, I'm *sorry.*"

Clarke stands over her. "Don't be," she says. She sees herself as some sort of exploding schematic, each piece neatly labeled. *So much anger in here,* she thinks. *So much hate. So much to take out on someone.*

She looks at Ballard, cowering on the floor.

"I think," Clarke says, "I'll start with you."

But her therapy ends before she can even get properly warmed up. A sudden noise fills the lounge—shrill, periodic, vaguely familiar. It takes a moment for Clarke to remember what it is. She lowers her foot.

Over in the Communications cubby, the telephone is ringing.

Jeanette Ballard is going home today.

For half an hour the 'scaphe has been dropping deeper into midnight. Now the Comm monitor shows it settling like a great bloated tadpole onto Beebe's docking assembly. Sounds of mechanical copulation reverberate and die. The overhead hatch drops open.

Ballard's replacement climbs down, already mostly 'skinned, staring impenetrably from eyes without pupils. His gloves are off; his 'skin is open up to the forearms.

Clarke sees the faint scars running along his wrists, and smiles a bit inside.

Was there another Ballard up there, waiting, she wonders, *in case I had been the one who didn't work out?*

Out of sight down the corridor, a hatch hisses open. Ballard appears in shirtsleeves, one eye swollen shut, carrying a single suitcase. She seems about to say something, but stops when she sees the newcomer. She looks at him for a moment. She nods briefly. She climbs into the belly of the 'scaphe without a word.

Nobody calls down to them. There are no salutations, no morale-boosting small talk. Perhaps the crew has been briefed. Perhaps they've figured it out on their own. The docking hatch swings shut. With a final clank, the 'scaphe disengages.

Clarke walks across the lounge and looks into the camera. She reaches between mirror fragments and rips its power line from the wall.

We don't need this anymore, she thinks, and she knows that somewhere far away, someone agrees.

She and the newcomer appraise each other with dead white eyes.

"I'm Lubin," he says at last.

Housecleaning

So. They say you're a beater.

Lubin stands in front of her, his duffel bag at his feet. Slavic; dark hair, pale skin, a face planed out by an underskilled woodworker. One thick eyebrow shading both eyes. Not tall—a hundred and eighty centimeters, maybe—but solid.

You look like a beater.

Scars. Not just on the wrists, on the face, too. Very faint, a webwork echo of old injuries. Too subtle for deliberate decoration, even if Lubin's tastes run to that, but too obvious for reconstructive work; medical technology learned how to erase such telltales decades ago. Unless—unless the injuries were *really* bad.

Is that it? Did something chew your face down to the bone, a long time ago?

Lubin reaches down, picks up his bag. His covered eyes betray nothing.

I've known beaters in my day. You fit. Sort of.

"Any preference which cubby I take?" he asks. It's strange, hearing that voice coming out of a face like his. It sounds almost pleasant.

Clarke shakes her head. "I'm second on the right. Take any of the others."

He steps past her. Daggers of reflective glass protrude from the edges of the far wall; within them, Lubin's fractured image disappears into the corridor at Clarke's back. She moves across the lounge to that jagged wall. *I should really clean this up one of these days . . . .*

She used to like the way the mirrors worked since Ballard's adjustments. The jigsaw reflections seem more creative, somehow. More impressionistic. Now, though, they're beginning to wear on her. Maybe it's time for another change.

A piece of Ken Lubin stares at her from the wall. Without thinking, she drives her fist into the glass. A shower of fragments tinkles to the floor.

You could be a beater. Just try it. Just fucking try it.

"Oh," Lubin says, behind her. "I—"

There's still enough mirror left to check; her face is free of any expression. She turns to face him.

"I'm sorry if I startled you," Lubin says quietly, and withdraws.

He does seem sorry, at that.

So. You're not a beater. Clarke leans against the bulkhead. *At least, not my kind of beater.* She's not exactly sure how she knows. There's some vital chemistry missing between them. Lubin, she thinks, is a very dangerous man. Just not to her.

She smiles to herself. *Beating means never having to say you're sorry.*

Until it's too late, of course.

She's tired enough of sharing the cubby with herself. Sharing it with someone else is something she likes even less.

Lenie Clarke lies on her bunk and scans the length of her own body. Past her toes, another Lenie Clarke stares coolly back. The jumbled topography of the forward bulkhead frames her reflected face like a tabletop junkyard turned on edge.

The camera behind that mirror must see the same thing she does, but distorted around the edges. Clarke figures on a wide-angle lens; the GA wouldn't want to leave the corners out of range. What's the point of running an experiment if you can't keep tabs on your subject animals?

She wonders if anyone's watching her now. Probably not; at least, nobody human. They'll have some machine, tireless and dispassionate, something that watches with relentless attention as she works or shits or gets herself off. It will be programmed to call flesh and blood if she does anything interesting.

Interesting. Who defines that parameter? Is it strictly in keeping with the nature of the experiment, or has someone programmed more personal tastes on the side? Does anyone else get off when Lenie Clarke does?

She twists on the bed and faces the headboard bulkhead. A spaghetti bundle of optical filaments erupts from the floor beside her pallet and crawls up the middle of the wall, disappearing into the ceiling; the seismic feeds, on their way to the Communications cubby. The air-conditioning inlet sighs across her cheek, just to one side. Behind it, a metal iris catches strips of light sectioned by the grating, ready to sphincter shut the moment delta-p exceeds some critical number of millibars per second. Beebe is a mansion with many rooms, each potentially self-isolating in case of emergency.

Clarke lies back on the bunk and lets her fingers drop to the deck. The telemetry cartridge on the floor is almost dry now, fine runnels of salt crusting its surface as the seawater evaporates. It's a basic broad-spectrum model, studded with half a dozen senses: seismic, temperature, flow, the usual sulfates and organics. Sensor heads disfigure its housing like the spikes on a mace.

Which is why it's here, now.

She closes her fingers around the carrying handle, lifts the cartridge off the deck. Heavy. Neutrally buoyant in seawater, of course, but 9.5 kilos in atmosphere, according to the specs. Mostly pressure casing, very tough. An active smoker at five hundred atmospheres wouldn't touch it.

Maybe it's a bit of overkill, sending it up against one lousy mirror. Ballard started the job with her bare hands, after all.

Odd that they didn't make them shatterproof.

But convenient.

Clarke sits up, hefting the cartridge. Her reflection looks back at her; its eyes, blank but not empty, seem somehow amused.

"Ms. Clarke? You okay?" It's Lubin. "I heard—"

"I'm fine," she says to the sealed hatch. There's glass all over the cubby. One stubborn shard, half a meter long, hangs in its frame like a loose tooth. She reaches out (mirror fragments tumble off her thighs) and taps it with one hand. It crashes to the deck and shatters.

"Just housecleaning," she calls.

Lubin says nothing. She hears him move away up the corridor.

He's going to work out fine. It's been a few days now and he's been scrupulous about keeping his distance. There's no sexual chemistry at all, nothing to set them at each other's throats. Whatever Ken Lubin did to Lana Cheung—whatever those two did to each other—won't be an issue here. Lubin's tastes are too specific.

For that matter, so are Clarke's.

She stands up, head bent to avoid the metal encrustations on the ceiling. Glass crunches under her feet. The bulkhead behind the mirror, freshly exposed, looks oily in the fluorescent light; a ribbed gray face with only two distinguishing features. The first is a spherical lens, smaller than a fingernail, tucked up in one corner. Clarke pulls it from its socket, holds it between thumb and forefinger for a second. A tiny glass eyeball. She drops it to the glittering deck.

There's also a name, stamped into one of the alloy ribs: HANSEN FABRICATION.

It's the first time she's seen a brand name since she arrived here, except for the GA logos pressed into the shoulders of their diveskins. That seems odd somehow. She checks the lightstrip running the length of the ceiling: white and featureless. An emergency hydrox tank next to the hatch: DOT test date, pressure specs, but no manufacturer.

She doesn't know if she should attach any significance to this.

Alone, now. Hatch sealed, surveillance ended—even her own reflection shattered beyond repair. For the first time, Lenie Clarke feels a sense of real safety here in the station's belly. She doesn't quite know what to do with it.

Maybe I could let my guard down a bit. Her hands go to her face.

At first she thinks she's gone blind; the cubby seems so dark to her uncapped eyes, walls and furniture receding into mere suggestions of shadow. She remembers turning the lights down in increments in the days since Ballard's departure, darkening this room, darkening every other corner of Beebe Station. Lubin's been doing it too, although they never talk about it.

For the first time she wonders at their actions. It doesn't make sense; eyecaps compensate automatically for changes in ambient light, always serve up the same optimum intensity to the retina. Why choose to live in a darkness you don't even perceive?

She nudges the lights up a bit; the cubby brightens. Bright colors jar the eye against a background of gray on gray. The hydrox tank reflects fluorescent orange; readouts wink red and blue and green; the handle on the bulkhead locker is a small exclamation of yellow. She can't remember the last time she noticed color; eyecaps draw the faintest images from darkness, but most of the spectrum gets lost in the process. Only now, when the lights are up, can color reassert itself.

She doesn't like it. It seems raw and out of place down here. Clarke puts her eyecaps back in, dims the lights to their usual minimal glow. The bulkhead fades to a comforting wash of blue pastels.

Just as well. Shouldn't get too careless anyway.

In a couple of days Beebe will be crawling with a full staff. She doesn't want to get used to exposing herself.

Neotenous

IT didn't look human at first. It didn't even look alive. It looked like a pile of dirty rags someone had thrown against the base of the Cambie pylon. Gerry Fischer wouldn't have looked twice if the Skytrain hadn't hissed overhead at exactly the right moment, strobing the ground with segmented strips of light.

He stared. Eyes, flashing in and out of shadow, stared back.

He didn't move until the train had slid away along its overhead track. The world fell back into muddy low contrast. The sidewalk. The strip of kudzu$_4$ below the track, gray and suffocating under countless drizzlings of concrete dust. Feeble cloudbank reflections of neon and laser from Commercial.

And this thing with the eyes, this rag pile against the pylon. A boy.

A young boy.

This is what you do when you really love someone, Shadow always said. *After all, the kid could* die *out here.*

"Are you okay?" he said at last.

The pile of rags shifted a little, and whimpered.

"It's okay. I won't hurt you."

"I'm lost," it said, in a very strange voice.

Fischer took a step forward. "You a ref?" The nearest refugee strip was over a hundred kilometers away, and well guarded, but sometimes someone would get out.

The eyes swung from side to side: *no.*

But then, Fischer thought, *what else would he say? Maybe he's afraid I'll turn him in.*

"Where do you live?" he asked, and listened closely to the answer:

"Orlando."

No hint of Asian or Hindian in that voice. Back when Fischer was a kid his mom would always tell him that disasters were color-blind, but he knew better now. The kid sounded N'Am; not a ref, then. Which meant there would probably be people looking for him.

Which, in a way, was too—

Stop it.

"Orlando," he repeated aloud. "You *are* lost. Where's your mom and dad?"

"Hotel." The rag pile detached itself from the pylon and shuffled closer. "Vanceattle." The words came out half-whistled, as though the kid was speaking through his sinuses. Maybe he had one of those, those—Fischer groped for the words—cleft palates, or something.

"Vanceattle? Which one?"

Shrug.

"Don't you have a watch?"

"Lost it."

You've got to help him, Shadow said.

"Well, um, look." Fischer rubbed at his temples. "I live close by. We can call from there."

There weren't that many Vanceattles in the lower mainland. The police wouldn't have to find out. And even if they did, they wouldn't charge him. Not for this. What was he supposed to do, leave the kid for body parts?

"I'm Gerry," Fischer said.

"Kevin."

Kevin looked about nine or ten. Old enough that he should know how to use a public terminal, anyway. But there was something wrong with him. He was too tall and skinny, and his limbs tangled up in themselves when he walked. Maybe he was brain-damaged. Maybe one of those nanotech babies that went bad. Or maybe his mother just spent too much time outdoors when she was pregnant.

Fischer led Kevin up to his two-room timeshare. Kevin dropped onto the couch without asking. Fischer checked the fridge: root beer. The boy took it with a nervous smile. Fischer sat down beside him and put a reassuring hand on Kevin's lap.

The expression drained from Kevin's face as though someone had pulled a plug.

Go *on*, Shadow said. He's not complaining, is he?

Kevin's clothes were filthy. Caked mud clung to his pants. Fischer reached over and began picking it off. "We should get you out of these clothes. Get you cleaned up. We can only take showers on even days here, but you could always take a sponge bath . . ."

Kevin just sat there. One hand gripped his drink, bony fingers denting the plastic; the other rested motionless on the couch.

Fischer smiled. "It's okay. This is what you do when you really—"

Kevin stared at the floor, trembling.

Fischer found a zipper, pulled. Pressed, gently. "It's okay. It's okay. Don't worry."

Kevin stopped shaking. Kevin looked up.

Kevin smiled.

"I'm not the one who should be worried here, asshole," he said in his whistling child's voice.

The jolt threw Fischer to the floor. Suddenly he was staring at the ceiling, fingers twitching at the ends of arms that had turned, magically, into dead weights. His whole nervous system sang like a tracery of high-tension wires embedded in flesh.

His bladder let go. Wet warmth spread out from his crotch.

Kevin stepped over him and looked down, all trace of

awkwardness gone from his movements. One hand still held the plastic cup. The other held a shockprod. ·

Very deliberately, Kevin upended his drink. Fischer watched the liquid snake down, almost casually, and splash across his face. His eyes stung; Kevin was a spindly blur in a wash of weak acid. Fischer tried to blink, tried again, finally succeeded.

One of Kevin's legs was swinging back at the knee.

"Gerald Fischer, you are under arrest—"

It swung forward. Pain erupted in Fischer's side.

"—for indecent assault of a minor—"

Back. Forward. Pain.

"—under Sections 151 and 152 of the N'Am Pacific Criminal Code."

The child knelt down and glared into his face. Up close the telltales were obvious; the depth of the eyes, the size of the pores in the skin, the plastic resilience of adult flesh soaked in androgen suppressants.

"Not to mention violation of yet *another* restraining order," Kevin added.

How long? Fischer wondered absently. Neural aftershock draped the whole world in gauze. *How many months did it take to stunt back down from man to child?*

"You have the right to—Ah, fuck."

And how long to reverse the reversal? Could·Kevin ever grow up again?

"You know your fucking rights better than I do."

This wasn't happening. The police wouldn't go this far, they didn't have the money, and anyway, why? How could anyone be willing to *change* themselves like that? Just to get Gerry Fischer? Why?

"I suppose I should call you in, shouldn't I? Then again, maybe I'll just let you lie here in your own piss for a while . . ."

Somehow, he got the feeling that Kevin was hurting more than he was. It didn't make sense.

It's okay, Shadow told him softly. It's not your fault. They just don't understand.

Kevin was kicking him again, but Fischer could hardly feel it. He tried to say something, anything, that would make his tormentor feel a little better, but his motor nerves were still fried.

He could cry, though. Different wiring.

It was different this time. It started out the same, the scans and the samples and the beatings, but then they took him out of the line and cleaned him up, and put him in a side room. Two guards sat him down at a table, across from a dumpy little man with brown moles all over his face.

"Hello, Gerry," he said, pretending not to notice Fischer's injuries. "I'm Dr. Scanlon."

"You're a shrink."

"Actually, I'm more of a mechanic." He smiled, a prissy little smile that said, *I've just been very clever but you're probably too stupid to get the joke.* Fischer decided he didn't like Scanlon much.

Still, his type had been useful before, with all their talk about *"competence"* and *"criminal responsibility."* It's not so much what you did, Fischer had learned, as why you did it. If you did things because you were evil, you were in real trouble. If you did the same things because you were sick, though, the doctors would sometimes cover for you. Fischer had learned to be sick.

Scanlon pulled a headband out of his breast pocket. "I'd like to talk to you for a little while, Gerry. Would you mind putting this on for me?"

The inside of the band was studded with sensor pads. It felt cool across his forehead. Fischer looked around the room, but he couldn't see any monitors or readouts.

"Great." Scanlon nodded to the guards. He waited until they'd left before he spoke again.

"You're a strange one, Gerry Fischer. We don't run into too many like you."

"That's not what the other doctors said."

"Oh? What did they say?"

"They said I was typical. They said, they said lots of the 151s used the same *rationale*."

Scanlon leaned forward. "Well, you know, that's true. It's a classic line: 'I was teaching her about her awakening sexuality, Doctor.' 'It's the parents' job to instruct their children, Doctor.' 'They don't like school, either, but it's for their own good.' "

"I never said those things. I don't even have kids."

"No, you don't. But the point is, pedophiles often claim to be acting in the best interests of the children. They turn sexual abuse into an act of altruism, if you will."

"It's *not* abuse. It's what you do if you really love someone."

Scanlon leaned back in his chair and studied Fischer for a few moments.

"That's what's so interesting about you, Gerry."

"What?"

"Everyone *uses* that line. You're the only person I've met who might actually *believe* it."

In the end, they said they could take care of the charges. He knew there had to be more to it than that, of course; they'd make him volunteer for some sort of experiment, or donate some of his organs, or submit to voluntary castration first. But the catch, when it came, wasn't any of those things. He almost couldn't believe it.

They wanted to give him a job.

"Think of it as community service," Scanlon said.

"Restitution to all of society. You'd be underwater most of the time, but you'd be well-equipped."

"Underwater where?"

"Channer Vent. About forty kilometers north of the Axial Volcano, on the Juan de Fuca Ridge. Do you know where that is, Gerry?"

"How long?"

"One year, minimum. You could extend that if you wanted to."

Fischer couldn't think of any reason why he would, but it didn't matter. If he didn't take this deal they'd stick a governor in his head for the rest of his life. Which might not be that long, when you thought about it.

"One year," he said. "Underwater."

Scanlon patted his arm. "Take your time, Gerry. Think about it. You don't have to decide until this afternoon."

Do it, Shadow urged. Do it or they'll cut into you and you'll *change*.

But Fischer wasn't going to be rushed. "So what do I do for one year, underwater?"

Scanlon showed him a vid.

"Jeez," Fischer said. "I can't do any of that."

"No problem." Scanlon smiled. "You'll learn."

He did, too.

A lot of it happened while he was sleeping. Every night they'd give him an injection, to help him learn, Scanlon said. Afterward a machine beside his bed would feed him dreams. He could never exactly remember them but something must have stuck, because every morning he'd sit at the console with his tutor—a real person, though, not a program—and all the text and diagrams she showed him would be strangely familiar. Like he'd known it all years ago, and had just forgotten. Now he remembered everything: plate tectonics and subduction zones, Archimedes Principle, the thermal conductivity of two-percent hydrox. Aldosterone.

Alloplasty.

He remembered his left lung after they cut it out, and the technical specs on the machines they put in its place.

Afternoons, they'd attach leads to his body and saturate his striated muscles with low-amp current. He was starting to understand what was going on now; the term was *"induced isometrics,"* and its meaning had come to him in a dream.

A week after the operation he woke up with a fever.

"Nothing to worry about," Scanlon told him. "That's just the last stage of your infection."

"Infection?"

"We shot you up with a retrovirus the day you came here. Didn't you know?"

Fischer grabbed Scanlon's arm. "Like a disease? You—"

"It's perfectly safe, Gerry." Scanlon smiled patiently, disentangling himself. "In fact, you wouldn't last very long down there without it; human enzymes don't work well at high pressure. So we loaded some extra genes into a tame virus and sent it in. It's been rewriting you from the inside out. Judging by your fever I'd say it's nearly finished. You should be feeling better in a day or so."

"Rewriting?"

"Half your enzymes come in two flavors now. They got the genes from one of those deepwater fish. Rattails, I think they're called." Scanlon patted Fischer on the shoulder. "So how does it feel to be part fish, Gerry?"

"Coryphaenoides armatus," Fischer said slowly.

Scanlon frowned. "What was that?"

"Rattails." Fischer concentrated. "Mostly dehydrogenases, right?"

Scanlon glanced at the machine by the bed. "I'm, um, not sure."

"That's it. Dehydrogenases. But they tweaked them to reduce the activation energy." He tapped his temple. "It's all here. Only I haven't done the tutorial yet."

"That's great," Scanlon said; but he didn't sound like he meant it.

One day they put him in a tank built like a piston, five stories tall; its roof could press down like a giant hand, squeezing whatever was inside. They sealed the hatch and flooded the tank with seawater.

Scanlon had warned him about the change. "We flood your trachea and your head cavities, but your lung and intestines aren't rigid so they just squeeze down. We're immunizing you against pressure, you see? They say it's a bit like drowning, but you get used to it."

It wasn't that bad, actually. Fischer's guts twisted in on themselves, and his sinuses burned like hell, but he'd take that over another bout with Kevin any day.

He floated there in the tank, seawater sliding through the tubes in his chest, and reflected on the queasy sensation of not breathing.

"They're getting some turbulence." Scanlon's voice came at him from all directions, as if the walls themselves were talking. "From your exhaust port."

A fine trail of bubbles was trickling from Fischer's chest. His eyecaps made everything seem marvelously clear, like a hallucination. "Just a bit of—"

Not his voice. His words, but spoken by something else, some cheap machine that didn't know about harmonics. One hand went automatically to the disk embedded in his throat.

"—hydrogen," he tried again. "No problem. Pressure'll squeeze them down when I get deep enough."

"Yeah. Still." Other words, muffled, as Scanlon spoke to someone else. Fischer felt something vibrate softly in his chest. The bubbles grew larger, then smaller. Then disappeared.

Scanlon was back. "Better?"

"Yeah." Fischer didn't know how he felt about this, though. He didn't really like having a chest full of machinery. He didn't really like having to breathe by chopping water into chunks of hydrogen and oxygen. But he *really* didn't like the idea of some tech he'd never even met, fiddling with his insides by remote control, reaching into his body and messing around in there without even asking. It made him feel—

Violated, right?

Sometimes Shadow was just a bitch. As if *she* hadn't been the one to put him up to it in the first place.

"We're going to kill the lights now, Gerry."

Darkness. The water hummed with the sound of vast machinery.

After a few moments he noticed a cold blue spark winking at him from somewhere overhead. It seemed to cast a lot more light than it should. As he watched, the inside of the tank reappeared in hazy shades of blue-on-black.

"Photoamps working okay?" Scanlon wanted to know.

"Uh-huh."

"What can you see?"

"Everything. The inside of the tank. The hatch. Sort of bluish."

"Right. Luciferin light source."

"It's not very bright," Fischer said. "Everything's sort of like, dusk."

"Well, it'd be pitch-black without your eyecaps."

And suddenly, it was.

"Hey."

"Don't worry, Gerry. Everything's fine. We just shut the light off."

He lay there in utter darkness. Floaters wriggled at the corner of his eye.

"How are you feeling, Gerry? Any sensation of falling? Claustrophobia?"

He felt almost peaceful.

"Gerry?"

"No. Nothing. I feel—fine—"

"Pressure's at two thousand meters."

"I can't feel it."

This might not be so bad after all. One year. One year . . .

"Dr. Scanlon," he said after a while. He was even getting used to the metallic buzz of his new voice.

"Right here."

"Why me?"

"What do you mean, Gerry?"

"I wasn't, you know, qualified. Even after all this training I bet there's lots of people who'd be better at this than me. Real engineers."

"It's not so much what you know," Scanlon said. "It's what you are."

He knew what he was. People had been telling him for as long as he could remember. He didn't see what the fuck that had to do with anything. "What's that, then?"

At first he thought he wasn't going to get an answer. But Scanlon finally spoke, and when he did there was something in his voice that Fischer had never heard before.

"Pre-adapted," was what he said.

Elevator Boy

The Pacific Ocean slopped two kilometers under his feet. He had a cargo of blank-eyed psychotics sitting behind him. And the lifter was being piloted by a large pizza with extra cheese. Joel Kita liked it all about as much as could be expected.

At least he *had* been expecting it, this time. For once the GA hadn't sprung one of their exercises in chaos theory onto his life without warning. He'd seen it coming almost a week in advance, when they'd sprung one onto Ray Stericker instead. Ray had been in this very cockpit, watching the pizza being installed and no doubt wondering when the term "job security" had become an oxymoron.

"I'm supposed to baby-sit it for a week," he had said then. Joel had climbed up into the 'scaphe for the usual preflight check and found his friend waiting by the controls. Ray had gestured up through the open hatchway to the lifter's cockpit, where a couple of techs were busy interfacing something to the controls. "Just in case it screws up in the field. Then I'm gone."

"Gone where?" Joel couldn't believe it. Ray had been on the Juan de Fuca run forever, even before the geothermal program. He'd even been an *employee,* back when such things were commonplace.

"Probably the Gorda circuit for a while. After that, who knows? They'll be upgrading everything before long."

Joel glanced up through the hatch. The techs were playing with a square vanilla box, half a meter on a side and about twice as thick as Kita's wrist. "What *is* the fucking thing? Some kind of autopilot?"

"With a difference. This takes off and lands. And all sorts of lovely things in between."

This was not good news. Humans had always been able to integrate 3-D spatial information better than the machines that kept trying to replace them. Not that machines couldn't recognize a tree or a building when such objects were pointed out to them, but they got real confused whenever you rotated any of those objects a few degrees. The shapes changed, contrast and shadow shifted, and it always took way too long for any of those arsenide pretenders to update its spatial maps and recognize that yes, it's still a tree, and no, it didn't morph into something else, dummy, you just changed your point of view.

In some places that wasn't a problem. Ocean surfaces, for example. Or controlled-access highways where the cars had their own ID transponders. Or even lashed to the underside of a giant squashed doughnut filled with buoyant vacuum, floating in midair. These had been respected and venerable environments for autopilots since well before the turn of the century.

Takeoffs and landings were a different scene altogether, though. Too many real objects going by too fast, too many things to keep an eye on. A few billion years of natural selection still had the edge when the fast lane got that crowded.

Until now, apparently.

"Let's get out of here." Ray dropped down onto the landing pad. Joel followed him out to the edge of the roof. Green tangled blankets of kudzu$_4$ spread out around them, shrouding the roofs of surrounding buildings. It always made Joel think post-apocalypse—weeds and ivy crawling back in from the wilderness to strangle the residue of some fallen civilization. Except, of course, these particular weeds were supposed to *save* civilization.

Way out by the coast, barely visible, streamers of

smoke dribbled into the sky from the refugee strip. *So much for civilization.*

"It's one of those smart gels," Ray said at last.

"Smart gels?"

"Head cheese. Cultured brain cells on a slab. The same things they've been plugging into the Net to fire-wall infections."

"I know what they are, Ray. I just can't fucking believe it."

"Well, believe it. They'll be coming for you too, give 'em enough time."

"Yeah. Probably." Joel let it sink in. "I wonder when."

Ray shrugged. "You've got some breathing space. All that unpredictable volcanic shit, things blowing up under you. Nastier than flying a hoover. Harder to replace you."

He looked back at the lifter, and the 'scaphe nestled into its underbelly.

"Won't take long, though."

Joel fished a derm out of his pocket; a tricyclic with a mild lithium chaser. He held it out without a word.

Ray just spat. "Thanks anyway. I *want* to feel pissed for a while, you know?"

And now, eight days later, Ray Stericker was gone.

He'd disappeared after his last shift, just the day before. Joel had tried to track him down, drag him out, piss him up, but he hadn't been able to find the man on site and Ray wasn't answering his watch. So here was Joel Kita, back on the job, alone except for his cargo: four very strange people in black suits, blank white lenses covering their eyes. They all had identical GA logos stamped onto their shoulders, tags with their surnames printed just below. At least the surnames were different, although the difference seemed trivial; male, female, large or small, they all seemed minor variants of the same make and model. *Ah yes, the Mk-5 was always such a nice boy. Kind of quiet, kept to himself. Who would've thought* . . .

Joel had seen rifters before. He'd ferried a couple out to Beebe about a month ago, just after construction had ended. One of them had seemed almost normal, had gone out of her way to chat and joke around as if trying to compensate for the fact that she looked like a zombie. Joel had forgotten her name.

The other one hadn't said a word.

One of the 'scaphe's tactical screens beeped a progress report. "Bottom's rising again," Joel called back. "Thirty-five hundred. We're almost there."

"Thanks," one of them—FISCHER, according to his shoulder tag—said. Everyone else just sat there.

A pressure hatch separated the 'scaphe's cockpit from the passenger compartment. If you sealed it you could use the aft chamber as an airlock, or even pressurize it for saturation dives if you didn't mind the hassle of decompression. You could also just swing the hatch shut if you wanted a bit of privacy, if you didn't like leaving your back exposed to certain passengers. That would be bad manners, of course. Joel tried idly to think of some socially acceptable excuse for slamming that big metal disk in their faces, but gave up after a few moments.

Now, the dorsal hatch—the one leading up into the lifter's cockpit—that one *was* closed, and that felt wrong. Usually they kept it open until just before the drop. Ray and Joel would shoot the shit for however long the trip would take—three hours, if you were going to Channer.

Yesterday, without warning, Ray Stericker had dropped the hatch shut fifteen minutes into the flight. He hadn't said an unnecessary word the whole time, had barely even used the intercom. And today—well, today there wasn't anyone up there to talk to anymore.

Joel looked out one of the side ports. The skin of the lifter blocked his view just a few centimeters on the other side; metal fabric stretched across carbon-fiber ribs, a gray expanse sucked into concave squares by the hard vacuum inside. The 'scaphe rode tucked into an oval hollow in the lifter's center. The only port that showed anything but gray skin was the one between Joel's feet; ocean, a long way down.

Not so far down now, though. He could hear the hisses and sighs of the lifter's ballast bags deflating overhead. Sharper sounds, more distant, cracked through the hull as electrical arcs heated the air in a couple of trim bags. This was still regular autopilot territory, but Ray used to do it all himself anyway. If it weren't for the closed hatch, Joel couldn't have told the difference.

The head cheese was doing a bang-up job.

He'd actually seen it a few days ago, during a delivery to an undersea rig just out of Gray's Harbor. Ray had hit a stud and the top of the box had slid away like white mercury, slipping back into a little groove at the edge of the casing and revealing a transparent panel underneath.

Beneath that panel, packed in clear fluid, was a ridged layer of goo, a bit too gray to be mozzarella. Dashes of brownish glass perforated the goo in neat parallel rows.

"I'm not supposed to open it up like this," Ray had said. "But fuck 'em. It's not as though the blighter's photosensitive."

"So what are those little brown bits?"

"Indium tin oxide over glass. Semiconductor."

"Jesus. And it's working right now?"

"Even as we speak."

"Jesus," Joel had said again. And then: "I wonder how you program something like this."

Ray had snorted at that. "You don't. You *teach* it.

Learns through positive reinforcement, like a bloody baby."

A sudden, smooth shift in momentum. Joel pulled back to the present; the lifter was hanging stable, five meters over the waves. Right on target. Nothing but empty ocean on the surface, of course; Beebe's transponder was thirty meters straight down. Shallow enough to hone in on, too deep to be a navigational hazard. Or to serve as a midwater hitching post for charter boats hunting Channer's legendary sea monsters.

The cheese printed out a word on the 'scaphe's tactical board: LAUNCH?

Joel's finger wavered over the OK key, then came down. Docking latches clanked open; the lifter reeled Joel Kita and his cargo down to the water. Sunlight squinted through viewports for a few seconds as the 'scaphe swung in its harness. A wavetop batted at the forward port.

The world jerked once, slewed sideways, and turned green.

Joel opened the ballast tanks and looked back over his shoulder. "Going down, folks. Your last glimpse of sunlight. Enjoy it while you can."

"Thanks," said FISCHER.

Nobody else moved.

Crush

Pre-adapted.

Even now, at the bottom of the Pacific Ocean, Fischer doesn't know what Scanlon meant by that.

He doesn't *feel* pre-adapted, not if that means he's supposed to be at home here. Nobody even talked to him on the way down. Nobody talked much to anyone else, either, but when they didn't talk to Fisher it seemed especially personal. And one of them, Brander—it's hard to tell with the eyecaps and all, but Fischer thinks Brander keeps looking at him, like they know each other from somewhere. Brander looks mean.

Everything's out in the open down here; pipes and cable bundles and ventilation ducts are all tacked onto the bulkheads in plain sight. He saw it on the vids before he came down, but those somehow left the impression of a brighter place, full of light and mirrors. The wall he's facing now, for instance; there should be a mirror there. But it's just a gray metal bulkhead with a greasy, unfinished sheen to it.

Fischer shifts his weight from one foot to the other. At one end of the lounge Lubin leans against a library pedestal, his capped eyes pointed at them with blank disinterest. Lubin's said only one thing to them in the five minutes they've been here:

"Clarke's still outside. She's coming in."

Something clanks under the floor. Water and nitrox mix, gurgling, nearby. The sound of a hatch swinging open, movement from below.

She climbs up into the lounge, droplets beading across her shoulders. Her diveskin paints her black below the neck, a skinny silhouette, almost sexless. Her hood is undone; blond hair, plastered against her skull, frames a face paler than Fischer's ever seen. Her mouth is a wide thin line. Her eyes, capped like his own, are blank white ovals in a child's face.

She looks around at them: Brander, Nakata, Caraco, Fischer. They look back, waiting.

She shrugs. "I'm changing the sodium on number two. A couple of you could come along, I guess."

She doesn't seem exactly human. There *is* something familiar about her, though.

What do you think, Shadow? Do I know her?

But Shadow isn't talking.

There's a street where none of the buildings have windows. The streetlamps shine down with a sick coppery light on masses of giant clams and big ropy brownish things emerging from mucous-gray cylinders (tubeworms, he remembers: *Riftia fuckinghugeous*, or something). Natural chimneys rise here and there above the invertebrate multitudes, pillars of basalt and silicon and crystallized sulfur. Every time Fischer visits the Throat, he thinks of really bad acne.

Lenie Clarke leads them on a flight down Main Street: Fischer, Caraco, a couple of cargo squids on remote. The generators lean up over them on both sides. A dark curtain billows across the road directly ahead, and it *sparkles*. A school of small fish darts around the edges of the streaming cloud.

"That's the problem," Lenie buzzes. She looks back at Fischer and Caraco. "Mud plume. Too big to redirect."

They've come past eight generators so far. That leaves six up ahead, drowning in silt. Double shift, even if they call out Lubin and Brander.

He hopes they don't have to. Not Brander, anyway.

Lenie fins off toward the plume. The squids whine softly behind, dragging their tools. Fischer steels himself to follow.

"Shouldn't we check thermal?" Caraco calls out. "I mean, what if it's hot?"

He was wondering that himself, actually. He's been wondering about such things ever since he overheard Caraco and Nakata comparing rumors from the Mendocino fracture. Nakata heard it was a really old minisub, with Plexiglas ports. Caraco heard they were thermoacrylate. Nakata said it got wedged inside the center of the rift zone. Caraco said no, it was just cruising over the seabed and a smoker blew up under it.

They agreed on how fast the viewports melted, though. Even the skeletons went to ash. Which didn't make much difference anyway, since every bone in every body had already been smashed by the ambient pressure.

Caraco makes a lot of sense, in Fischer's opinion, but Lenie Clarke doesn't even answer. She just fins off into that black sparkly cloud and disappears. At the spot she disappears the mud glows suddenly, a phosphorescent wake. The fish swarm toward it.

"She doesn't even care, sometimes," Fischer buzzes softly. "Like, whether she lives or dies . . ."

Caraco looks at him for a moment, then kicks off toward the plume.

Clarke's voice buzzes out of the cloud. "Not much time."

Caraco dives into the roiling wall with a splash of light. A knot of fish—a couple of them are a fair size now, Fischer sees—swirl in her wake.

Go *on*, Shadow says.

Something moves.

He spins around. For a moment there's only Main Street, fading in distance.

Then something big and black and . . . and *lopsided* appears from behind one of the generators.

"*Jeez.*" Fischer's legs move of their own volition. "They're coming!" he tries to yell. The vocoder scales it down to a croak.

Stupid. Stupid. They warned us, the sparkles bring in the little fish and the little fish bring in the big fish and if we don't watch it we just get in the way.

The plume is right in front of him now, a wall of sediment, a river on the bottom of the ocean. He dives in. Something nips lightly at his calf.

Everything goes black, with occasional sparkles. He

turns his headlight on; the flowing mud swallows the beam half a meter from his face.

But Clarke can see it somehow: "Turn it off."

"I can't see—"

"Good. Maybe they won't either."

He kills the light. In the darkness he gropes the gas billy from its sheath on his leg.

Caraco, from a distance: "I thought they were blind. . . ."

"Some of them."

And they've got other senses to fall back on. Fischer runs through the list: *smell, sound, pressure waves, bioelectric fields* . . . Nothing *relies* on vision down here. It's just one of the options.

If the plume blocks *only* light, they're fucked.

But even as he watches, the darkness is lifting. Black murk turns brown, then almost gray. Faint light filters in from the floodlamps on Main Street.

It's the eyecaps, he realizes. *They're compensating. Cool.*

He still can't see very far, though. It's like being caught in dirty fog.

"Remember." Clarke, very close. "They're not as tough as they look. They probably won't do much real damage."

A sonar pistol stutters nearby. "I'm not getting anything," Caraco buzzes. Milky sediment swirls on all sides. Fischer puts his arm out; it fades at the elbow.

"Oh shit." Caraco.

"Are you—"

"Something's on my leg something's Christ it's big—"

"Lenie—" Fischer cries.

A bump from behind. A slap on the back of his head. A shadow, black and spiny, fades into the murk.

Hey, that wasn't so—

Something clamps onto his leg. He looks down: jaws, teeth, a monstrous head fading away into the murk.

Oh Jeez—

He jams his billy against scaly flesh. Something gives, like gelatin. A soft thump. The flesh bloats, ruptures; bubbles explode from the rip.

Something else smashes him from behind. His chest is in a vise. He lashes out, blindly. Mud and ash and black blood billow into his face.

He grabs blindly, twists. There's a broken tooth in his hand, half as long as his forearm; he tightens his grip and it splinters. He drops it, brings the billy around and jams it into the thing on his side. Another explosion of meat and compressed CO_2.

The pressure lifts from his chest. Whatever's clamped onto his leg isn't moving. Fischer lets himself sink, drifts down against the base of a barite chimney.

Nothing charges him.

"Everyone okay." Lenie's vocoded monotone. Fischer grunts yes.

"Thank God for bad nutrition," Caraco buzzes. "We're fucked if these guys ever get enough vitamins."

Fischer reaches down, pries the dead monster's jaws off his calf. He wishes he had breath to catch.

Shadow?

Right here.

Was this what it was like for you?

No. This didn't take so long.

He lies against the bottom and tries to shut his eyes. He can't; the diveskin bonds to the surface of the eye-caps, traps the eyelids in little cul-de-sacs. *I'm sorry, Shadow. I'm so sorry.*

I know, she says. It's okay.

———

Lenie Clarke stands naked in Medical, spraying the bruises on her leg. No, not naked; the caps are still on her eyes. All Fischer can see is skin.

It's not enough.

A trickle of blood crawls down her side from just below the water intake. She absently wipes it away and reloads the hypo.

Her breasts are small, almost adolescent bumps. No hips. Her body's as pale as her face, except for the bruises and the fresh pink seams that access the implants. She looks anorexic.

She's the first adult Fischer's ever wanted.

She looks up and sees him in the doorway. "Strip down," she tells him, and goes back to work.

He splits his skin and starts to peel. Lenie finishes with her leg and stabs an ampoule into the cut in her side. The blood clots like magic.

"They warned us about the fish," Fischer says, "but they said they were really fragile. They said we could just beat them off with our hands if we had to."

Lenie sprays the cut in her side with a hypo, wipes off the residue. "You're lucky they told you that much." She pulls her diveskin tunic off a hanger, slides into it. "They barely mentioned the giantism when they sent us down."

"That's stupid. They must've known."

"They say this is the only vent where the fish get this big. That they've found, anyway."

"Why? What's so special here?"

Lenie shrugs.

Fischer has stripped to the waist. Lenie looks at him. "Leggings too. It got your calf, right?"

He shakes his head. "That's okay."

She looks down. His diveskin's only a couple of millimeters thick, it doesn't hide anything. He feels his erection going soft under her gaze.

Lenie's cold white eyes track back to his face. Fischer feels his face heating before he remembers: she can't see his eyes. No one can.

It's almost safe in here.

"Bruising's the biggest problem," Lenie says at last. "They don't puncture the diveskin all that often, but the force of the bite still gets through." Her hand is on his arm, firm and professional, probing the edges of Fischer's injury. It hurts, but he doesn't mind.

She uncaps a tube of anabolic salve. "Here. Rub this in."

The pain fades on contact. His flesh goes warm and tingly where he applies the ointment. He reaches out, a little bit scared, and touches Lenie's arm. "Thanks."

She twists out of reach without a word, bending down to seal the 'skin on her leg. Fischer watches the leggings slide up her body. They seem almost alive. They *are* almost alive, he remembers. The 'skin's got these *reflexes*, changes its permeability and thermal conductivity in response to body temperature. Maintains, what's the word, homeostasis.

Now he watches it swallowing Lenie's body like some slick black amoeba but she's showing through underneath, black ice instead of white but still the most beautiful creature he's ever seen. She's so far away. There's someone inside telling him to watch it—

—*Go away, Shadow*—

—but he can't help himself, he can almost *touch* her, she's bent over sealing her boots and his hand caresses the air just above her shoulder, traces the outline of her curved back so close it could feel her body heat if that stupid diveskin wasn't in the way, and—

And she straightens, bumping into his hand. Her face comes up; something burns behind her eyecaps. He pulls back but it's too late; her whole body's gone rigid and furious.

I just touched her. I didn't do anything wrong I just touched her—

She takes a single step forward. "Don't do that again," she says, her voice so flat he wonders for a second how her vocoder could be working out of the water.

"I'm not—I didn't—"

"I don't care," she says. "Don't do it again."

Something moves at the corner of his eye. "Problem, Lenie? Need a hand?" Brander's voice.

She shakes her head. "No."

"Okay, then." Brander sounds disappointed. "I'll be upstairs."

Movement again. Sounds, receding.

"I'm *sorry*," Fischer says.

"Fine," Lenie says, and brushes past him into the wetroom.

Autoclave

Nakata nearly bumps into her at the base of the ladder. Clarke glares; Nakata moves aside, baring teeth in a submissive primate smile.

Brander's in the lounge, pecking at the library: "You—?"

"I'm fine." She isn't, but she's getting there. This anger is nowhere near critical mass; it's just a reflex, really, a spark budded off from the main reservoir. It decays exponentially with elapsed time. By the time she reaches her cubby she's almost feeling sorry for Fischer.

Not his fault. He didn't mean any harm.

She closes the hatch behind her. It's safe to hit something now, if she wants. She looks around halfheartedly for a target, finally just drops onto her bunk and stares at the ceiling.

Someone raps on metal. "Lenie?"

She rises, pushes at the hatch.

"Hey Lenie, I think I've got a bad slave channel on one of the squids. I was wondering if you could—"

"Sure." Clarke nods. "Fine. Only not right now, okay, um—"

"Judy," says Caraco, sounding slightly miffed.

"Right. Judy." In fact, Clarke hasn't forgotten. But Beebe's way too crowded these days. Lately Clarke's learned to lose the occasional name. It helps keep things comfortably distant.

Sometimes.

"Excuse me," she says, brushing past Caraco. "I've got to get outside."

In a few places, the rift is almost gentle.

Usually the heat stabs up in boiling muddy pillars or jagged bolts of superheated liquid. Steam never gets a chance to form at three hundred atmospheres, but thermal distortion turns the water into a column of writhing liquid prisms, hotter than molten glass. Not here, though. In this one spot, nestled between lava pillows and safe from Beebe's prying ears, the heat wafts up through the mud like a soft breeze. The underlying bedrock must be porous.

She comes here when she can, keeping to the bottom en route to foil Beebe's sonar. The others don't know about this place yet; she'd just as soon keep it that way. Sometimes she comes here to watch convection stir the mud into lazy curlicues. Sometimes she splits the seals on her 'skin, basks face and arms in the thirty-degree seep.

Sometimes she just comes here to sleep.

She lies with the shifting mud at her back, staring up into blackness. This is how you fall asleep when you can't close your eyes; you stare into the dark, and when you start seeing things you know you're dreaming.

Now she sees herself, the high priestess of a new troglodyte society. She was the first one here, deep at peace while the others were still being cut open and reshaped by grubby dryback hands. She's the founding mother, the template against which other, rawer recruits trace themselves. They come down and they see that her eyes are always capped, and they go and do likewise.

But she knows it isn't true. The rift is the real creative force here, a blunt hydraulic press forcing them all into shapes of its own choosing. If the others are anything like her it's because they're all being squeezed in the same mold.

And let's not forget the GA. If Ballard was right, they made sure we weren't too different to start with.

There are all the superficial differences, of course. A bit of racial diversity. Token beaters, token victims, males and females equally represented . . .

Clarke has to smile at that. Count on Management to jam a bunch of sexual dysfunctionals together and then make sure the gender ratio is balanced. *Nice of them to try and see that nobody gets left out.*

Except for Ballard, of course.

But at least they learn from their mistakes. Dozing at three thousand meters, Lenie Clarke wonders what their next one will be.

Sudden, stabbing pain in the eyes. She tries to scream; smart implants feel tongue and lips in motion, mistranslate:

"Nnnnaaaaaah. . . ."

She knows the feeling. She's had it once or twice before. She dives blindly on a random heading. The pain in her head leaps from intense to unbearable.

"Aaaaaa—"

She twists back in the opposite direction. A bit better. She trips her headlamp, kicking as hard as she can. The world turns from black to solid brown. Zero viz. Mud seething on all sides. Somewhere close by she hears rocks splitting open.

Her headlamp catches the outcropping looming up a split second before she hits it. The shock rocks her skull, runs down her spine like a small earthquake. There's a different flavor of pain up there now, mingling with the searing in her eyes. She gropes blindly around the obstacle, keeps going. Her body feels—*warm*—

It takes a lot of heat to get through a diveskin, especially a class four. Those things are *built* for thermal stress.

Eyecaps, on the other hand . . .

Black. The world is black again, and clear. Clarke's headlamp stabs out across open space, lays a jiggling footprint on the mud a good ten meters away.

The view's still rippling, though.

The pain seems to be fading. She can't be sure. So many nerves have been screaming for so long that even the echoes are torture. She clutches her head, still kicking; the movement twists her around to face the way she came.

Her secret hideaway has exploded into a wall of mud and sulfur compounds, boiling up from the seabed. Clarke checks her thermistor; 45°C, and she's several meters away. Boiled fish skeletons spin in the thermals. Geysers hiss farther in, unseen.

The seep must have burst through the crust in an instant; any flesh caught in that eruption would have boiled off the bone before anything as elaborate as a flight reflex could cut in. A shudder shakes Clarke's body. Another one.

Just luck. Just stupid luck I was far enough away. I

*could be dead now. I could be dead I could be dead I
could be dead—*

Nerves fire in her thorax; she doubles over. But you
can't sob without breathing. You can't cry with your
eyes pinned open. The routines are all there, stuttering
into action after years of dormancy, but the pieces they
work on have all been changed. The whole body wakes
up in a straitjacket.

—dead dead dead—

That small, remote part of her kicks in, the part she
saves for these occasions. It wonders, off in the distance,
at the intensity of her reaction. This was hardly the first
time that Lenie Clarke thought she was going to die.

But this was the first time in years that it seemed to
matter.

Waterbed

Taking off his diveskin is like gutting himself.

He can't believe how much he's come to depend on
it, how hard it is to come out from inside. The eyecaps
are even harder. Fischer sits on his pallet, staring at the
sealed hatch while Shadow whispers, *It's okay, you're
alone, you're safe.* Half an hour goes by before he can
bring himself to believe her.

Finally, when he bares his eyes, the cubby lights are
so dim he can hardly see. He turns them up until the
room is twilit. The eyecaps sit in the palm of his hand,
pale and opaque in the semidarkness, like jellied circles
of eggshell. It's strange to blink without feeling them
under his eyelids. He feels so *exposed.*

He has to do it, though. It's part of the process. That's
what this is all about; opening yourself up.

Lenie's in her cubby, just centimeters away. If it

wasn't for this bulkhead Fischer could reach right out and touch her.

This is what you do when you really love someone, Shadow said way back then. So he does it now, to himself. For Shadow.

Thinking about Lenie.

Sometimes he thinks Lenie's the only other real person on the whole rift. The others are robots; glass robot eyes, matte black robot bodies, lurching through programmed routines that do nothing but keep other, bigger machines running. Even their names sound mechanical. Nakata. Caraco.

Not Lenie, though. There's someone inside her 'skin, her eyes may be glassed-in but they're not glass. She's *real*. Fischer knows he can touch her.

Of course, that's why he keeps getting into trouble. He keeps touching. But Lenie would be different, if only he could break through. She's more like Shadow than all the others ever were. Older, though.

No older than I'd be now, Shadow murmurs, and maybe that's it.

His mouth moves—*I'm so sorry, Lenie*—and no sound comes out. Shadow doesn't correct him.

This is what you do, she'd said, and then she'd begun to cry. As Fischer cries now. As he always does, when he comes.

The pain wakes him, sometime later. He's curled up on the pallet, and something's cutting into his cheek: a little piece of broken glass.

A mirror.

He stares at it, confused. A silver glass shard with a dark bloody tip, like a small tooth. There's no mirror in his cubby.

He reaches up and touches the bulkhead behind his

pillow. Lenie's there, Lenie's just the other side. But here, on *this* side there's a dark line, a rim of shadow he never noticed before. His eyes follow it around the edge of the wall, a gap about half a centimeter wide. Here and there little bits of glass are still wedged into that space.

There used to be a mirror covering this whole bulkhead. Just like Scanlon's vids. And it wasn't just removed, judging from the little fragments left behind. Somebody smashed it out.

Lenie. She went through the whole station, before the rest of them came down, and she smashed all the mirrors. He doesn't know why he's so sure, but somehow it seems like exactly the sort of thing Lenie Clarke would do when no one was looking.

Maybe she doesn't like to see herself. Maybe she's ashamed.

Go talk to her, Shadow says.

I can't.

Yes you can. I'll help you.

He picks up the tunic of his 'skin. It slithers around his body, its edges fusing together along the midline of his chest. He steps over the sleeves and leggings still spilled across the deck, reaches down for his eyecaps.

Leave them there.

No!

Yes.

I can't, she'll see me . . . .

That's what you want, isn't it? Isn't it?

She doesn't even like me, she'll just—

Leave them. I *said* I'll help you.

He leans against the closed hatch, eyes shut, his breathing loud and rapid in his ears.

Go on. Go *on.*

The corridor outside is in deep twilight. Fischer moves

along it to Lenie's sealed hatch. He touches it, afraid to knock.

From behind, someone taps his shoulder.

"She's out," Brander says. His 'skin is done right up to his neck, arms and legs completely sealed. His capped eyes are blank and hard. And there's the usual edge in his voice, that same familiar tone saying, *Just give me an excuse, asshole, just do anything* . . .

Maybe he wants Lenie too.

Don't get him mad, Shadow says.

Fischer swallows. "I just wanted to talk to her."

"She's *out.*"

"Okay. I'll . . . I'll try later."

Brander reaches out, pokes Fischer's face. His finger comes away sticky.

"You're cut," he says.

"It's nothing. I'm okay."

"Too bad."

Fischer tries to edge past Brander to his own cubby. The corridor pushes them together.

Brander clenches his fists. "Don't you fucking touch me."

"I'm not, I'm just trying to—I mean . . ." Fischer falls silent, glances around. No one else anywhere.

Deliberately, Brander relaxes.

"And for Christ's sake put your eyes back in," he says. "Nobody wants to look in there."

He turns and walks away.

They say Lubin sleeps out here. Lenie too, sometimes, but Lubin hasn't slept in his bunk since the rest of them came down. He keeps his headlight off, and he stays away from the lit part of the Throat, and nothing bothers him. Fischer heard Nakata and Caraco talking about it on the last shift.

It's starting to sound like a good idea. The less time he spends in Beebe these days, the better.

The station is a dim faraway blotch, glowing to Fischer's left. Brander's in there. He goes on duty in three hours. Fischer figures he can just stay out here until then. He doesn't really need to go inside much. None of them do. There's a little desalinator piggybacked on his electrolyzer in case he gets thirsty, and a bunch of flaps and valves that do things he doesn't want to think about, when he has to piss or take a dump.

He's getting a bit hungry, but he can wait. He's fine out here as long as nothing attacks him.

Brander just won't let him alone. Fischer doesn't know what Brander's got against him—

Oh yes you do, says Shadow.

—but he knows that look. Brander wants him to fuck up real bad.

The others keep out of it, for the most part. Nakata, the nervous one, just keeps out of everyone's way. Caraco acts like she couldn't care less if he boiled alive in a smoker. Lubin just sits there, looking at the floor and smoldering; even Brander leaves him alone.

And Lenie. Lenie's cold and distant as a mountaintop. No, Fischer's not getting any help with Brander. So when it comes to a choice between the monsters out here or the one in there, it's an easy call.

Caraco and Nakata are doing a hull check back at the station. Their distant voices buzz distractingly along Fischer's jaw. He shuts his receiver off and settles down behind an outcropping of basalt pillows.

Later, he can't remember drifting off.

"Listen, cocksucker. I just did two shifts end to end because you didn't show up for work when you were supposed to. Then half another shift *looking* for you. We thought you were in trouble. We *assumed* you were in trouble. Don't tell me—"

Brander pushes Fischer up against the wall.

"Don't tell me," he says again, "that you weren't. You don't want to say that."

Fischer looks around the ready room. Nakata watches from the opposite bulkhead, jumpy as a cat. Lubin rattles around in the equipment lockers, his back to the proceedings. Caraco racks her fins and edges past them to the ladder.

"Carac—"

Brander slams him hard against the wall.

Caraco, her foot on the bottom rung, turns and watches for a moment. A smile ghosts across her face. "Don't look at me, Gerry my man. This is your problem." She climbs away overhead.

Brander's face hovers a few centimeters away. His hood is still sealed, except for the mouth flap. His eyes look like translucent glass balls embedded in black plastic. He tightens his grip.

"So, cocksucker?"

"I'm . . . sorry—" Fischer stammers.

"You're sorry." Brander glances over his shoulder, includes Nakata in the joke. "He's sorry."

Nakata laughs, too loudly.

Lubin clanks in the locker, still ignoring them all. The airlock begins cycling.

"I don't think," Brander says, raising his voice over the sudden gurgle, "that you're sorry *enough*."

The 'lock swings open. Lenie Clarke steps out, fins in one hand. Her blank eyes sweep across the room; they don't pause at Fischer. She carries her fins to the drying rack without a word.

Brander punches Fischer in the stomach. Fischer doubles over, gasping; his head smashes into the airlock hatch. He can't catch his breath. The deck scrapes his cheek. Brander's boot is almost touching his nose.

"Hey." Lenie's voice, distant, not particularly interested.

"Hey yourself, Lenie. He's got it coming."

"I know." A moment passes. "Still."

"Judy got nailed by a viperfish, looking for him. She could've been killed."

"Maybe." Lenie sounds as if she's very tired. "So why isn't Judy here?"

"*I'm* here," Brander says.

Fischer's lung is working again. Gulping air, he pushes himself up against the bulkhead. Brander glares at him. Lubin's back in the room now, just off to one side. Watching.

Lenie stands in the middle of the ready room. She shrugs.

"What?" Brander demands.

"I don't know." She glances indifferently at Fischer. "It's just, he . . . he just fucked up. He didn't mean any har—"

She stops. Fischer gets the sense that she's looking straight through him, through the bulkhead, right out into the abyss itself to something only she can see. Whatever it is, she doesn't like it much.

"Ah, fuck it." She heads for the ladder. "None of my business anyway."

Lenie, please . . .

Brander turns back to Fischer as she climbs out of sight. Fischer stares back. Endless seconds go by. Brander's fist hovers in mid-air.

It lashes out almost too fast to see. Fischer reels, catches himself on a conduit. Lights swarm across his left eye. He blinks them away, hanging on to the bulkhead. Everything hurts.

Brander unclenches his fist. "Lenie's way too nice,"

he remarks, flexing his fingers. "Personally, I don't care whether you meant any harm or not."

Doppelgänger

Beebe's almost as soundproof as the inside of an echo chamber.

Lenie Clarke sits on her bunk and listens to the walls. She can't hear any actual words, but a sudden impact of flesh against metal was clear enough a few minutes ago. Now, low voices converse out in the lounge. Water gurgles through a pipe somewhere.

She thinks she hears something moving downstairs.

She lays her ear against a random pipe. Nothing. Another; a hiss of compressed gas. A third; the faint, tinny echo of slow footsteps, scraping across the lower deck. After a moment a muted hum vibrates through the plumbing.

The medical scanner.

It's none of my business. It's between them. Brander's got his reasons, and Fischer—

He didn't mean any harm.

Fischer's nothing. He's a pathetic, twisted asshole, nobody's problem but his own. It's too bad he gets under Brander's skin like that, but life's not guaranteed to be fair. No one knows that better than Lenie Clarke. She knows what it's like. She remembers the fists out of nowhere, the million little things you didn't even know you'd done wrong until it was too late. Nobody'd helped *her.* She'd managed, though. Sex worked, sometimes, as a diversionary tactic. Other times you just had to run.

He didn't mean any harm.

She shakes her head.

Well I fucking didn't either!

The sound sinks in before the pain does. A dull, solid

thud, like a fish hitting a floodlight. Blood oozes from the torn skin of her knuckles, the droplets almost black to her filtered vision. The stinging that follows is a welcome distraction.

The bulkhead, of course, is completely unmarked.

Out in the lounge, the conversation has stopped. Clarke sits rigid on the pallet, sucking her hand. Eventually, the voices start up again.

Almost time to go on shift with Nakata and Brander. Clarke looks around her cubby, hesitating. There's something she has to do before she opens the hatch, something important, and she can't quite remember what it is. Her eyes keep coming back to the same wall, looking for something that isn't—

The mirror. For some reason, she wants to see what she looks like. That's odd. She can't remember feeling that way for—well, for a long time. But it's no big deal. She'll just sit here until the feeling goes away. She doesn't have to step outside, she doesn't even have to stand up, until she feels normal again.

When in doubt, stay out of sight.

"Alice?"

The hatch is closed. There's no answer.

"She's in there." Brander stands at the end of the corridor, the lounge behind him. "She didn't go in more than ten minutes ago."

Clarke knocks again, harder. "Alice? It's almost time."

Brander turns on his heel—"I'll go get our stuff together"—and steps out of sight.

Beebe's hatches do not lock, for safety reasons. Still, Clarke hesitates. She knows how *she'd* feel if someone just walked into her private space without being invited.

But she said she was up for another shift. And I did knock. . . .

She spins the wheel in the center of the hatch. The mimetic seal around the rim softens and retracts. Clarke pulls the hatch open, peers inside.

Alice Nakata lies twitching on her bunk, eyes closed, 'skin partially peeled. Leads trail from insertion points on her face and wrists, drape away to a lucid dreamer on the bedside shelf.

She goes to sleep ten minutes before her shift starts? It doesn't make sense. Besides, Nakata was just downstairs with the rest of them. With Fischer. How could anyone fall asleep after *that*?

Clarke steps closer, studies the telltales on the device; induced REM's cranked to maximum and the alarm's disabled. Nakata would have been out in seconds. Hell, at those settings she'd drift off in the middle of a gang rape.

Lenie Clarke nods approvingly. *Nice trick.*

Reluctantly she touches the wake-up stud. Sleep drains from Nakata's face; her expression changes abruptly. Asian eyes flicker, open wide and dark.

Clarke steps back, startled. Alice Nakata has taken her eyecaps off.

"Time to go, Alice," she says softly. "Sorry to wake you. . . ."

She is, too. She's never seen Nakata smile before. It would have been nice if it could have lasted.

Brander's sealing a broadband sensor into its casing when Clarke drops into the lounge. "She'll catch up with us," she tells him, and turns to the drying rack for her fins.

Directly in front of her, the Med hatch is sealed. No sounds, human or mechanical, filter through from inside.

"Oh yeah. He's still in there." Brander raises his voice

a fraction. "Good fucking thing, too, while I'm around."

"He didn't m—" *Shut up! Shut the fuck up!*

"Lenie?"

She turns to see his hand dropping away. Brander's actually a lot more touchy-feely than you'd expect, sometimes he almost forgets himself around her.

But it's okay. He doesn't mean any harm either.

"Nothing," Clarke says, grabbing her fins.

Brander carries the sensor over to the airlock, drops it in with some other trinkets and cycles them through. Gurgles and clunks accompany their passage into the abyss.

"Only—"

He looks at her, his face framing a question around empty eyes.

"What have you got against Fischer?" she says, nearly whispering.

You know exactly what he's got against Fischer. It's none of your business. Stay out of it.

Brander's face hardens like setting cement. "He's a fucking freak. He diddles little kids."

I know. "Who says?"

"Nobody has to *say.* I can see his kind coming ten klicks away."

"If you say so." Clarke listens to her own voice. Cool. Distant, almost bored. Good.

"He looks at me funny. Hell, have you seen the way he looks at *you?*" Metal clanks against metal. "If he so much as touches me I'll fucking kill him."

"Yeah. Well, it wouldn't take much. He just sits there and takes whatever you dish out, you know, he's so—passive. . . ."

Brander snorts. "Why do you care, anyway? He creeps you out as much as the rest of us. I saw what happened in Medical last week."

The airlock hisses. A green light flashes on its side.

"I don't know," Lenie says. "You're right, I guess. I know what he is."

Brander swings the 'lock open and steps inside. Clarke holds the edge of the hatch.

"There's something else, though," she says, almost to herself. "Something's—missing. He doesn't fit."

"None of us fits," Brander growls. "That's the whole fucking point."

She closes the hatch. There's enough room for two in there—the other Rifters generally drop out in pairs—but she prefers to go through alone. It's a small thing. Nobody comments on it.

Not his fault. Not Brander's, not Fischer's. Not Dad's. Not mine.

Nobody's fucking fault.

The airlock flushes beside her.

Angel

The seabed is glowing. Cracks in the rock flicker comforting shades of orange, like hot coals, and he knows that's thermal; the scalding rivulets feel warm even through his 'skin, his thermistor leaps around every time the current twitches. But there are places here where the rocks shine green, and others where they shine blue. He doesn't know whether to thank biology or geochemistry. All he knows is that it's beautiful. It's a city from high up, at night. It's a vid of the northern lights he saw once, only sharper and brighter. It's a brush fire in emeralds.

In a way he's almost grateful to Brander. If it weren't for Brander he'd never have come upon this place. He'd be sitting in Beebe with the rest of them, hooked into the library or hiding in his cubby, safe and dry.

But Beebe's no refuge with Brander inside. Beebe's a gauntlet. So today Fischer just stayed away when his shift ended, crawled off across the ocean floor, exploring. Now, somewhere far from the Throat, he discovers *real* sanctuary.

Don't fall asleep, Shadow says. If you miss your shift again it'll just give him an excuse.

So what? He won't find me out here.

You can't stay outside forever. You've got to eat sometime.

I know, I know. Be quiet.

He's the only person to have ever seen this place. How long has it been here? How many millions of years has this little oasis been glowing peacefully in the night, a pocket universe all to itself?

Lenie would like it out here, Shadow says.

Yeah.

A rattail cruises into view about half a meter up, its underside a jigsaw of reflected color. It thrashes once, suddenly; violent shivers run the length of its body. The water around it shimmers with heat distortion. The fish spins lopsidedly, tail-down, in the wake of the little eruption. Its body turns white in seconds, begins to fray at the edges.

Four hundred eight degrees Centigrade: that's maximum recorded temperature for hot seeps on the Juan de Fuca Ridge. Fischer thinks back for the temperature rating on diveskin copolymer.

One-fifty.

He sculls up into the water column a bit, just in case. As soon as he clears bottom clutter he feels the faint, regular tapping of Beebe's sonar against his insides.

That's odd. This far out, he shouldn't be able to feel the signal, not unless they'd really cranked it up. And they wouldn't do *that* unless—

He checks the time.

Oh no. Not again.

By the time he makes it back to the Throat they're

halfway through stripping number four. They open a space on the line for him. Lenie doesn't want to hear his apologies. She doesn't want to talk to him at all. That hurts, but Fischer can't really blame her. Maybe he can make it up to her soon. Maybe he can take her sight-seeing.

It's not Brander's shift, thank God. He's back at Beebe. But Fischer's getting hungry again.

Maybe he's in his cubby. Maybe I can just eat and go to bed. Maybe—

He's sitting right there, all alone in the lounge, glaring up from his meal as soon as Fischer climbs into the room.

Don't get him mad.

Too late. He's always *mad.*

"I—thought we should clear some things up," he tries.

"Fuck off."

Fischer reaches the galley table, pulls out a chair.

"Don't bother," Brander says.

"Look, this place is small enough as it is. We've got to at least *try* to get along, you know? I mean, that's *assault*. It's *illegal*."

"So arrest me."

"Maybe you're not really mad at me at all," Fischer stops for a moment, surprised. *Maybe that's it.* "Maybe you've mixed me up with someone—"

Brander stands up.

Fischer pushes on: "Maybe someone *else* did something to you once, and—"

Brander comes around the table, very deliberately.

"I haven't got you mixed up with anybody. I know exactly what you are."

"No, you don't, we never even *saw* each other until a couple of weeks ago!" *Of course that's it. It's not me at all, it's someone else!* "Whatever happened to you—"

"Is none of your fucking business, and if you say one more word I'll fucking *kill* you."

Let's just go, Shadow pleads. Let's leave, this is only making things worse.

But Fischer stands his ground. Suddenly everything seems so clear. "It wasn't me," he says quietly. "What happened—I'm sorry. But it wasn't me, you *know* it wasn't."

For a moment he thinks he might actually be getting through. Brander's face untwists a little, the knots of flesh and eyebrow unkinking just a bit around those featureless white eyes, and Fischer can almost see that face wearing something other than rage.

But then he feels something moving, it's his own arm reaching out *Shadow no you'll ruin everything* but Shadow's not listening, she's crooning, Don't get him mad, don't get him mad don't get him mad—

This is what you *do*.

The growl starts low in Brander's throat, rising, like a distant wave pushed higher and higher out of the sea as it rushes shoreward.

". . . don't *you fucking TOUCH ME!*"

And nothing goes dead fast enough.

It stings at first. Then he feels clotted blood break around his eyelid, sees a fuzzy line of red light. He tries to bring his hand to his face. It hurts.

Something cold and wet, soothing. More clots come away.

"*Nnnnnn . . .*"

Someone is poking at his eyes. He tries to struggle, but all he can do is move his head feebly from side to side. That hurts even more.

"Don't move."

Lenie's voice.

"Your right eyecap's damaged. It could be gouging your cornea."

He relents. Lenie's fingers push between lids that feel as puffy as pillows. There's a sudden pressure on his eyeball, a tug of suction. A slurping sound, and the feel of ragged edges dragged across his pupil.

The world goes dark. "Hang on," Lenie says. "I'll turn up the lights."

There's still a reddish tinge to everything, but at least he can see.

He's in his cubby. Lenie Clarke leans over him, a bit of glistening wet membrane in one hand.

"You were lucky. He'd have ripped your costochondrals if your implants hadn't been packed in behind them." She drops the ruined cap out of sight, picks up a cartridge of liquid skin. "As it is, he only broke a couple of ribs. Lots of bruises. Mild concussion, maybe, but you'll have to go to Medical to be sure. Oh, and I'm pretty sure he broke your cheekbone too."

She sounds as if she's reading a grocery list.

"Why not—" Warm salt floods his mouth. His tongue does some careful exploring; his teeth are still intact, at least. "—in Medical now?"

"It would have been a bitch getting you down the ladder. Brander wasn't going to help. Everyone else is outside." She sprays foam across his bicep. It pulls his skin as it dries.

"Not that they'd be any help either," she adds.

"Thanks . . ."

"I didn't do anything. Just dragged you in here, basically."

He wants desperately to touch her.

"What is it with you, Fischer?" she asks after a while. "Why don't you ever fight back?"

"Wouldn't work."

"Are you kidding? You know how *big* you are? You could take Brander apart if you just stood up to him."

Shadow says it only makes things worse. You fight back, it only gets them madder.

"Shadow?" Lenie says.

"What?"

"You said—"

"Didn't say anything . . ."

She watches him for a few moments.

"Okay," she says at last. She stands up. "I'll call up and send for a replacement."

"No. That's okay."

"You're injured, Fischer."

Medical tutorials whisper inside his head. "We've got stuff downstairs."

"You still wouldn't be able to work for a week. More than twice that before you'd fully healed."

"They planned for accidents. When they set up the schedules."

"And how are you going to keep clear of Brander until then?"

"I'll stay outside more," he says. "Please, Lenie."

She shakes her head. "You're crazy, Fischer." She turns to the hatch, undogs it. "None of my business, of course. I just don't think—"

Turns back.

"Do you like it down here?" she asks.

"What?"

"Do you get off, being down here?"

It should be a stupid question. Especially now. Somehow it isn't.

"Sort of," he says at last, realizing it for the first time.

She nods, blinking over white space. "Dopamine rush."

"Dopa—?"

"They say we get hooked on it. Being down here.

Being—scared, I guess." She smiles faintly. "That's the rumor, anyway."

Fischer thinks about that. "Not so much I get off on it. More like, just used to it. You know?"

"Yeah." She turns and pushes the hatch open. "For sure."

There's this praying mantis a meter long, all black with chrome trim, hanging upside down from the ceiling of the Medical cubby. It's been sleeping up there ever since Fischer first arrived. Now it hovers over his face, jointed arms clicking and dipping like crazy articulated chopsticks. Every now and then one of its feelers winks red light, and Fischer can smell the scent of his own flesh cauterizing. It kind of bothers him. What's even worse is, he can't move his head. The neuroinduction field in the Med table has got him paralyzed from the neck up. He keeps wondering what would happen if the focus slipped, if that damping energy ended up pointing at his lung. At his *heart*.

The mantis stops in midmotion, its antennae quivering. It keeps completely still for a few seconds. "Hello, er—Gerry, isn't it?" it says at last. "I'm Dr. Troyka."

It sounds like a woman.

"How are we doing here?" Fischer tries to answer, but his head and neck are still just so much dead meat. "No, don't try to answer," the mantis says. "Rhetorical question. I'm checking your readouts now."

Fischer remembers: the medical equipment can't always do everything on its own. Sometimes, when things get too complicated, it calls up the line to a human backup.

"Wow," says the mantis. "What happened to you? No, don't answer that, either. I don't want to know." An accessory arm springs into sight and passes back and forth across Fischer's line of sight. "I'm going to override the damping field for a moment. It might hurt a bit. Try not to move when that happens, except to answer my questions."

Pain floods across Fischer's face. It's not too bad. Familiar, even. His eyelids feel scratchy, and his tongue is dry. He tries blinking; it works. He closes his mouth, rubs his tongue against swollen cheeks. Better.

"I don't suppose you want to come back up?" Dr. Troyka asks, hundreds of kilometers away. "You know these injuries are bad enough to warrant a recall."

Fischer shakes his head. "That's okay. I can stay here."

"Uh-huh." The mantis doesn't sound surprised. "I've been hearing that a fair bit lately. Okay, I'm going to wire your cheekbone back together, and I'll be planting a little battery under your skin. Just below the right eye. It'll basically kick your bone cells into overdrive, speed up the healing process. It's just a couple of millimeters across, you'll feel like you've got sort of a hard pimple. It may itch, but try not to pick at it. When you're healed up you can just squeeze it out like a zit. Okay?"

"Okay."

"All right, Gerry. I'm going to turn the field back on and get to work." The mantis whirs in anticipation.

Fischer holds up a hand. "Wait."

"What is it, Gerry?"

"What . . . what time is it, up there?" he asks.

"It's oh-five-ten. Pacific daylight. Why?"

"It's early."

"Sure is."

"I guess I got you up," Fischer says. "Sorry."

"Nonsense." Digits on the end of mechanical arms wiggle absently. "I've been up for hours. Graveyard shift."

"Graveyard?"

"We're on duty around the clock, Gerry. There's a lot of geothermal stations out there, you know. You—you keep us pretty busy, as a rule."

"Oh," Fischer says. "Sorry."

"Forget it. It's my job." There's a humming, somewhere in the back of his head; for a moment Fischer can feel the muscles of his face going slack. Then everything goes numb, and the mantis swoops down on him like a predator.

He knows better than to open up outside.

It doesn't kill you, not right away. But seawater's a lot saltier than blood; let it inside and osmosis sucks the water from the epithelial cells, shrivels them down to viscous little blobs. Rifter kidneys are modified to speed up water reclamation when that happens, but it's not a long-term solution, and it costs. Organs wear out faster, urine turns to oil. It's best to just keep sealed up. Your insides soak in seawater too long, they sort of *corrode*, implants or no implants.

But that's another one of Fischer's problems. He never takes the long view.

The face seal is a single macromolecule fifty centimeters long. It wraps back and forth along the line of the jaw like the two sides of a zipper, with hydrophobic side-chains for teeth. A little blade on the index of Fischer's left glove can split them apart. He runs it along the seal and the 'skin opens neatly around his mouth.

He doesn't feel much of anything at first. He was half expecting the ocean to charge up his nose and burn his sinuses, but of course all his body cavities are already packed with isotonic saline. The only immediate change is that his face gets cold, numbing the chronic ache of torn flesh a bit. Deeper pain pulses under one eye, where Dr. Troyka's wires hold the bones of his face together;

microelectricity tingles along those lines, press-gangs bonebuilding osteoblasts into high gear.

After a couple of moments he tries to gargle. That doesn't work, so he settles for gaping like a fish and wriggling his tongue around. That does it. He gets his first taste of raw ocean, coarse and saltier than the stuff that pumps him up inside.

On the seabed in front of him, a swarm of blind shrimp feeds in the current from a nearby vent. Fischer can see right through them. They're like little chunks of glass with blobs of organs jiggling around inside.

It must be fourteen hours since he's eaten, but there's no fucking way he's going back to Beebe with Brander still inside. The last time he tried, Brander was actually standing guard in the lounge, waiting for him.

What the hell. It's just like krill. People eat this stuff all the time.

They have a strange taste. Fischer's mouth is going numb from the cold, but there's still a faint sense of rotten eggs, dilute and barely detectable. Not bad other than that, though. Better than Brander by a long shot.

When the convulsions hit fifteen minutes later, he's not so sure.

"You look like shit," Lenie says.

Fischer hangs on to the railing, looks around the lounge. "Where—"

"At the Throat. On shift with Lubin and Caraco."

He makes it to the couch.

"Haven't seen you for a while," Lenie remarks. "How's your face doing?"

Fischer squints at her through a haze of nausea. Lenie Clarke is actually making small talk. She's *never* done that before. He's still trying to figure out why when his stomach clamps down again and he pitches onto the floor. By now nothing comes up but a few dribbles of sour fluid.

His eyes trace the pipes tangling along the ceiling. After a while Lenie's face blocks the view, looking down from a great height.

"What's wrong?" She seems to be asking out of idle curiosity, no more.

"Ate some shrimp," he says, and retches again.

"You ate—from *outside*?" She bends down and pulls him up. His arms drag along behind on the deck. Something hard bumps his head; the railing around the downstairs ladder.

"Fuck," Lenie says.

He's on the floor again, alone. Receding footsteps. Dizziness. Something presses against his neck, pricks him with a soft hiss.

His head clears almost instantly.

Lenie's leaning in, closer than she's ever been. She's even touching him, she's got one hand on his shoulder. He stares down at that hand, feeling a stupid sort of wonder, but then she pulls it away.

She's holding a hypo. Fischer's stomach begins to settle.

"Why," she says softly, "would you do a stupid thing like that?"

"I was hungry."

"So what's wrong with the dispenser?"

He doesn't answer.

"Oh," Lenie says. "Right."

She stands up and snaps the spent cartridge out of the hypo. "This can't go on, Fischer. You know that."

"He hasn't got me in two weeks."

"He hasn't *seen* you in two weeks. You only come in when he's on shift. And you're missing your own shifts more and more. Doesn't make you too popular with the rest of us." She cocks her head as Beebe creaks around them. "Why don't you just call up and get them to take you home?"

Because I do things to children, and if I leave here they'll cut me open and change me into something else. . . .

Because there are things outside that almost make it worthwhile . . .

Because of you . . .

He doesn't know if she'd understand any of those reasons. He decides not to risk it.

"Maybe you could talk to him," he manages.

Lenie sighs. "He wouldn't listen."

"Maybe if you tried, at least—"

Her face hardens. "I *have* tried. I—"

She catches herself.

"I can't get involved," she whispers. "It's none of my business."

Fischer closes his eyes. He feels as if he's going to cry. "He just doesn't let up. He really hates me."

"It's not you. You're just—filling in."

"Why did they put us together? It doesn't make sense!"

"Sure it does. Statistically."

Fischer opens his eyes. "What?"

Lenie's pulling one hand down across her face. She seems very tired.

"We're not people here, Fischer. We're a cloud of data points. Doesn't matter what happens to you or me or Brander, just as long as the mean stays where it's supposed to and the standard deviation doesn't get too big."

Tell her, Shadow says.

"Lenie—"

"Anyway." Lenie shrugs the mood away. "You're crazy to eat anything that near a rift zone. Didn't you learn about hydrogen sulfide?"

He nods. "Basic training. The vents spit it out."

"And it builds up in the benthos. They're toxic. Which I guess you know now anyway."

She starts down the ladder, stops on the second rung.

"If you really want to go native, try feeding farther from the rift. Or go for the fish."

"The fish?"

"They move around more. Don't spend all their time soaking in the hot springs. Maybe they're safe."

"The fish," he says again. He hadn't thought of that.

"I said *maybe*."

Shadow, I'm so sorry . . .

Shush. Just look at all the pretty lights.

So he looks. He knows this place. He's on the bottom of the Pacific Ocean. He's back in fairyland. He thinks he comes here a lot now, watches the lights and bubbles, listens to the deep rocks grinding against each other.

Maybe he'll stay this time, watch the whole thing working, but then he remembers he's supposed to be somewhere else. He waits, but nothing specific comes to him. Just a feeling that he should be doing something somewhere else. Soon.

It's getting harder to stay here anyway. There's a vague pain hanging around his upper body somewhere, fading in and out. After a while he realizes what it is. His face hurts.

Maybe this beautiful light is hurting his eyes.

That can't be right. His caps should take care of all that. Maybe they're not working. He seems to remember something that happened to his eyes a while back, but it doesn't really matter. He can always just leave. Suddenly, wonderfully, all of his problems have easy answers.

If the light hurts, all he has to do is stay in the dark.

Feral

"Hey," Caraco buzzes as they come around the corner. "Number five."

Clarke looks. Five's fifteen meters away and the water's a bit murky this shift. Still, she can see something big and dark sticking to the intake vent. Its shadow twitches down along the casing like an absurdly stretched black spider.

Clarke fins forward a few meters, Cacaro at her side. The two women exchange looks.

Fischer, hanging upside down against the mesh. It's been eight days since anyone's seen him.

Clarke gently sets down her carry bag; Caraco follows her lead. Two or three kicks bring them to within five meters of the intake. Machinery hums omnipresently, makes a sound deep enough to feel.

He's facing away from them, drifting from side to side, tugged by the gentle suction of the intake vent. The vent's grillwork is fuzzy with rooted growing things; small clams, tubeworms, shadow crabs. Fischer pulls squirming clumps from the intake, leaves them to drift or to fall to the street below. He's cleaned maybe two meters square so far.

It's nice to see he still takes some duties seriously.

"Hey. Fischer," Caraco says.

He spins around as if shot. His forearm flails toward Clarke's face; she raises her own just in time. In the next instant he's bowled past her. She kicks, steadies herself. Fischer's heading for the darkness without looking back.

"Fischer," Clarke calls out. "Stop. It's okay."

He stops kicking for a moment, looks back over his shoulder.

"It's me," she buzzes. "And Judy. We won't hurt you."

Barely visible now, he rotates to a stop and turns to face them. Clarke risks a wave.

"Come on, Fischer. Give us a hand."

Caraco comes up behind her. "Lenie, what are you doing?" She's turned her vocoder down to a hiss. "He's too far gone, he's—"

Clarke cranks her own vocoder down. "Shut up, Judy." Up again. "What do you say, Fischer? Earn your pay."

He's coming back into the light, hesitantly, like a wild animal lured by the promise of food. Closer, Clarke can see the line of his jaw moving up and down under his hood. The motions are jerky, erratic, as though he's learning them for the first time.

Finally a noise comes out. "Oh—kay—"

Caraco goes back and retrieves their gear. Clarke offers a scraper to Fischer. After a moment he takes it, clumsily, and follows them back to number five.

"Jussst like," Fischer buzzes. "Old. T-times."

Caraco looks at Clarke. Clarke says nothing.

Near the end of the shift she looks around. "Fischer?"

Caraco pokes her head out from an access tunnel. "He's gone?"

"When did you see him last?"

Caraco's vocoder ticks a couple of times; the machinery always misinterprets "*hmmm.*" "Half hour ago, maybe."

Clarke puts her own vocoder on high. "Hey Fischer! You still around?"

No answer.

"Fischer, we're heading back in a bit. If you want to come along . . ."

Caraco just shakes her head.

Shadow

It's a nightmare.

There's light everywhere, blinding, painful. He can barely move. Everything has such hard edges, and everywhere he looks the boundaries are too sharp. Sounds are like that too, clanks and shouts, every noise an exclamation of pain. He barely knows where he is. He doesn't know why he's there.

He's drowning.

"UNNNNNSEEEEELLLLLHHHHH IZZZZZMMMMOOUUUUUTH..."

The tubes in his chest suck at emptiness. The rest of his insides strain to inflate, but there's nothing there to fill them. He thrashes, panicky. Something gives with a snap. Sudden pain resonates in some faraway limb, floods the rest of his body a moment later. He tries to scream, but there's nothing inside to push out.

"HHIZZMMMOUTHFORRRKKKRRI ISSAAAAAKHEEEZSSUFFUK-KATE—"

Someone pulls part of his face off. His insides fill with a rush; not the cold saline he's used to, but it helps. The burning in his chest eases.

"BIGGFFUKKINNGGMMISSTTAAKE—"

Pressure, painful and uneven. Things are holding him down, holding him up, banging into him. The noise is tinny, deafening. He remembers a sound—

—*gravity*—

—that applies somehow, but he doesn't know what it means. And then everything's spinning, and everything's familiar and horrible except for one thing, one glimpse of a face that calms him somehow—

Shadow?

—and the weight's gone, the pressure's gone, ice-

water calms his insides as he spirals back with her, outside again, where she used to be years ago—

She's showing him how to do it. She creeps into his
room after the shouting stops, she crawls under the
covers with him and she starts stroking his penis.

"Dad says this is what you do when you really love
somebody," she whispers. And that scares him because
they don't even *like* each other, he just wants her to go
away and leave them all alone.

"Go away. I *hate* you," he says, but he's too afraid to
move.

"That's okay, then you don't have to do it for me."
She's trying to laugh, trying to pretend he was just kidding.

And then, still stroking: "Why are you always so
mean to me?"

"I'm not mean."

"Are too."

"You're not supposed to be here."

"Can't we just be friends?" She rubs up against him.
"I can do this whenever you want—"

"Go away. You can't stay here."

"I *can*, maybe. If it works out, they said. But we have
to like each other or they could send me back—"

"Good."

She's crying now, she's rubbing against him so hard
the bed shakes: "*Please can't you like me please I'll do
anything I'll even—*"

But he never finds out what she'll even do because
that's when the door slams open and whatever happens
after that, Gerry Fischer can't remember.

Shadow, I'm so sorry. . . .

But she's back with him now, in the cold and the dark
where it's safe. Somehow. Beebe's a dim gray glow in
the distance. She floats against that backdrop like a black
cardboard cutout.

"Shadow . . ." Not his voice.

"No." Not hers. "Lenie."

"Lenie. . . ."

Twin crescents, thin as fingernails, reflect from her eyes. Even in two dimensions she's beautiful.

Mangled words buzz from her throat: "You know who I am? You can understand me?"

He nods, then wonders if she can see it. "Yeah."

"You don't—Lately you're sort of gone, Fischer. Like you've forgotten how to be human."

He tries to laugh, but the vocoder can't handle it. "It comes and goes, I think. I'm . . . lucid now, anyway. That's the word, isn't it?"

"You shouldn't have come back inside." Machinery strips any feeling from her words. "He says he'll kill you. Maybe you should just stay out of his way."

"Okay," he says, and thinks it actually might be.

"I can bring food out, I guess. They don't care about that."

"That's okay. I can—go fishing."

"I'll call for a 'scaphe. It can pick you up out here."

"No. I can swim back up myself if I want to. Not far."

"Then I'll tell them to send someone."

"No."

A pause. "You can't swim all the way back to the mainland."

"I'll stay down here . . . a while. . . ."

A tremor growls softly along the seabed.

"You sure?" Lenie says.

"Yeah." His arm hurts. He doesn't know why.

She turns slightly. The dim reflections vanish from her eyes for a long moment.

"I'm sorry, Gerry."

"Okay."

Lenie's silhouette twists around and faces back toward Beebe. "I should get going."

She doesn't leave. She doesn't say anything for almost a minute.

Then: "Who's Shadow?"

More silence.

"She's a. . . . friend. When I was young."

"She means a lot to you." Not a question. "Do you want me to send her a message?"

"She's dead," Fischer says, marveling that he's really known it all along.

"Oh."

"Didn't mean to," he says. "But she had her own mom and dad, you know, why did she need *mine*? She went back where she belonged. That's all."

"Where she belonged," Lenie buzzes, almost too softly to hear.

"Not my fault," he says. It's hard to talk. It didn't used to be this hard.

Someone's touching him. Lenie. Her hand is on his arm, and he knows it's impossible but he can feel the warmth of her body through his 'skin.

"Gerry."

"Yes?"

"Why wasn't she with her own family?"

"She *said* they hurt her. She always said that. That's how she got in. She *used* it, it always worked. . . ."

Not *always*, Shadow reminds him.

"And then she went back," Lenie murmurs.

"I didn't mean to."

A sound comes out of Lenie's vocoder, and he has no idea what it is. "Brander's right, isn't he. About you and kids."

Somehow he knows she's not accusing him. She's just checking.

"That's what you—do," he tells her. "When you really love someone."

"Oh, Gerry. You're so completely fucked up."

A string of clicks taps faintly on the machinery in his chest.

"They're looking for me," she says.

"Okay."

"Be careful, okay?"

"You could stay. Here."

Her silence answers him.

"Maybe I'll come out and visit sometimes," she buzzes at last. She rises up into the water, turns away.

" 'Bye," Shadow says. It's the first time she's spoken aloud since she came inside, but Fischer doesn't think Lenie notices the difference.

And then she's gone, for now.

But she comes out here all the time. Alone, sometimes. He knows it isn't over. And when she goes back and forth with the others, doing all the things *he* used to do, he'll be there, off where no one can see. Checking up. Making sure she's okay.

Like her own guardian angel. Right, Shadow?

A couple of fish flicker dimly in the distance.

Shadow . . . ?

BALLET

Dancer

A week later Fischer's replacement comes down on the 'scaphe. Nobody stands watch in Communications anymore; machines don't care if they have an audience. Sudden clanking reverberates through Beebe Station and Clarke stands alone in the lounge, waiting for the ceiling to open up. Compressed nitrox hisses overhead, blowing seawater back to the abyss.

The hatch drops open. Green incandescence spills into the room. He climbs down the ladder, diveskin sealed, only his face exposed. His eyes, already capped, are featureless glass balls. But they aren't as dead as they should be, somehow. Something stares through those blank lenses, and it almost *shines*.

His blind eyes scan the compartment like radar dishes. They lock on to hers: "You're Lenie Clarke?" The voice is too loud, too normal. *We talk in whispers here,* Clarke realizes.

They are not alone now. Lubin, Brander, Caraco have appeared at the edges of her vision, drifting into the room like indifferent wraiths. They take up positions around the edge of the lounge, waiting. Fischer's replacement doesn't seem to notice them. "I'm Acton," he tells Clarke. "And I bring gifts from the overworld. Behold!" He extends his clenched fist, opens it palm up. Clarke sees five metal cylinders there, each no more than two centimeters long. Acton turns slowly, theatrically, showing his trinkets to the other rifters. "One for each of you," he says. "They go into your chest, right next to the seawater intake."

Overhead, the docking hatch swings shut. From behind it a postcoital tattoo, metal on metal, heralds the shuttle's escape to the surface. They wait there for a few moments: rifters, newcomer, five new gadgets to dilute their humanity a little further. Finally, Clarke reaches out to touch one. "What do they do?" she says, her voice neutral.

Acton snaps his fingers shut, stares about the lounge with eyeless intensity. "Why, Ms. Clarke," he replies, "they tell us when we're dead."

In Communications, Acton spills his trinkets onto a control console. Clarke stands behind him, filling the cubby. Caraco and Brander look in through the hatchway.

Lubin has disappeared.

"The program's only four months old," Acton says, "and it's lost two people at Piccard, one each at Cousteau and Link, and Fisher makes five. Not the kind of record you want to trumpet to the world, eh?"

Nobody says anything. Clarke and Brander stand impassive; Caraco shifts on her feet. Acton sweeps his blank shiny eyes over them all. "Christ but you're a lively lot. You sure Fischer's the only one down here who cashed in?"

"These things are supposed to save our lives?" Clarke asks.

"Nah. They don't care *that* much about us. These just help you find the bodies."

He turns to the console, plays it with practiced fingers. The topographic display flashes to life on the main screen. "Mmmm." Acton traces along the luminous contours with one finger. "So this is Beebe here in the center, and this must be the rift proper—Jesus, there's a lot of geography out here." He points at a cluster of hard green rectangles halfway to the edge of the screen. "These are the generators?"

Clarke nods.

Acton picks up one of the little cylinders. "They say they've already sent down the software for these things." Silence. "Well, I guess we'll find out, won't we?" He fingers the object in his hand, presses one end of it.

Beebe Station screams aloud.

Clarke jerks back at the sound; her head cracks painfully against an overhead pipe. The station continues to howl, wordless and despairing.

Acton touches a control; the scream stops as if guillotined.

Clarke glances at the others, shaken. They appear unmoved. Of course. For the first time she wonders what their eyes would show, naked.

"Well," Acton says, "we know the audio alarm works. But you get a visual signal too." He points at the screen: Dead center, within the phosphor icon that is Beebe, a crimson dot pulses like a heart under glass.

"It keys on myoelectricity in the chest," he explains. "Goes off automatically if your heart stops."

Behind her, Clarke feels Brander turning for the hatchway.

"Maybe my etiquette is out of date—" Acton says.

His voice is suddenly very quiet. Nobody else seems to notice.

"—but I've always thought it was—rude—to walk away when someone's talking to you."

There's no obvious threat in the words. Acton's tone seems pleasant enough. It doesn't matter. In an instant Clarke sees all the signs again: the reasoned words, the deadened voice, the sudden slight tension of a body rising to critical mass. Something familiar is growing behind Acton's eyecaps.

"Brander," she says quietly, "why don't you hang around and hear the man out?"

Behind her, the sounds of motion stop.

Before her, Acton relaxes ever so slightly.

Within her, something deeper than the rift stirs in its sleep.

"They're a snap to install," Acton says. "It takes about five minutes. GA says deadman switches are standard issue from now on."

I know you, she thinks. *I don't remember but I'm sure I've seen you before somewhere. . . .*

A tiny knot forms in her stomach. Acton smiles at her, as though sending some secret greeting.

Acton is about to be baptized. Clarke is looking forward to it.

They stand together in the airlock, their diveskins clinging like shadows. The deadman switch, newly installed, itches in Clarke's chest. She remembers the first time she dropped into the ocean this way, remembers the person who held her hand through that drowning ordeal.

That person is gone now. The deep sea broke her and spat her out. Clarke wonders if it will do the same to Acton.

She floods the airlock.

By now the feeling is almost sensual; her insides folding flat, the ocean rushing into her, cold and unstoppable as a lover. At 4°C the Pacific slides through the plumbing in her chest, anesthetizing the parts of her that can still feel. The water rises over her head; her eyecaps show her the submerged walls of the lock with crystal precision.

It's not like that with Acton. He's trying to fall in on himself; he only falls into Clarke. She senses his panic, watches him convulse, sees his knees buckle in a space far too narrow to permit collapse.

He needs more room, she thinks, smiling to herself, and opens the outer hatch. They drop.

She glides down and out, arcing away from under Beebe's oppressive bulk. She leaves the floodlit circle behind, skims into the welcoming darkness with her headlight doused. She feels the presence of the seabed a couple of meters beneath her. She's free again.

After a few moments she remembers Acton. She turns back the way she came. Beebe's floodlamps stain the darkness with dirty light; the station, bloated and angular, pulls against the cables holding it down. Light pours from its lower surface like feeble rocket exhaust. Pinned facedown in that glare, Acton lies unmoving on the bottom.

Reluctantly she swims closer. "Acton?"

He doesn't move.

"Acton?" She's back in the light now. Her shadow cuts him in half.

At last he looks up. "It'ssss—"

He seems surprised by the sound of his own transmuted voice.

He puts his hand to his throat. "I'm not—breathing—" he buzzes.

She doesn't answer.

He looks back down. There's something on the bottom, a few centimeters from his face. Clarke drifts closer; a tiny shrimplike creature trembles on the substrate.

"What is it?" Acton asks.

"Something from the surface. It must have come down on the 'scaphe."

"But it's—dancing—"

She sees. The jointed legs flex and snap, the carapace arches to some insane inner rhythm. It seems so brittle a life; perhaps the next spasm, or the next, will shatter it.

"It's a seizure," she says after a while. "It doesn't

belong here. The pressure makes the nerves fire too fast, or something."

"Why doesn't that happen to us?"

Maybe it does. "Our implants. They pump us full of neuroinhibitors whenever we go outside."

"Oh. Right," Acton buzzes softly. Gently he reaches out to the creature. Takes it in the palm of his hand.

Crushes it.

Clarke hits him from behind. Acton bounces off the seabed, his hand flying open; fragments of shell, of watery flesh swirl in the water. He kicks, rights himself, stares at Clarke without speaking. His eyecaps shine almost yellow in the light.

"You asshole," Clarke says very quietly.

"It didn't belong here," Acton buzzes.

"Neither do we."

"It was suffering. You said so yourself."

"I said the nerves fired too fast, Acton. Nerves carry pleasure as well as pain. How do you know it wasn't dancing for fucking *joy*?"

She pushes off the bottom and kicks furiously into the abyss. She wants to reach into Acton's body and tear everything out, sacrifice that gory tangle of viscera and machinery to the monsters at the rift. She can't remember ever being so angry. She tells herself she doesn't know why.

Gurgles and clanks from below. Clarke looks down through the lounge hatch in time to see the airlock spill open. Brander backs out, supporting Acton.

Acton's 'skin is laid open at the thigh.

He bends over, removing his flippers. Brander's are already off; he turns to Clarke as she climbs down the ladder. "He met his first monster. Gulper eel."

"I met my fucking monster, all right," Acton says in

a low voice. And Clarke sees it coming a fraction of a second before—

—Acton is on Brander, left fist swinging like a bolo on the end of his arm, once twice three times and Brander's on the floor, bleeding. Acton's bringing his foot back when Clarke gets in front of him, her hands raised to protect herself, crying, "Stop it stop it's not his fault!" but somehow it's not Acton she's pleading with it's something inside of him coming out, and she'd do anything if it would only please God go back where it came from—

It stares through Acton's milky eyes and snarls, "The fucker saw it coming at me! He let that thing tear my leg open!"

Clarke shakes her head. "Maybe not. You know how dark it is out there, I've been down here longer than anyone and they sneak up on me all the time, Acton. Why would Brander want to hurt you?"

She hears Brander coming to his feet behind her. His voice carries over her shoulder: "Brander sure as shit wants to hurt him *now*—"

She cuts him off. "Look, I can handle this." Her words are for Brander; her eyes remain locked with Acton's. "Maybe you should go to Medical, make sure you're okay."

Acton leans forward, tensed. The thing inside waits and watches.

"This asshole—" Brander begins.

"*Please*, Mike." It's the first time she has ever used his first name.

There's a moment of silence.

"Since when did *you* ever get involved?" he says behind her.

It's a good question. Brander's footsteps shuffle away before she can think of an answer.

Something in Acton goes back to sleep.

"You'd better go there too," Clarke says to him. "Later."

"Nah. It wasn't that tough. I was surprised how feeble it was, after I got over the *size* of the fucking thing."

"It ripped your diveskin. If it could do that, it wasn't as weak as you think. At least check it out; your leg might be lacerated."

"If you say so. Although I'll bet Brander needs Medical more than I do." He flashes a predatory grin, and moves to pass her.

"You might also consider reining in your temper," she says as he brushes past.

Acton stops. "Yeah. I was kind of hard on him, wasn't I?"

"He won't be as eager to help you out the next time you get caught in a smoker."

"Yeah," he says again. Then: "I don't know, I've always been sort of—you know—"

She remembers a word someone else used, after the fact. "Impulsive?"

"Right. But really I'm not that bad. You just have to get used to me."

Clarke doesn't answer.

"Anyhow," he says, "I guess I owe your friend an apology."

My friend. And by the time she gets over that jarring idea, she's alone again.

Five hours later Acton's in Medical. Clarke passes the open hatchway and glances in; he sits on the examination table, his 'skin undone to the waist. There's something wrong with the image. She stops and leans through the hatch.

Acton has opened himself up. She can see the flesh peeled back around the water intake, the places where meat turns to plastic, the tubes that carry blood and the ones that carry antifreeze. He holds a tool in one hand; it disappears into the cavity, the spinning thing on its tip whirring quietly.

Acton hits a nerve somewhere, and jumps as if shocked.

"Are you damaged?" Clarke asks.

He looks up. "Oh. Hi."

She points at his dissected thorax. "Did the gulper—"

He shakes his head. "No. No, it just bruised my leg a bit. I'm just making some adjustments."

"Adjustments?"

"Fine-tuning." He smiles. "Settling-in stuff."

It doesn't work. The smile is hollow somehow. Muscles stretch lips in the usual way, but the gesture's imprisoned in the lower half of his face. Above it, his capped eyes stare cold as drifted snow, innocent of any topography. She wonders why it's never bothered her before, and realizes that this is the first time she's ever seen a rifter smile.

"That's not supposed to be necessary," she says.

"What's not?" Acton's smile is beginning to wear on her.

"Fine-tuning. We're supposed to be self-adjusting."

"Exactly. I'm adjusting myself."

"I mean—"

"I know what you mean," Acton says. "I'm—customizing the job." His hand moves around inside his rib cage as if autonomous, tinkering. "I figure I can get better performance if I nudge the settings just a bit outside the approved specs."

Clarke hears a brief, lilliputian screech of metal against metal.

"How?" she asks.

Acton withdraws his hand, folds flesh back over the

hole. "Not exactly sure yet." He runs another tool along the seam in his chest, sealing himself. He shrugs back into his 'skin, seals that as well. Now he's as whole as any rifter.

"I'll let you know next time I go outside," he says, laying a casual hand on Clarke's shoulder as he squeezes past.

She almost doesn't flinch.

Acton stops. He seems to look right around her.

"You're nervous," he says slowly.

"Am I."

"You don't like being touched." His hand rests on her collarbone like an insult.

She remembers: She has the same armor that he does. She relaxes fractionally. "It's not a general thing," she lies. "Just some people."

Acton seems to weigh the gibe, decide whether it's worthy of a response. His hand withdraws.

"Kind of an unfortunate quirk in a place as small as this," he says, turning away.

Small? I've got the whole goddamn ocean! But Acton's already climbing upstairs.

The new smoker is erupting again. Water shoots scalding from the chimney at the north end of the Throat, curdles and mixes with deep icy saline; microbes caught in the turbulence luminesce madly. The water fills with the hiss of unformed steam, aborted by the weight of three hundred atmospheres.

Acton is ten meters above the seabed, awash in rippling blue light.

She glides up from underneath. "Nakata said you were still out here," she buzzes at him. "She said you were waiting for this thing to go off."

He doesn't even look at her. "Right."

"You're lucky it did. You could have been waiting out here for days." Clarke turns away, aims herself at the generators.

"And I think," Acton says, "it'll stop in a minute or two."

She twists around and faces him. "Look, all these eruptions are . . ." She rummages for the word, "chaotic."

"Uh-huh."

"You can't predict them."

"Hey, the Pompeii worms can predict them. The clams and brachyurans can predict them. Why not me?"

"What are you talking about?"

"They can tell when something's going to blow. Take a look around sometime, you'll see for yourself. They react before it even happens."

She looks around. The clams are acting just like clams. The worms are acting just like worms. The brachyurans scurry around the bottom the way brachyurans always do. "React how?"

"Makes sense, after all. These vents can feed them or parboil them. After a few million years they've learned to read the signs, right?"

The smoker hiccoughs. The plume wavers, light dimming at its edges.

Acton looks at his wrist. "Not bad."

"Lucky guess," Clarke says, her vocoder hiding uncertainty.

The smoker manages a couple of feeble bursts and subsides completely.

Acton drifts closer. "You know, when they first sent me down here I thought this place would be a real shithole. I figured I'd just knuckle down and do my time and get out. But it's not like that. You know what I mean, Lenie?"

I know. But she doesn't answer.

"I thought so," he says, as though she has. "It's really kind of . . . well, beautiful, in a way. Even the monsters, once you get to know 'em. We're all beautiful."

He seems almost gentle.

Clarke dredges her memory for some sort of defense. "You couldn't have known," she says. "Way too many variables. It's not computable. Nothing down here's computable."

An alien creature looks down at her and shrugs. "Computable? Probably not. But *knowable*—"

There's no time for this, Clarke tells herself. *I've got to get to work.*

"—that's something else again," Acton says.

She never figured him for a bookworm. Still, there he is again, plugged into the library. Stray light from the eyephones leaks across his cheeks.

He seems to be spending a lot of time in there these days. Almost as much time as he spends outside.

Clarke glances down at the flatscreen as she wanders past. It's dark.

"Chemistry," Brander says from across the lounge.

She looks at him.

Brander jerks his thumb at the oblivious Acton. "That's what he's into. Weird shit. Boring as hell."

That's what Ballard was into, just before . . . Clarke fingers a spare headset from the next terminal.

"Ooh, you're walking a fine line there," Brander remarks. "Mr. Acton doesn't *like* people reading over his shoulder."

Then Mr. Acton will be in privacy mode and I won't be able to. She sits down and slips the headset on. Acton has not invoked privacy; Clarke taps into his line without any trouble. The eyephone lasers etch text and formulae across her retinas. Serotonin. Acetylcholine. Neuropeptide moderation. Brander's right: it's really boring.

Someone's touching her.

She does not yank the headset off. She removes it calmly. She doesn't even flinch, this time. She will not give him the satisfaction.

Acton has turned in his chair to face her, headset dangling around his neck. His hand is on her knee.

"Glad to see we have common interests," he says quietly. "Not that surprising, though. We do share a certain . . . chemistry . . ."

"That's true." She stares back, safe behind her eyecaps. "Too bad I'm allergic to shitheads."

He smiles. "Of course, it would never work. The ages are all wrong." He stands up, returns the headset to its hook.

"I'm not nearly old enough to be your father."

He crosses the lounge and climbs downstairs.

"What an asshole," Brander remarks.

"He's more of a prick than Fischer ever was. I'm surprised you're not picking fights with *him* all the time."

Brander shrugs. "Different dynamic. Acton's just an asshole. Fischer was a fucking *pervert*."

Not to mention that Fischer never fought back. She keeps the insight to herself.

Concentric circles, glowing emerald. Beebe Station sits on the bull's-eye. Intermittent blobs of weaker light litter the display: fissures and jagged rock outcroppings, endless muddy plains, the Euclidean outlines of human machinery all reduced to a common acoustic currency.

There's something else out there too, part Euclid, part Darwin. Clarke zooms in. Human flesh is too much like seawater to return an echo, but bones show up okay. The machinery inside is even clearer, it shouts at the faintest sonar signal. Clarke focuses the display, points at a translucent green skeleton with clockwork in its chest.

"That him?" Caraco says.

Clarke shakes her head.

"Maybe it is. Everyone else is—"

"It's not him." Clarke touches a control. The display zooms back to maximum range. "You sure he's not in his quarters?"

"He left the station seven hours ago. Hasn't been back since."

"Maybe he's just hugging the bottom. Maybe he's behind a rock."

"Maybe." Caraco sounds unconvinced.

Clarke leans back in her chair. The back of her head touches the rear wall of the cubby. "Well, he's doing his job okay. When he's off shift he can go wherever he likes, I guess."

"Yeah, but this is the third time. He's always *late*. He just wanders in whenever he likes—"

"So what?" Clarke, suddenly tired, rubs the bridge of her nose between thumb and forefinger. "We don't run on dryback schedules here, you know that. He pulls his weight, don't fuck with him."

"Well, Fischer was always getting shit for being l—"

"Nobody cared if Fischer was late," Clarke cuts in. "They just—wanted an excuse."

Caraco leans forward. "I don't like him," she confides.

"Acton? No reason you should. He's psycho. We all are, remember?"

"But he's different, somehow. You know that."

"Lubin nearly killed his wife down at Galápagos before they assigned him here. Brander's got a history of attempted suicide."

Something changes in Caraco's stance. Clarke can't be sure, but the other woman's gaze seems to have dropped to the deck. *Touched a nerve there, I guess.*

She continues, more gently. "You're not worried

about the rest of us, are you? So what's so special about Acton?"

"Oh," Caraco says. "Look."

On the tactical display, something has just moved into range.

Clarke zooms in on the new reading; it's too distant for good resolution, but there's no mistaking the hard metallic blip in its center.

"Acton," she says.

"Um . . . how far?" Caraco asks in a hesitant voice.

Clarke checks. "He's about nine hundred meters out. Not too bad, if he's using a squid."

"He's not. He never does."

"Hmm. At least he seems to be beelining in." Clarke looks up at Caraco. "You two are on shift when?"

"Ten minutes."

"No big deal. He'll be fifteen minutes late. Half hour, tops."

Caraco stares at the display. "What's he *doing* out there?"

"I don't know," Clarke says. She wonders, not for the first time, if Caraco really belongs down here. She just doesn't seem to get it sometimes.

"I was wondering if you could maybe talk to him," Caraco says.

"Acton? Why?"

"Nothing. Forget it."

"Okay." Clarke rises from the Communications chair. Caraco backs out of the hatchway to let her past.

"Um, Lenie . . ."

Clarke turns.

"What about you?" Caraco asks.

"Me?"

"You said Lubin nearly killed his wife. Brander tried to kill himself. What did you do, I mean, to . . . qualify?"

Clarke watches her steadily.

"I mean, I guess, if it's not too—"

"You don't understand," Clarke says, her voice absolutely level. "It's not how much shit you've raised that suits you for the rift. It's how much you've survived."

"I'm sorry." Caraco manages, with eyes utterly devoid of feeling, to look abashed.

Clarke softens a bit. "In my case," she says, "mostly I just learned to roll with the punches. I haven't done much worth bragging about, you know?"

I'm sure enough working on it, though.

She doesn't know how it could have happened so fast. He's been here only two weeks, yet the 'lock can barely contain his eagerness to get outside. The chamber floods, she feels a single shiver scurry along his body; and before she can move, Acton hits the latch and they drop outside.

He coasts out from under the station, his trajectory an effortless parallel of her own. Clarke fins off toward the Throat. She feels Acton at her side, although she cannot see him. His headlamp, like hers, stays dark; for her it's become a gesture of respect to the more delicate lanterns that dwell here.

She doesn't know what Acton's reasoning is.

He doesn't speak until Beebe's a dirty yellow smudge behind them. "Sometimes I wonder why we ever go back inside."

It can't be happiness in that voice. How could any emotion make it through the mechanical gauntlet that lets people speak out here?

"I fell asleep near the Throat yesterday," he says.

"You're lucky something didn't eat you," she tells him.

"They're not so bad. You just have to know how to relate to them."

Clarke wonders if he relates to other species with the same subtlety that he relates to his own. She keeps the question to herself.

They swim through sparse, living starlight for a while. Another smudge glimmers ahead, weak and sullen; the Throat, dead on target. It's been months now since Clarke has even thought of the guide rope that's supposed to lead them back and forth, like blind troglodytes. She knows where it is, but she never uses it. Other senses come awake down here. Rifters don't get lost.

Except Fischer, maybe. And Fischer was lost long before he came down here.

"So what happened to Fischer, anyway?" Acton says.

The chill starts in her chest, reaches her fingers before the sound of Acton's voice has died away. *It's a coincidence. It's a perfectly normal question to ask.*

"I said—"

"He disappeared," Clarke says.

"They told me that much," Acton buzzes back. "I thought you might have a bit more insight."

"Maybe he fell asleep outside. Maybe something ate him."

"I doubt that."

"Really? And what makes you such an expert, Acton? You've been down here for what, two weeks now?"

"Only two weeks? Seems longer. Time stretches when you're outside, doesn't it?"

"At first," Clarke says.

"You know why Fischer disappeared?"

"No."

"He outlived his usefulness."

"Ah." Her machine parts turn it into half creak, half growl.

"I'm serious, Lenie." Acton's mechanical voice does not change. "You think they're going to let you stay down here forever? You think they'd let people like us down here at all if they had any choice?"

She stops kicking. Her body continues to coast. "What are you talking about?"

"Use your head, Lenie. You're smarter than I am, inside at least. You've got the keys to the city here—you've got the keys to the whole fucking seaboard, and you're still acting like a victim." Acton's vocoder gurgles indecipherably—a laugh, mistransposed? A snarl?

More words: "They count on that, you know."

Clarke starts kicking again, stares ahead to the brightening glow of the Throat.

It isn't there.

There's a moment's disorientation—*We can't be lost, we were headed right for it, has the power gone out?*—before she sees the familiar streak of coarse yellow light, bearing four o'clock.

How could I have gotten turned around like that?

"We're here," Acton says.

"No. The Throat's way over—"

A nova flares beside her, drenching the abyss with blinding light. It takes Clarke's eyecaps a moment to adjust; when the starbursts have faded from her eyes, the ocean is a muddy black backdrop for the bright cone from Acton's headlamp.

"Don't," she says. "It gets so dark when you do that, you can't see anything—"

"I know. I'll turn it off in a moment. Just look."

His beam shines down on a small rocky outcropping rising from the mud, no more than two meters across. Jagged cookie-cutter flowers litter its surface, radial clusters shining garish red and blue in the artificial light. Some of them lie flat along the rock face. Others are contorted into frozen calcareous knots, clenched around things Clarke can't see.

Some of them move, slowly.

"You brought me out here to look at starfish?" She tries, and fails, to squeeze some hint of bored contempt through the vocoder. But inside, there's a distant, frightened amazement that he *has* led her here, that she could be guided, utterly unsuspecting, so completely off course. *And how* did *he find this place? No sonar pistol, compass doesn't work worth shit this close to the Throat . . .*

"I figured you probably hadn't looked at them very closely before," Acton says. "I thought you might be interested."

"We don't have time for this, Acton."

His hands reach down into the light and lock on to one of the starfish. They peel it slowly from the rock; there are filaments of some kind along the creature's underside, anchoring it to the substrate. Acton's efforts tear them free, a few at a time.

He holds the animal up for Clarke's inspection. Its upper surface is colored stone, encrusted with calcareous spicules. Acton flips it over. The underside writhes with hundreds of thick squirming threads, jammed into dense rows along the length of each arm. Each thread has a tiny sucker at its tip.

"A starfish," Acton tells her, "is the ultimate democracy."

Clarke stares, quietly repelled.

"This is how they move," Acton is saying. "They walk along on all these tube feet. But the weird thing is, they have no brains at all. Not surprising for a democracy."

Rows of squirming maggots. A forest of translucent leeches, groping blindly into the water.

"So there's nothing to coordinate the tube feet, they all move independently. Usually that's not a problem; they all tend to go toward food, for example. But it's not unusual for a third of these feet to be pulling in some other direction entirely. The whole animal's a living tug-of-war. Sometimes, some really stubborn tube feet just don't give up, and they literally get torn out at the roots when the others move the body someplace they don't want to go. But hey: majority rules, right?"

Clarke extends a tentative finger. Half a dozen tube feet latch on to it. She can't feel them through her 'skin. Anchored, they look almost delicate, like filaments of milky glass.

"But that's nothing," Acton says. "Watch this."

He rips the starfish in half.

Clarke pulls back, shocked and angry. But there's something in Acton's posture, in that barely visible outline behind his lamp, that makes her pause.

"Don't worry, Lenie," he says. "I haven't killed it. I've *bred* it."

He drops the torn halves. They flutter like leaves to the seabed, trailing bits of bloodless entrail.

"They regenerate. Didn't you know that? You can tear them into pieces and each piece grows back the missing parts. It takes time, but they recover. Only, you end up with more of them. Damn hard to kill these guys.

"Understand, Lenie? Tear them to pieces, they come back stronger."

"How do you know all this?" she asks in a metallic whisper. "Where do you come from?"

He lays an icy black hand on her arm. "Right here. This is where I was born."

She doesn't think it absurd. In fact, she barely hears him. Her mind is somewhere else entirely, terrified by a sudden realization.

Acton is touching her, and she doesn't mind.

Of course, the sex is electric. It always is. The familiar has reasserted itself, here in the cramped space of Clarke's cubby. They can't both lie on the pallet at the same time but they manage somehow, Acton on his knees, then Clarke, squirming around each other in a metal nest lined with ducts and vents and bundles of optical cabling. They navigate each others' seams and scars, tonguing puckers of metal and pale flesh, unseen and all-seeing behind their corneal armor.

For Clarke it's a new twist, this icy ecstasy of a lover without eyes. For the first time she feels no need to avert her face, no threat to fragile intimacy; at first, when Acton moved to take out his caps, she stopped him with a touch and a whisper and he seemed to understand.

They cannot lie together afterward so they sit side by side, leaning into each other, staring at the hatch two meters in front of them. The lights are turned too low for dryback vision; Clarke and Acton see a room suffused in pale fluorescence.

Acton reaches out and fingers a shard of glass sticking from an empty frame on one wall. "There used to be a mirror here," he remarks.

Clarke nibbles his shoulder. "There were mirrors everywhere. I—took them down."

"Why? A few mirrors would open the place up a bit. Make it larger."

She points. Several torn wires, fine as threads, hang from a hole in the frame. "They had cameras behind them. I didn't like that."

Acton grunts. "I don't blame you."

They sit without speaking for a bit.

"You said something outside," she says. "You said you were born down here."

Acton hesitates, then nods. "Ten days ago."

"What did you mean?"

"You should know," he says. "You witnessed my birth."

She thinks back. "That was when the gulper got you. . . ."

"Close." Acton grins his cold eyeless grin, puts an arm around her. "Actually, the gulper sort of catalyzed it, if I remember. Think of it as a midwife."

An image pops into her mind: Acton in Medical, vivisecting himself.

"Fine-tuning," she says.

"Uh-huh." He gives her a squeeze. "And I've got you to thank for it. You gave me the idea."

"Me?"

"You were my mother, Len. And my father was this spastic little shrimp that ended up way over its head. He died before I was born, actually: I killed him. You weren't very happy about that."

Clarke shakes her head. "You're not making sense."

"You telling me you haven't noticed the change? You telling me I'm the same person I was when I came down?"

"I don't know," she says. "Maybe I've just gotten to know you better."

"Maybe. Maybe I have, too. I don't know, Len, I just seem more . . . *awake* now, I guess. I see things differently. You must have noticed."

"Yeah, but only when you're—"

Outside.

"You did something to your inhibitors," she whispers.

"Reduced the dosage a bit."

She grasps his arm. "Karl, those chemicals keep you from spazzing out every time you go outside. You fuck with this stuff, you're risking a seizure as soon as the 'lock floods."

"I *have* been fucking with it, Lenie. You see any change in me that isn't an improvement?"

She doesn't answer.

"It's all about action potential," he tells her. "Your nerves have to build up a certain charge before they can fire—"

"And at this depth they'd fire all the time. Karl, please—"

"Shh." He lays a gentle finger on her lips but she brushes it away, suddenly angry.

"I'm serious, Karl. Without those drugs your nerves short-circuit, you burn out, I *know*—"

"You only know what they tell you," he snaps. "Why don't you try working things out yourself for once?"

She falls silent, stung by his disapproval. A space opens between them on the pallet.

"I'm not a fool, Lenie," Acton says, more quietly. "I just reduced the settings a bit. Five percent. Now when I go outside it takes a bit less of a stimulus for my nerves to fire, that's all. It—it wakes you up, Len; I'm more aware of things, I'm more alive somehow."

She watches him, unspeaking.

"Of course they *say* it's dangerous," he says. "They're scared shitless of you already. You think they're going to give you even more of an edge?"

"They're not scared of us, Karl."

"They should be." His arm goes back around her. "Wanna try it?"

It's as though she's suddenly outside, still naked. "No."

"There's nothing to worry about, Len. I've already done the guinea-pig work on myself. Open up to me and I could make the adjustments myself, it'd take ten minutes."

"I'm not up for it, Karl. Not yet, anyway. Maybe one of the others is."

He shakes his head. "They don't trust me."

"You can't blame them."

"I don't." He grins, showing teeth as sharp and white as eyecaps. "But even if they did trust me, they wouldn't do anything unless you thought it was okay."

She looks at him. "Why not?"

"You're in charge here, Len."

"Bullshit. They never told you that."

"They didn't have to. It's obvious."

"I've been down here longer than them. So's Lubin. That doesn't matter to anyone."

Acton frowns briefly. "No, I don't think it does. But you're still leader of the pack, Len. Head wolf. A-fucking-kayla."

Clarke shakes her head. She searches her memory for something, anything, that would contradict Acton's absurd claim. She comes up empty.

She feels a little sick inside.

He gives her a squeeze. "Tough luck, lover. I guess the clothes don't fit so well after being a career victim your whole life, eh?"

Clarke stares at the deck.

"Think about it, anyway," Acton whispers in her ear. "I guarantee you'll feel twice as alive as you do now."

"That happens anyway," Clarke reminds him. "Whenever I go outside. I don't need to screw up my internals for that." *Not those internals, anyway.*

"This is different," he insists.

She looks at him and smiles, and hopes he doesn't push it. *How can he expect me to let him cut me open like that?* she wonders, and then wonders if maybe someday she will, if the fear of losing him might somehow grow large enough to force her other fears into submission. It wouldn't be the first time.

Twice as alive, Acton says. Hiding behind her smile, Clarke considers: Twice as much of her life. Not a great prospect, so far.

There's a light from behind; it chases her shadow out along the seabed. She can't remember how long it's been there. She feels a momentary chill—

—Fischer?—

—before common sense sets in. Gerry Fischer wouldn't use a headlamp.

"Lenie?"

She revolves on her own axis, sees a silhouette hovering a few meters away. Cyclopean light glares from its forehead. Clarke hears a subvocal buzz, the corrupted equivalent of Brander clearing his throat. "Judy said you were out here," he explains.

"Judy." She means it as a question, but her vocoder loses the intonation.

"Yeah. She sort of, keeps tabs on you sometimes."

Clarke considers that a moment. "Tell her I'm harmless."

"It's not like that," he buzzes. "I think she just . . . worries . . ."

Clarke feels muscles twitching at the corners of her mouth. She thinks she might be smiling.

"So I guess we're on shift," she says, after a moment.

The headlight bobs up and down. "Right. A bunch of clams need their asses scraped. More quantum science."

She stretches, weightless. "Okay. Let's go."

"Lenie . . ."

She looks up at him.

"Why do you come—I mean, why *here*?" Brander's headlight sweeps the bottom, comes to rest on an outcropping of bone and rotted flesh. A skeletal smile stitches its way across the lit circle. "Did you kill it, or something?"

"Yeah, I—" She falls silent, realizing: *He means the whale.*

"Nah," she says instead. "It just died on its own."

Of course, she wakes up alone. They still try to sleep together sometimes, after sex has made them too lazy to go outside. But the bunk is too small. The most they can manage is a sort of diagonal slouch: feet on the floor, necks bent up against the bulkhead, Acton cradling her like a living hammock. If they're unlucky they really do fall asleep like that. It takes hours to get the kinks out afterward. Way more trouble than it's worth.

So she wakes up alone. But she misses him anyway.

It's early. The schedules handed down from the GA are increasingly irrelevant—circadian rhythms lose their way in the incessant darkness, fall slowly out of phase— but the rubbery timetable that remains leaves hours before her shift starts. Lenie Clarke is awake in the middle of the night. It seems like a stupid and obvious thing to say, months from the nearest sunrise, but right now it seems especially true.

In the corridor she turns for a moment in the direction of his cubby before she remembers. He's never in there anymore. He's never even inside, unless he's eating or working or being with her. He's barely slept in his quarters almost since they got involved. He's getting almost as bad as Lubin.

Caraco is sitting silently in the lounge, unmoving, obeying her own inner clock. She looks up as Clarke crosses to Comm.

"He went out about an hour ago," she says softly.

Sonar picks him up fifty meters southeast, barely echoing above the bottom clutter. Clarke heads for the ladder.

"He showed us something the other day," Caraco says after her. "Ken and me."

Clarke looks back.

"A smoker, way off in one corner of the Throat. It had this weird fluted vent, and it made singing sounds, almost . . ."

"Mmm."

"He really wanted us to know about it, for some rea-

son. He was really excited. He's—he's kind of strange
out there, Lenie . . ."

"Judy," Clarke says neutrally, "why are you telling
me this?"

Caraco looks away. "Sorry. I didn't mean anything."

Clarke starts down the ladder.

"Just be careful, okay?" Caraco calls after her.

He's curled up when Clarke reaches him, knees
tucked under his chin, floating a few centimeters above
a stone garden. His eyes are open, of course. She reaches
out, touches him through two layers of reflex copolymer.

He barely stirs. His vocoder emits sporadic ticking
noises.

Lenie Clarke curls herself around him. In a womb of
freezing seawater, they sleep on until morning.

Short-circuit

I won't give in.

It would be so easy. She could live out there, stay the
fuck away from this creaking eggshell except to eat and
bathe and do whatever parts of her job demand an atmosphere. She could spend her whole life flying across the
seabed. Lubin does. Brander and Caraco and even Nakata are starting to.

Lenie Clarke knows she doesn't belong in here. None
of them do.

But at the same time, she's scared of what *outside*
might do to her. *I could end up like Fischer. It would
be so easy to just—slip away. If a hot seep or mud slide
didn't get me first.*

Lately she's been valuing her own life quite a lot.
Maybe that means she's losing it. What kind of a rifter
cares about living? But there it is: The rift is starting to
scare her.

That's bullshit. Complete, total bullshit.

Who *wouldn't* be scared?

Scared. Yes. Of Karl. Of what you'll let him do to you.

It's been, what, a week now?—

Two days.

—two days since she's slept outside. Two days since she decided to incarcerate herself in here. She goes outside to work, and comes back as soon as each shift ends. No one's mentioned the change to her. Perhaps no one's noticed; if they don't come back to Beebe themselves after work, they scatter off across the seabed to do whatever they do in splendid, freezing isolation.

She knew Acton would notice, though. He'd notice, and miss her, and follow her back inside. Or maybe he'd try and talk her back out, fight with her when she resisted. But he's shown no sign at all. He spends as much time out there as he ever did. She still sees him, of course. At mealtimes. At the library. Once for sex, during which neither spoke of anything important. And then gone again, back into the ocean.

He didn't enter into any pact with her. She didn't even tell him about her pact with herself. Still, she feels betrayed.

She needs him. She knows what that means, sees her own footprints crowding the road ahead, but reading the signs and changing course are two completely different things. Her insides are twisting with the need to go, whether out to him or just *out*, she can't say. But as long as he's outside and she's in Beebe, Lenie Clarke can tell herself that she's still in control.

It's progress, sort of.

Now, curled up in her cubby with the hatch sealed tight, she hears the subterranean gurgle of the airlock. She comes up off the bed as though radio-controlled.

Noises, flesh against metal, hydraulics and pneumatics. A voice. Lenie Clarke is on her way to the wetroom.

He's brought a monster inside with him. It's an anglerfish, almost two meters long, a jellylike bag of flesh with teeth half the length of Clarke's forearm. It lies quivering on the deck, its insides exploded through its own mouth in the near vacuum of Beebe's sea-level atmosphere. Dozens of miniature tails, twitching feebly, sprout everywhere from its body.

Caraco and Lubin, in the middle of some task, look over from the engineering 'lock. Acton stands beside his catch; his thorax, still inflating, hisses softly.

"How did you fit it inside the 'lock?" Clarke wonders.

"More to the point," Lubin says, coming over, "why bother?"

"What're all those tails?" Caraco says.

Acton grins at them. "Not tails. Mates."

Lubin's face doesn't change. "Really."

Clarke leans forward. Not just tails, she sees now; some of them have those extra fins along the side and back. Some of them have gills. A couple of them even have eyes. It's as though a whole school of tiny anglers are boring into this big one. Some are in only as far as their jaws, but others are buried right down to the tail.

Another thought strikes her, even more revolting; the big fish doesn't need its mouth anymore. It's just *engulfing* the little ones across its body wall, like some giant devolving microbe.

"Group sex on the rift," says Acton. "All the big ones we've been seeing, they're female. The males are these little finger-sized fuckers here. Not many dating opportunities this far down, so they just latch on to the first female they can find, and they sort of *fuse*—their heads get absorbed, their bloodstreams link together. They're parasites, get it? They worm into her side and they spend their whole lives feeding off her. And there's a fuck of a lot of them, but she's bigger than they are, she's stronger, she could eat them alive if she just—"

"He's been in the library again," Caraco remarks.

Acton looks at her for a moment. Deliberately, he points at the bloated carcass on the deck. "That's us." He grabs one of the parasitic males, rips it free. "This is everyone else. Get it?"

"Ah," Lubin says. "A metaphor. Clever."

Acton takes a single step toward the other man. "Lubin, I am getting awfully fucking tired of you."

"Really." Lubin doesn't seem the least bit threatened.

Clarke moves; not directly between them, just off to one side, forming the apex of a human triangle. She has absolutely no idea what to do if this comes to blows. She has no idea what to say to stop that from happening.

Suddenly, she's not even sure that she wants to.

"Come on, you guys." Caraco leans back against the drying rack. "Can't you settle this some other way? Maybe you could just whip out a ruler and compare your dicks or something."

They stare at her.

"Watch it, Judy. You're getting pretty cocky there."

Now they're staring at Clarke.

Did I say that?

For a long, long moment nothing happens. Then Lubin grunts and goes back to the workshop. Acton watches him go; then, deprived of an immediate threat, he steps back into the airlock.

The dead angler shivers on the deck, bristling with infestation.

"Lenie, he's really getting weird," Caraco says as the 'lock floods. "Maybe you should just let him go."

Clarke just shakes her head. "Go where?"

She even manages a smile.

She was looking for Karl Acton, but somehow she's found Gerry Fischer instead. He looks sadly down at her through the length of a long tunnel. He seems to be a whole ocean away. He doesn't speak but she senses sadness, disappointment. *You lied to me,* that feeling says. *You said you'd come and see me and you lied. You've forgotten all about me.*

He's wrong. She hasn't forgotten him at all. She's only tried to.

She doesn't say it aloud, of course, but somehow he reacts to it anyway. His feelings change; sadness fades, something colder seeps up in its place, something so deep and so old that she can't think of words to describe it.

Something pure.

From behind, a touch on her shoulder. She spins, instantly alert, hand closing around her billy.

"Hey, calm down. It's me." Acton's silhouette hangs against a faint wash of light from the direction of the Throat. Clarke relaxes, pushes gently at his chest. Says nothing.

"Welcome back," Acton says. "Haven't seen you out here for a while."

"I was—I was looking for you," she says.

"In the mud?"

"What?"

"You were just floating there, facedown."

"I was—" She feels a vestige of disquiet, but she can't remember what to attach it to. "I must have drifted off. I was dreaming. It's been so long since I slept out here, I—"

"Four days, I think. I missed you."

"Well, you could have come inside."

Acton nods. "I tried. But I could never get all of me through the airlock, and the part that I could—well, it was sort of a poor substitute. If you'll remember."

"I don't know, Karl. You know how I feel—"

"Right. And I know you like it out here as much as I do. Sometimes I feel like I could just stay out here forever." He pauses for a moment, as if weighing alternatives. "Fischer's got it right."

Something goes cold. "Fischer?"

"He's still out here, Len. You know that."

"You've seen him?"

"Not often. He's pretty skittish."

"When do . . . I mean—"

"Only when I'm alone. And pretty far from Beebe."

She looks around, inexplicably frightened. *Of course you can't see him. He isn't here. And even if he was, it's still too dark to . . .*

She forces herself to leave her headlamp doused.

"He's . . . I think he's really hooked in to you, Len. But I guess you know that too."

No. No, I didn't. I don't. "He talks to you?" She doesn't know why she'd resent that.

"No."

"Then how?"

Acton doesn't answer for a moment. "I don't know. I just got that impression. But he doesn't talk. It's . . . I don't know, Len. He just hangs around out there and watches us. I don't know if he's what we'd consider . . . sane, I guess—"

"He watches us," she says, buzzing low and level.

"He knows we're together. I think . . . I think he figures that connects me and him somehow." Acton is silent for a bit. "You cared about him, didn't you?"

Oh yes. It always starts off so innocently. *You cared about him, that's nice,* and then it's *did you find him attractive* and then *well you must have done something or he wouldn't keep hitting on you* and then *you fucking slut I'll—*

"Lenie," Acton says. "I'm not trying to start anything."

She waits and watches.

"I know there was nothing going on. And even if there was, I know it's no threat."

She's heard this part before, too.

"Now that I think about it, that's always been my problem," Acton muses. "I always had to go on what other people told me, and people—People lie all the time, Len, you know that. So no matter how many times she swears she's not fucking around on you, or even that she doesn't *want* to fuck around on you, how can you ever really *know*? You can't. So the default assumption is, she's lying. And being lied to all the time, that's a damn good reason for—well, for doing what I do sometimes."

"Karl—you know—"

"I know *you* don't lie to me. You don't even hate me. That's kind of a change."

She reaches out to touch the side of his face. "I'd say that's a good call. I'm glad you trust me."

"Actually, Len, I don't *have* to trust you. I just *know*."

"What do you mean? How?"

"I'm not sure," he says. "It's something to do with the changes."

He waits for her to respond.

"What are you saying, Karl?" she says at last. "Are you saying you can read my mind?"

"No. Nothing like that. I just, well, I identify with you more. I can—It's kind of hard to explain—"

She remembers him levitating beside a luminous smoker: *The Pompeii worms can predict them. The clams and brachyurans can predict them. Why not me?*

He's tuned in, she realizes. *To everything. He's even tuned in to the bloody worms, that's what he—*

He's tuned in to Fischer—

She tongues the light switch. A bright cone stabs into the abyss. She sweeps the water around them. Nothing.

"Have the others seen him?"

"I don't know. I think Caraco caught him on sonar once or twice."

"Let's go back," Clarke says.

"Let's not. Stay awhile. Spend the night."

She looks straight into his empty lenses. "Please, Karl. Come with me. Sleep inside for a bit."

"He's not dangerous, Len."

"That's not it." *At least, that's not all.*

"What, then?"

"Karl, has it ever occurred to you that you might be developing some sort of dependence on this nerve rush of yours?"

"Come on, Len. The rift gives us all a rush. That's why we're down here."

"We get a rush because we're fucked in the head. That doesn't mean we should go out of our way to augment the effect."

"Lenie—"

"Karl." She lays her hands on his shoulders. "I don't know what happens to you out here. But whatever it is, it scares me."

He nods. "I know."

"Then please, please try it my way. Try sleeping inside again, just for a while. Try not to spend every waking moment climbing around on the bottom of the ocean, okay?"

"Lenie, I don't like myself inside. *You* don't even like me inside."

"Maybe. I don't know. I just—I just don't know how to deal with you when you're like this."

"When I'm not about to beat the shit out of anyone? When I'm acting like a rational human being? If we'd had this conversation back at Beebe we'd be throwing things at each other by now." He falls silent for a moment. Something changes in his posture. "Or do you *miss* that somehow?"

"No. Of course not," she says, surprised at the thought.

"Well, then—"

"Please. Just indulge me. What harm can it do?"

He doesn't answer. But she has a sneaking suspicion that he could.

She has to give him credit. His reluctance shows in every move, but he's even first through the airlock. Something happens to him as it drains, though; the air rushes into him and—displaces something else, somehow. She can't quite put her finger on it. She wonders why she's never noticed it before.

As a reward, she takes him directly into her cubby. He fucks her up against the bulkhead, violently, with no discretion at all. Animal sounds echo through the hull. She wonders, as he comes, if the noise is bothering the others.

"Have any of you," Acton says, "thought about why things are so fucking grotty down here?"

It's a strange and wondrous occasion, as rare as a planetary conjunction. All the circadian clocks have drifted together for an hour or two, drawn everyone to dinner at the same time. Almost everyone; Lubin is nowhere to be seen. Not that he ever contributes much to the conversation anyway.

"What do you mean?" Caraco says.

"What do you *think* I mean? Look around, for Christ's sake!" Acton waves his arm, taking in the lounge. "The place is barely big enough to stand up in. Everywhere you look there's fucking pipes and cables. It's like living in a service closet."

Brander frowns around a mouthful of rehydrated potato.

"They were on a very strict schedule," Nakata suggests. "It was important to get everything online as quickly as possible. Perhaps they just didn't have time to make everything as cushy as they could have."

Acton snorts. "Come on, Alice. How much extra time would it take to program the blueprints for decent headroom?"

"I feel a conspiracy theory coming on," Brander remarks. "So go on, Karl. Why's the GA going out of its way to make us bump our heads all the time? They breeding us for short height, maybe? So we'll eat less?"

Lenie Clarke feels Acton tensing; it's like a small shock wave pushed out by his clenching muscles, a pulse of tension that ripples through the air and breaks against her 'skin. She rests one calming hand casually on his thigh, under the table. It's a calculated risk, of course. It would piss him off even more if Acton thought he was being patronized.

This time he relaxes a little. "I think they're trying to keep us off balance. I think they deliberately designed Beebe to stress us out."

"Why?" Caraco again, tense but civil.

"Because it gives them an advantage. The more time we spend being on edge, the less time we have to think about what we could do to them if we really wanted to."

"And what's that?"

"Use your head, Judy. We could black out the grid from the Charlottes down to Portland."

"They'd just switch feeds," Brander says. "There are other deep stations."

"Yeah. And they're all staffed by people just like us." Acton slaps the table with one hand. "Come *on*, you guys. They don't *want* us down here. They *hate* us, we're sickos that beat up our wives and eat our babies for breakfast. If it weren't for the fact that anyone else would flip out down here—"

Clarke shakes her head. "But they could get us out of the loop completely if they wanted. Just automate everything."

"Hallelujah." Acton brings his hands together in sarcastic applause. "The woman's got it at last."

Brander leans back in his chair. "Give it a rest, Acton. Haven't you ever worked for the GA before? You ever work for *any* sort of bureaucracy?"

Acton's gaze swivels, locks on to the other man. "What's your point?"

Brander looks back with a hint of a sneer on his face. "My point, *Karl*, is that you're reading way too much into this. So they made the ceiling too low. So their interior decorator's not worth shit. So what else is new? The GA just isn't that scared of you." He takes in Beebe with a wave of his arm. "This isn't some subtle psychological war. Beebe was just designed by incompetent bozos." Brander stands up, takes his plate to the galley. "If you don't like the headroom, stay outside."

Acton looks at Lenie Clarke, his face utterly devoid of expression. "Oh, I'd like to. Believe me."

He's hunched over the library terminal, 'phones on his ears, 'phones on his eyes, the flatscreen blanked as usual to hide his litsearch from view. As if anything in the database could really be personal. As if the GA would ever ration out any fact worth hiding.

She's learned not to bother him when he's like this. He's hunting in there, he resents any distraction, as though the files he's after might somehow escape if he looks the other way. She doesn't touch him. She doesn't run a gentle finger along his arm or try to work the knots from his shoulders. Not anymore. There are some mistakes that Lenie Clarke can learn from.

He's actually helpless in a strange way; cut off from the rest of Beebe, deaf and blind to the presence of people who are by no means friends. Brander could come up behind him right now and plant a knife in his back. And yet everyone leaves him alone. It's as though his sensory exile, this self-imposed vulnerability, is some sort of brazen dare that no one has the guts to take him up on. So Acton sits at the keyboard—tapping at first, now stabbing—in his own private datasphere, and his deaf blind presence somehow dominates the lounge out of all proportion to his physical size.

"FUCK!"

He tears the 'phones from his face and slams his fist down on the console. Nothing even cracks. He glares around the lounge, white eyes blazing, and settles on Nakata over in the galley. Lenie Clarke, wisely, has avoided eye contact.

"This database is fucking ancient! They stick us down this fucking black anus for months at a time and they don't even give us a link to the Net!"

Nakata spreads her hands. "The Net's infected," she says, nervously. "They send us scrubbed downloads every month or s—"

"I fucking know that." Acton's voice is suddenly, ominously calm. Nakata takes the hint and falls silent.

He stands up. The whole room seems to shrink down around him. "I've got to get out of here," he says at last. He takes a step toward the ladder, glances at Clarke. "Coming?"

She shakes her head.

"Suit yourself."

Caraco, maybe. She's made overtures in the past.

Not that Clarke ever took them. But things are changing. There aren't just two Karl Actons anymore. There used to be; all of her partners have been twosomes, in fact. There's always been a host, some magnetic chassis whose face and name never mattered because it would change without warning. And providing continuity, riding along behind each twinkling pair of eyes, there's always been the thing inside, and it *never* changes. Nor, to be honest, would Lenie Clarke know what to do if it did.

Now there's something new: the thing *out*side. So far at least, it has shown no trace of violence. It does seem to have X-ray vision, which could be even worse.

Lenie Clarke has always slept with the thing inside. Until now, she'd always just assumed it was for want of an alternative.

She taps lightly on Caraco's hatch. "Judy? You there?" She should be; she's nowhere else in Beebe, and sonar can't find any trace of her outside.

No answer.

It can wait.

No. It's waited long enough.

How would I feel if—

She isn't me.

The hatch is closed but not dogged. Clarke pulls it open a few centimeters and peers inside.

Somehow they've managed to pull it off. Alice Nakata and Judy Caraco spoon around each other on that tiny bunk. Their eyes dart restlessly beneath closed lids. Nakata's dreamer stands guard beside them, its tendrils pasted to their bodies.

Clarke lets the hatch hiss shut again.

It was a stupid idea anyhow. What would she know?

She wonders how long they've been together, though. She never even saw that coming.

"Your boyfriend isn't here," Lubin calls in. "We were supposed to top up the coolant on number seven."

Clarke calls up the topographic display. "How long ago?"

"Oh four hundred."

"Okay." Acton's half an hour late. That's unusual; he's been going out of his way to be punctual these days, a grudging concession to Clarke in the name of group relations. "I can't find him on sonar," she reports. "Unless he's hugging the bottom. Hang on."

She leans out of the Comm cubby. "Hey. Anybody see Karl?"

"He left a while ago," Brander calls from the wetroom. "Maintenance on seven, I think."

Clarke punches back into Lubin's channel. "He's not here. Brander says he left already. I'll keep looking."

"Okay. At least his deadman switch hasn't gone off." Clarke can't tell whether Lubin thinks that's good or bad.

Movement at the corner of her eye. She looks up; Nakata's standing in the hatchway.

"Have you found him?" she asks.

Clarke shakes her head.

"He was in Medical, just before he left," Nakata says. "He was open. He said he was making some adjustments—"

Oh God.

"He said they improved performance outside, but he didn't explain. He said he would show me later. Maybe something went wrong."

External camera display, ventral view. The image flickers for a moment, then clears; on the screen, a scalloped circle of light lies across a flat muddy plain, transected by the knife-edge shadows of anchor cables. Near the edge of that circle is a black human figure, facedown, its hands held to either side of its head.

She wakes up the close acoustics. "Karl! Karl, can you hear me?"

He reacts. His head twists around, faces up into the floods; his eyecaps reflect featureless white glare into the camera. He's shaking.

"His vocoder," Nakata says. There's sound coming from the speaker, soft, repetitive, mechanical. "It's— stuttering—"

Clarke's already in the wetroom. She knows what Acton's vocoder is saying. She knows, because the same word is repeating over and over in her own head.

No. No. No. No. No.

No obvious motor impairment. He's able to make it back inside on his own; stiffens, in fact, when Clarke tries to help him. He strips his gear and follows her into Medical without a word.

Nakata, diplomatically, closes the hatch behind them.

Now he sits on the examination table, stone-faced. Clarke knows the routine; get his 'skin off, his eyecaps out. Check autonomic pupil response and reflex arcs. Stab him, draw off the usual samples: blood gases, acetylcholine, GABA, lactic acid.

She sits down beside him. She doesn't want his eyecaps out. She doesn't want to see behind them.

"Your inhibitors," she says at last. "How far down are they?"

"Twenty percent."

"Well." She tries for a light touch. "At least we know your limit now. Just nudge them back up to normal."

Almost imperceptibly, he shakes his head.

"Why not?"

"Too late. I went over some sort of threshold. I don't think—it doesn't feel reversible."

"I see." She puts one tentative hand on his arm. He doesn't react. "How *do* you feel?"

"Blind. Deaf."

"You're not, though."

"You asked how I *felt*," he says, still expressionless.

"Here." She takes the NMR helmet down from its hook. Acton lets her strap it across his skull. "If there's anything wrong, this should—"

"There's something wrong, Len."

"Well." The helmet writes its impressions across the diagnostic display. Clarke's got the same medical expertise they all have, stuffed into her mind by machines that hijacked her dreams. Still, the raw data mean nothing to her. It's almost a minute before the display prints out an executive summary.

"Your synaptic calcium's way down." She's careful not to show her relief. "Makes sense, I guess. Your neurons fire too often, eventually they run out of something."

He looks at the screen, saying nothing.

"Karl, it's okay." She leans toward his ear, one hand on his shoulder. "It'll fix itself. Just put your inhibitors back up to normal; demand goes down, supply keeps up. No harm done."

He shakes his head again. "Won't work."

"Karl, look at the readout. You're going to be fine."

"Please don't touch me," he says, not moving at all.

Critical Mass

Clarke catches a glimpse of fist before it hits her eye. She staggers back against the bulkhead, feels some protruding rivet or valve catch the back of her head. The world drowns in explosions of afterlight.

He's lost control, she thinks dully. *I win.* Her knees collapse under her; she slides down the wall, sits with a heavy thud on the deck. She considers it a matter of some pride that she's kept utterly silent through all this.

I wonder what I did to set him off. She can't remember. Acton's fist seems to have knocked the past few minutes out of her head. *Doesn't matter anyway. Same old dance.*

But this time there seems to be someone on her side. She can hear shouts, sounds of a scuffle. She hears the sick jarring thud of flesh against bone against metal, and for once, none of it seems to be hers.

"You *cocksucker*! I'll rip your fucking balls off!"

Brander's voice. Brander is sticking up for her. He always was the gallant one. Clarke smiles, tastes salt. *Of course, he never quite forgave Acton for that tiff over the gulper, either* . . .

Her vision is starting to clear, in one eye at least. There's a leg right in front of her, another to one side. She looks up; the legs meet at Caraco's crotch. Acton and Brander are in her cubby too; Clarke's amazed that they can all fit.

Acton, his mouth bloody, is under siege. Brander's hand is at his throat. Acton has the wrist of that hand caught in a grip of his own; while Clarke watches, his other arm lashes out and glances off Brander's jaw.

"Stop it," she mumbles.

Caraco hits Acton's temple twice in rapid succession. Acton's head snaps sideways, he snarls, but he doesn't release his grip on Brander.

"I said *stop it*!"

This time they hear her. The struggle slows, pauses; fists remain poised, no holds break, but they're all looking at her now.

Even Acton. Clarke looks up into his eyes, looks behind them. She can see nothing staring back but Acton
himself. *You were there before*, she remembers. *I'm almost sure of it. Count on you to get Karl into a losing
fight and then bugger off* . . .

She braces herself against the bulkhead and pushes
slowly erect. Caraco moves aside, helps her up.

"I'm flattered by all the attention, folks," Clarke says,
"and I want to thank you for stopping by, but I think we
can handle this on our own from here on in."

Caraco puts a protective hand on her shoulder. "You
don't have to put up with this shit." Her eyes, somehow
venomous through the shielding, are still locked on Acton. "None of us do."

One corner of Acton's mouth pulls back in a small,
bloody sneer.

Clarke endures Caraco's touch without flinching. "I
know that. And thanks for stepping in. But please, just
leave us alone for a while."

Brander doesn't loosen his grip on Acton's throat. "I
don't think that's a very good—"

*"Will you get your fucking hands off him and leave
us alone!"*

They back off. Clarke glares after them, dogs the
hatch to keep them out. "Goddamned nosy neighbors,"
she grumbles, turning back to Acton.

His body sags in the sudden privacy, all the anger and
bravado evaporating as she watches.

"Want to tell me why you're being such an asshole?"
she says.

Acton collapses on her pallet. He stares at the deck,
avoiding her eyes. "Don't you know when you're being
fucked over?"

Clarke sits down beside him. "Sure. Getting punched
out is pretty much a giveaway."

"I'm trying to *help* you. I'm trying to help *all* of you."

He turns and hugs her, body shaking, cheek pressed against hers, face aimed at the bulkhead behind her shoulder. "Oh God Lenie I'm so sorry you're the last person in the whole fucking world I want to hurt—"

She strokes him without speaking. She knows he means it. They always do. She still can't bring herself to blame any of them.

He thinks he's alone in there. He thinks it's all his own doing.

Briefly, an impossible thought: *Maybe it is. . . .*

"I can't go on with this," he says. "Staying inside."

"It'll get better, Karl. It's always hard at first."

"Oh God, Len. You don't have a clue. You still think I'm some sort of junkie."

"Karl—"

"You think I don't know what addiction is? You think I can't tell the difference?"

She doesn't answer.

He manages a small, sad laugh. "I'm losing it, Len. You're forcing me to lose it. Why in God's name do you want me this way?"

"Because this is who you are, Karl. Outside isn't you. Outside's a distortion."

"Outside I'm not an asshole. Outside I don't make everyone hate me."

"No." She hugs him. "If controlling your temper means seeing you turn into something else, seeing you doped up all the time, then I'll take my chances with the original."

Acton looks at her. "I hate this. Jesus Christ, Len. Won't you ever get tired of people who kick the shit out of you?"

"That's a really nasty thing to say," she remarks quietly.

"I don't think so. I can remember some things I saw

out there, Len. It's like you need—I mean God, Lenie, there's so much *hate* in all of you. . . ."

She's never heard him speak like this. Not even outside. "You've got a bit of that in you, too, you know."

"Yeah. I thought it made me different. I thought it gave me—an edge, you know?"

"It does."

He shakes his head. "Oh, no. Not next to you."

"Don't underrate yourself. You don't see me trying to take on the whole station."

"That's just it, Len. I blow it off all the time, I waste it on stupid shit like this. But you—you hoard it." His expression changes, she's not exactly sure what to. Concern, maybe. Worry. "Sometimes you scare me more than Lubin does. You never lash out, or beat on anybody—Christ, it's a major event when you even raise your voice—so it just builds up. It's got its upside, I guess." He manages a soft laugh. "Hatred's a great fuel source. If anything ever—activated you, you'd be unstoppable. But now, you're just—toxic. I don't think you really know how much hate you've got in you."

Pity?

Something inside her goes suddenly cool. "Don't play therapist with me, Karl. Just because your nerves fire too fast doesn't mean you've got second sight. You don't know me that well."

Of course not. Or you wouldn't be with me.

"Not in here." He smiles, but that strange, sick expression keeps showing through behind. "Outside, at least, I can see things. In here I'm blind."

"You're in the land of the blind," she says curtly. "It's not a drawback."

"Really? Would *you* stay here if it meant getting your eyes cut out? Would you stay someplace that rotted your brain out piece by piece, turned you from a human being into a fucking monkey?"

Clarke considers. "If I was a monkey to begin with, maybe."

Uh-oh. Sounded too flippant by half, didn't I?

Acton looks at her for a moment. Something else does too, drowsily, with one eye open.

"At least *I* don't get my endorphins by playing victim," he says, slowly. "You should really be a bit more careful who you choose to look down on."

"And you," Clarke replies, "should save the pious lectures for those rare occasions when you actually know what you're talking about."

He rises off the bed and glares at her, fists carefully unclenched.

Clarke does not move. She feels her whole body hardening from the inside out. She deliberately lifts her head until she's looking straight into Acton's hooded eyes.

It's in there now, fully awake. She can't see Acton at all anymore. Everything's back to normal.

"Don't even try," she says. "I gave you a couple of shots for old times' sake, but if you lay a hand on me again I swear I'll fucking kill you."

She marvels inwardly at the strength in her voice; it sounds like iron.

They stare at each other for an endless moment.

Acton's body turns on its heel and undogs the hatch. Clarke watches it step out of the cubby; Caraco, waiting in the corridor, lets it by without a word. Clarke holds herself utterly still until she hears the 'lock beginning to cycle.

He didn't call my bluff.

Except this time, she's not sure that that's all it was.

He doesn't see her.

It's been days since they've said anything to each other. Even their schedules have diverged. Tonight, as she was trying to sleep, she heard him come out of the abyss again and climb up into the lounge like some invading sea creature. He does it now and then when the place is deserted, when everyone is either outside or sealed into their cubicles. He sits there at the library, diving through his 'phones down endless virtual avenues, desperation in every movement. It's as though he has to hold his breath whenever he comes inside; once she saw him tear the headset off his skull and flee outside as though his chest would burst. When she picked up the abandoned headset, the results of his litsearch were still glowing in the eyephones. Chemistry.

Another time he turned on his way out, to see her standing in the corridor. He smiled. He even said something: "—*sorry*—" is what she heard, but there may have been more. He didn't stay.

Now his hands rest, unmoving, on the keyboard. His shoulders are shaking. He doesn't make any sound at all. Lenie Clarke closes her eyes for a moment, wondering whether to approach him. When she looks again the lounge is empty.

She can tell exactly where he's going. His icon buds off of Beebe and crawls away across the display, and there's only one thing in that direction.

When she gets there he's crawling across its back, digging a hole with his knife. Clarke's eyecaps can barely find enough light to see by, this far from the Throat; Acton cuts and slices in the light of her headlamp, his shadow writhing away across a horizon of dead flesh.

He's dug a crater, maybe half a meter across, half a meter deep. He's cut through the stratum of blubber below the skin and is tearing through the brown muscle beneath. It's been months now since this creature landed here. Clarke marvels at its preservation.

The abyss likes extremes, she muses. *If it isn't a pressure cooker, it's a fridge.*

Acton stops digging. He just floats there, staring down at his handiwork.

"What a stupid idea," he buzzes at last. "I don't know what gets into me sometimes." He turns to face her; his eyecaps reflect yellow. "I'm sorry, Lenie. I know this place was special to you somehow, I didn't mean to . . . well, desecrate it, I guess."

She shakes her head. "It's okay. It's not important."

Acton's vocoder gurgles; in air, it would be a sad laugh. "I give myself too much credit sometimes, Len. Whenever I'm inside, and I'm fucking up and I don't know what to do, I figure all I've got to do is come outside and the scales will fall off my eyes. It's like, religious faith almost. All the answers. Right out here."

"It's okay," Clarke says again, because it seems better than saying nothing.

"Only sometimes the answer doesn't really do much for you, you know? Sometimes the answer's just: 'Forget it. You're fucked.' " Acton looks back down at the dead whale. "Would you turn the light off?"

The darkness swallows them like a blanket. Clarke reaches through it and brings Acton to her. "What were you trying to do?"

That mechanical laugh again. "Something I read. I was thinking—"

His cheek brushes against hers.

"I don't know what I was thinking. When I'm inside I'm a fucking lobo case, I get these stupid ideas and even when I get back out it takes awhile before I really wake up and realize what a dork I've been. I wanted to study an adrenal gland. Thought it would help me figure out how to counter ion depletion at the synapse junctions."

"You know how to do that." ·

"Well, it was just bullshit anyway. I can't think straight in there."

She doesn't bother to argue.

"I'm sorry," Acton buzzes after a while.

Clarke strokes his back. It feels like two sheets of plastic rubbing together.

"I think I can explain it to you," he adds. "If you're interested."

"Sure." But she knows it won't change anything.

"You know how there's this strip in your brain that controls movement?"

"Okay."

"And if, say, you became a concert pianist, the part that runs your fingers would actually spread out, take up more of the strip to meet the increased demand for finger control. But you lose something, too. The adjacent parts of the strip get crowded out. So maybe you couldn't wiggle your toes or curl your tongue as well as you could before you started practicing."

Acton falls silent. Clarke feels his arms, cradling her loosely from behind.

"I think something like that happened to me," he says, after a while.

"How?"

"I think something in my brain got exercised, and it spread out and crowded some other parts away. But it only works in a high-pressure environment, you see, it's the pressure that makes the nerves fire faster. So when I go back inside, the new part shuts down and the old parts have been—well, lost."

Clarke shakes her head. "We've been through this, Karl. Your synapses just ran low on calcium."

"That's not all that happened. That's not even a problem anymore, I've brought my inhibitors up again. Not all the way, but enough. But I still have this new part, and I still can't find the old ones." She feels his chin on the top of her head. "I don't think I'm exactly human anymore, Len. Which, considering the kind of human I was, is probably just as well."

"And what does it do, exactly? This new part?"

He takes awhile to answer. "It's almost like getting an extra sense organ, except it's . . . diffuse. Intuition, only with a really hard edge."

"Diffuse, with a hard edge."

"Yeah, well. That's the problem when you try to explain smell to someone without a nose."

"Maybe it's not what you think. I mean, something's changed, but that doesn't mean you can really just—look into people like that. Maybe it's just some sort of mood disorder. Or a hallucination, maybe. You can't *know*."

"I know, Len."

"Then you're right." Anger trickles up from her internal reservoir. "You're not human anymore. You're less than human."

"Lenie—"

"Humans have to *trust*, Karl. There's no big deal about putting your faith in something you know for certain. I want you to trust me."

"Not know you."

She tries to hear sadness on that synthetic voice. In Beebe, maybe, it would have come through. But in Beebe he would never had said that.

"Karl—"

"I can't come back."

"You're not yourself out here." She pushes away, spins around; she can just barely distinguish his silhouette.

"You want me to be—" she hears confusion in the

words, even through the vocoder, but she knows it's not a question—"hateful."

"Don't be an idiot. I've had more than my fill of assholes, believe me. But Karl, this is just some kind of cheap trick. Step out of the magic booth, you're Mr. Nice Guy. Step back in, you're the Sea Tac Strangler. It's not *real*."

"How do you know?"

She keeps her distance, suddenly knowing the answer. It's only real if it hurts. It's only real if it happens slowly, painfully, each step carved in shouts and threats and thrown punches.

It's only real if Lenie Clarke is the one to make him change.

She doesn't tell him any of this, of course. But she's afraid, as she turns and leaves him there, that she doesn't have to.

She comes instantly out of sleep, tense and completely alert. There's darkness—the lights are off, she's even blanked the readouts on the wall—but it's the close, familiar darkness of her own cubby. Something is tapping on the hull, regular and insistent.

From outside.

Out in the corridor there's light enough for rifter eyes. Nakata and Caraco stand motionless in the lounge. Brander sits at the library; the screens are dark, the headsets all hanging on their pegs.

The sound ticks through the lounge, fainter than before but easily audible.

"Where's Lubin?" Clarke asks softly. Nakata tilts her head towards the hull: *Outside somewhere.*

Clarke climbs downstairs and into the airlock.

———

"We thought you'd gone over," she says. "Like Fischer."

They float between Beebe and the sea floor. Clarke reaches out to him. Acton reaches back.

"How long has it been?" The words come out as faint, metallic sighs.

"Six days. Maybe seven. I've been putting off—calling up for a replacement—"

He doesn't react.

"We saw you on sonar sometimes," she adds. "For a while. Then you disappeared."

Silence.

"Did you get lost?" she asks after a while.

"Yeah."

"But you're back now."

"No."

"Karl—"

"I need you to promise me something, Lenie."

"What?"

"Promise me you'll do what I did. The others too. They'll listen to you."

"You know I can't—"

"Five percent, Lenie. Maybe ten. If you keep it that low you'll do okay. Promise."

"Why, Karl?"

"Because I wasn't wrong about everything. Because sooner or later they're going to have to get rid of you, and you need every edge you can get."

"Come inside. We can talk about it inside, everyone's there."

"There's strange things happening out there, Len. Out past sonar range, they're—I don't know what they're doing. They don't tell us. . . ."

"Come inside, Karl."

He shakes his head. He seems almost unused to the gesture.

"—can't—"

"Then don't expect me—"

"I left a file in the library. It explains things. As much as I could, when I was in there. Promise me, Len."

"No. *You* promise. Come inside. Promise we'll work it out."

"It kills too much of me," he sighs. "I pushed it too far. Something burned out, I'm not even completely whole out here anymore. But you'll be okay. Five or ten percent, no more."

"I need you," she buzzes, very quietly.

"No," he says. "You need Karl Acton."

"What's that supposed to mean?"

"You need what he did to you."

All the warmth goes out of her then. What's left is a slow, freezing boil.

"What is this, Karl? Some grand insight you got while spirit-walking around in the mud? You think you know me better than I do?"

"You know—"

"Because you don't, you know. You don't know shit about me, you never did. And you don't really have the balls to find out, so you run off into the dark and come back spouting all this pretentious bullshit." She's goading him, she knows she's goading him but he's just not reacting. Even one of his outbursts would be better than this.

"It's saved under 'Shadow'," he says.

She stares at him without speaking.

"The file," he adds.

"What's wrong with you?" She's beating at him now, pounding as hard as she can but he's not hitting back, he's not even *defending* himself for Christ's sake *why don't you fight back asshole why don't you just get it over with, just beat the shit out of me until the guilt covers us both and we'll promise never to do it again and—*

But even anger deserts her now. The inertia of her attack pushes them away from each other. She catches herself on an anchor cable. A starfish, wrapped around the line, reaches blindly out to touch her with the tip of one arm.

Acton continues to drift.

"Stay," she says.

He brakes and holds position without answering, dim and gray and distant.

There are so many things denied her out here. She can't cry. She can't even close her eyes. So she stares at the seabed, watches her own shadow stretch off into the darkness. "Why are you doing this?" she asks, exhausted, and wonders who she meant the question for.

His shadow flows across her own. A mechanical voice answers:

"This is what you do when you really love someone."

She jerks her head up in time to see him disappear.

Beebe's quiet when she returns. The wet slap of her feet on the deck is the only sound. She climbs into the lounge and finds it empty. She takes a step toward the corridor that leads to her cubby.

Stops.

In Comm, a luminous icon inches toward the Throat. The display lies for effect; in reality Acton is dark and unreflective, no more luminous than she is.

She wonders again if she should try and stop him. She could never overpower him by force, but perhaps she just hasn't thought of the right thing to say. Perhaps if she just gets it right she can call him back, compel his return through words alone. *Not a victim anymore*, he said once. Perhaps she's a siren instead.

She can't think of anything to say.

He's almost there now. She can see him gliding between great bronze pillars, bacterial nebulae swirling in his wake. She imagines his face aimed down, scanning, relentless, hungry. She can see him homing in on the north end of Main Street.

She shuts off the display.

She doesn't have to watch this. She knows what's going on, and the machines will tell her when it's over. She couldn't stop them if she tried, not unless she smashed them into junk. That, in fact, is exactly what she wants to do. But she controls herself. Quiet as stone, Lenie Clarke sits in the Command cubby staring at a blank screen, waiting for the alarm.

N E K T O N

DRYBACK

Jump-Start

He dreamed of water. He always dreamed of water. He dreamed the smell of dead fish in rotten nets, and rainbow puddles of gasoline shimmering off the Steveston jetty, and a home so close to the shoreline you could barely get insurance. He dreamed of a time when waterfront meant something, even the muddy brown stretch where the Fraser hemorrhaged into the Strait of Georgia. His mother was standing over him, beaming *a vital ecological resource, Yves. A staging ground for migrating birds. A filter for the whole world.* And little Yves Scanlon smiled back, proud that he alone of all his friends— well, not *friends* exactly, but maybe they would be *now*—would grow up appreciating nature firsthand, right here in his new backyard. One and a half meters above the high-tide line.

And then, as usual, the real world kicked in the doors and electrocuted his mother in mid-smile.

Sometimes he could postpone the inevitable. Sometimes he could fight the jolt from his bedside dreamer, keep it from dragging him back for just a few more seconds. Thirty years of random images would flash across his mind in those moments: falling forests, bloating deserts, ultraviolet fingers reaching ever deeper into barren seas. Oceans creeping up shorelines. Vital ecological resources turning into squatting camps for refugees. Squatting camps turning into intertidal zones.

And Yves Scanlon was awake again, sweat-soaked, teeth clenched, jump-started.

God, no. I'm back.

The real world.

Three and a half hours. Only three and a half hours . . .

It was all the dreamer would allow him. Sleep stages one through four got ten minutes each. REM got thirty, in deference to the incompressibility of the dream state. A seventy-minute cycle, run three times nightly.

You could freelance. Everyone else does.

Freelancers chose their own hours. Employees—those few that remained—got their hours chosen for them. Yves Scanlon was an employee. He frequently reminded himself of the advantages: you didn't have to fight and scramble for a new contract every six months. You had stability, of a sort. If you performed. If you kept on performing. Which meant, of course, that Yves Scanlon couldn't afford the nightly nine and a half hours that was optimal for his species.

Servitude for security, then. No day passed when he didn't hate the choice he'd made. Someday, perhaps, he'd even hate it more than he feared the alternative.

"Seventeen items on high priority," said the workstation as his feet hit the floor. "Four broadcast, twelve Net, one phone. Broadcast and phone items are clean. Net items were disinfected on entry, with a forty-percent chance that encrypted bugs slipped through."

"Up the disinfectant," Scanlon said.

"That will destroy any encrypted bugs, but might also destroy up to five percent of the legitimate data. I could just dump the risky files."

"Disinfect them. What's on midlist?"

"Eight hundred sixty-three items. Three hundred twenty-seven broad—"

"Dump it all." Scanlon headed for the bathroom, stopped. "Wait a minute. Play the phone call."

"This is Patricia Rowan," the station said in a cold, clipped voice. "We may be encountering some personnel problems with the deep-sea geothermal program. I'd like to discuss them with you. I'll have your return call routed direct."

Shit. Rowan was one of the top corpses on the West Coast. She'd barely even acknowledged him since he'd been hired on at the GA. "Is there a priority on that call?" Scanlon asked.

"Important but not urgent," the workstation replied.

He could have breakfast first, maybe go through his mail. He could ignore all those reflexes urging him to drop everything and jump like a trained seal to immediate attention. They needed him for something. About time. About goddamned time.

"I'm taking a shower," he told the workstation, hesitantly defiant. "Don't bother me until I come out."

His reflexes, though, didn't like it at all.

"—that 'curing' victims of multiple-personality disorder is actually tantamount to serial murder. The issue has remained controversial in the wake of recent findings that the human brain can potentially contain up to one hundred forty fully-sentient personalities without significant sensory/motor impairment. The tribunal will also consider whether encouraging a multiple personality to reintegrate voluntarily—again, a traditionally therapeutic act—should be redefined as assisted suicide. Crosslinked to next item under cognition and legal."

The workstation fell silent.

Rowan wants to see me. The VP in charge of the GA's whole Northwest franchise wants to see me. Me.

He was thinking into sudden silence. Scanlon realised the workstation had stopped talking. "Next," he said.

"Fundamentalist acquitted of murder in the destruction of a smart gel," the station recited. "Tagged to—"

Didn't she say I'd be working with her, though? Wasn't that the deal when I first came on?

"—AI, cognition, and legal."

Yeah. That's what they said. Ten years ago.

"Ahh—summary, nontechnical," Scanlon told the machine.

"Victim was a smart gel on temporary loan to the Ontario Science Center as part of a public exhibit on artificial intelligence. Accused admitted to the act, stating that neuron cultures"—the workstation changed voices, neatly inserting a sound bite—"*desecrate the human soul.*

"Expert defense witnesses, including a smart gel online from Rutgers, testified that neuron cultures lack primitive evolved midbrain structures necessary to experience pain, fear, or a desire for self-preservation. Defense argued that the concept of a 'right' is intended to protect individuals from unwarranted suffering. Since smart gels are incapable of physical or mental distress of any sort, they have no rights to protect regardless of their level of self-awareness. This reasoning was eloquently summarized during the defense's closing statement: 'Gels themselves don't care whether they live or die. Why should we?' The verdict is under appeal. Cross-linked to next item under AI and World News."

Scanlon swallowed a mouthful of powdered albumin. "List expert defense witnesses, names only."

"Phillip Quan. Lily Kozlowski. David Childs—"

"Stop." Lily Kozlowski. He knew her, from back at UCLA. An expert witness. Shit. *Maybe* I *should have kissed a few more asses in grad school . . .*

Scanlon snorted. "Next."

"Net infections down fifteen percent."

Problems with the rifters, she said. I wonder . . .

"Summary, nontechnical."

"Viral infections on the Internet have declined fifteen percent in the past six months, due to the ongoing installation of smart gels at critical nodes along the Net's backbone. Digital infections find it nearly impossible to infect smart gels, each of which has a unique and flexible system architecture. In light of these most recent results, some experts are predicting a safe return to casual E-mail by the end of—"

"Ah, fuck. Cancel."

Come on, Yves. You've been waiting for years for those idiots to recognize your abilities. Maybe this is it. Don't blow it by looking too eager.

"Waiting," said the station.

Only, what if she doesn't wait? What if she gets impatient and goes for someone else? What if—

"Tag the last phone call and reply." Scanlon stared at the dregs of his breakfast while the connection went up.

"Admin," said a voice that sounded real.

"Yves Scanlon for Patricia Rowan."

"Dr. Rowan is occupied. Her simulator is expecting your call. This conversation is being monitored for quality-control purposes." A click, and another voice that sounded real: "Hello, Dr. Scanlon."

His Master's voice.

Muckraker

It rumbles up the slope from the abyssal plain, bouncing an echo that registers five hundred meters outside Beebe's official sonar range. It's moving at almost ten meters a second, not remarkable for a submarine but this thing's so close to the bottom it *has* to be running on treads. Six hundred meters out it crosses a small spreading zone and slews to a stop.

"What is it?" wonders Lenie Clarke.

Alice Nakata fiddles with the focus. The unknown has started up again at a crawl, edging along the length of the spread at less than one meter per second.

"It's feeding," Nakata says. "Polymetallic sulfides, perhaps."

Clarke considers. "I want to check it out."

"Yes. Shall I notify the GA?"

"Why?"

"It is probably foreign. It might not be legal."

Clarke looks at the other woman.

"There are fines for unauthorized incursions into territorial waters," Nakata says.

"Alice, really." Clarke shakes her head. "Who cares?"

Lubin is off the scope, probably sleeping on the bottom somewhere. They leave him a note. Brander and Caraco are out replacing the bearings on number six; a tremor cracked the casing last shift, jammed two thousand kilograms of mud and grit into the works. Still, the other generators are more than able to take up the slack. Brander and Caraco grab their squids and join the parade.

"We should keep our lights down," Nakata buzzes as they leave the Throat. "And stay very close to the bottom. It may frighten easily."

They follow the bearing, their lights dimmed to embers, through darkness almost impenetrable even to rifter eyes. Caraco pulls up beside Clarke: "I'm heading into the wild blue yonder after this. Wanna come?"

A shiver of secondhand revulsion tickles Clarke's insides; from Nakata, of course. Nakata used to join Caraco on her daily swim up Beebe's transponder line, until about two weeks ago. Something happened up at the deep scattering layer—nothing dangerous, apparently, but it left Alice absolutely cold at the prospect of going anywhere near the surface. Caraco's been pestering the others to pace her ever since.

Clarke shakes her head. "Didn't you get enough of a workout slurping all that shit out of number six?"

Caraco shrugs. "Different muscle groups."

"How far up do you go now?"

"Almost to a thousand. Another month and I'll be lapping all the way to the surface."

A sound has been rising around them, so gradually that Clarke can't pin down the moment she first noticed it; a grumbling, mechanical noise, the distant sound of rocks being pulverized between great molars.

Flickers of nervousness flash back and forth in the group. Clarke tries to rein herself in. She knows what's coming, they all do, it's not nearly as dangerous as the risks they face every shift. It's not dangerous at all—

—unless it's got defenses we don't know about—

—but that *sound,* the sheer *size* of this thing on the scope—*We're all scared. We know there's nothing to be afraid of, but all we can hear are teeth gnashing in the darkness. . . .*

It's bad enough dealing with her own hardwired apprehension. It doesn't help to be tuned in to everyone else's.

A faint pulse of surprise from Brander, in the lead. Then from Nakata, next in line, a split second before Clarke herself feels a slap of sluggish turbulence. Caraco, forewarned, barely radiates anything when the plume washes over her.

The darkness has become fractionally more absolute, the water itself more viscous. They hold station in a stream that's half mud, seawater.

"Exhaust wake," Brander vibrates. He has to raise his voice slightly to be heard over the sound of feeding machinery.

They turn and follow the trail upstream, keeping to the plume's edge more by touch than sight. The ambient grumble swells to full-blown cacophony, resolves into a dozen different voices: pile drivers, muffled explosions, the sounds of cement mixers. Clarke can barely think above the waterborne racket, or the rising apprehension in four separate minds, and suddenly it's *right there*, just for a moment, a great segmented tread climbing up around a gear wheel two stories high, rolling away in the murk.

"*Jesus*. It's fucking *huge*." Brander, his vocoder cranked.

They move together, aiming their squids high and cruising up at an angle. Clarke tastes the thrill from three other sets of adrenals, adds her own and sends it back, a vicarious feedback loop. With their lamps on minimum, the viz can't be more than three meters; even in front of Clarke's face the world is barely more than shadows on shadows, dimly lit by headlights bobbing to either side.

The top of the tread slides below them for a moment, a jointed moving road several meters across. Then a plain of jumbled metal shapes, fading into view barely ahead, fading out again almost instantly: exhaust ports, sonar domes, flow-meter ducts. The din fades a little as they move toward the center of the hull.

Most of the protuberances are smoothed back into hydrodynamic teardrops. Close up, though, there's no shortage of handholds. Caraco's smoldering headlight is the first to settle down onto the machine; her squid paces along above her. Clarke sets her own squid to heel and joins the others on the hull. So far there's been no obvious reaction to their presence.

They huddle together, heads close to converse above the ambient noise.

"Where's it from?" Brander wonders.

"Probably Korea," Nakata buzzes back. "I did not see any registry markings, but it would take a long time to check the whole hull."

Caraco: "Bet you wouldn't find anything anyway. If they were going to risk sneaking it this far into foreign territory, they wouldn't be stupid enough to leave a return address."

The rumbling metal landscape pulls them along. A couple of meters up, barely visible, their riderless squids trail patiently behind.

"Does it know we're here?" asks Clarke.

Alice shakes her head. "It kicks up a lot of shit from the bottom so it ignores close contacts. Bright light might scare it, though. It *is* trespassing. It might associate light with getting caught."

"Really." Brander lets go for a moment, drifts back a few meters before catching another handhold. "Hey Judy, want to go exploring?"

Caraco's vocoder emits static; Lenie feels the other woman's laughter from inside. Caraco and Brander leap away into the murk like black gremlins.

"It moved very fast," Nakata says. There's a sudden small blot of insecurity radiating from inside her, but she talks over it. "When if first showed up on sonar. It was moving way too fast. It wasn't safe."

"Safe?" Lenie frowns to herself. "It's a machine, right? No one inside."

Nakata shakes her head. "Too fast for a machine in complex terrain. A person could do it."

"Come on, Alice. These things are robots. Besides, if there was anyone inside we'd be able to *feel* them, right? You feel anyone other than the four of us?" Nakata tends to be a bit more sensitive than the others in matters of fine-tuning.

"I—don't think so," Nakata says, but Clarke senses uncertainty. "Maybe I—It's a big machine, Lenie. Maybe the pilot is just too far away—"

Brander and Caraco are plotting something. They're both out of sight—even their squids have left to keep them in range—but they're easily close enough for

Clarke to sense a rising anticipation. She and Nakata exchange looks.

"We better see what they're up to," Clarke says. The two of them head off across the muckraker.

A few moments later, Brander and Caraco materialize in front of them. They're crouched to either side of a metal dome about thirty centimeters across. Several dark fisheyes stare out from its surface.

"Cameras?" Clarke asks.

"Nope," Caraco says.

"Photocells," Brander adds.

Lenie feels the beat before a punchline. "Are you sure this is a good—"

"Let there be light!" cries Judy Caraco. Beams stab out from her headlamp and Brander's, bathing the fisheyes at full intensity.

The muckraker stops dead. Inertia pushes Clarke forward; she grabs and regains her balance, unexpected silence ringing in her ears. In the wake of that incessant noise, she feels almost deaf.

"Whoa," Brander buzzes into the stillness. Something ticks through the hull once, twice, three times.

The world lurches back into motion. The landscape rotates around them, throws them together in a tangle of limbs. By the time they've sorted themselves out they're accelerating. The muckraker is grumbling again, but with a different voice; no lazy munching on polymetallics now, just a straight beeline for international waters. Within seconds Clarke is hanging on for dear life.

"Yee-haw!" Caraco shouts.

"Bright light might scare it?" Brander calls from somewhere behind. "I would say *so!*"

Strong feelings on all sides. Lenie Clarke tightens her grip and tries to sort out which ones are hers. Exultation spiked with primal, giddy fear; that's Brander and Caraco. Alice Nakata's excited almost despite herself, but with more worry in the mix; and here, buried somewhere down deep, almost a sense of . . . She can't tell, really.

Discontent? Unhappiness?

Not really.

Is that me? But that doesn't feel right either.

Bright light pins Clarke's shadow to the hull, disappears an instant later. She looks back; Brander's up above her somehow, swinging back and forth on a line trailing up into the water—*could've sworn that wasn't there before*—his beam waving around like a demented lighthouse. Ribbons of muddy water stream past just above the deck, their edges writhing in textbook illustrations of turbulent flow.

Caraco pushes off the hull and flies back up into the water. Her silhouette vanishes into the murk, but her headlamp comes to rest and starts dipping around just behind Brander's. Clarke looks over at Nakata, still plastered against the hull. Nakata's feeling a little sick now, and even more worried about something. . . .

"It is not *happy*!" Nakata shouts.

"Hey; come on, groundhogs!" Caraco's voice buzzes faintly. "Fly!"

Discontent. Something not expected.

Who is *that?* Clarke wonders.

"Come *on*!" Caraco calls again.

What the hell. Can't hang on much longer anyway. Clarke lets go, pushes off; the top of the muckraker races on beneath. Heavy water drags the momentum from her. She kicks for altitude, feels sudden expectation from behind—and in the next second something slams against her back, pushing her forward again. Implants lurch against her rib cage.

"Jesus Christ!" Brander buzzes in her ear. "Get a grip, Lenie!"

He's caught her on his way past. Clarke reaches out and grabs the line that he and Caraco are attached to.

It's only as thick as her finger, and too slippery to hang on to. She looks back and sees that the other two have looped it around their chests and under their arms, leaving their hands more or less free. She tries the same trick, drag arching her back, while Caraco calls out to Nakata.

Nakata is not eager to let go. They can feel that, even though they can't see her. Brander angles back and forth, tacking his body like a rudder; the three of them swing in a grand, barely controlled arc, knotted into the middle of their tether. "Come on, Alice! Join the human kite! We'll catch you!"

And Nakata's coming, she's coming, but she's doing it her own way. She's climbed sideways against the current, hand over hand, until she found the place where the line joins the deck. Now she's letting drag push her back along the filament to them.

Clarke has finally secured herself in a loop. Speed digs the line into her flesh; it's already starting to hurt. She doesn't feel much like a human kite. Bait on a hook is more like it. She twists around to Brander, points at the line: "What *is* this, anyway?"

"VLF antennae. Unspooled when we scared it. Probably crying for help."

"It won't get any, will it?"

"Not on this side of the ocean. It's probably just making a last call so its owners'll know what happened. Sort of a suicide note."

Caraco, entangled a bit farther back, twists around at that. "Suicide? You don't suppose these things self-destruct?"

Sudden concern settles over the human kite. Alice Nakata tumbles into them.

"Maybe we ought to let it go," Clarke says.

Nakata nods emphatically. "It is not happy." Her disquiet radiates through the others like a warning light.

It takes a few moments to disentangle themselves

from the antennae. It whips past and away, trailing a small float like a traffic cone. Clarke tumbles, lets the water brake her. Machine roars recede into grumbles, into mere tremors.

The rifters hang in empty midwater, silence on all sides.

Caraco points a sonar pistol straight down, fires. "Jeez. We're almost thirty meters off the bottom."

"We lose the squids?" Brander says. "That thing was really moving."

Caraco raises her pistol, takes a few more readings. "Got 'em. They're not all that far off, actually, I—Hey."

"What?"

"There's five of them. Closing fast."

"Ken?"

"Uh-huh."

"Well. He's saving us a swim, anyway," Brander says.

"Did anyone—"

They turn. Alice Nakata starts again: "Did anyone else feel it?"

"Feel what?" Brander begins, but Clarke is nodding.

"Judy?" Nakata says.

Caraco radiates reluctance. "I—There was something, maybe. Didn't get a good fix on it. I assumed it was one of you guys."

"What," Brander says. "The muckraker? I thought—"

A black cipher rises in their midst. His squid cruises straight up from underneath like a slow missile. It hovers overhead when he releases it. A couple of meters below, four other squids bob restlessly at station-keeping, noses up.

"You lost these," Lubin buzzes.

"Thanks," Brander replies.

Clarke concentrates, tries to tune Lubin in. She's only going through the motions, of course. He's dark to them.

He's always been dark, fine-tuning didn't change him a bit. Nobody knows why.

"So what's going on?" he asks. "Your note said something about a muckraker."

"It got away from us," Caraco says.

"It was not happy," Nakata repeats.

"Yeah?"

"Alice got some sort of feeling off of it," Caraco says. "Lenie and me too, sort of."

"Muckrakers are unmanned," Lubin remarks.

"Not a man," Nakata says. "Not a person. But . . ." She trails off.

"I felt it," Clarke says. "It was alive."

Lenie Clarke lies on her bunk, alone again. Really alone. She can remember a time, not so long ago, when she reveled in this kind of isolation. Who would have thought that she'd miss *feelings?*

Even if they are someone else's.

And yet it's true. Every time Beebe takes her in, some vital part of her falls away like a half-remembered dream. The airlock clears, her body reinflates, and her awareness turns flat and muddy. The others just *vanish.* It's strange; she can see them, hear them the way she always could. But if they don't move and she closes her eyes, she's got no way of *knowing* they're here.

Now her only company is herself. Just one set of signals to process in here. Nothing jamming her.

Shit.

Blind, or naked. That was the choice. It nearly killed her. *My own damn fault, of course. I was just* asking *for it.*

She was, too. She could have just left everything the way it was, quietly deleted Acton's file before anyone else found out about it. But there'd been this debt. Something owed to the ghost of the Thing Outside, the thing that didn't snarl or blame or lash out, the thing that, finally, took the Thing Inside away where it couldn't hurt her anymore. Part of Lenie Clarke still hates Acton for that, on some sick level where conditioned reflex runs the show; but even down there, she thinks maybe he did it for her. Like it or not, she owed him.

So she paid up. She called the others inside and played the file. She told them what he'd said, that last time, and she didn't ask them to turn their backs on his offering even though she desperately hoped they would. If she had asked, perhaps, they might have listened. But one by one, they split themselves open and made the changes. Mike Brander, out of curiosity. Judy Caraco, out of skepticism. Alice Nakata, afraid of being left behind. Ken Lubin, unsuccessfully, for reasons he kept to himself.

She clenches her eyelids, remembers rules changing overnight. Careful appearances suddenly meant nothing; blank eyes and ninja masks were just cosmetic affectations, useless as armor. *How are you feeling, Lenie Clarke? Horny, bored, upset? So easy to tell, though your eyes are hidden behind those corneal opacities. You could be terrified. You could be pissing in your 'skin and everyone would know.*

Why did you tell them? Why did you tell them? Why did you tell *them?*

Outside, she watched the others change. They moved around her without speaking, one connecting smoothly with another to lend a hand or a piece of equipment. When she needed something from one of them, it was there before she could speak. When they needed something from her they had to ask aloud, and the choreography would falter. She felt like the token cripple in a dance troupe. She wondered how much of her they could see, and was afraid to ask.

Inside, sometimes, she would try. It was safer there; the thread that connected the rest of them fell apart in atmosphere, put everyone back on equal terms. Brander spoke of a heightened awareness of the presence of others; Caraco compared it to body language. "Just sort of makes up for the eyecaps," she said, apparently expecting Clarke to feel reassured at that.

But it was Alice Nakata who finally remarked, almost offhandedly, that other people's feelings could be . . . distracting. . . .

Lenie Clarke's been tuned for a while now. It's not so bad. No precise telepathic insights, no sudden betrayals. It's more like the sensation from a ghost limb, the ancestral memory of a tail you can almost feel behind you. And Clarke knows now that Nakata was right. Outside, the feelings of the others trickle into her, masking, diluting. Sometimes she can even forget she has any of her own.

There's something else, too, a familiar core in each of them, dark and writhing and angry. That doesn't surprise her. They don't even talk about it. Might as well discuss the fact that they all have five fingers on each hand.

Brander's busy at the library; Clarke can hear Nakata in Comm, on the phone.

"According to this," Brander says, "they've started putting smart gels in muckrakers."

"Mmm?"

"It's a pretty old file," he admits. "It'd be nice if the GA would download a bit more often, infections or no infections. I mean, we *are* single-handedly keeping the Western world safe from brownouts, it wouldn't kill them to—"

"Gels," Clarke prompts.

"Right. Well, they've always needed neural nets in those things, you know, they wander around some pretty hairy topography—you hear about those two muckrakers that got caught up in the Aleutian Trench?—anyway, navigation through complex environments generally needs a net of some sort. Usually it's gallium-arsenide-based, but even those don't come close to matching a human brain for spatial stuff. They still just *crawled* when it came to figuring seamounts, that sort of thing. So they've started replacing them with smart gels."

Clarke grunts. "Alice said it was moving too fast for a machine."

"Probably was. And smart gels are made out of real neurons, so I guess we tune in to them the same way we tune in to each other. At least, judging by what you guys felt—Alice said it wasn't happy."

"It wasn't." Clarke frowns. "It wasn't unhappy either, actually. It wasn't really an emotion at all, it was just—well, *surprised*, I guess. Like, like a sense of—divergence. From what was expected."

"Hell, I *did* feel that," Brander says. "I thought it was *me*."

Nakata emerges from Comm. "Still no word on Karl's replacement. They say the new recruits still are not through training. Cutbacks, they say."

By now it's a running joke. The GA's new recruits have to be the slowest learners since the eradication of Down's syndrome. Almost four months now and Acton's replacement still hasn't materialized.

Brander waves one hand dismissively. "We've been doing okay with five." He shuts down the library and stretches. "Anyone seen Ken, by the way?"

"He is just outside," Nakata says. "Why?"

"I'm with him next shift; got to set up a time. His rhythm's been a bit wonky the past couple of days."

"How far out is he?" Clarke asks suddenly.

Nakata shrugs. "Maybe ten meters, when I last checked."

He's in range. There are limits to fine-tuning. You can't feel someone in Beebe from as far as the Throat, for example. But ten meters, easy.

"He's usually farther out, isn't he?" Clarke speaks softly, as if afraid of being overheard. "Almost off the scope, most times. Or working on that weird contraption of his."

They don't know why they can't tune Lubin in. He says they're all dark to him, too. Once, about a month ago, Brander suggested doing an exploratory NMR; Lubin said he'd rather not. He sounded pleasant enough, but there was something about his tone, and Brander hasn't brought the subject up since.

Now Brander points his eyecaps at Clarke, a half-smile on his face. "I dunno, Len. Do *you* want to call him a liar to his face?"

She doesn't answer.

"Oh." Nakata breaks the silence before it can get too awkward. "There is something else. Until our replacement arrives they are sending someone down for ... They called it routine evaluation. That doctor, the one who—you know—"

"Scanlon." Lenie is careful not to spit out the word.

Nakata nods.

"What the hell for?" Brander growls. "It's not enough we're already shorthanded, we've got to sit still while *Scanlon* has another go at us?"

"It's not like before, they say. He's just going to observe. While we work." Nakata shrugs. "They say it is completely routine. No interviews or sessions or anything."

Caraco snorts. "There better not be. I'd let them cut out my other lung before I'd take another session with that prick."

"So, you were repeatedly buggered by a trained Dobermans while your mom charged admission,'" Brander recites in a fair imitation of Scanlon's voice. "'And how did that make you *feel*, exactly?'"

"'Actually I'm more of a *mechanic*,'" Caraco chimes in. "Did he give you that line?"

"He seemed nice enough to me," Nakata says hesitantly.

"Well, that's his job: to seem nice." Caraco grimaces. "He's just no fucking *good* at it." She looks over at Clarke. "So what do you think, Len?"

"I think he overplayed the empathy card," Clarke says after a moment.

"No, I mean how do we handle this?"

Clarke shrugs, vaguely irritated. "Why ask me?"

"He better not get in my way. Dumpy little turd." Brander spares a blank look at the ceiling. "Now why can't they design a smart gel to replace *him*?"

Scream

TRANS/OFF1/210850:2132

This is my second night in Beebe. I've asked the participants not to alter their behavior in my presence, since I'm here to observe routine station operations. I'm pleased to report that my request is being honored by everyone involved. This is gratifying insofar as it minimizes "observer effects," but it may present problems given that the rifters do not keep reliable schedules. This makes it difficult to plan one's time with them, and in fact there's one employee—Ken Lubin—whom I haven't seen since I arrived. Still, I have plenty of time.

The rifters tend to be withdrawn and uncommunicative—a layperson might call them *sullen*—but this is entirely in keeping with the profile. The station itself seems to be well-maintained and is operating smoothly, despite a certain disregard for standard protocols.

When the lights go out in Beebe Station, you can't hear anything at all.

Yves Scanlon lies on his bunk, not listening. He does not hear any strange sounds filtering in through the hull. There is no reedy, spectral keening from the seabed, no faint sound of howling wind because he knows that, down here, no wind is possible. Imagination, perhaps. A trick of the brain stem, an auditory hallucination. He's not the slightest bit superstitious; he's a scientist. He does not hear the ghost of Karl Acton moaning on the seabed.

In fact, concentrating, he's quite certain he hears nothing at all.

It really doesn't bother him, being stuck in a dead man's quarters. After all, where else *is* there? It's not as though he's going to move in with one of the vampires. And besides, Acton's been gone for months now.

Scanlon remembers the first time he heard the recording. Four lousy words: "We lost Acton. Sorry." Then she hung up. Cold bitch, Clarke. Scanlon once thought something might happen between her and Acton, it was a jigsaw match from the profiles, but you wouldn't know it from that phone call.

Maybe it's her, he muses. *Maybe it's not Lubin after all, maybe it's Clarke.*

"We lost Acton." So much for eulogy. And Fischer before Acton, and Everitt over at Linke. And Singh before Everitt. And—

And now Yves Scanlon is here, in their place. Sleeping on their bunk, breathing their air. Counting the seconds, in darkness and quiet. In dark—

Jesus Christ, what is—

And quiet. Everything's quiet. Nothing's moaning out there.

Nothing at all.

TRANS/OFF1/220850:0945

We're all mammals, of course. We therefore have a circadian rhythm which calibrates itself to ambient photoperiod. It's been known for some time that when people are denied photoperiodic cues their rhythms tend to lengthen, usually stabilizing between twenty-seven and thirty-six hours. Adherence to a regular twenty-four hour work schedule is usually sufficient to keep this from happening, so we didn't expect a problem in the deep stations. As an added measure I recommended that a normal photoperiod be built into Beebe's lighting systems; the lights are programmed to dim slightly between 2200 and 0700 every day.

The participants have apparently chosen to ignore these cues. Even during "daytime" they keep ambient lighting dimmer than my suggested "nocturnal" levels. (They also prefer to leave their eyecaps in at all times, for obvious reasons; although I had not predicted this behavior, it is consistent with the profile.) Work schedules are somewhat flexible, but this is to be expected given that their sleep cycles are always shifting in relation to each other. Rifters do not wake up in time to perform their duties; they perform their duties whenever two or more of them happen to be awake. I suspect that they also work alone sometimes, a safety violation, but I have yet to confirm this.

For the moment, these unorthodox behaviors do not appear to be serious. Necessary work seems to get done on time, even though the station is currently understaffed. However, I believe the situation is potentially problematic.

Efficiency could probably be improved by stricter adherence to a twenty-four-hour diel cycle. Should the GA wish to ensure such adherence, I would recommend proteoglycan therapy for the participants. Hypothalamic rewiring is another possibility; it is more invasive, but would be virtually impossible to subvert.

Vampires. That's a good metaphor. They avoid the light, and they've taken out all the mirrors. That could be part of the problem right there. Scanlon had very sound reasons for recommending mirrors in the first place.

Most of Beebe—all of it, except for his cubby—is too dark for uncapped vision. Maybe the vampires are trying to conserve energy. A high priority, sitting here next to eleven thousand megawatts' worth of generating equipment. Still, these people are all under forty; they probably can't imagine a world without rationed power.

Bullshit. There's logic, and there's vampire logic. Don't confuse the two.

For the past two days, leaving his cubby has been like creeping out into some dark alleyway. He's finally given in and capped his eyes like the rest of them. Now Beebe's bright enough, but so pale. Hardly any color at all. As though the cones have been sucked right out of his eyes.

Clarke and Caraco lean against the ready-room bulkhead, watching with their white, white eyes as he checks out his diving armor. No vampire vivisection for Yves Scanlon, no sirree. Not for this short a tour. Preshmesh and acrylic all the way.

He fingers a gauntlet; chain mail, with links the size of pinheads. He smiles. "Looks okay."

The vampires just watch and wait.

Come on, Scanlon, you're the mechanic. They're machines like everyone else. They just need more of a tune-up. You can handle them.

"Very nice tech," he remarks, setting the armor back down. "Of course, it's not much next to the hardware *you* folks are packing. What's it like to be able to turn into a fish at will?"

"Wet," Caraco says, and a moment later looks at Clarke. Checking for approval, maybe.

Clarke just keeps staring at him. At least, he thinks she's staring. It's so damn hard to tell.

Relax. She's only trying to psych you out. The usual stupid dominance games.

But he knows it's more than that. Deep down, the rifters just don't like him.

I know what they are. That's why.

Take a dozen children, any children. Beat and mix thoroughly until some lumps remain. Simmer for two to three decades; bring to a slow, rolling boil. Skim off the full-blown psychotics, the schizoaffectives, the multiple personalities, and discard. (There were doubts about Fischer, actually; but then, who *doesn't* have an imaginary friend at some point?)

Let cool. Serve with dopamine garnish.

What do you get? Something bent, not broken. Something that fits into cracks too twisted for the rest of us.

Vampires.

"Well," Scanlon says into the silence. "Everything checks out. Can't wait to try it on." Without waiting for a reply—without exposing himself to the lack of one—he climbs upstairs. At the edge of his vision, Clarke and Caraco exchange looks. Scanlon glances back, rigorously casual, but any smiles have disappeared by the time he scans their faces.

Go ahead, ladies. Indulge yourselves while you can. The lounge is empty. Scanlon passes through it and into the corridor. *You've got maybe five years before you're obsolete.* His cubby—Acton's cubby—is third on the left. *Five years, before all this can run itself without your help.* He opens the hatch; brilliant light spills out, blinding him for a moment while his eyecaps compensate. Scanlon steps inside, swings the hatch shut. Sags against it.

Shit. No locks.

After a while he lies back on his bunk, stares up at a congested ceiling.

Maybe we should have waited after all. Not let them rush us. If we'd just taken the time to do it right from the start...

But they hadn't had the time. Total automation at start-up would have delayed the whole program longer than civilized appetites were willing to wait. And the vampires were already there, after all. They'd be so much use in the short run, and then they'd be sent home, and they'd be glad to leave this place. Who wouldn't be?

The possibility of addiction never even came up.

It seems insane on the face of it. How could anyone get addicted to a place like this? What kind of paranoia has seized the GA, that they'd worry about people refusing to *leave*? But Yves Scanlon is no mere layperson, he's not fooled by the merely apparent. He's beyond anthropomorphism. He's looked into all those undead eyes, up there in his world, down here in theirs, and he knows: Vampires live by different rules.

Maybe they *are* too happy here. It's one of two questions Yves Scanlon has set out to answer. Hopefully they won't figure that out while he's still down here. They dislike him enough as it is.

It's not their fault, of course. It's just the way they're programmed. They can't help hating him, any more than he can help the reverse.

———

Preshmesh is better than surgery. That's about the most he can say for it.

The pressure jams all those tiny interlocking plates together, and they don't seem to stop clenching until they're a micron away from grinding his body to pulp. There's a stiffness in the joints. It's perfectly safe, of course. Perfectly. And Scanlon can breathe unpressurized air when he goes outside, and nobody's had to carve out half his chest in the meantime.

He's been out now for about fifteen minutes. Beebe's just a few meters away. Clarke and Brander escort him on his maiden voyage, keeping their distance. Scanlon kicks, rises clumsily from the bottom; the mesh lets him swim like a man with splinted limbs. Vampires skim the edge of his vision like effortless shadows.

His helmet seems like the center of the universe. Wherever he looks, an infinite weight of black ocean presses in against the acrylic. A tiny flaw down by the neck seal catches his eye; he stares, horrified, as a hairline crack grows across his field of vision.

"Help! Get me in!" He kicks furiously toward Beebe. Nobody answers.

"My helmet! My hel—" The crack isn't just growing now: it's *squirming*, twitching laterally across the corner of the helmet bubble like—like—

Yellow featureless eyes staring in from the ocean. A black hand, silhouetted in Beebe's halo, reaching for his face—

"Ahhh—"

A thumb grinds down on the crack in Scanlon's helmet. The crack smears, *bursts*; fine gory filaments smudge against the acrylic. The back half of the hairline peels off and writhes loose into the water, coiling, uncoiling—

Dying. Scanlon pants with relief. *A worm. Some stupid*

*fucking roundworm on my faceplate and I thought I was
going to die, I thought—*

Oh Christ. I've made a complete fool of myself.

He looks around. Brander, hanging off his right shoulder, points to the gory remnants sticking to the helmet.
"If it ever really cracked, you wouldn't have time to
complain. You'd look just like that."

Scanlon clears his throat. "Thanks. Sorry, I—Well,
you know I'm new here. Thanks."

"By the way."

Clarke's voice. Or what's left of it, after the machinery does its job. Scanlon flails around until she comes
into view overhead.

"How long are you going to be checking up on us?"
she asks.

Neutral question. Perfectly reasonable.

*In fact, you've got to wonder why nobody asked it
before . . .*

"A week at least." His heart is slowing down again.
"Maybe two. As long as it takes to make sure things are
running smoothly."

She's silent for a second. Then: "You're lying." It
doesn't sound like an accusation, somehow; just a simple
observation. Maybe it's the vocoder.

"Why do you say that?"

She doesn't answer. Something else does; not quite a
moan, not quite a voice. Not quite faint enough to ignore.

Scanlon feels the abyss trickling down his back. "Did
you hear that?"

Clarke slips down past him to the seabed, rotating to
keep him in view. "Hear? What?"

"It was . . ." Scanlon listens. A faint tectonic rumble.
That's all. "Nothing."

She pushes off the bottom at an angle, slides up
through the water to Brander. "We're on shift," she

buzzes at Scanlon. "You know how the 'lock works."

The vampires vanish into the night.

Beebe shines invitingly. Alone and suddenly nervous, Scanlon retreats to the airlock.

But I wasn't lying. I wasn't. He hasn't had to, yet. Nobody's asked the right questions.

Still. It seems odd that he has to remind himself.

TRANS/OFFI/230850:0830

I'm about to embark on my first extended dive. Apparently, the participants have been asked to catch a fish for one of the Pharm consortiums. Washington/Rand, I believe. I find this a bit puzzling—usually Pharms are only interested in bacteria, and they use their own people for collecting—but it provides the participants with a change from the usual routine, and it provides me an opportunity to watch them in action. I expect to learn a great deal.

Brander is slouched at the library when Scanlon comes through the lounge. His fingers rest unmoving on the keypad. Eyephones hang unused in their hooks. Brander's empty eyes point at the flatscreen. The screen is dark.

Scanlon hesitates. "I'm heading out now. With Clarke and Caraco."

Brander's shoulders rise and fall, almost indiscernibly. A sigh, perhaps. A shrug.

"The others are at the Throat. You'll be the only—I mean, will you be running tender from Comm?"

"You told us not to change the routine," Brander says, not looking up.

"That's true, Michael. But—"

Brander stands. "So make up your mind." He disappears down the corridor. Scanlon watches him go. *Nat-*

urally this has to go into my report. Not that you care.
You might, though. Soon enough.

Scanlon drops into the wetroom and finds it empty.
He struggles into his armor single-handed, taking an extra few moments to ensure that the helmet bubble is
spotless. He catches up with Clarke and Caraco just outside; Clarke is checking out a quartet of squids hovering
over the seabed. One of them is tethered to a specimen
canister resting on the bottom, a pressure-proof coffin
over two meters long. Caraco sets it for neutral buoyancy; it rises a few centimeters.

They set off without a word. The squids tow them
into the abyss; the women in the lead, Scanlon and the
canister following behind. Scanlon looks back over his
shoulder. Beebe's comforting lights wash down from
yellow to gray, then disappear entirely. Feeling a sudden
need for reassurance, he trips through the channels on
his acoustic modem. There: the homing beacon. *You're*
never really lost down here as long as you can hear that.

Clarke and Caraco are running dark. Not even their
squids are shining.

Don't say anything. You don't want them to change
their routine, remember?

Not that they would anyway.

Occasional dim lights flash briefly at the corner of his
eye, but they always vanish when he looks at them. After
an endless few minutes a bright smear fades into view
directly ahead, resolves into a collection of copper beacons and dark angular skyscrapers. The vampires avoid
the light, head around it at an angle. Scanlon and cargo
follow helplessly.

They set up just off the Throat, at the borderline between light and dark. Caraco unlatches the canister as
Clarke rises into the column above them; she's got
something in her right hand, but Scanlon can't see what

it is. She holds it up as though displaying it to an invisible crowd.

It gibbers.

It sounds like a very loud mosquito at first. Then it Dopplers down to a low growl, slides back up into erratic high frequency.

And now, finally, Lenie Clarke turns her headlight on.

She hangs up there like some crucified ascendant, her hand whining at the abyss, the light from her head sweeping the water like, like—

—*a dinner bell,* Scanlon realizes as something charges out of the darkness at her, almost as big as she is, and Jesus, the *teeth* on it—

It swallows her leg up to the crotch. Lenie Clarke takes it all in stride. She jabs down with a billy that's magically appeared in her left hand. The creature bloats and bursts in a couple of places; clumps of bubbles erupt like silvery mushrooms through flesh, shudder off into the sky. The creature thrashes, its gullet a monstrous scabbard around Clarke's leg. The vampire reaches down and dismembers it with her bare hands.

Caraco, still fiddling with the canister, looks up. "Hey, Len. They wanted it *intact.*"

"Wrong kind," Clarke buzzes. The water around her is full of torn flesh and flashing scavengers. Clarke ignores them, turning slowly, scanning the abyss.

Caraco: "Behind you; four o'clock."

"Got it," Clarke says, spinning to a new bearing.

Nothing happens. The shredded carcass, still twitching, drifts toward the bottom, scavengers sparkling on all sides. Clarke's handheld voicebox gurgles and whines.

How—Scanlon moves his tongue in his mouth, ready to ask aloud.

"Not now," Caraco buzzes at him, before he can.

There's nothing there. What are they keying on?

It comes in fast, unswerving, from the precise direction Lenie Clarke is facing. "That'll do," she says.

A muffled explosion to Scanlon's left. A thin contrail of bubbles streaks from Caraco to monster, connecting the two in an instant. The thing jerks at a sudden impact. Clarke slips to one side as it thrashes past, Caraco's dart embedded in its flank.

Clarke's headlight goes out, her voicebox falls silent. Caraco stows the dart gun and swims up to join her. The two women maneuver their quarry down toward the canister. It snaps at them, weak and spastic. They push it down into the coffin, seal the top.

"Shooting fish for a barrel," Caraco buzzes.

"How did you know it was coming?" Scanlon asks.

"They always come," Caraco says. "The sound fools them. And the light."

"I mean, how did you know which direction? In advance?"

A moment's silence.

"You just get a feel for it after a while," Clarke says finally.

"That," Caraco adds, "and this." She holds up a sonar pistol, tucks it back under her belt.

The convoy re-forms. There's a prescribed drop-off point for monsters, a hundred meters away from the Throat. (The GA has never been keen on letting outsiders wander too far into its home turf.) Once again the vampires leave light for darkness, Scanlon in tow. They travel through a world utterly without form, save for the scrolling circle of mud in his headlight. Suddenly Clarke turns to Caraco.

"I'll go," she buzzes, and peels away into the void.

Scanlon throttles his squid, edges up beside Caraco.

"Where's she off to?"

"Here we are," Caraco says. They coast to a halt. Caraco fins back to the droned squid and touches a control;

buckles disengage, straps retract. The canister floats free. Caraco cranks down the buoyancy and it settles down on a clump of tubeworms.

"Len—Uh, Clarke," Scanlon prods.

"They need an extra hand back at the Throat. She went to help out."

Scanlon checks his modem channel. Of course it's the right one; if it wasn't, he wouldn't be able to hear Caraco. Which means that Clarke and the vampires at the Throat must have been using a different frequency. Another safety violation.

But he's not a fool, he knows the story. They've only switched channels because *he's* here. They're just trying to keep him out of the loop.

Par for the course. First the fucking GA, now the hired help—

A sound, from behind. A faint electrical whine. The sound of a squid starting up.

Scanlon turns around. "Caraco?"

His headlamp sweeps across canister, squid, seabed, water.

"Caraco? You there?"

Canister. Squid. Mud.

"Hello?"

Empty water.

"Hey! Caraco! What the *hell*—"

A faint thumping, very close by.

He tries to look everywhere at once. One leg presses against the coffin.

The coffin is rocking.

He lays his helmet against its surface. Yes. Something inside, muffled, wet. Thumping. Trying to get out.

It can't. No way. It's just dying in there, that's all.

He pushes away, drifts up into the water column. He feels very exposed. A few stiff-legged kicks take him back to the bottom. Slightly better.

"Caraco? Come *on*, Judy—"

Oh Jesus. She left me here. She just fucking left *me out here.*

He hears something moaning, very close by.

Inside his helmet, in fact.

TRANS/OFFI/230850:2026

I accompanied Judy Caraco and Lenie Clarke outside today, and witnessed several events that concern me. Both participants swam through unlit areas without headlamps and spent significant periods of time isolated from dive buddies; at one point, Caraco simply left me on the seabed without warning. This is potentially life-threatening behavior, although of course I was able to find my way back to Beebe using the homing beacon.

I have yet to receive an explanation for all this. The v—
——The other personnel are presently gone from the station. I can find two or three of them on sonar; I suppose the rest are just hidden in the bottom clutter. Once again, this is extremely unsafe behavior.

Such recklessness appears to be typical here. It implies a relative indifference to personal welfare, an attitude entirely consistent with the profile I developed at the onset of the rifter program. (The only alternative is that they simply do not appreciate the dangers involved in this environment, which is unlikely.)

It is also consistent with a generalized post-traumatic addiction to hostile environments. This doesn't constitute evidence per se, of course, but I have noted one or two other things which, taken together, may be cause for concern. Michael Brander, for example, has a history which ranges from caffeine and sympathomimetic abuse to limbic hot-wiring. He's known to have brought a substantial supply of phencyclidine derms with him to Beebe; I've just located it in his cubby and I was surprised to find that it has barely been touched. Phencyclidine is not, physiologically speaking, addictive—exogenous-drug addicts are screened out of the program—but the fact remains that Brander had a habit when he came down here, a habit which he has since abandoned. I have to wonder what he's replaced it with.

The wetroom.

"*There* you are. Where did you go?"

"Had to recover this cartridge. Bad sulfide head."

"You could have told me. I was supposed to come along on your rounds anyway, remember? You just left me out there."

"You got back."

"*That's*—That's not the point, Judy. You don't leave someone alone at the bottom of the ocean without a word. What if something had happened to me?"

"We go out alone all the time. It's part of the job. Watch that, it's slippery."

"Safety procedures are also part of the job. Even for you. And especially for me, Judy, I'm a complete fish out of water here, heh-heh. You can't expect me to know my way around."

". . ."

"Excuse me?"

"We're shorthanded, remember? We can't always afford to buddy up. And you're a big strong man—well, you're a man, anyway. I didn't think you needed baby-sit—"

"*Shit! My hand!*"

"I told you to be careful."

"*Ow.* How much does the fucking thing weigh?"

"About ten kilos, without all the mud. I guess I should've rinsed it off."

"I guess so. I think one of the heads gouged me on the way down. Shit, I'm bleeding."

"Sorry about that."

"Yeah. Well, look, Caraco. I'm sorry if baby-sitting rubs you the wrong way, but a little more baby-sitting and Acton and Fisher might still be alive, you know? A little more baby-sitting and—Did you hear that?"

"What?"

"From outside. That—moaning, sort of—"

". . ."

"Come on, C—Judy. You must've heard it!"

"Maybe the hull shifted."

"No. I *heard* something. And this isn't the first time, either."

"I didn't hear anything."

"You'd—Where are you going? You just came *in*! Judy . . ."

Clank. Hiss.

". . . don't go. . . ."

TRANS/OFFI/250850:2120

I've asked each of the participants to submit to a routine sweep under the Medical scanner—or rather, I've asked most of them directly, and asked them to pass the word on to Ken Lubin, whom I've seen a few times now but haven't actually spoken to yet. (I have twice attempted to engage Mr. Lubin in conversation, without success.) The participants know, of course, that Medical scans do not require physical contact on my part, and they're well able to run them at their own convenience without me even being present. Still, although no one has explicitly refused my request, there has been a notable lack of enthusiasm in terms of actual compliance. It's fairly obvious (and entirely consistent with my profile) that they consider it something of an intrusion, and will avoid it if possible. To date I've managed to get rundowns on only Alice Nakata and Judy Caraco. I've appended their binaries to this entry; both show elevated production of dopamine and norepinephrine, but I can't establish whether this began before or after their present tour of duty. GABA and other inhibitor levels were slightly up, too, left over from their previous dive (less than an hour before the scan).

The others, so far, haven't been able to "find the time" for an exam. In the meantime I've resorted to going over stored scanner records of old injuries. Not surprisingly, physical injuries are common down here, although they've become much less frequent as of late. There are no cases of head trauma on record, however—at least, nothing that would warrant an NMR. This effectively limits my brainchemistry data to what the participants are willing to provide on request—not much, so far. If this doesn't change, the bulk of my analysis will have to be based on behavioral observations. As medieval as that sounds.

Who could it be? Who?

When Yves Scanlon first sank into the abyss he had two questions on his mind. He's chasing the second one now, lying in his cubby, shielded from Beebe by a pair of eyephones and the personal database in his shirt pocket. For now, he's gone mercifully blind to plumbing and condensation.

He's not deaf, though. Unfortunately. Every now and then he hears footsteps, or low voices, or—just maybe— the distant cry of something unimaginable in pain; but then he speaks a little louder into the pickup, drowns unwelcome sounds with barked commands to scroll up, link files, search for keywords. Personnel records dance across the inside of his eyes, and he can almost forget where he is.

His interest in this particular question has not been

sanctioned by his employers. *They know about it, though—yes sirree they know. They just don't think I do.*

Rowan and her cronies are such assholes. They've been lying to him from the start. Scanlon doesn't know why. He'd have been okay with it, if they'd just leveled with him. But they kept it under wraps. As though he wouldn't be able to figure it out for himself.

It's bloody obvious. There's more than one way to make a vampire. Usually you take someone who's fucked in the head, and you train them. But why couldn't you take someone who's already trained, and then fuck them in the head? It might even be cheaper.

You can learn a lot from a witch hunt. All that repressed-memory hysteria back in the nineteen nineties, for example: so many people suddenly remembering abuse, or alien abduction, or dear old grandma stirring a cauldron of stewed babies. It didn't take much, no one had to go in and physically rewire the synapses; the brain's gullible enough to rewire *itself* if you coax it. Most of those poor bozos didn't even know they were doing it. These days, it only takes a few weeks' worth of hypnotherapy. The right suggestions, delivered just the right way, can inspire memories to build themselves out of bits and pieces. Sort of a neurological cascade effect. And once you *think* you've been abused, well, why wouldn't your psyche shift to match?

It's a good idea. Someone else thought so, too, at least that's what Scanlon heard from Mezzich a couple of weeks ago. Nothing official, of course, but there may already be a few prototypes in the system. Someone right here in Beebe, maybe, a walking testament to Induced False Memory Syndrome. Maybe Lubin. Maybe Clarke. Could be anyone, really.

They should have told me.

They told him, all right. They told him, when he first started, that he was coming in on the ground floor. *You'll have input on pretty much everything,* was what Rowan had promised. *The design work, the follow-ups.* They even offered him automatic coauthorship on all unclassified publications. Yves Scanlon was supposed to be a fucking *equal.* And then they shut him off in a little room, mumbling to recruits while *they* made all the decisions up on the thirty-fifth fucking floor.

Standard corporate mentality. Knowledge was power. Corpses never told anybody *anything.*

I was an idiot to believe them as long as I did. Sending up my recommendations, waiting for them to honor a promise or two. And this is the bone they throw me. Stick me at the bottom of the fucking ocean with these post-traumatic head cases because no one else wants to get shit on their hands.

I mean, fuck. I'm so far out of the loop I have to coax rumors from a has-been hack like Mezzich?

Still. He wonders who it might be. Brander or Nakata, maybe. Her record shows a background in geothermal engineering and high-pressure tech, and he's got a master's in systems ecology with a minor in genomics. Too much education for your average vampire. Assuming there *is* such a thing.

Wait a second. Why should I trust these flies? After all, if Rowan's keeping this thing under wraps she might not be stupid enough to leave clues lying around in the GA personnel records.

Scanlon ponders the question. Suppose the files have been modified. Maybe he should check out the *least* likely candidates. He orders an ascending sort by educational background. Lenie Clarke. Premed dropout, basic virtual-tech ed. The GA hired her away from the Hongcouver aquarium. PR department.

Hmm. Someone with Lenie Clarke's social skills, in public relations? Not likely. I wonder if—

Jesus. There it is again.

Yves Scanlon strips the 'phones from his eyes and stares at the ceiling. The sound seeps in through the hull, barely audible.

I'm almost getting used to it, actually.

It sighs through the bulkhead, recedes, dies. Scanlon waits. He realizes he's holding his breath.

There. Something very far away. Something very—

Lonely. It sounds so lonely.

He knows how it feels.

The lounge is empty, but something casts a faint shadow through the Communications hatchway. A soft voice from inside: Clarke, it sounds like. Scanlon eavesdrops for a few seconds. She's reciting supply consumption rates, listing the latest bits of equipment to break down. A routine call up to the GA, from the sound of it. She hangs up just before he steps into view.

She's sitting slumped in her chair, a cup of coffee within easy reach. They eye each other for a moment, without speaking.

"Anyone else around?" Scanlon wonders.

She shakes her head.

"I thought I heard something, a few minutes ago."

She turns back to face the console. A couple of icons flash on the main display.

"What are you doing?"

She makes a vague gesture to the console. "Running tender. Thought you'd like that, for a change."

"Oh, but I said—"

"Not to change the routine," Clarke cuts in. She seems tired. "Do you always expect blind obedience from your subjects?"

"Is that what you think I meant?"

She snorts softly, still not looking back.

"Look," Scanlon says, "Are you sure you didn't hear

something, like—like—" *like a ghost, Clarke? A sound like poor dead Acton might make, watching his own remains rotting out there on the rift?*

"Don't worry about it," she says.

Aha. "So you *did* hear something." *She knows what it is, too. They all do.*

"What I hear," she says, "is my own concern."

Take a hint, Scanlon. But there's nowhere else to go, except back to his cubby. And the prospect of being alone, right now—Somehow, even the company of a vampire seems preferable.

She turns around to face him again. "Something else?"

"Not really. Just can't seem to sleep." Scanlon dons a disarming smile. "Just not used to the pressure, I guess." *That's right. Put her at ease. Acknowledge her superiority.*

She just stares at him

"I don't know how you take it, month after month," he adds.

"Yes you do. You're a psychiatrist. You *chose* us."

"Actually, I'm more of a mechanic."

"Of course," she says, expressionless. "It's your job to keep things broken."

Scanlon looks away.

She stands up and takes a step toward the hatchway, her tending duties apparently forgotten. Scanlon stands aside. She brushes past, somehow avoiding physical contact in the cramped space.

"Look," he blurts out, "how about a quick review of the tending procedure? I'm not all that familiar with this equipment."

It's too obvious. He knows she sees through it before the words are even out of his mouth. But it's also a perfectly reasonable request from someone in his role. Routine evaluation, after all.

She watches him for a moment, her head cocked a bit

to one side. Her face, expressionless as usual, somehow conveys the impression of a slight smile. Finally she sits down again.

She taps on a menu. "This is the Throat." A cluster of luminous rectangles nested in a background of contour lines. "Thermal readout." The image erupts into psychedelic false color, red and yellow hot spots pulsing at irregular intervals along the main fissure. "You don't usually bother with thermal when you're tending," Clarke explains. "When you're out there you find that stuff out sooner firsthand anyway." The psychedelia fades back to green and gray.

And what happens if someone gets taken by surprise out there and you don't have the readings in here to know they're in trouble? Scanlon doesn't ask aloud. Just another cut corner.

Clarke pans, finds a pair of alphanumeric icons. "Alice and Ken." Another red hot-spot slides into view in the upper left corner of the display.

No, wait a minute; she turned thermal off. . . .

"Hey," Scanlon says, "that's a *deadman switch—*"

No audio alarm. Why isn't there an alarm?—His eyes dart across the half-familiar console. *Where is it, where—* Shit—

The alarm's been disabled.

"*Look!*" Scanlon points at the display. "Can't you—"

Clarke looks up at him, almost lazily. She doesn't seem to understand.

He jabs his thumb down. "Somebody just *died* out there!"

She looks at the screen, slowly shakes her head. "No—"

"You stupid bitch, you cut off the alarm!"

He hits a control icon. The station starts howling. Scanlon jumps back, startled, bumps the bulkhead. Clarke watches him, frowning slightly.

"What's wrong with you?" He reaches out and grabs her by the shoulders. *"Do something!* Call Lubin, call—" The alarm is deafening. He shakes her, hard, pulls her up out of the chair—

And remembers, too late: *You don't touch Lenie Clarke.*

Something happens in her face. It almost *crumples*, right there in front of him. Lenie Clarke the ice queen is suddenly nowhere to be seen. In her place there's only a beaten, blind little kid, body shaking, mouth moving in the same pattern over and over, he can't hear over the alarm but her lips shape the words, *I'm sorry I'm sorry I'm sorry—*

All in the few scant seconds before she crystallizes.

She seems to harden against the sound, against Scanlon's assault. Her face goes completely blank. She rises out of the chair, centimeters taller than she should be. One hand comes up, grabs Yves Scanlon by the throat. Pushes.

He staggers backward into the lounge, flailing. The table appears to one side; he reaches out, steadies himself.

Suddenly, Beebe falls silent again.

Scanlon takes a deep breath. Another vampire has appeared in his peripheral vision, standing impassively at the mouth of the corridor; he ignores it. Directly ahead, Lenie Clarke is sitting down again in Communications, her back turned. Scanlon steps forward.

"It's Karl," she says before he can speak.

It takes a moment to register: *Acton.*

"But—that was months ago," Scanlon says. "You *lost* him."

"We lost him." She breathes, slowly. "He went down a smoker. It erupted."

"I'm sorry," Scanlon says. "I—didn't know."

"Yeah." Her voice is tight with controlled indiffer-

ence. "He's too far down to—We can't get him back.
Too dangerous." She turns to face him, impossibly calm.
"Deadman switch still works, though. It'll keep screaming until the battery runs down." She shrugs. "So we
keep the alarm off."

"I don't blame you," Scanlon says softly.

"Imagine," Clarke tells him, "how much your approval comforts me."

He turns to leave.

"Wait," she says. "I can zoom in for you. I can show
you exactly where he died, maximum rez."

"That's not necessary."

She stabs controls. "No problem. Naturally you're interested. What kind of mechanic wouldn't want to know
the performance specs of his own creation?" She re-
shapes the display like a sculptor, hones it down and
down until there's nothing left but a tangle of faint green
lines and a red pulsing dot.

"He got wedged into an ancillary crevice," she says.
"Looks like a tight fit even now, when all the flesh has
been boiled away. Don't know how he managed to get
down there when he was all in one piece." There's no
stress in her voice at all. She could be talking about a
friend's vacation.

Scanlon can feel her eyes on him; he keeps his on the
screen.

"Fischer," he says. "What happened to him?"

From the corner of his eye: she starts to tense, turns
it into a shrug. "Who knows? Maybe Archie got him."

"Archie?"

"Archie Toothis." Scanlon doesn't recognize the
name; it's not in any of his files, as far as he knows. He
considers, decides not to push it.

"Did *Fischer's* deadman go off, at least?"

"He didn't have one." She shrugs. "The abyss can kill

you any number of ways, Scanlon. It doesn't always leave traces."

"I'm—I'm sorry if I upset you, Lenie."

One corner of her mouth barely twitches.

And he *is* sorry. Even though it's not his fault. *I didn't make you what you are,* he wants to say. *I didn't smash you into junk, that was someone else. I just came along afterward and found a use for you. I gave you a purpose, more of a purpose than you ever had back there.*

Is that really so bad?

He doesn't dare ask aloud, so he turns to leave. And when Lenie Clarke lays one finger, very briefly, on the screen where Acton's icon flashes, he pretends not to notice.

TRANS/OFFI/260850:1352

I recently had an interesting conversation with Lenie Clarke. Although she didn't admit so openly—she is very well defended, and quite expert at hiding her feelings from laypeople—I believe that she and Karl Acton were sexually involved. This is a heartening discovery, insofar as my original profiles strongly suggested that such a relationship would develop. (Clarke has a history of relationships with Intermittent Explosives.) This adds a measure of empirical confidence to other, related predictions regarding rifter behavior.

I have also learned that Karl Acton, rather than simply disappearing, was actually killed by an erupting smoker. I don't know what he was doing down there—I'll continue to investigate—but the behavior itself seems foolish at best and quite possibly suicidal. Suicide is not consistent either with Karl Acton's DSM or ECM profiles, which must have been accurate when first derived. Suicide, therefore, would imply a degree of basic personality change. This is consistent with the trauma-addiction scenario. However, some sort of physical brain injury can not be ruled out. My search of the medical logs didn't turn up any head injuries, but was limited to living participants. Perhaps Acton was ... different ...

Oh. I found out who Archie Toothis is. Not in the personnel files at all. The library. *Architeuthis*: giant squid.

I think she was kidding.

Bulrushes

At times like this it seems as if the world has always been black.

It hasn't, of course. Joel Kita caught a hint of ambient blue out the dorsal port just ten minutes ago. Right before they dropped through the deep scattering layer; pretty thin stuff compared to the old days, he's been told, but still impressive. Glowing siphonophores and flashlight fish and all. Still beautiful.

That's a thousand meters above them now. Right here there's nothing but the thin vertical slash of Beebe's transponder line. Joel has put the 'scaphe into a lazy spin during the drop, forward floods sweeping the water in a descending corkscrew. The transponder line swings past the main viewport every thirty seconds or so, keeping time, a bright vertical line against the dark.

Other than that, blackness.

A tiny monster bumps the port. Needle teeth so long the mouth can't close, an eel-like body studded with glowing photophores—fifteen, twenty centimeters long, tops. It's not even big enough to make a sound when it hits and then it's gone, spinning away above them.

"Viperfish," Jarvis says.

Joel glances around at his passenger, hunched up beside him to take advantage of what might laughingly be

called "the view." Jarvis is some sort of cellular physi-
ologist out of Rand/Washington U., here to collect a
mysterious package in a plain brown wrapper.

"See many of those?" he asks now.

Joel shakes his head. "Not this far down. Kind of unusual."

"Yeah, well, this whole area is unusual. That's why
I'm here."

Joel checks tactical, nudges a trim tab.

"Now, viperfish, they're not supposed to get any bigger than the one you just saw," Jarvis remarks. "But
there was a guy, oh, back in the 1930s—Beebe his name
was, the same guy they named—Anyway, he swore he
saw one that was over two meters long."

Joel grunts. "Didn't know people came down here
back then."

"Yeah, well, they were just starting out. And everyone
had always thought deepwater fish were these puny little
midgets, because that's all they ever brought up in their
trawls. But then Beebe sees this big ripping viperfish,
and people start thinking hey, maybe we only caught
little ones because all the big ones could outswim the
trawls. Maybe the deep sea really *is* teeming with giant
monsters."

"It's not," Joel says. "At least, not that I've seen."

"Yeah, well, that's what most people think. Every
now and then you get pieces of something weird wash-
ing up, though. And of course there's Megamouth. And
your garden-variety giant squid."

"They never get down this far. I bet none of your other
giants do, either. Not enough food."

"Except for the vents," Jarvis says.

"Except for the vents."

"Actually," Jarvis amends, "except for *this* vent."

The transponder line swings past, a silent metronome.

"Yeah," says Joel after a moment. "Why is that?"

"Well, we're not sure. We're working on it, though. That's what I'm doing here. Gonna bag one of those scaly mothers."

"You're kidding. How? We going to butt it to death with the hull?"

"Actually, it's already been bagged. The rifters got it for us a couple of days ago. All we do is pick it up."

"I could do that solo. Why'd you come along?"

"Got to check to make sure they did it right. Don't want the canister blowing up on the surface."

"And that extra tank you strapped onto my 'scaphe? The one with the biohazard stickers all over it?"

"Oh," Jarvis says. "That's just to sterilize the sample."

"Uh-huh." Joel lets his eyes run over the panels. "You must pull a lot of weight back onshore."

"Oh? Why's that?"

"I used to make the Channer run a lot. Pharmaceutical dives, supply trips to Beebe, ecotourism. A while back I shuttled some corpse type out to Beebe; he said he was staying for a month or so. The GA calls me three days later and tells me to go pick him up. I show up for the run and they tell me it's canceled. No explanation."

"Pretty strange," Jarvis remarks.

"You're the first run I've had to Channer in three weeks. You're the first run *anyone's* had, from what I can tell. So, you pull some weight."

"Not really." Jarvis shrugs in the half-light. "I'm just a research associate. I go where they tell me, just like you. Today they told me to go and pick up an order of fish to go."

Joel looks at him.

"You were asking why they got so big," Jarvis says, deking to the right. "We figure it's some kind of endo-symbiotic infection."

"No shit."

"Say it's easier for some microbe to live inside a fish

than out in the ocean—less osmotic stress—so once inside, it's pumping out more ATP than it needs."

"ATP," Joel says.

"High-energy phosphate compound. Cellular battery. Anyway, it spits out this surplus ATP, and the host fish can use it as extra growth energy. So maybe Channer Vent's got some sort of unique bug that infects teleost fishes and gives 'em a growth spurt."

"Pretty weird."

"Actually, happens all the time. Every one of your own cells is a colony, for that matter. You know, nucleus, mitochondria, chloroplasts if you're a plant—"

"I'm not." Whitecap tourist faces flash through his mind. *More than I can say for some folks . . .*

"—those all used to be free-living microbes in their own right. A few billion years ago something ate them, but it couldn't digest them properly so they all just kept living inside the cytoplasm. Eventually they struck up a deal with the host cell, took over housecleaning tasks and such-like, in lieu of rent. Voilà: your modern eukaryotic cell."

"So what happens if this Channer bug gets into a person? We all grow three meters high?"

A polite laugh. "Nope. People stop growing when they reach adulthood. So do most vertebrates, actually. Fish, on the other hand, keep growing their whole lives. And *deepwater* fish—those don't do anything *except* grow, if you know what I mean."

Joel raises his eyebrows.

Jarvis holds up his hands. "I know, I know. Your baby finger is bigger than your average deepsea fish. But that just means they're short of fuel; when they *do* gas up, believe me, they use it for growth. Why waste calories just swimming around when you can't see anything anyway? In dark environments it makes more sense for predators to sit and wait. Whereas if you grow big enough, maybe you'll get too big for *other* predators, you see?"

"Mmm."

"Of course, we're basing the whole theory on a couple of samples that got dragged up without any protection against temperature or pressure changes." Jarvis snorts. "Might as well have sent them in a paper bag. But this time we're doing it right—Hey, is that *light* I see down there?"

There's a vague yellow glow smudging the darkness directly below. Joel calls up a topographic display: Beebe. The geothermal array over at the rift proper lays out a sequence of hard green echoes bearing 340°. And just to the left of that, about a hundred meters off the easternmost generator, something squirts a unique acoustic signature at four-second intervals.

Joel taps commands to the dive planes. The 'scaphe pulls out of its spiral and coasts off to the northeast. Beebe Station, never more than a bright stain, fades to stern.

The ocean floor resolves suddenly in the 'scaphe's headlights: bone-gray ooze slides past, occasional outcroppings, great squashed marshmallows of lava and pumice. In the cockpit a flashing point of light slo-mos toward the center of the topographic display.

Something charges them from overhead; the dull wet sound of its impact reverberates briefly through the hull. Joel looks up through the dorsal port but sees nothing. Several more impacts, staggered. The 'scaphe whirs implacably onward.

"There."

It looks almost like a lifeboat canister, almost three meters long. Readouts twinkle from a panel on one rounded end. It's resting on a carpet of giant tubeworms, their feathery crowns extended in full filter-feeding mode. Joel thinks of the baby Moses, nestled in a clump of mutant bulrushes.

"Wait a second," Jarvis says. "Kill the lights first."

"What for?"

"You don't need them, do you?"

"Well, no. I can use instruments if I have to. But why—"

"Just do it, okay?" Jarvis, the chatterbox, is suddenly all business.

Darkness floods the cockpit, retreats a bit before the glow of the readouts. Joel grabs a pair of eyephones off a hook to his left. The sea floor reappears before him courtesy of the ventral photoamps, faded to blue-and-black.

He coaxes the 'scaphe into position directly above the canister, listens to the clank and creak of grapples flexing beneath the deck; metal claws the color of slate extend across his field of view.

"Spray it before you pick it up," Jarvis says.

Joel reaches out and taps the control codes without looking. The 'phones show him a nozzle extending from Jarvis's tank, taking aim like a skinny cobra.

"Do it."

The nozzle ejaculates gray-blue murk, sprays back and forth along the length of the canister, sweeping the benthos on either side. The tubeworms yank back into their tunnels and shut the doors; the whole featherduster forest vanishes in an instant, leaving a crowd of sealed leathery tubes.

The nozzle spews its venom.

One of the tubes opens, almost hesitantly. Something dark and stringy drifts out, twitching. The gray plume sweeps across it; it sags, lifeless, across the sill of its burrow. Other tubes are opening now. Invertebrate corpses slump back into sight.

"What's in this stuff?" Joel whispers.

"Cyanide. Rotenone. Some other things. Sort of a cocktail."

The nozzle sputters for a few seconds and runs dry. Automatically Joel retracts it.

"Okay," Jarvis says. "Let's grab it and go home."

Joel doesn't move.

"Hey," Jarvis says.

Joel shakes his head, plays the machinery. The 'scaphe extends its arms in a metal hug, pulls the canister off the bottom. Joel strips the 'phones from his eyes and taps the controls. They begin rising.

"That was a pretty thorough rinse," Joel remarks after a while.

"Yes. Well, the sample's costing us a fair bit. Don't want to contaminate it."

"I see."

"You can turn the lights back on," Jarvis says. "How long before we break the surface?"

Joel trips the floods. "Twenty minutes. Half hour."

"I hope the lifter pilot doesn't get too bored." Jarvis is all chummy again.

"There is no pilot. It's a smart gel."

"Really? You don't say." Jarvis frowns. "Those are scary things, those gels. You know one suffocated a bunch of people in London a few years back?"

Yes, Joel's about to say, but Jarvis is back in spew mode. "No shit. It was running the subway system over there, perfect operational record, and then one day it just forgets to crank up the ventilators when it's supposed to. Train slides into station fifteen meters underground, everybody gets out, no air, *boom.*"

Joel's heard this before. The punch line's got something to do with a broken clock, if he remembers it right.

"These things teach themselves from experience, right?" Jarvis continues. "So everyone just assumed it had learned to cue the ventilators on something obvious. Body heat, motion, CO_2 levels, you know. Turns out instead it was watching a clock on the wall. Train arrival

correlated with a predictable subset of patterns on the
digital display, so it started the fans whenever it saw one
of those patterns."

"Yeah. That's right." Joel shakes his head. "And van-
dals had smashed the clock, or something."

"Hey. You *did* hear about it."

"Jarvis, that story's ten years old if it's a day. That
was way back when they were starting out with these
things. Those gels have been debugged from the molecules up since then."

"Yeah? What makes you so sure?"

"Because a gel's been running the lifter for the better
part of a year now, and it's had plenty of opportunity to
fuck up. It hasn't."

"So you like these things?"

"Fuck no," Joel says, thinking about Ray Stericker.
Thinking about himself. "I'd like 'em a lot better if they
did screw up sometimes, you know?"

"Well, I don't like 'em *or* trust 'em. You've got to
wonder what they're up to."

Joel nods, distracted by Jarvis's digression. But then
his mind returns to dead tube worms, and undeclared
no-dive zones, and an anonymous canister drenched with
enough poison to kill a fucking city.

I've got to wonder what all *of us are.*

Ghosts

It's hideous.

Nearly a meter across. Probably smaller when Clarke
started working on it, but it's a real monster now. Scanlon thinks back to his v-school days, and remembers:
Starfish are supposed to be all in one plane. Flat disks
with arms. Not this one. Clarke has grafted bits and
pieces together at all angles and produced a crawling

Gordian knot, some pieces red, some purple, some white. Scanlon thinks the original body may have been orange, before.

"They regenerate," she buzzes at his shoulder. "And they've got really primitive immune systems, so there's no tissue-rejection problems to speak of. It makes them easier to fix if something goes wrong with them."

Fix. As if this is actually some sort of improvement. "So, it was broken?" Scanlon asks. "What was wrong with it, exactly?"

"It was scratched. It had this cut on its back. And there was another starfish nearby, all torn up. Way too far gone for even me to help, but I figured I could use some of the pieces to patch this little guy together."

This little guy. *This little guy* drags itself around between them in slow, pathetic circles, leaving tangled tracks in the mud. Filaments of parasitic fungus trail from ragged seams not quite healed. Extra limbs, asymmetrically grafted, catch on rocks; the body lurches, perpetually unstable.

Lenie Clarke doesn't seem to notice.

"How long ago—I mean, how long have you been doing this?"

Scanlon's voice is admirably level; he's certain it conveys nothing but friendly interest. But somehow she knows. She's silent for a second, and then she points her undead eyes at him and she says, "Of course. It makes you sick."

"No, I'm just—well, fascinated, I—"

"You're disgusted," she buzzes. "You shouldn't be. Isn't this exactly the sort of thing you'd expect from a rifter? Isn't that why you sent us down here in the first place?"

"I know what you think, Lenie," Scanlon tries, going for the light touch. "You think we get up every morning and ask ourselves, *How can we best fuck over our employees today?*"

She looks down at the starfish. " 'We'?"

"The GA."

She floats there while her pet monster squirms in slow motion, trying to right itself.

"We're not evil, Lenie," Scanlon says after a while. If only she'd look at him, see the earnest expression on his helmeted face. He's practiced it for years.

But when she does look up, finally, she doesn't even seem to notice. "Don't flatter yourself, Scanlon," she says. "You don't have the slightest control over what you are."

TRANS/OFFI/280850:1043

There's no doubt that the ability to function down here stems from attributes which would, under other conditions, qualify as "dysfunctional." These attributes not only permit long-term exposure to the rift; they may also intensify as a *result* of that exposure. Lenie Clarke, for example, has developed a mutilation neurosis which she could not have had prior to her arrival here. Her fascination with an animal which can be easily "fixed" when broken has fairly obvious roots, notwithstanding a number of horribly botched attempts at "repair." Judith Caraco, who used to run indoor marathons prior to her arrest, compulsively swims up and down Beebe's transponder line. The other participants have probably developed corresponding habits.

Whether these behaviors are indicative of a physiological addiction, I cannot yet say. If they are, I suspect that Kenneth Lubin may be the farthest along. During conversation with some of the other participants I have learned that Lubin may actually *sleep* outside on occasion, which can not be considered healthy by anyone's standards. I would be better able to understand the reason for this if I had more particulars about Lubin's background. Of course, his file as provided is missing certain relevant details.

On the job, the participants work unexpectedly well together, given the psychological baggage each of them carries. Duty shifts carry an almost uncanny sense of coordination. They seem choreographed. It's almost as if—

This is a subjective impression, of course, but I believe that rifters do in fact share some heightened awareness of each other, at least when they're outside. They may also have a heightened awareness of *me*—either that, or they've made some remarkably shrewd guesses about my state of mind.

No. Too . . . too—

Too easy to misinterpret. If the haploids back on shore read that, they might think the vampires have the upper hand. Scanlon deletes the last few lines, considers alternatives.

There's a word for his suspicions. It's a word that describes one's experience in an isolation tank, or in VR with all the inputs blanked, or—in extreme cases—when someone cuts the sensory cables of the central nervous system. It describes that state of sensory deprivation in which whole sections of the brain go dark for want of input. The word is Ganzfeld.

It's very quiet in a Ganzfeld. Usually the temporal and occipital lobes seethe with input, signals strong enough to swamp any competition. When those fall silent, though, the mind can sometimes make out faint whispers in the darkness. It imagines scenes that have a curious likeness to those glowing on a television in some distant room, perhaps. Or it feels a faint emotional echo, familiar but not, somehow, firsthand.

Statistics suggest that these sensations are not entirely imaginary. Experts of an earlier decade—people much like Yves Scanlon, except for their luck in being in the right place at the right time—have even found out where the whispers come from.

It turns out that protein microtubules, permeating each and every neuron, act as receivers for certain weak signals at the quantum level. It turns out that consciousness itself is a quantum phenomenon. It turns out that under certain conditions conscious systems can interact directly, bypassing the usual sensory middlemen.

Not a bad payoff for something that started a hundred years ago with halved Ping-Pong balls taped over someone's eyes.

Ganzfeld. That's the ticket. Don't talk about the ease with which these creatures stare through you. Forget the endpoint: Dissect the process.

Take control.

I believe some sort of Ganzfeld effect may be at work here. The dark, weightless abyssal environment might impoverish the senses enough to push the signal-to-noise ratio past threshold. My observations suggest that the women may be more sensitive than the men, which is consistent with their larger corpus callosa and consequent advantage in intercortical processing speed.

Whatever the cause of this phenomenon, it has yet to affect me. Perhaps it just takes a little time.

Oh, one other thing. I was unable to find any record of Karl Acton using the medical scanner. I've asked Clarke and Brander about this; neither could remember Acton actually using the machine. Given the number of injuries on record for everyone else, I find this surprising.

Yves Scanlon sits at the table and forces himself to eat with a mouth gone utterly dry. He hears the vampires moving downstairs, moving along the corridor, moving just behind him. He doesn't turn around. He mustn't show any weakness. He can't betray any lack of confidence.

Vampires, he knows now, are like dogs. They can smell fear.

His head is full of sampled sounds, looping endlessly. *You're not among friends here, Scanlon. Don't make us into enemies.* That was Brander, five minutes ago, whispering in Scanlon's ear before dropping down into the wetroom. And Caraco *click click click*ing her bread knife against the table until he could barely hear himself think. And Nakata and that stupid *giggle* of hers. And Patricia Rowan, sometime in the imagined future, sneering *Well, if you can't even handle a routine assignment without starting a revolt, it's no wonder we didn't trust you . . .*

Or perhaps, echoing back along a different timeline, a terse call to the GA: *We lost Scanlon. Sorry.*

And underlying it all, that long, hollow, icy sound, slithering along the floor of his brain. That thing. That thing that nobody mentions. The voice in the abyss. It sounds nearby tonight, whatever it is.

Not that that matters to the vampires. They're sealing their 'skins while Scanlon sits frozen at the end of his meal, they're grabbing their fins, dropping outside in ones and twos, deserting him. They're going out there, with the moaning thing.

Scanlon wonders, over the voices in his head, if it can get inside. If this is the night they bring it back with them.

The vampires are all gone. After a while, even the voices in Scanlon's head start to fade. Most of them.

This is insane. I can't just sit here.

There's one voice he didn't hear tonight. Lenie Clarke just sat there through the whole fiasco, watching.

Clarke's the one they look to, all right. She doesn't talk much, but they pay attention when she does. Scanlon wonders what she tells them, when he's not around.

Can't just sit here. And it's not that bad. It's not as though they really threatened me—

You're not among friends here, Scanlon.

—not explicitly.

He tries to figure out exactly where he lost them. It seemed like a reasonable enough proposition. The prospect of shorter tours shouldn't have put them off like that. Even if they are addicted to this godawful place, it was just a *suggestion*. Scanlon went out of his way to be completely nonthreatening. Unless they took exception to his mention of their carelessness in the safety department. But that should have been old news; they not only knew the chances they were taking, they flaunted them.

Who am I kidding? That's not when I lost them. I shouldn't have mentioned Lubin, shouldn't have used him as an example.

It made so much sense at the time, though. Scanlon *knows* Lubin's an outsider, even down here. Scanlon's not an idiot, he can read the signs even behind the eyecaps. Lubin's different from the other vampires. Using him as an example should have been the safest thing in the world. Scapegoats have been a respected part of the therapeutic arsenal for hundreds of years.

Look, you want to end up like Lubin? He sleeps outside, for Christ's sake!

Scanlon puts his head in his hands. *How was I supposed to know they* all *did?*

Maybe he should have. He could have monitored sonar more closely. Or timed them when they went into their cubbies, seen how long they stayed inside. There were things he could have done, he knows.

Maybe I really did fuck up. Maybe. If only I'd—

Jesus, that sounds close. What is—
Shut up! Just shut the fuck up!

Maybe it shows up on sonar.

Scanlon takes a breath and ducks into Comm. He's had basic training on the gear, of course; it's all pretty intuitive anyway. He didn't really need Clarke's grudging tutorial. A few seconds' effort elicits a tactical overview: vampires, strung like beads on an invisible line between Beebe and the Throat. Another one off to the west, heading for the Throat; probably Lubin. Random topography. Nothing else.

As he watches, the four icons closest to Beebe edge a pixel or two closer to Main Street. The fifth in line is way out ahead, almost as far out as Lubin. Nearly at the Throat already.

Wait a second.

Vampires: Brander, Caraco, Clarke, Lubin, Nakata. Right.

Icons: One, two, three, four, five—

Six.

Scanlon stares at the screen. *Oh shit.*

Beebe's phone link is very old-school; a direct line, not even routed through the telemetry and Comm servers. It's almost Victorian in its simplicity, guaranteed to stay on line through any systems crash short of an implosion. Scanlon has never used it before. Why should he? The moment he calls home he's admitting he can't do the job by himself.

Now he hits the call stud without a moment's hesitation. "This is Scanlon, Human Resources. I've got a bit of a—"

The line stays dark.

He tries again. Dead.

Shit shit shit. Somehow, though, he isn't surprised.

I could call the vampires. I could order them to come back in. I have the authority. It's an amusing thought for a few moments.

At least the Voice seems to have faded. He thinks he can hear it, if he concentrates, but it's so faint it could even be his imagination.

Beebe squeezes down on him. He looks back at the tactical display, hopefully. *One, two, three, f—*
Oh shit.

He doesn't remember going outside. He remembers struggling into his preshmesh, and picking up a sonar pistol, and now he's on the seabed, under Beebe. He takes a bearing, checks it, checks it again. It doesn't change.

He creeps away from the light, toward the Throat. He fights with himself for endless moments, wins; his headlamp stays doused. No sense in broadcasting his presence.

He swims blind, hugging the bottom. Every now and then he takes a bearing, resets his course. Scanlon zigzags across the sea floor. Eventually the abyss begins to lighten before him.

Something moans, directly ahead.

It doesn't sound lonely anymore. It sounds cold and hungry and utterly inhuman. Scanlon freezes like a night creature caught in headlights.

After a while the sound goes away.

The Throat glimmers half-resolved, maybe twenty meters ahead. It looks like a spectral collection of buildings and derricks set down on the moon. Murky copper light spills down from floods set halfway up the generators. Scanlon circles, just beyond the light.

Something moves, off to the left.

An alien sigh.

He flattens down onto the bottom, eyes closed. *Grow*

*up, Scanlon. Whatever it is, it can't hurt you. Nothing
can bite through preshmesh.*

Nothing flesh and blood.

He refuses to finish the thought. He opens his eyes.

When it moves again, Scanlon is staring right at it.

A black plume, jetting from a chimney of rock on the
seabed. And this time it doesn't just sigh; it *moans*.

*A smoker. That's all it is. Acton went down one of
those.*

Maybe this one—

The eruption peters out. The sound whispers away.

*Smokers aren't supposed to make sounds. Not like
that, anyway.*

Scanlon edges up to the lip of the chimney. Fifty degrees Celsius. Inside, anchored about two meters down,
is some sort of machine. It's been built out of things that
were never meant to fit together; rotary blades spinning
in the vestigial current, perforated tubes, pipes anchored
at haphazard angles. The smoker is crammed with junk.

And somehow, the water jets through it and comes
out singing. Not a ghost. Not an alien predator, after all.
Just—windchimes. Relief sweeps through Scanlon's
body in a chemical wave. He relaxes, soaking in the
sensation, until he remembers:

Six contacts. Six.

And here he is, floodlit, in full view.

Scanlon retreats back into darkness. The machinery
behind his nightmares, exposed and almost pedestrian,
has bolstered his confidence. He resumes his patrol. The
Throat rotates slowly to his right, a murky monochrome
graphic.

Something fades into view ahead, floating above an
outcropping of featherworms. Scanlon slips closer, hides
behind a convenient piece of rock.

Vampires. Two of them.

They don't look the same.

Vampires usually look alike out here, it's almost impossible to tell them apart. But Scanlon's sure he's never seen one of these two before. It's facing away from him, but there's still something—it's too tall and thin, somehow. It moves in furtive starts and twitches, almost birdlike. Reptilian. It carries something under one arm.

Scanlon can't tell what sex it is. The other vampire, though, looks female. The two of them hang in the water a few meters apart, facing each other. Every now and then the female gestures with her hands; sometimes she moves too suddenly and the other one jumps a little, as if startled.

He clicks through the voice channels. Nothing. After a while the female reaches out, almost tentatively, and touches the reptile. There's something almost gentle—in an alien way—about the way she does that. Then she turns and swims off into the darkness. The reptile stays behind, drifting slowly on its axis. Its face comes into view.

Its hood seal is open. Its face is so pale that Scanlon can barely tell where skin ends and eyecaps begin; it almost looks as if this creature *has* no eyes.

The thing under its arm is the shredded remains of one of Channer's monster fish. As Scanlon watches, the reptile brings it up to its mouth and tears off a chunk. Swallows.

The voice in the Throat moans in the distance, but the reptile doesn't seem to notice.

Its uniform has the usual GA logo stamped onto the shoulders. The usual name tag underneath.

Who—?

Its blank empty face sweeps right past Scanlon's hiding place without pausing. A moment later it's facing away again.

It's all alone out there. It doesn't *look* dangerous.

Scanlon braces against his rock, pushes off. Water

pushes back, slowing him instantly. The reptile doesn't see him. Scanlon kicks. He's only a few meters away when he remembers.

Ganzfeld effect. What if there's some Ganzfeld effect down h—

The reptile spins suddenly, staring directly at him.

Scanlon lunges. Another split second and he wouldn't even have come close, but fortune smiles; he catches on to one of the creature's fins as it dives away. Its other foot lashes back, bounces off the helmet. Again, lower down; Scanlon's sonar pistol spins away from his belt.

He hangs on. The reptile comes at him with both fists, utterly silent. Scanlon barely feels the blows through his preshmesh. He hits back with the familiar desperation of a childhood punching bag, cornered again, feeble self-defense his only option.

Until it dawns on him that this time, somehow, it's *working*.

He's not facing the neighborhood bully here. He's not paying the price for careless eye contact with some australopithecine at the local drink'n'drug. He fighting a spindly little freak that's trying to *get away*. From *him*. This guy is downright *feeble*.

For the first time in his life, Yves Scanlon is winning a fight.

His first connects, a chain-mail mace. The enemy jerks and struggles. Scanlon grabs, twists, wrestles his quarry into an armlock. His victim flails around, utterly helpless.

"You're not going anywhere, friend." Finally, a chance to try out that tone of easy contempt he's been practicing since the age of seven. It sounds good. It sounds confident, in control. "Not until I find out just what the *fuck* is—"

The lights go out.

The whole Throat goes dark, suddenly and without fuss. It takes a few seconds to blink away the afterimagés; finally, in the extreme distance, Scanlon makes out a very faint gray glow. Beebe.

It dies as he watches. The creature in his arms has grown very still.

"Let him go, Scanlon."

"Clarke?" It might be Clarke. The vocoders don't mask everything, there are subtle differences that Scanlon's just beginning to recognize. "Is that you?" He gets his headlamp on, but no matter where he points it there's nothing to see.

"You'll break his arms," the voice says. *Clarke. Got to be.*

"I'm not that"— *strong*—"clumsy," Scanlon says to the abyss.

"You don't have to be. His bones have decalcified." A momentary silence. "He's fragile."

Scanlon loosens his grip a bit. He twists back and forth, trying to catch sight of something. Anything. All that comes into view is his prisoner's shoulder patch.

Fischer.

But he went missing—Scanlon counts back—*seven months ago!*

"Let him *go*, cocksucker." A different voice, this time. Brander's.

"*Now*," it buzzes. "Or I'll fucking *kill* you."

Brander? Brander actually defending a pedophile? How the hell did that happen?

It doesn't matter now. There are other things to worry about.

"Where are you?" Scanlon calls out. "What are you so afraid of?" He doesn't expect such an obvious goad to work. He's just buying time, trying to delay the inevitable. He can't just let Fischer *go*; he's out of options the moment that happens.

Something moves, just to the left. Scanlon spins; a flurry of motion out there, maybe a hint of limbs caught in the beam. Too many for one person. Then nothing.

He tried to do it, Scanlon realizes. *Brander just tried to kill me, and they held him back.*

For now.

"Last chance, Scanlon." Clarke again, close and invisible, as though she's humming in his ear. "We don't have to lay a hand on you, you know? We can just leave you here. You don't let him go in ten seconds and I swear you'll never find your way back. One."

"And even if you did," adds another voice—Scanlon doesn't know who—"We'd be waiting for you there."

"Two."

He checks the helmet dashboard laid out around his chin. The vampires have shut off Beebe's homing beacon.

"Three."

He checks his compass. The readout won't settle. No surprise there; magnetic navigation is a joke on the rift.

"Four."

"Fine," Scanlon tries. "Leave me here. I don't care. I'll—"

"Five."

"—just head for the surface. I can last for *days* in this suit." *Sure. As if they'll just let you float away with their—What is Fischer to them, anyway? Pet? Mascot?*

"Six."

Role model?

"Seven."

Oh God. Oh God.

"Eight."

"Please," he whispers.

"Nine."

He opens his arms. Fischer dives away into the dark. Stops.

Turns back and hangs there in the water, five meters away.

"Fischer?" Scanlon looks around. For all he can tell, they are the only two particles in the universe. "Can you understand me?"

He extends his arm. Fischer starts, like a nervous fish, but doesn't bolt.

Scanlon scans the abyss. "Is this how you want to end up?" he calls out.

Nobody answers.

"You have any idea what seven months of sensory deprivation does to your mind? You think he's even *close* to being human anymore? Are you going to spend the rest of your lives rooting around here in the mud, eating worms? Is that what you want?"

"What we want," something buzzes from the darkness, "is to be left alone."

"That's not going to happen. No matter what you do to me. You can't stay down here forever."

Nobody bothers to disagree. Fischer continues to float before him, his head cocked to one side.

"Listen, C—Lenie. Mike. All of you." The headlight beam sweeps back and forth, empty. "It's just a *job*. It's not a lifestyle." But Scanlon knows that's a lie. All these people were rifters long before the job existed.

"They'll come for you," he says softly, and he doesn't know whether it's a threat or a warning.

"Maybe we won't be here," the abyss replies at last.

Oh God. "Look, I don't know what's happening down here, but you can't *want* to stay here, nobody in their—I mean—Jesus, *where are you*?"

No answer. Only Fischer.

"This wasn't how it was supposed to go," Scanlon says, pleading.

And then, "I never meant for—I mean, I didn't—"

And then only "I'm *sorry*. I'm sorry . . ."

And then nothing at all, except the darkness.

Eventually the lights come back on. Beebe beeps reassuringly on its designated channel. Gerry Fischer is gone by then; Scanlon isn't sure when he left.

He's not sure the others were ever there. He swims back to Beebe, alone.

They probably didn't even hear me. Not really. Which is a shame, because there at the end he was actually telling the truth.

He wishes he could pity them. It should be easy; they hide in the dark, they hide behind their eyecaps as though photocollagen is some sort of general anesthetic. They warrant the pity of real people. But how can you pity someone who's somehow better off than you are? How can you pity someone who, in some sick way, seems to be happy?

How can you pity someone who scares you to death?

And besides, they walked all over me. I couldn't control them at all. Have I made a single real choice since I came down?

Sure. I gave them Fischer, and they let me live.

Yves Scanlon wonders, briefly, how to put *that* into the official record without making himself look like a complete screwup.

In the end, he doesn't really care.

TRANS/OFFI/300850:1043

I have recently encountered evidence of. . . . that is, I believe . . .

The behavior of Beebe Station personnel is distinctively . . .

I have recently participated in a telling exchange with station personnel. I managed to avoid outright confrontation, although . . .

Ah, fuck it.

T minus twenty minutes, and except for Yves Scanlon, Beebe is deserted.

It's been like this for the past couple of days. The vampires just don't come inside much anymore. Maybe they're deliberately excluding him. Maybe they're just reverting to their natural state. He can't tell.

It's just as well. By now, the two sides have very little left to say to each other.

The shuttle should be almost here. Scanlon summons his resolve: When they come, they're not going to find him hiding in his cubby. He's going to be in the lounge, in plain view.

He takes a breath, holds it, listens. Beebe creaks and drips around him. No other sounds of life.

He gets off the pallet and presses an ear against the bulkhead. Nothing. He undogs the cubby hatch, opens it a few centimeters, peers out.

Nothing.

His suitcase has been packed for hours. He grabs it off the deck, swings the hatch all the way open, and strides purposefully down the corridor.

He sees the shadow just before he enters the lounge, a dim silhouette against the bulkhead. A part of him wants to turn and run back to his cubby, but it's a much smaller part than it used to be. Most of him is just tired. He steps forward.

Lubin is waiting there, standing motionless beside the ladder. He stares through Scanlon with eyes of solid ivory.

"I wanted to say good-bye," he says.

Scanlon laughs. He can't help it.

Lubin watches impassively.

"I'm sorry," Scanlon says. He doesn't feel even slightly amused. "It's just—You never even said *hello*, you know?"

"Yes," Lubin says. "Well."

Somehow, there's no sense of threat about him this time. Scanlon can't quite understand why; Lubin's background file is still full of holes, the rumors are still festering over Galápagos; even the other vampires keep their distance from this one. But none of that shows through right now. Lubin just stands there, shifting his weight from one foot to the other. He looks almost vulnerable.

"So they're going to be bringing us back early," he says.

"I honestly don't know. It's not my decision."

"But they sent you down to—prepare the way. Like John the Baptist."

It's a very strange analogy, coming from Lubin. Scanlon says nothing.

"Did you—Didn't they *know* we wouldn't want to come back? Didn't they count on it?"

"It wasn't like that." But he wonders, more than ever, what the GA knew.

Lubin clears his throat. He seems very much to want to say something, but doesn't.

"I found the windchimes," Scanlon says at last.

"Yes."

"They scared the hell out of me."

Lubin shakes his head. "That's not what they were for."

"What *were* they for?"

"Just—a hobby, really. We've all got hobbies here. Lenie does her starfish. Alice—dreams. This place has a way of taking ugly things and lighting them in a certain way, so they almost look beautiful." A shrug. "I build memorials."

"Memorials."

Lubin nods. "The windchimes were for Acton."

"I see."

Something drops onto Beebe with a clank. Scanlon jumps.

Lubin doesn't react. "I'm thinking of building another set," he says. "For Fischer, maybe."

"Memorials are for dead people. Fischer's still alive." *Technically, anyway.*

"Okay, then. I'll make them for you."

The overhead hatch drops open. Scanlon grips his suitcase and starts to climb, one-handed.

"Sir—"

Scanlon looks down, surprised.

"I—" Lubin stops himself. "We could have treated you better," he says at last.

Scanlon knows, somehow, that this is not what Lubin intended to say. He waits. But Lubin offers nothing more.

"Thanks," Scanlon says, and climbs out of Beebe forever.

The chamber he rises into is wrong. He looks around, disoriented; this isn't the usual shuttle. The passenger compartment is too small, the walls studded with an array of nozzles. Forward, the cockpit hatch is sealed. A strange face looks back through the porthole as the ventral hatch swings shut.

"Hey . . ."

The face disappears. The compartment resonates with the sound of metal mouths disengaging. A slight lurch and the 'scaphe is rising free.

A fine aerosol mist hisses from the nozzles. It stings Scanlon's eyes. An unfamiliar voice reassures him from the cabin speaker. Nothing to worry about, it says. Just a routine precaution.

Everything's just fine.

SEINE

Entropy

MAYBE things are getting out of hand, Lenie Clarke wonders.

The others don't seem to care. She hears Lubin and Caraco talking up in the lounge, hears Brander trying to sing in the shower—*as if we didn't all get enough abuse during our childhoods*—and envies their unconcern. Everyone hated Scanlon—well, not *hate*, exactly, that's a bit strong—but there was at least a sort of—

Contempt—

That's the word. Contempt. Back on the surface, Scanlon ticked everyone. No matter what you said to him, he'd nod, make little encouraging noises, do everything to convince you that he was on your side. Except actually agree with you, of course. You didn't need fine-tuning to see through that shit; everyone down here already had too many Scanlons in their past, the official sympathizers, the instant friends who gently encouraged you to go back home, drop the charges, carefully pretending it was *your* interests being served. Back then Scanlon was just another patronizing bastard with a shaved deck, and if fortune put him down here on rifter turf for a while, who could be blamed for having a little fun with him?

But we could have killed him.

He started it. He attacked Gerry. He was holding him hostage.

As if the GA's going to make any sort of allowance for that . . .

So far, Clarke's kept her doubts to herself. It's not that she fears no one will listen to her. She fears the exact opposite. She doesn't *want* to change anybody's mind. She's not out to rally the troops. Initiative is a prerogative of leaders; she doesn't want the responsibility. The last thing she wants to be is

Leader of the pack, Len. Head wolf. A-fucking-kayla.

Acton's been dead for months and he's still laughing at her.

Okay. Scanlon was a nuisance at worst. At best he was an amusing diversion. "Shit," Brander said once. "You tune him in out there? I bet the *GA* doesn't even take him seriously." The Grid needs them, and it's not going to pull the plug just because a few rifters had some fun with an asshole like Scanlon. Makes sense.

Still, Clarke can't help thinking about consequences. She's never been able to avoid them in the past.

Brander's finally out of the shower; his voice drifts down from the lounge. Showers are an indulgence down here, hardly necessary when you live inside a self-flushing semipermeable diveskin but a sheer hot hedonistic pleasure just the same. Clarke grabs a towel off the rack and heads up the ladder before anyone else can cut in.

"Hey, Len." Caraco, seated at the table with Brander, waves her over. "Check out the new look."

Brander's in real shirtsleeves. He doesn't even have his caps in.

His eyes are brown.

"Wow." Clarke doesn't know what else to say. Those eyes look really strange. She looks around, vaguely uncomfortable. Lubin's over on the sofa, watching. "What do you think, Ken?"

Lubin shakes his head. "Why do you want to look like a dryback?"

Brander shrugs. "Don't know. I just felt like giving my eyes a rest for a couple of hours. I guess seeing Scanlon down here in shirtsleeves all the time." Not that anyone would even *think* of popping their caps in front of Scanlon.

Caraco affects an exaggerated shudder. "Please. Tell me he's not your new role model."

"He wasn't even my old one," Brander says.

Clarke can't get used to it. "Doesn't it bother you?" — *Walking around naked like that?*

"Actually, the only thing that bothers me is I can't see squat. Unless someone wants to turn up the lights . . ."

"So anyway." Caraco picks up the thread of some previous conversation. "You came down here why?"

"It's safe," Brander says, blinking against his own personal darkness.

"Uh-huh."

"*Saf*er, anyway. You were up there not so long ago. Didn't you see it?"

"I think what I saw up there was sort of skewed. That's why I'm down here."

"You never thought that things were getting, well, top-heavy?"

Caraco shrugs. Clarke, imagining steamy needles of water, takes a step toward the corridor.

"I mean, look how fast the Net changed," Brander says. "It wasn't that long ago you could just sit in your living room and go all over the world, remember? Anywhere could link up with anywhere else, for as long as they liked."

Clarke turns back. She remembers those days. Vaguely.

"What about the bugs?" she asks.

"There weren't any. Or there were, but they were really simple. Couldn't rewrite themselves, couldn't handle different operating systems. Just a minor inconvenience at first, really."

"But there were these laws they taught us in school," Caraco says.

Lenie remembers: "Explosive speciation. Brookes' Laws."

Brander holds up a finger. " 'Self-replicating information strings evolve as a sigmoid-difference function of replication error rate and generation time.' " Two fingers. " 'Evolving information strings are vulnerable to parasitism by competing strings with sigmoid-difference functions of lesser wavelength.' " Three. " 'Strings under pressure from parasites develop random substring-exchange protocols as a function of the wavelength ratio of the host and parasite sigmoid functions.' Or something like that."

Caraco looks at Clarke, then back at Brander. "What?"

"Life evolves. Parasites evolve. Sex evolves to counter the parasites. Shuffles the genes so the parasites have to shoot for a moving target. Everything else—species diversity, density-dependence, everything—it all follows from those three laws. You get a self-replicating string past a certain threshold, it's like a nuclear reaction."

"Life explodes," Clarke murmurs.

"Actually, *information* explodes. Organic life's just a really slow example. Happened a lot faster in the Net."

Caraco shakes her head. "So what? You're saying you came down here to get away from bugs in the Internet?"

"I came down here to get away from *entropy.*"

"I think," Clarke remarks, "you've got one of those language disorders. Dyslexia or something."

But Brander's going full tilt now. "You've heard the phrase 'entropy increases'? Everything falls apart eventually. You can postpone it for a while, but that takes energy. The more complicated the system, the more energy it needs to stay in one piece. Back before us everything was sun-powered, all the plants were like these little solar batteries that everything else could build on.

Only now we've got this society that's on an exponential complexity curve, and the Net's on the same curve, only a lot *steeper*, right? So we're all balled up in this run-away machine, it's got so complicated it's always on the verge of flying apart, and the only thing that prevents that is all the energy we feed it."

"Bad news," Caraco says. Clarke doesn't think she's really getting the point, though.

"Good news, actually. They'll always need more energy, so they'll always need us. Even if they ever *do* get fusion figured out."

"Yeah, but—" Caraco's frowning all of a sudden. "If you say it's exponential, then it hits a wall eventually, right? The curve goes straight up and down."

Brander nods. "Yup."

"But that's infinity. There's no way you could keep things from falling apart, no matter how much power we pump out. It'd never be enough. Sooner or later—"

"Sooner," says Brander. "And that's why I'm staying right here. Like I said, it's safer."

Clarke looks from Brander to Caraco to Brander. "That is just so much bullshit."

"How so?" Brander doesn't seem offended.

"Because we'd have heard about it before now. Especially if it's based on some kind of physical law everyone knows about. They couldn't keep something like that under wraps, people would keep figuring it out for themselves."

"Oh, I think they have," Brander says mildly, smiling from naked brown eyes. "They'd just rather not think about it too much."

"Where do you get all this, Mike?" Clarke asks. "The library?"

He shakes his head. "Got a degree. Systems ecology, artificial life."

Clarke nods. "I always thought you were too smart to be a rifter."

"Hey. A rifter's the smartest thing to *be* right now."

"So you chose to come down here? You actually applied?"

Brander frowns. "Sure. Didn't you?"

"I got a phone call. Offered me this new high-paying career, even said I could go back to my old job if it didn't work out."

"What was your old job?" Caraco wonders.

"Public relations. Mostly Honquarium franchises."

"You?"

"Maybe I wasn't very good at it. What about you?"

"Me?" Caraco bites her lip. "It was sort of a deal. One year with an option to renew, in lieu of prosecution." The corner of her mouth twitches. "Price of revenge. It was worth it."

Brander leans back in his chair, looks around Clarke. "What about you, Ken? Where'd *you* come—"

Clarke turns to follow Brander's stare. The sofa's empty. Down the corridor, Clarke can hear the shower door swinging shut.

Shit.

Still, it'll only be a short wait. Lubin's already been inside for four hours straight, he'll be gone in no time. And it's not as though there's any shortage of hot water.

"They should just shut the whole bloody Net down for a while," Caraco is saying behind her. "Just pull the plug. Bugs wouldn't be able to handle *that*, I bet."

Brander laughs, comfortably blind. "Probably not. Of course, neither would the rest of us."

Carousel

She's been staring at the screen for two minutes and she still can't see what Nakata's going on about. Ridges and fissures run along the display like long green wrinkles. The Throat returns its usual echoes, crammed especially close to center screen because Nakata's got the range topped out. Occasionally, a small blip appears between two of the larger ones: Lubin, lazing through an uneventful shift.

Other than that, nothing.

Lenie Clarke bites her lip. "I don't see any—"

"Just wait. I know I saw it."

Brander looks in from the lounge. "Saw what?"

"Alice says she's got something bearing three-twenty."

Maybe it's Gerry, Clarke muses. But Nakata wouldn't raise the alarm over *that.*

"It was just—*There!*" Nakata jabs her finger at the display, vindicated.

Something hovers at the very edge of Beebe's vision. Distance and diffraction make it hazy, but to bounce any kind of signal at that range it's got to have a lot of metal. As Clarke watches, the contact fades.

"Not one of us," Clarke says.

"It's big." Brander squints at the panel; his eyecaps reflect through white slits.

"Muckraker?" Clarke suggests. "A sub, maybe?"

Brander grunts.

"There it is again," Nakata says.

"There *they* are," Brander amends. Two echoes tease the edge of the screen now, almost indiscernible. Two large, unidentified objects, now rising just barely clear of the bottom clutter, now sinking back down into mere noise.

Gone.

"Hey," Clarke says, pointing. There's a tremor rippling along the seismo display, setting off sensors in a wave from the northwest. Nakata taps commands, gets a retrodict bearing on the epicenter. Three-twenty.

"There is nothing scheduled to be out there," she says.

"Nothing anyone bothered to tell us about, anyway." Clarke rubs the bridge of her nose. "So who's coming?"

Brander nods. Nakata shakes her head. "I'll wait for Judy."

"Oh, that's right. She's going all the way today, isn't she? Surface and back?"

"Yes. She should be back in maybe an hour."

"Okay." Brander's on his way downstairs. Clarke reaches past Nakata and taps into an outside channel. "Hey, Ken. Wake up."

I tell myself I know this place, she muses. *I call this my home.*

I don't know anything.

Brander cruises just below her, lit from underneath by a seabed on fire. The world ripples with color, blues and yellows and greens so pure it almost hurts to look at them. A dusting of violet stars coalesces and sweeps across the bottom; a school of shrimp, royally luminous.

"Has anyone been—" Clarke begins, but she feels wonder and surprise from Brander. It's obvious he hasn't seen this before. And Lubin—"It's news to me," Lubin answers aloud, as dark as ever.

"It's gorgeous," Brander says. "We've been down here how long, and we never even knew this place existed . . ."

Except Gerry, maybe. Every now and then Beebe's sonar picks someone up in this direction, when everyone else is accounted for. Not this far out, of course, but who knows how far afield Fischer—or whatever Fischer's become—wanders these days?

Brander drops away from his squid and coasts down, one arm outstretched. Clarke watches him scoop something off the bottom. A faint tingle clouds her mind for a moment—that indefinable sense of some other mind working nearby—and she's past him, her own squid towing her away.

"Hey, Len," Brander buzzes after her. "Check this out."

She releases the throttle and arcs back. Brander's got a glassy jointed creature in the palm of his hand. It looks a bit like that shrimp Acton found, back when—

"Don't hurt it," she says.

Brander's mask stares back at her. "Why would I hurt it? I just wanted you to see its eyes."

There's something about the way Brander's radiating. It's as though he's a little bit out of sync with himself somehow, as though his brain is broadcasting on two bands at once. Clarke shakes her head. The sensation passes.

"It doesn't *have* eyes," she says, looking.

"Sure it does. Just not on its head."

He flips it over, uses thumb and forefinger to pin it upside-down against the palm of his other hand. Rows of limbs—legs, maybe, or gills—scramble uselessly for purchase. Between them, where joints meet body, a row of tiny black spheres stare back at Lenie Clarke.

"Weird," she says. "Eyes on its *stomach*."

She's feeling it again: a strange, almost prismatic sense of fractured awareness.

Brander lets the creature go. "Makes sense. Seeing as how all the light down here comes from below." Suddenly he looks at Clarke, radiating confusion. "Hey, Len, you feeling okay?"

"Yeah, I'm fine."

"You seem kind of—"

"*Split*," they say, simultaneously.

Realization. She doesn't know how much of it is hers and how much she's tuning in from Brander, but suddenly they both know.

"There's someone else here," Brander says unnecessarily.

Clarke looks around. *Lubin.* She can't see him.

"Shit. You think that's it?" Brander's scanning the water too. "You think ol' Ken is finally starting to tune in?"

"I don't know."

"Who else could it be?"

"I don't know. Who else is out here?"

"Mike. Lenie." Lubin's voice, faintly, from somewhere ahead.

Clarke looks at Brander. Brander looks back.

"Right here," Brander calls, edging his volume up.

"I found it," Lubin says, invisibly distant.

Clarke launches off the bottom and grabs her squid. Brander's right beside her, sonar pistol out and clicking. "Got him," he says after a moment. "That way."

"What else?"

"Don't know. Big, anyhow. Three, four meters. Metallic."

Clarke tweaks the throttle. Brander follows. A riot of fractured color unspools below them.

"There."

Ahead of them, a mesh of green light sections the bottom into squares.

"What—"

"Lasers," Brander says, "I think."

Emerald threads float perfectly straight, a luminous profusion of right angles a few centimeters off the bottom. Beneath them, drab metal pipes run along the rock; tiny prisms erupt at regular intervals along their length, like spines. Each prism, an interstice; from each interstice, four beams of coherent light, and four, and four, a wire-frame checkerboard overlaid against bedrock.

They cruise two meters above the grid. "I'm not sure," Brander grates, "but I think it's all just one beam. Reflected back across itself."

"Mike—"

"I see it," he says.

At first it's just a fuzzy green column resolving out of the middle distance. Nearness brings clarity; the beams crisscrossing the ocean floor converge in a circle here, bend vertically up to form the luminous bars of a cylindrical cage. Within that cage a thick metal stalk rises out of the seabed. A great disk flowers at its top, spreads out like some industrial parasol. The spokes of laser light stream down from its perimeter and bounce endlessly away along the bottom.

"It's like a—a carousel," Clarke buzzes, remembering an old picture from an even older time. "Without horses . . ."

"Don't block those beams," Lubin buzzes. He's hanging off to one side, aiming a sonar pistol at the structure. "They're too weak to hurt you unless you get it in the eye, but you don't want to interfere with what they're doing."

"And that is?" Brander says.

Lubin doesn't answer.

What in the world—But Clarke's confusion is only partly directed at the mechanism before her. The rest dwells on a disorienting sense of alien cognition, very strong now, not her, not Brander, but somehow familiar.

Ken? That you?

"This isn't what we saw on sonar," Brander's saying. Clarke feels his confusion even as he talks over it. "Whatever we saw was moving around."

"Whatever we saw was probably planting this," Lubin buzzes. "It's long gone by now."

"But what *is* . . ." Brander's voice trails down to a mechanical croak.

No. It's not Lubin. She knows that now.

"It's thinking," she says. "It's *alive*."

Lubin's got another instrument out now. Clarke can't

see the visual readout but its telltale *tick tick tick*ing carries through the water.

"It's radioactive," he says.

Alice Nakata's voice comes to them in the endless darkness between Beebe and the Land of the Carousel.

"—*Judy*—" it whispers, almost too faint to make out. "—*scatter—lay*—"

"Alice?" Clarke's got her vocoder cranked loud enough to hurt her own ears. "We can't hear you. Say again?"

"—*just—no sign*—"

Clarke can barely distinguish the words. Somehow, though, she can hear the fear in them.

A small tremor shudders past, raising clouds of mud and swamping Nakata's signal. Lubin throttles up his squid and pulls away. Clarke and Brander follow suit. Somewhere in the darkness ahead, Beebe draws closer in decibel fractions.

The next words they hear manage to cut through the noise: "Judy's gone!"

"Gone?" Brander echoes. "Gone where?"

"She just disappeared!" The voice hisses softly from every direction. "I was talking to her. She was up above the deep scattering layer, she was—I was telling her about the signal we saw and she said she saw something too, and then she was *gone* . . ."

"Did you check sonar?" Lubin wants to know.

"Yes! Yes of course I checked the sonar!" Nakata's words are increasingly clear. "As soon as she was cut off I checked but I saw nothing for sure. There was something, maybe, but the scattering layer is very thick today, I could not be sure. And it's been fifteen minutes now and she still hasn't come back—"

"Sonar wouldn't pick her up anyway," Brander says softly. "Not through the DSL."

Lubin ignores him. "Listen, Alice. Did she say what she saw?"

"No. Just something, she said, and then I heard nothing more."

"Your sonar contact. How big?"

"I don't know! It was just there for a second, and the layer—"

"Could it have been a sub? Alice?"

"I don't know!" the voice cries, disembodied and anguished. "Why would it? Why would anyone?"

Nobody answers. The squids race on.

Ecdysis

They dump her out of the airlock, still caught in the tangleweb. She knows better than to fight under these conditions, but the situation's got to change pretty soon. She thinks they may have tried gassing her in the 'lock. Why else would they leave their headsets on after the lock had drained? What about that faint hiss that lasted a few seconds too long after blowdown? It's a pretty subtle cue, but you don't spend most of a year on the rift without learning what an airlock sounds like. There was something a bit off about that one.

No matter. You'd be surprised how much O_2 can be electrolyzed from just the little bit of water left sloshing around in the ol' thoracic plumbing. Judy Caraco can hold her breath until the cows come home, whatever the fuck *that* means. And now, maybe they think their gas-chamber-that-blows-like-an-airlock has got her doped or unconscious or just very laid-back. Maybe now they'll take her out of this fucking net.

She waits, limp. Sure enough there's a soft electrical

cackle and the web falls away, all those sticky molecular tails polarizing flat like Velcro slicking down to cat fur. She stares out through glassy unblinking eyecaps—no cues they can read *there*—and counts three, with maybe more behind her.

They're zombies, or something.

Their skin looks rotten with jaundice. Fingernails are barely distinguishable from fingers. Faces are slightly distorted, blurred behind stretched, yellowish membrane. Waxy, dark ovals protrude through the film where their mouths should be.

Body condoms, Caraco realizes after a moment. *What is this? Do they think I'm contagious?*

And a moment later: *Am I?*

One of them reaches toward her, holding something like a handgun.

She lashes out with one arm. She'd rather have kicked—more strength in the legs—but the refsuckers that brought her in didn't bother taking off her flippers. She connects: A nose, it feels like. A nose under latex. A satisfying crunch. Someone's found sudden cause to regret their own presumption.

There's a moment's shocked silence. Caraco uses it, flips onto her side and swings one flippered foot backward, heel first, into the back of someone's knee. A woman cries out, a startled face topples past, a smear of red hair plastered against its cheek, and Judy Caraco is reaching down to get those big clown-foot flippers off in time to—

The tip of a shockprod hovers ten centimeters from her nose. It doesn't waver a millimeter. After a moment's indecision—*how far can I push this, anyway?*—Caraco stops moving.

"Get up," says the man with the prod. She can barely see, through the condom, shadows where his eyes should be.

Slowly she takes off her fins and stands. She never had a chance, of course. She knew that all along. But they obviously want her alive for something, or they would never have bothered bringing her on board. And she, in turn, wants to make it clear that these fuckers are *not* going to intimidate her, no matter *how* many of them there are.

There's catharsis to be had even in a losing fight.

"Calm down," the man says—one of four, she sees now, including the one backing out of the compartment with a red stain spreading under his caul. "We're not trying to hurt you. But you know you shouldn't have tried to leave."

"Leave?" His clothes—all of their clothes—are uniform but not uniforms: loose-fitting white jumpsuits with an unmistakable look of disposability. No insignia. No name tags. Caraco turns her attention to the sub itself.

"Now we're going to get you out of that diveskin," the prodmaster continues. "And we're going to give you a quick medical workup. Nothing too intrusive, I assure you."

Not a large craft, judging from the curvature of the bulkhead. But fast. Caraco knew that from the moment it resolved out of the murk above her. She didn't see much, then, but she saw enough. This boat has wings. It could lap an orca on steroids.

"Who *are* you guys?" she asks.

"Your cooperation would make us all very grateful," Prodmaster says, as if she hasn't spoken. "And then maybe you can tell us exactly what you're trying to escape from out here in the middle of the Pacific."

"Escape?" Caraco snorts. "I was doing *laps*, you idiot."

"Uh-huh." He returns his shockprod to a holster on his belt, leaves one hand resting lightly on the handle.

The gun is back, in different hands. It looks like a

cross between a staple gun and a circuit tester. The redhead pushes it firmly onto Caraco's shoulder. Caraco
controls the urge to push back. A faint electrical tingle
and her diveskin drops away in pieces. There go her
arms. There go her legs. Her torso splits like a molting
insect and drops away, short-circuited. She stands utterly
'skinned, surrounded by strangers. A naked mulatto
woman looks back at her from a mirror on the bulkhead.
Somehow, even stripped, she looks strong. Her eyes,
brilliant white in that dark face, are cold and invulner-
able. She smiles.

"That wasn't too bad, was it?" There's a trained kindness to the other woman's voice. *Almost like I didn't just
dump her on the deck.*

They lead her through a passageway to a table in a
compact Med cubby. The redhead places a membrane-
sheathed hand on Caraco's arm, her touch just slightly
sticky; Caraco shrugs it off. There's only room for two
others in here besides Caraco. Three squeeze in: the redhead, the prodmaster, and a shorter male, a bit chubby.
Caraco looks at his face, but she can't see details under
the condom.

"I hope you can see *out* of that thing better than I can
see in," she says.

A soft background humming, too monotonous to register until now, rises subtly in pitch. There's a sense of
sudden acceleration; Caraco staggers a bit, catches herself on the table.

"If you could just lie back, Ms. Caraco—"

They stretch her out on the table. The chubby male
pastes a few leads at strategic points along her body and
proceeds to take very small pieces out of her. "No, this
isn't good. Not at all." Cantonese accent. "Poor epithelial turgor, you know dive*skin*'s only an expression, you
weren't supposed to *live* in it." The touch of his fingers
on her skin: like the redhead's, thin sticky rubber. "Now

look at you," he says. "Half your sebaceous glands are shut down, your vit K's low, you haven't been taking your UV, either, have you?"

Caraco doesn't answer. Mr. Canton continues to draw samples on her left. At the other side of the table, the redhead offers what she probably thinks is a reassuring smile, mostly hidden behind the oval mouthpiece.

Down at Caraco's feet, just in front of the hatchway, Prodmaster stands motionless.

"Yes, too much time sealed up in that diveskin," says Mr. Canton. "Did you *ever* take it off? Even outside?"

The redhead leans forward confidentially. "It's important, Judy. There could be health complications. We really should know if you ever opened up outside. For an emergency of some kind, maybe."

"If your 'skin was—punctured, for example." Mr. Canton affixes some kind of ocular device onto the membrane over his left eye, peers into Caraco's ear. "That scar on your leg, for instance. Quite large."

The redhead runs a finger along the crease in Caraco's calf. "Yeah. One of those big fish, I guess?"

Caraco stares up at her. "You guess."

"That must have been a deep wound." Mr. Canton again. "Is it?"

"Is it what?"

"A souvenir from one of those famous monsters?"

"You don't have my medical records?"

"It would be easier if you'd save us the trouble of looking them up," the redhead explains.

"You in a hurry?"

Prodmaster takes a step forward. "Not really. We can wait. But in the meantime, maybe we should get those eyecaps out."

"*No.*" The thought scares her to the core. She's not sure why.

"You don't need them anymore, Ms. Caraco." A

smile, a civilized baring of teeth. "You can relax. You're on your way home."

"Fuck that. They stay in." She sits up, feels the leads tearing off her flesh.

Suddenly her arms are pinned. Mr. Canton on one side, the redhead on the other.

"Fuck you." She lashes out with one foot. It goes low, catches Prodmasters' shock stick and flips it right out of the holster and onto the deck. Prodmaster jumps back out of the cubby, leaving his weapon behind. Suddenly Caraco's arms are free. Mr. Canton and the redhead are backing right off, squeezing along the walls of the compartment as though desperate to avoid physical contact—

As well you might be, she thinks, grinning. *Don't try your cute little power games with me, assholes—*

The Oriental shakes his head, a mixture of sadness and disapproval. Judy Caraco's body *hums,* right down in the bones, and goes completely limp.

She falls back onto the neoprene padding, nerves singing in the table's neuroinduction field. She tries to move but all her motor synapses are shorted out. The machines in her chest twitch and stutter, listening for orders, interpreting static.

Her lung sighs flat under its own weight. She can't summon the strength to fill it up again.

They're tying her down. Wrists, ankles, chest, all strapped and cinched back against the table. She can't even blink.

The humming stops. Air rushes down her throat and fills her chest. It feels good to gasp again. "How's her heart?" Prodmaster.

"Good. Bit of defib at first, but okay now."

Mr. Canton bends over from the head of the table: maggot skin stretched across a human face. "It's okay, Ms. Caraco. We're just here to help you. Can you understand?"

She tries to talk. It's an effort. "g-g-g-g-G—A—"

"What?"

"Th-this is Scanlon's work. Right? S-Scanlon's fucking revenge."

Mr. Canton looks up at someone beyond Caraco's field of view.

"Industrial psych." The redhead's voice. "No one important."

He looks back down. "Ms. Caraco, I don't know what you're talking about. We're going to take your eyecaps out now. It won't do you any good to struggle. Just relax."

Hands hold her head in position. Caraco clamps her eyes shut; they pry the left one open. She stares into something like a big hypo with a disk on the end. It settles on her eyecap, bonds with a faint sucking sound.

It pulls away. Light floods in like acid.

She wrenches her head to one side and shuts her eye against the stinging. Even filtered through her closed eyelid the light burns, an orange fire bringing tears. Then they have her again, twisting her head forward, fumbling at her face—

"Turn the lights down, you idiot! She's photosensitive!"

The redhead?

"—Sorry. We kept them at half, I thought—"

The light dims. Her eyelids go black.

"Her irises haven't had to work for almost a year," the redhead snaps. "Give her a chance to adjust, for Christ's sake."

She's in charge here?

Footsteps. A rattle of instruments.

"Sorry about that, Ms. Caraco. We've lowered the lights now, is that better?"

Go away. Leave me alone.

"Ms. Caraco, I'm sorry, but we still have to remove your other cap."

She keeps her eyes squeezed shut. They pull the cap out of her face anyway. The straps loosen around her body, drop off. She hears them backing away.

"Ms. Caraco, we've turned the lights down. You can open your eyes."

The lights. I don't care about the fucking lights. She curls up on the table and buries her face in her hands.

"She doesn't look so tough now, does she?"

"Shut up, Burton. You can be a real asshole sometimes, you know that?"

The sound of an airtight hatch hissing shut. A dense, close silence settles on Caraco's eardrums.

An electrical hum. "Judy." The redhead's voice: not in person this time. From a speaker somewhere. "We don't want this to be any worse than it has to be."

Caraco holds her knees tightly against her chest. She can feel the scars there, a raised web of old tissue from the time they cut her open. Eyes still shut, she runs her fingers along the ridges.

I want my eyes back.

But all she has now are these naked, fleshy things that anyone can see. She opens them the merest crack, peeks between her fingers. She's alone.

"We have to know some things, Judy. For your own good. We need to know how you found out."

"Found out what?" she cries, her face in hands. "I was just . . . exercising. . . ."

"It's okay, Judy. There's no hurry. You can rest now, if you want. Oh, and there are clothes in the drawer on your right."

She shakes her head. She doesn't care about clothes, she's been naked in front of worse monsters than these. It's only skin.

I want my eyes.

Alibis

Dead air from the speaker.

"Did you copy that?" Brander says after five seconds have passed.

"Yes. Yes, of course." The line hums for a second. "It just comes as a bit of a shock, that's all. It's just— very bad news."

Clarke frowns, and says nothing.

"Maybe she got detoured by a current at the thermocline," the speaker suggests. "Or caught up in a Langmuir cell. Are you sure she isn't still above the scattering layer somewhere?"

"*Of course* we're su—" Nakata bursts out, and stops. Ken Lubin has just laid a cautionary hand on her shoulder.

There's a moment's silence.

"It *is* night up there," Brander says finally. The deep scattering layer rises with darkness, spreads thin near the surface until daylight chases it back down. "And we'd be able to get her voice channel even if sonar couldn't get through. But maybe we should go up there ourselves and look around."

"No. That won't be necessary," says the speaker. "In fact, it might be dangerous, until we know more about what happened to Caraco."

"So we don't even *look* for her?" Nakata looks at the others, outrage and astonishment mingling on her face. "She could be hurt, she could be—"

"Excuse me, Ms.—"

"Nakata! Alice Nakata. I cannot believe—"

"Ms. Nakata, we *are* looking for her. We've already scrambled a search team to scour the surface. But you're in the middle of the Pacific Ocean. You simply don't have the resources to cover the necessary volume." A deep breath, carried flawlessly down four hundred kilometers of fiberop. "On the other hand, if Ms. Caraco is at all mobile, she'll most likely try and make it back to Beebe. If you want to search, your best odds are to look close to home."

Nakata looks helplessly around the room. Lubin stands expressionless; after a moment he puts one finger to his lips. Brander glances back and forth between them.

Lenie Clarke looks away.

"And you don't have any idea what might have happened to her?" the GA asks.

Brander grits his teeth. "I *said*, some kind of sonar spike. No detail. We thought *you* might be able to tell us something."

"I'm sorry. We don't know. It's just unfortunate that she wandered so far from Beebe. The ocean, it's—well, not always safe. It's even possible a squid got her. She *was* at the right depth."

Nakata's head is shaking. *"No,"* she whispers.

"Be sure and call if anything turns up," the speaker says. "We're setting up the search plan now, so if there's nothing else—"

"There is," Lubin says.

"Oh?"

"There's an unmanned installation a few klicks northwest of us. Recently installed."

"Really?"

"You don't know about it?"

"Hang on, I'm punching it up." The speaker falls briefly silent. "Got it. My God, that's way out of your backyard. I'm surprised you even picked it up."

"What is it?" Lubin says. Clarke watches him, the hairs on her neck stirring.

"Seismology rig, it says here. OSU put it down there

for some study on natural radioactives and tectonics.
You should really keep away from it, it's a bit hot.
Carrying some calibration isotopes."

"Unshielded?"

"Apparently."

"Doesn't that scramble the onboard?" Lubin wants to
know.

Nakata stares at him, openmouthed and angry. "Who
cares! Judy's *missing*!"

She's got a point. Lubin barely even talks to the other
rifters; coming from him, this interchange with the drybacks almost qualifies as babbling.

"Says here it's an optical processor," the speaker says
after a brief pause. "Radiation doesn't bother it. But I
think Al—Ms. Nakata is right; your first priority—"

Lubin reaches past Brander and kills the connection.

"Hey," Brander says sharply.

Nakata gives Lubin a blank angry stare and disappears
from the hatchway. Clarke hears her retreat into her cubby
and dog the hatch. Brander looks up at Lubin. "Maybe it
hasn't dawned on you, Ken, but Judy just might be dead.
We're kind of upset about that. Alice especially."

Lubin nods, expressionless.

"So I've got to wonder why you chose this moment
to grill the GA about the technical specs on a fucking
seismic rig."

"That's not what it is," Lubin says.

"Yeah?" Brander rises, twisting up out of the console
chair. "And just what—"

"Mike," says Clarke.

"What?"

She shakes her head. "They said an *optical* CPU."

"So the fuck *wh*—" Brander stops in midepithet. Anger drains from his face.

"Not a gel," Clarke says. "A chip. That's what they're
saying."

"But why lie to us?" Brander asks. "When we can just go out there and *feel*—"

"They don't know we can do that, remember?" She lets out a little smile, like a secret shared between friends. "They don't know anything about us. All they've got is their files."

"Not anymore," Brander reminds her. "Now they've got Judy."

"They've got us too," Lubin adds. "Quarantined."

"Alice. It's me."

A soft voice through hard metal: "Come—"

Clarke pulls the hatch open, steps through.

Alice Nakata looks up from her pallet as the hatch sighs shut. Almond eyes, dark and startling, reflect in the dimmed light. One hand goes to her face: "Oh. Excuse me, I'll . . ." She fumbles at the bedhead compartment, where her eyecaps float in plastic vials.

"Hey. No problem." Clarke reaches out, stops just short of touching Nakata's arm. "I like your eyes, I've always—well . . ."

"I should not be sulking in here anyway," Nakata says, rising. "I'm going outside."

"Alice—"

"I am *not* going to just let her disappear out there. Are you coming?"

Clarke sighs. "Alice, the GA's right. There's just too much volume. If she's still out there, she knows where we are."

" 'If'? Where else would she be?"

Clarke looks at the deck, reviewing possibilities.

"I—I think the drybacks took her," she says at last. "I think they'll take us, too, if we go after her."

Nakata stares at Clarke with disquieting human eyes. "Why? Why would they do that?"

"I don't know."

Nakata sags back on the pallet. Clarke sits down beside her.

Neither woman speaks for a while.

"I'm sorry," Clarke says at last. She doesn't know what else to say. "We all are."

Alice Nakata stares at the floor. Her eyes are bright, but not overflowing. "Not all," she whispers. "Ken seemed more interested in—"

"Ken had his reasons. They're lying to us, Alice."

"They always lied to us," Nakata says softly, not looking up. And then: "I should have been there."

"Why?"

"I don't know. If there'd been two of us, maybe . . ."

"Then we'd have lost both of you."

"You don't know that. Maybe it wasn't the drybacks at all, maybe she just ran into something . . . living."

Clarke doesn't speak. She's heard the same stories Nakata has. Confirmed reports of people getting eaten by Archie date back over a hundred years. Not many, of course; humans and giant squid don't run into each that often. Even rifters swim too deep for such encounters.

As a general rule.

"That's why I stopped going up with her, did you know that?" Nakata shakes her head, remembering. "We ran into something alive, up midwater. It was horrible. Some kind of jellyfish, I think. It *pulsed*, and it had these thin watery tentacles that stretched out of sight, just hanging there in the water. And it had all these—these stomachs. Like fat squirming slugs. And each one had its own mouth, and they were all opening and closing. . . ."

Clarke screws up her face. "Sounds lovely."

"I didn't even see it. It was quite translucent, and I was not looking and I bumped into it and it started *ejecting* pieces of itself. The main body just went completely dark and pulled into itself and pulsed away and all these shed stomachs and mouths and tentacles were left behind, they were all glowing and writhing as though they were in pain. . . ."

"I think I'd stop going up there, too, after that."

"The strange thing was, I envied it in a way." Nakata's eyes brim, spill over, but her voice doesn't change. "It must be nice to just be able to—to cut yourself off from the parts that give you away."

Clarke smiles, imagining. "Yes." She realizes, suddenly, that only a few centimeters separate her from Alice Nakata. They're almost touching.

How long have I been sitting here? she wonders. She shifts on the pallet, pulls away out of habit.

"Judy didn't see it that way," Nakata's saying. "She felt sorry for the *pieces*. I think she was almost angry with the main body, do you believe it? She said it was this blind stupid blob, she said—what did she say?—'fucking typical bureaucracy, first sign of trouble it sacrifices the very parts that keep it fed.' That's what she said."

Clarke smiles. "That sounds like Judy."

"She never takes shit from anyone," Nakata says. "She always fights back. I like that about her, I could never do that. When things get bad I just . . ." She glances at the little black device stuck on the wall beside her pillow. "I dream."

Clarke nods and says nothing. She can't remember Alice Nakata ever being so talkative.

"It's so much better than VR, you have much more control. In VR you are stuck with someone else's dreams."

"So I hear."

"You have never tried it?" Nakata asks.

"Lucid dreaming? A couple of times. I never got into it."

"No?"

Clarke shrugs. "My dreams don't have much . . . detail." *Or too much, sometimes.* She nods at Nakata's machine. "Those things wake me up just enough to notice how vague everything is. Or sometimes, when there *is* any detail, it's something really stupid. Worms crawling through your skin or something."

"But you can control that. That is the whole point. You can *change* it."

In your dreams, maybe. "But you have to see it first. Just sort of spoiled the effect for me, I guess. And mostly there were those big, vague gaps."

"Ah." A flicker of a smile. "For myself that is not a problem. The world is pretty vague to me even when I am awake."

"Well." Clarke smiles back, tentatively. "Whatever works."

More silence.

"I just wish I *knew*," Nakata says finally.

"I know."

"You knew what happened to Karl. It was bad, but you *knew*."

"Yes."

Nakata glances down. Clarke follows, notices that her own hands have somehow clasped around Nakata's. She supposes it's a gesture of support. It feels okay. She squeezes, gently.

Nakata looks back up. Her dark naked eyes still startle, somehow.

"Lenie, she did not *mind* me. I pulled away, and I dreamed, and sometimes I just went crazy and she put up with all of it. She understood—she under*stands*."

"We're rifters, Alice." Clarke hesitates, decides to risk it. "We all understand."

"Except Ken."

"You know, I think maybe Ken understands more than we give him credit for. I don't think he meant to be insensitive before. He's on our side."

"He is very strange. He is not here for the same reason we are."

"And what reason is that?" Clarke asks.

"They put us here because this is where we belong," Nakata says, almost whispering. "With Ken, I think— they just didn't dare put him anywhere *else*."

Brander's on his way downstairs when she gets back to the lounge. "How's Alice?"

"Dreaming," Clarke says. "She's okay."

"None of us are okay," Brander says. "Borrowed time all around, you ask me."

She grunts. "Where's Ken?"

"He left. He's never coming back."

"What?"

"He went over. Like Fischer."

"Bullshit. Ken's not like Fischer. He's the farthest thing from Fischer."

"We know that." Brander jerks a thumb at the ceiling. "*They* don't. He went over. That's the story he wants us to sell upstairs, anyway."

"Why?"

"You think that motherfucker told *me*? I agreed to play along for now, but I don't mind telling you I'm getting a bit tired of his bullshit." Brander climbs down a rung, looks back. "I'm heading back out myself. Gonna check out the carousel. I think some serious observations are in order."

"Want some company?"

Brander shrugs. "Sure."

"Actually," Clarke remarks, "just *company* doesn't cut it anymore, does it? Maybe we'd better be—what's the word—"

"Allies," Brander says.

She nods. "Allies."

QUARANTINE

Bubble

FOR a week now, Yves Scanlon's world had measured five meters by eight. In all that time he had not seen another living soul.

There were plenty of ghosts, though. Faces passed across his workstation, full of cheerful concern about his comfort, his diet, whether the latest gastrointestinal tap had made him uncomfortable. There were poltergeists, too. Sometimes they possessed the medical teleoperator that hung from the ceiling, made it dance and stab and steal slivers of flesh from Scanlon's body. They spoke with many voices, but rarely said anything of substance.

"It's probably nothing, Dr. Scanlon," the teleop said once, a talking exoskeleton. "Just a preliminary report from Rand/Washington, some new pathogen on the rift—probably benign. . . ."

Or, in a pleasant female voice: "You're obviously in exc—good health; I'm sure there's nothing to worry about. Still, you know how careful we have to be these days, even acne would mutate into a plague if we let it, heh-heh-heh—now, just another two cc's. . . ."

After a few days Scanlon had stopped asking.

Whatever it was, he knew it had to be serious. The world was full of nasty microbes, new ones spawned by accident, old ones set free from dark corners of the world, common ones mutated into novel shapes. Scanlon had been quarantined before a couple of times. Most people had. It usually involved technicians in body condoms, nurses trained to maintain spirits with a well-timed joke. He'd never heard of everything being done by remote control before.

Maybe it was a security issue. Maybe the GA didn't want the news leaking out, so they'd minimized the personnel involved. Or maybe—maybe the potential danger was so great that they didn't want to risk live techs.

Every day Scanlon discovered some new symptom. Shortness of breath. Headaches. Nausea. He was astute enough to wonder if any of them were real.

It occurred to him, with increasing frequency, that he might not get out of there alive.

Something resembling Patricia Rowan haunted his screen every now and then, asking questions about vampires. Not even a ghost, really. A simulation, masquerading as flesh and blood. Its machinery showed through in subtle repetitions, derivative conversational loops, a fixation on keyword over concept. Who was in charge down there? it wanted to know. Did Clarke carry more weight than Lubin? Did Brander carry more weight than Clarke? As if anyone could glean the essence of those twisted, fantastic creatures with a few inept questions. How many years had it taken Scanlon to achieve his level of expertise?

It was rumored that Rowan didn't like real-time phone conversations. Corpses were always paranoid about security or some such thing. Still, it made Scanlon angry. It was her fault that he was here now, after all. Whatever he'd caught on the rift, he'd caught because she'd ordered him down there, and now all she sent to him were *puppets*? Did she really consider him that inconsequential?

He never complained, of course. His aggression was too passionately passive. Instead, he toyed with the model she sent. It was easy to fool, programmed to look for certain words and phrases in answers to any given question. Just a trained dog, really, grabbing and fetching at the right set of commands. It was only when it ran back home, eager jaws clamped around some utterly useless bit of trivia, that its master would realize how truly ambiguous certain key phrases could be. . . .

He lost count of the times he sent it back, sated on junk food. It kept returning, but it never learned.

He patted the teleop. "*You're* probably smarter than that doppelgänger of hers, you know. Not that that's saying much. But at least you get your pound of flesh on the first try."

Surely by now Rowan knew what he was doing. Maybe this was some sort of game. Maybe, eventually, she'd admit defeat, come seek an audience in person. That hope kept him playing. Without it, he would have given up and cooperated out of sheer boredom.

On the first day of his quarantine he'd asked one of the ghosts for a dreamer, and been refused. Normal circadian metabolism was a prerequisite for one of the tests, it said; they didn't want his tissues cheating. For several days after that, Scanlon hadn't been able to sleep at all. Then he'd fallen into a dreamless abyss for twenty-eight hours. When he'd finally awakened, his body had ached from an unremembered wave of microsurgical strikes.

"Impatient little bastard, aren't you?" he'd murmured to the teleop. "Can't even wait until I'm awake? I hope it was good for you." He'd kept his voice low, in case there were any active pickups in the room. None of the workstation ghosts seemed to know anything about psychology; they were all physiologists and Tinkertoy jocks. If they'd caught him talking to a machine, they might think he was going crazy.

Now he was sleeping a full nine hours daily. Unpredictable attacks by the poltergeists cost him maybe an hour on top of that. Crew reports and IPD profiles, none of which ever seemed to come from Beebe Station, appeared regularly in his terminal: another four or five hours a day.

The rest of the time he watched television.

Strange things happening out there. A mysterious underwater explosion on the MidAtlantic Ridge, big enough for a nuke but no confirmation one way or the other. Israel and Tanaka-Krueger had both recently reactivated their nuclear testing programs, but neither admitted to any knowledge of this particular blast. The usual protests from corps and countries alike. Things were getting even testier than usual. Just the other day, it had come out that N'AmPac, several weeks earlier, had responded to a relatively harmless bit of piracy on the part of a Korean muckraker by blowing it out of the water.

Regional news was just as troubling. An estimated three hundred dead after a firebomb took out most of the Urchin Shipyards outside Portland. It was a fairly hefty death toll for two A.M., but Urchin property abutted the Strip and a number of refs had been caught in the firestorm. No known motive. Certain similarities to a much smaller explosion a few weeks earlier and a few hundred kilometers farther north, in the Coquitlam Burb. That one had been attributed to gang warfare.

And speaking of the Strip: More unrest among refugees forever hemmed in along the coastline. The usual rationale from the usual municipal entities. Waterfront's the only available real estate these days, and besides, can you imagine what it would cost to install sewer systems for seven million if we let them come *inland*?

Another quarantine, this time over some nematode recently escaped from the headwaters of the Ivindo. No news of anything from the North Pacific. Nothing from Juan de Fuca.

Two weeks into his sentence Scanlon realized that the

· symptoms he'd imagined earlier had all disappeared. In
fact, in a strange way he actually felt better than he had
in years. Still they kept him locked up. There were more
tests to be done.

Over time his initial sharp fears subsided to a chronic
dull ache in the stomach, so diffuse he barely felt it
anymore. One day he awoke with a sense of almost frantic relief. Had he really ever thought that the GA might
wall him away forever? Had he really been so paranoid?
They were taking good care of him. Naturally: He was
important to them. He'd lost sight of that at first. But
the vampires were still problematic, or Rowan wouldn't
be trolling her puppet through his workstation. And the
GA had chosen Yves Scanlon to study that problem because they knew he was the best man for the job. Now
they were just protecting their investment, making sure
he was healthy. He laughed out loud at that earlier, panicky self. There was really nothing to worry about.

Besides, he kept up with the news. It was safer in here.

Enema

He only spoke to it at night, of course.

After the day's samples and scans, when it was folded
up against the ceiling with its lights doused. He didn't
want the ghosts listening in. Not that it embarrassed him
to confide in a machine. Scanlon knew far too much
about human behavior to worry over such a harmless
quirk. Lonely end-users were always falling in love with
VR simulations. Programmers bonded with their own
creations, instilling imaginary life into every utterly predictable response. Hell, people even talked to their *pillows* if they were really short of alternatives. The brain
wasn't fooled, but the heart took comfort in the pretense.
It was perfectly natural, especially during periods of pro-

longed isolation. Nothing to worry about at all.

"They need me," Scanlon told it now, the ambient lighting damped down until he could barely see. "I know vampires, I know them better than anyone. I've lived with them. I've survived them. These—these *drybacks* up here only *use* them." He looked up. The teleop hung above him like a bat in the dim light, and didn't interact, and somehow that was the most comforting thing of all.

"I think Rowan's giving in. Her *puppet* said she was going to try and find some time."

No answer.

Scanlon shook his head at the sleeping machine. "I'm losing it, you know? I'm turning into a complete brain stem, is what I'm doing."

He didn't admit it often these days. Certainly not with the same sense of horror and uncertainty that he'd felt even a week before. But after all he'd been through lately, it was only natural that he'd have some adjustments to make. Here he was, quarantined, possibly infected by some unknown germ. Before that, he'd been through a gauntlet that would have driven most people right over the brink. And before *that* . . .

Yes, he'd been through a lot. But he was a professional. He could still turn around, take a good hard look at himself. More than most people could do. Everyone had doubts and insecurities, after all. The fact that he was strong enough to admit to his didn't make him a freak. Quite the contrary.

Scanlon stared across to the far end of the room. A window of isolation membrane stretched across the upper half of that wall, looked through to a small dark chamber that had been empty since his arrival. Patricia Rowan would be there soon. She would get firsthand benefit of Scanlon's new insights, and if she didn't already know how valuable he was, she'd be convinced after he spoke to her. The long wait for recognition was almost over. Things were about to make a huge change for the better.

Yves Scanlon reached up and touched a dormant metal claw. "I like you better like this," he remarked. "You're less . . . hostile.

"I wonder who you'll sound like tomorrow. . . ."

It sounded like some kid fresh out of grad school. It acted like one, too. It wanted him to drop his pants and bend over.

"Stuff it," Scanlon said at first, his public persona firmly in place.

"Exactly my intention," said the machine, wiggling a pencil-shaped probe on the end of one arm. "Come on, Dr. Scanlon. You know it's for your own good."

In fact he didn't know any such thing. He'd been wondering lately if the indignities he suffered in here might be due entirely to some repressed asshole's misdirected sadism. Just a few months ago it would have driven him crazy. But Yves Scanlon was finally starting to see his place in the universe, and was discovering that he could afford to be tolerant. Other people's pettiness didn't bother him nearly as much as it used to. He was above it.

He did, however, stop to pull the curtain across the window before undoing his belt. Rowan could show up at any time.

"Don't move," said the poltergeist. "This won't hurt. Some people even enjoy it."

Scanlon did not. The realization came as a bit of a relief.

"I don't see the hurry," he complained. "Nothing goes in or out of me without you people turning a valve somewhere to let it past. Why not just take what I send down the toilet?"

"We do that, too," the machine said, coring. "Since you got here, in fact. But you never know. Some stuff degrades pretty quickly when it leaves a body."

"If it degrades that fast, then why am I still in quarantine?"

"Hey, I didn't say it was harmless. Just said it might have turned into something else. Or maybe it *is* harmless. Maybe you just pissed off someone upstairs."

Scanlon winced. "The people upstairs like me just fine. What are you looking for, anyway?"

"Pyranosal RNA."

"I'm—I'm not sure I remember what that is."

"No reason you should. It's been out of fashion for three and a half billion years."

"No shit."

"Don't you wish." The probe withdrew. "It was all the rage in primordial times, until—"

"Excuse me," said Patricia Rowan's voice.

Scanlon glanced automatically over to the workstation. She wasn't there. The voice was coming from behind the curtain.

"Ah. Company. I've got what I came for, anyway." The arm swung around and neatly inserted the soiled probe into a dumbwaiter. By the time Scanlon had his pants back up, the teleop had folded into neutral.

"See you tomorrow," said the poltergeist, and fled. The teleop's lights went out.

She was here.

Right in the next room.

Vindication was at hand.

Scanlon took a breath and pulled back the curtain.

Patricia Rowan stood in shadow on the other side. Her eyes glittered with faint mercury: almost vampire eyes, but diluted. Translucent, not opaque.

Her contacts, of course. Scanlon had tried a similar pair once. They linked in to a weak RF signal from your watch, scrolled images across your field of view at a virtual range of forty centimeters. Patricia Rowan saw Scanlon and smiled. Whatever else she saw through those magical lenses, he could only guess.

"Dr. Scanlon," she said. "It's good to see you again."

He smiled back. "I'm glad you came by. We have a lot to talk about—"

Rowan nodded, opened her mouth.

"—and although your dopplegängers are perfectly adequate for normal conversation, they tend to lose a lot of the nuances—"

Closed it again.

"—especially given the kind of information you seem to be interested in."

Rowan hesitated a moment. "Yes. Of course. We, um, we need your insights, Dr. Scanlon." Yes. Good. Of course. "Your report on Beebe was quite—well, interesting, but things have changed somewhat since you filed it."

He nodded thoughtfully. "In what way?"

"Lubin's gone, for one thing."

"Gone?"

"Disappeared. Dead, perhaps, although apparently there's no signal from his deadman. Or possibly just—regressed, like Fischer."

"I see. And have you learned whether anyone at the other stations has gone over?" It was one of the predictions he'd made in his report.

Her eyes, rippling silver, seemed to stare at a point just beside his left shoulder. "We can't really say. Certainly we've had some losses, but rifters tend not to be very forthcoming with details. As we expected, of course."

"Yes, of course." Scanlon tried on a contemplative

look. "So Lubin's gone. Not surprising. He was definitely closest to the edge. In fact, if I remember, I predicted—"

"Probably just as well," Rowan murmured.

"Excuse me?"

She shook her head, as if clearing it of some distraction. "Nothing. Sorry."

"Ah." Scanlon nodded again. No need to harp on Lubin if Rowan didn't want to. He'd made lots of other predictions. "There's also the matter of the Ganzfeld effect I noted. The remaining crew—"

"Yes, we've spoken with a couple of—other experts about that."

"And?"

"They don't think the rift environment is, 'sufficiently impoverished' is the way they put it. Not sufficiently impoverished to function as a Ganzfeld."

"I see," Scanlon felt part of his old self bristling. He smiled, ignoring it. "How do they explain my observations?"

"Actually . . ." Rowan coughed. "They're not completely convinced you *did* observe anything significant. Apparently there was some evidence that your report was dictated under conditions of—well, personal stress."

Scanlon carefully froze his smile into place. "Well. Everyone's entitled to their opinion."

Rowan said nothing.

"Although the fact that the rift is a stressful environment shouldn't come as news to any real *expert*," Scanlon continued. "That was the whole point of the program, after all."

Rowan nodded. "I don't disbelieve you, Doctor. I'm not really qualified to judge one way or the other."

True, he didn't say.

"And in any event," Rowan added, "you were there. They weren't."

Scanlon relaxed. Of course she'd put his opinion ahead of those other *experts*, whoever they were. He was the one she'd chosen to go down there, after all.

"It's not really important," she said now, dismissing the subject. "Our immediate concern is the quarantine."

Mine as well as theirs. But of course he didn't let that on. It wouldn't be—professional—to seem too concerned about his own welfare right now. Besides, they were treating him fine in here. At least he knew what was going on.

"—yet," Rowan finished.

Scanlon blinked. "What? Excuse me?"

"I said, for obvious reasons we've decided not to recall the crew from Beebe just yet."

"I see. Well, you're in luck. They don't want to leave."

Rowan stepped closer to the membrane. Her eyes faded in the light. "You're sure of this."

"Yes. The rift is their home, Ms. Rowan, in a way a layperson probably couldn't understand. They're more alive down there than they ever were on land." He shrugged. "Besides, even if they wanted to leave, what could they do? They're hardly going to swim all the way back to the mainland."

"They might, actually."

"What?"

"It's possible," Rowan admitted. "Theoretically. And we—we caught one of them, leaving."

"What?"

"Up in the euphotic zone. We had a sub stationed up there, just to—keep an eye on things. One of the rifters—Cracker, or—" A glowing thread wriggled across each eye. "Caraco, that's it. Judy Caraco. She was heading straight for the surface. They figured she was making a break for it."

Scanlon shook his head. "Caraco does laps, Ms. Rowan. It was in my report."

"I know. Perhaps your report should have been more widely distributed. Although, her *laps* never took her that close to the surface before. I can see why they—" Rowan shook her head. "At any rate, they took her. A mistake, perhaps." A faint smile. "Those happen, sometimes."

"I see," Scanlon said.

"So now we're in something of a situation," Rowan went on. "Maybe the Beebe crew thinks that Caraco was just another accidental casualty. Or maybe they're getting suspicious. So do we let it lie, hope things blow over? Will they make a break if they think we're covering something up? Will some go and some stay? Are they a group, or a collection of individuals?"

She fell silent.

"A lot of questions," Scanlon said after a while.

"Okay, then. Here's just one. Would they obey a direct order to stay on the rift?"

"They might stay on the rift," Scanlon said. "But not because you ordered them to."

"We were thinking, maybe Lenie Clarke," Rowan said. "According to your report she's more or less the leader. And Lubin's—Lubin *was*—the wild card. Now he's out of the picture, perhaps Clarke could keep the others in line. If we can reach Clarke."

Scanlon shook his head. "Clarke's not any sort of leader, not in the conventional sense. She adopts her own behaviors independently, and the others just—follow her lead. It's not the usual authority-based system as you'd understand it."

"But if they follow her lead, as you say . . ."

"I suppose," Scanlon said slowly, "she's the most likely to obey an order to stay on site, no matter how

hellish the situation. She's hooked on abusive relationships, after all." He stopped.

"You could always try telling them the truth," he suggested.

She nodded. "It's a possibility, certainly. And how do
you think they'd react?"

Scanlon said nothing.

"Would they trust us?" Rowan asked.

Scanlon smiled. "Do they have any reason to?"

"Perhaps not.". Rowan sighed. "But no matter what
we tell them the issue's the same. What will they do
when they learn they're stuck down there?"

"Probably nothing. That's where they want to be."

Rowan glanced at him curiously. "I'm surprised you'd
say that, Doctor."

"Why?"

"There's no place I'd rather be than my own apart-
ment. But the moment anyone put me under house arrest
I'd want very much to leave it, and I'm not even slightly
dysfunctional."

Scanlon let the last part slide. "That's a point," he
admitted.

"A very basic one," she said. "I'm surprised someone
with your background would miss it."

"I didn't *miss* it. I just think other factors *outweigh*
it." On the outside, Scanlon smiled. "As you say, you're
not at all dysfunctional."

"No. Not yet, anyway." Rowan's eyes clouded with a
sudden flurry of data. She stared into space for a moment
or two, assessing. "Excuse me. Bit of trouble on another
front." She focused again on Scanlon. "Do you ever feel
guilty, Yves?"

He laughed, cut himself off. "Guilty? Why?"

"About the project. About—what we did to them."

"They're happier down there. Believe me. I know."

"Do you."

"Better than anyone, Ms. Rowan. You know that. That's why you came to me today."

She didn't speak.

"Besides," Scanlon said, "nobody drafted them. It was their own free choice."

"Yes," Rowan agreed softly. "Was."

And extended her arm through the window.

The isolation membrane coated her hand like liquid glass. It fit the contours of her fingers without a wrinkle, painted palm and wrist and forearm in a transparent sheath, pulled away just short of her elbow and stretched back to the windowpane.

"Thanks for your time, Yves," Rowan said.

After a moment Scanlon shook the proffered hand. It felt like a condom, slightly lubricated. "You're welcome," he said. Rowan retracted her arm, turned away. The membrane smoothed behind her like a soap bubble.

"But—" Scanlon said.

She turned back. "Yes?"

"Was that all you wanted?" he said.

"For now."

"Ms. Rowan, if I may. There's a lot about the people down there you don't know. A lot. I'm the only one who can give it to you."

"I appreciate that, Y—"

"The whole geothermal program hinges on them. I'm sure you see that."

She stepped back toward the membrane. "I do, Dr. Scanlon. Believe me. But I have a number of priorities right now. And in the meantime, I know where to find you." Once more she turned away.

Scanlon tried very hard to keep his voice level: "Ms. *Rowan*—"

Something changed in her then, a subtle hardening of posture that would have gone unnoticed by most people.

Scanlon saw it as she turned back to face him. A tiny pit opened in his stomach.

He tried to think of what to say.

"Yes, Dr. Scanlon," she said, her voice a bit too level.

"I know you're busy, Ms. Rowan, but—how much longer do I have to stay in here?"

She softened fractionally. "Yves, we still don't know. In a way it's just another quarantine, but it's taking longer to get a handle on this one. It's from the bottom of the ocean, after all."

"What is it, exactly?"

"I'm not a biologist." She glanced at the floor for a moment, then met his eyes again. "But I can tell you this much: You don't have to worry about keeling over dead. Even if you have this thing. It doesn't really attack people."

"Then why—"

"Apparently there are some—agricultural concerns. They're more afraid of the effect it might have on certain plants."

He considered that. It made him feel a little better.

"I really have to go now." Rowan seemed to consider something for a moment, then added, "And no more dopplegängers. I promise. That was rude of me."

Turncoat

She'd told the truth about the dopplegängers. She'd lied about everything else.

After four days Scanlon left a message in Rowan's cache. Two days later he left another. In the meantime he waited for the spirit which had thrust its finger up his ass to come back and tell him more about primordial biochemistry. It never did. By now even the other ghosts weren't visiting very often, and they barely said a word when they did.

Rowan didn't return Scanlon's calls. Patience melted into uncertainty. Uncertainty simmered into conviction. Conviction began to gently boil.

Locked up in here for three fucking weeks and all she gives me is a ten-minute courtesy call. Ten lousy minutes of my-experts-say-you're-wrong and it's-such-a-basic-point-I-can't-believe-you-missed-it and then she just walks away. She just fucking smiles and walks away.

"Know what I *should* have done," he growled at the teleop. It was the middle of the day but he didn't care anymore. Nobody was listening, they'd deserted him in here. They'd probably forgotten all about him. "What I *should* have done is rip a hole in that fucking membrane when she was here. Let a little of whatever's in *here* out to mix with the air in *her* lungs. Bet *that'd* inspire her to look for some answers!"

He knew it was fantasy. The membrane was almost infinitely flexible, and just as tough. Even if he succeeded in cutting it, it would repair itself before any mere gas molecules could jump through. Still, it was satisfying to think about.

Not satisfying enough. Scanlon picked up a chair and hurled it at the window. The membrane caught it like a form-fitting glove, enfolded it, let it fall almost to the floor on the other side. Then, slowly, the window tightened down to two dimensions. The chair toppled back into Scanlon's cell, completely undamaged.

And to think she'd had the fucking *temerity* to lecture him with that inane little homily about house arrest! As though she'd caught him in some sort of *lie*, when he'd suggested the vampires might stay put. As though she thought he was *covering* for them.

Sure, he knew more about vampires than anyone. That didn't mean he *was* one. That didn't mean—

We could have treated you better, Lubin had said, there at the last. *We.* As though he'd been speaking for all of them. As though, finally, they were *accepting* him. As though—

But vampires were damaged goods, always had been. That was the whole point. How could Yves Scanlon qualify for membership in a club like *that*?

He knew one thing, though. He'd rather be a vampire than one of these assholes up *here.* That was obvious now. Now that the pretenses were dropping away and they didn't even bother talking to him anymore. They exploited him and then they shunned him; they used him just like they used the vampires. He'd always known that deep down, of course. But he'd tried to deny it, kept it stifled under years of accommodation and good intentions and misguided efforts to fit in.

These people were the enemy. They'd always been the enemy.

And they had him by the balls.

He spun around and slammed his fist into the examination table. It didn't even hurt. He continued until it did. Panting, knuckles raw and stinging, he looked around for something else to smash.

The teleop woke up enough to hiss and spark when the chair bounced off its central trunk. One of the arms wiggled spastically for a moment. A faint smell of burnt insulation. Then nothing. Only slightly dented, the teleop slept on above a litter of broken paradigms.

"Tip for the day," Scanlon snarled at it. "Never trust a dryback."

HEAD CHEESE

Theme and Variation

A tremor shivers through bedrock. The emerald grid fractures into a jagged spiderweb. Strands of laser light bounce haphazardly into the abyss.

From somewhere within the carousel, a subtle discontent. Intensified cogitation. The displaced beams waver, begin realigning themselves.

Lenie Clarke has seen and felt all of this before. This time she watches the prisms on the seabed, rotating and adjusting themselves like tiny radio-telescopes. One by one the disturbed beams lie back down, parallel, perpendicular, planar. Within seconds the grid is completely restored.

Emotionless satisfaction. Cold alien thoughts nearby, reverting.

And farther away, something else coming closer. Thin and hungry, like a faint reedy howl in Clarke's mind. . . .

"Ah, shit," Brander buzzes, diving for the bottom.

It streaks down from the darkness overhead, mindlessly single-minded, big as Clarke and Brander put together. Its eyes reflect the glow from the seabed. It slams into the top of the carousel, mouth open, bounces away with half its teeth broken.

It has no thoughts, but Lenie Clarke can feel its emotions. They don't change. Injury never seems to faze these monsters. Its next attack targets one of the lasers. It skids around the roof of the carousel and comes up from underneath, swallowing one of the beams. It rams the emitter, and thrashes.

A sudden vicarious tingle shoots along Clarke's spine.

The creature sinks, twitching. Clarke feels it die before it touches bottom.

"Jesus," she says. "You *sure* the laser didn't do that?"

"No. Way too weak," Brander tells her. "Didn't you feel it? An electric shock?"

She nods.

"Hey," Brander realizes. "You haven't seen this before, have you?"

"No. Alice told me about it, though."

"The lasers lure them in sometimes, when they wobble."

Clarke eyes the carcass. Neurons hiss faintly inside it. The body's dead, but it can take hours for the cells to run down.

She glances back at the machinery that killed them. "Lucky none of us touched that thing," she buzzes.

"I was keeping my distance anyway. Lubin said it wasn't hot enough to be dangerous, but, well . . ."

"I was tuned in to the gel when it happened," she says. "I don't think it—"

"The gel never even notices. I don't think it's hooked into the defense system." Brander looks up at the metal structure. "No, our head cheese has far too much on its mind to waste its time worrying about fish."

She looks at him. "You know what it is, don't you?"

"I don't know. Maybe."

"Well?"

"I said I don't know. Just got some ideas."

"Come on, Mike. If you've got ideas, it's only because the rest of us have been out here taking notes for the past two weeks. Give."

He floats above her, looking down. "Okay," he says at last. "Let me just dump what you got today and run it against the rest. Then, if it pans out . . ."

"About time." Clarke grabs her squid off the bottom and tweaks the throttle. "Good."

Brander shakes his head. "I don't think so. Not at all."

"Okay, then. Smart gels are especially suited for coping with rapid changes in topography, right?"

Brander sits at the library. In front of him, one of the flatscreens cycles through a holding pattern. Behind, Clarke and Lubin and Nakata do the same.

"So there are two ways for your topographic environment to change rapidly," he continues. "One, you move quickly through complex surroundings. That's why we're getting gels in muckrakers and ATVs these days. Or you could sit still, and let your *surroundings* change."

He looks around. Nobody says anything. "Well?"

"So it's thinking about earthquakes," Lubin remarks. "The GA told us that much."

Brander turns back to the console. "Not just any earthquake," he says, a sudden edge in his voice. "The *same* earthquake. Over and over again."

He touches an icon on the screen. The display rearranges itself into a pair of axes, x and y. Emerald script glows adjacent to each line. Clarke leans forward: TIME, says the abscissa. ACTIVITY, says the ordinate.

A line begins to crawl left to right across the display.

"This is a mean composite plot of every time we ever watched that thing," Brander explains. "I tried to pin some sort of units onto the y-axis, but of course all we can tune in is 'now it's thinking hard,' or 'now it's slacking off.' So you'll have to settle for a relative scale. What you're seeing now is just baseline activity."

The line shoots about a quarter of the way up the scale, flattens out.

"Here it's started thinking about something. I can't correlate this to any real events like local tremors, it just seems to start on its own. An internally generated loop, I think."

"Simulation," Lubin grunts.

"So it's thinking along like this for a while," Brander continues, ignoring him, "and then, voilà . . ." Another jump, to halfway up the *y*-axis. The line holds its new altitude for a few pixels, slides into a gentle decline for a pixel or two, then jumps again. "So here it started thinking quite hard, starts to relax, then starts thinking even harder." Another, smaller jump, another gradual decline. "Here it's even more lost in thought, but it takes a nice long break afterward." Sure enough, the decline continues uninterrupted for almost thirty seconds.

"And right about *now* . . ."

The line shoots almost to the top of the scale, fluctuates near the top of the graph. "And here it just about gives itself a hemorrhage. It goes on for a while, then—"

The line plummets vertically.

"—drops right back to baseline. Then there's some minor noise—I think it's storing its results or updating its files or something—and the whole thing starts all over again." Brander leans back in his chair, regards the others with his hands clasped behind his head. "That's all it's been doing. As long as we've been watching it. The whole cycle takes about fifteen minutes, give or take."

"That's it?" Lubin says.

"Some interesting variations, but that's the basic pattern."

"So what does it mean?" Clarke asks.

Brander leans forward again, toward the library. "Suppose you were an earthquake tremor, starting here on the rift and propagating east. Guess how many faults you'd have to cross to get to the mainland."

Lubin nods and says nothing.

Clarke eyes the graph, guesses: *Five.*

Nakata doesn't even blink, but then Nakata hasn't done much of anything for days.

Brander points to the first jump. "Us. Channer Vent."

The second: "Juan de Fuca, Coaxial Segment." Third: "Juan de Fuca, Endeavour Segment." Fourth: "Beltz Minifrac." The last and largest: "Cascadia Subduction Zone."

He waits for their reaction. Nobody says anything. Faintly, from outside, comes the sound of windchimes in mourning.

"Jesus. Look, any simulation is computationally most intensive whenever the number of possible outcomes is greatest. When a tremor crosses a fault, it triggers ancillary waves perpendicular to the main direction of travel. Makes for very hairy calculations at those points, if you're trying to model the process."

Clarke stares at the screen. "Are you sure about this?"

"Christ, Len, I'm basing it on stray emissions from a blob of fucking nerve tissue. Of course I'm not sure. But I'll tell you this much: If you assume that this first jump represents the initial quake, and this last dropoff is the mainland, and you also assume a reasonably constant speed of propagation, these intermediate spikes fall almost exactly where Cobb, Beltz, and Cascadia would be. I don't think that's a coincidence."

Clarke frowns. "But doesn't that mean the model stops running as soon as it reaches N'AmPac? I would've thought that's when they'd be *most* interested."

Brander bites his lip. "Well, that's the thing. The lower the activity near the end of a run, the longer the run seems to last."

She waits. She doesn't have to ask. Brander's far too proud of himself not to explain further.

"And if you assume that lower end-run activity reflects a smaller predicted quake, the cheese spends more time thinking about quakes with lower shoreline impact. Usually, though, it just stops when it hits the coast."

"There's a threshold," Lubin says.

"What?"

"Every time it predicts a coastal quake above a certain threshold, the model shuts down and starts over. Unacceptable losses. It spends more time thinking about the milder ones, but so far they've all resulted in unacceptable losses."

Brander nods slowly. "I was wondering about that."

"Stop wondering." Lubin's voice is even more dead than usual. "That thing's only got one question on its mind."

"What question?" Clarke asks.

"Lubin, you're being paranoid," Brander snorts. "Just because it's a bit radioactive—"

"They lied to us. They took Judy. Even you're not naive enough—"

"What question?" Clarke asks again.

"But why?" Brander demands. "What would be the point?"

"Mike," Clarke says, softly and clearly, *"shut up."*

Brander blinks and falls silent. Clarke turns to Lubin. "What question?"

"It's watching the local plates. It's asking, What happens on N'AmPac if there's an earthquake here, right now?" Lubin parts his lips in an expression few would mistake for a smile. "So far it hasn't liked the answer. But sooner or later predicted impact's going to fall below some critical level."

"And then what?" Clarke says. *As if I didn't know.*

"Then it blows up," says a small voice.

Alice Nakata is talking again.

Ground Zero

Nobody speaks for a long time.

"That's insane," Lenie Clarke says at last.

Lubin shrugs.

"So you're saying it's some kind of a bomb?"

He nods.

"A bomb big enough to cause an earthquake three, four hundred kilometers away?"

"No," Nakata says. "All of those faults it would have to cross, they would stop it. Firewalls."

"Unless," Lubin adds, "one of those faults is just about ready to slip on its own."

Cascadia. Nobody says it aloud. Nobody has to. One day, five hundred years ago, the Juan de Fuca Plate developed an attitude. It got tired of being endlessly ground under North America's heel. So it just stopped sliding, hung on by its fingernails, and dared the rest of the world to shake it free. So far the rest of the world hasn't been able to. But the pressure's been building now for half a millennium. It's only a matter of time.

When Cascadia lets go, a lot of maps are going to end up in recyc.

Clarke looks at Lubin. "You're saying even a small bomb here could kick Cascadia loose. You're saying the big one, right?"

"That's what he's saying," Brander confirms. "So why, Ken old buddy? This some sort of Asian real-estate scam? A terrorist attack on N'AmPac?"

"Wait a minute." Clarke holds up a hand. "They're not trying to *cause* an earthquake. They're trying to *avoid* one."

Lubin nods. "You set off a fusion charge on the rift, you trigger a quake. Period. How serious depends on conditions at detonation. This thing is just holding itself back until it causes as little damage as possible, back onshore."

Brander snorts. "Come on, Lubin, isn't this all kind of excessive? If they wanted to take us out, why not just come down here and shoot us?"

Lubin looks at him, empty-eyed. "I don't believe

you're that stupid, Mike. Perhaps you're just in denial."

Brander rises out of his chair. "Listen, *Ken*—"

"It's not us," Clarke says. "It's not *just* us. Is it?"

Lubin shakes his head, not taking his eyes off Brander.

"They want to take out *everything*. The whole rift."

Lubin nods.

"*Why*?"

"I don't know," Lubin says.

Figures, Clarke muses. *I just never get a break.*

Brander sinks back into his chair. "What are you smiling at?"

Clarke shakes her head. "Nothing."

"We must *do* something," Nakata says.

"No shit, Alice." Brander looks back at Clarke. "Any ideas?"

Clarke shrugs. "How long do we have?"

"If Lubin's right, who knows? Tomorrow, maybe. Ten years from now. Earthquakes are classic chaotic systems, and the tectonics around here change by the minute. If the Throat slips a millimeter, it could make the difference between a shiver and a meltdown."

"Perhaps it is a small-yield device," Nakata suggests hopefully. "It is a ways away, and all this water might damp down the shock wave before it reaches us."

"No," Lubin says.

"But we do not *know*—"

"Alice," Brander says, "It's almost two hundred kilometers to Cascadia. If this thing can generate P-waves strong enough to kick it loose at that range, we're not going to ride it out here. We might not get vaporized, but the shock wave would tear us into little pieces."

"Perhaps we can disable it somehow," Clarke says.

"No." Lubin is flat and emphatic.

"Why not?" Brander says.

"Even if we get past its front-line defense, we're only

seeing the top of the structure. The vitals are buried."

"If we can get in at the top, there might be access—"

"Chances are it's set for damped detonation if tampered with," Lubin says. "And there are others we haven't found."

Brander looks up. "And how do you know that?"

"There have to be. At this depth it would take almost three hundred megatons to generate a bubble even half a kilometer across. If they want to take out any significant fraction of the vent, they'll need multiple charges, distributed."

There's a moment's silence.

"Three hundred megatons," Brander repeats at last. "You know, I can't tell you how *disturbed* I am to find that you know such things."

Lubin shrugs. "It's basic physics. It shouldn't intimidate anyone who isn't completely innumerate."

Brander is standing again, his face only centimeters from Lubin's.

"And I am getting pretty fucking disturbed by you too, Lubin," he says through clenched teeth. "Who the fuck *are* you, anyway?"

"Mike," Clarke begins.

"No, I fucking *mean* it. We don't know shit about you, Lubin. We can't tune you in, we sell your bullshit story to the drybacks for you and you *still* haven't explained why, and now you're mouthing off like some kind of fucking secret agent. You want to call the shots, say so. Just drop this bullshit man-with-no-name routine."

Clarke takes a small step back. *Okay. Fine. If he thinks he can fuck with Lubin, he's on his own.*

But Lubin isn't showing any of the signs. No change in stance, no change in breathing, his hands stay unclenched at his sides. When he speaks, his voice is calm and even. "If it'll make you feel any better, by all means;

call upstairs and tell them I'm still alive. Tell them you lied. If they—"

The eyes don't change. That flat white stare persists while the flesh around it *twitches*, suddenly, and now Clarke *can* see the signs, the slight lean forward, the subtle cording of veins and tendons in the throat. Brander sees them too. He's standing still as a dog caught in headlights.

Fuck fuck fuck he's going to blow. . . .

But she's wrong again. Impossibly, Lubin relaxes. "As for your endearing desire to get to know me,"—laying a casual hand on Brander's shoulder—"you're luckier than you know that that hasn't happened."

Lubin takes back his hand, steps toward the ladder. "I'll go along with whatever you decide, as long as it doesn't involve tampering with nuclear explosives. In the meantime, I'm going outside. It's getting close in here."

He drops through the floor. Nobody else moves. The sound of the airlock flooding seems especially loud.

"*Jesus*, Mike," Lenie breathes at last.

"Since when was he calling the shots?" Brander seems to have regained some of his bravado. He casts a hostile glance through the deck. "I don't trust that fucker. No matter what he says. Probably tuning us in right now."

"If he is, I doubt he's picking up anything you haven't already shouted at him."

"Listen," says Nakata. "We must *do* something."

Brander throws his hands in the air. "What choice is there? If we don't disarm the fucking thing, we either get the hell out of here or we sit around and wait to get incinerated. Not really a tough decision if you ask me."

Isn't it? Clarke wonders.

"We cannot leave by the surface," Nakata points out. "If they got Judy—"

"So we hug the bottom," Brander says. "Right. Scam

their sonar. We'd have to leave the squids behind, they'd be too easy to track."

Nakata nods.

"Lenie? What?"

Clarke looks up. Brander and Nakata are both staring at her. "I didn't say anything."

"You look like you don't approve."

"It's three hundred klicks to Vancouver Island, Mike. Minimum. It could take over a week to make it without squids, assuming we don't get lost."

"Our compasses work fine once we're away from the rift. And it's a pretty big continent, Len; we'd have to try pretty hard *not* to bump into it."

"And what do we do when we get there? How would we make it past the Strip?"

Brander shrugs. "Sure. For all we know, the refs could eat us alive, if our tubes don't choke on all the shit floating around back there. But really, Len, would you rather take your chances with a ticking nuke? It's not like we're drowning in options."

"Sure." Clarke moves one hand in a gesture of surrender. "Fine."

"Your problem, Len, is you've always been a fatalist," Brander pronounces.

She has to smile at that. *Not always.*

"There is also the question of food," Nakata says. "To bring enough for the trip will slow us considerably."

I don't want to leave, Clarke realizes. *Even now. Isn't that stupid.*

"—don't think speed is much of a concern," Brander is saying. "If this thing goes off in the next few days, an few extra meters per hour won't do us much good anyway."

"We could travel light and forage on the way," Clarke muses, her mind wandering. "Gerry does okay."

"Gerry," Brander repeats, suddenly subdued.

A moment's silence. Beebe shivers with the small distant cry of Lubin's memorial.

"Oh God," Brander says softly. "That thing can really get on your nerves after a while."

Software

There was a sound.

Not a voice. It had been days since he'd heard any voice but his own. Not the food dispenser or the toilet. Not the familiar crunch of his feet over dismembered machinery. Not even the sound of breaking plastic or the clang of metal under assault; he'd already destroyed everything he could, given up on the rest.

No, this was something else. A hissing sound. It took him a few moments to remember what it was.

The access hatch, pressurizing.

He craned his neck until he could see around the corner of an intervening cabinet. The usual red light glowed from the wall to one side of the big metal ellipse. It turned green as he watched.

The hatch swung open. Two men in body condoms stepped through, light from behind throwing their shadows along the length of the dark room. They looked around, not seeing him at first.

One of them turned up the lights.

Scanlon squinted up from the corner. The men were wearing sidearms. They looked down at him for a few moments, folds of isolation membrane draped around their faces like leprous skin.

Scanlon sighed and pulled himself to his feet. Fragments of bruised technology tinkled to the floor. The guards stood aside to let him pass. Without a word they followed him back outside.

Another room. A strip of light divided it into two dark halves. It speared down from a recessed groove in the ceiling, bisecting the wine draperies and the carpet, laying a bright band across the conference table. Tiny bright hyphens reflected from Perspex workpads set into the mahogany.

A line in the sand. Patricia Rowan stood well back on the other side, her face halflit in profile.

"Nice room," Scanlon remarked. "Does this mean I'm out of quarantine?"

Rowan didn't face him. "I'm afraid I'll have to ask you to stay on your side of the light. For your own safety."

"Not yours?"

Rowan gestured at the light without looking. "Microwave. UV too, I think. You'd fry if you crossed it."

"Ah. Well, maybe you've been right all along." Scanlon pulled a chair out from the conference table and sat down. "I developed a real symptom the other day. My stools seem a bit off. Intestinal flora not working properly, I guess."

"I'm sorry to hear it."

"I thought you'd be pleased. It's the closest thing to vindication you've got to date."

Neither person spoke for nearly a minute.

"I . . . I wanted to talk," Rowan said at last.

"So did I. A couple of weeks ago." And then, when she didn't respond: "Why now?"

"You're a therapist, aren't you?"

"Neurocognitist. And we haven't *talked*, as you put it, for decades. We prescribe."

She lowered her face.

"You see, I have—" she began.

"—Blood on my hands," she said a moment later.

"Then you really don't want me. You want a priest."

"They don't talk either. At least, they don't say much."

The curtain of light hummed softly, like a bug zapper.

"Pyranosal RNA," Scanlon said, after a moment. "Five-sided ribose ring. A precursor to modern nucleic acids, pretty widespread about three and a half billion years ago. The library says it would've made a perfectly acceptable genetic template on its own; faster replication than DNA, fewer replication errors. Never caught on, though."

Rowan said nothing. She may have nodded, but it was hard to tell.

"So much for your story about an 'agricultural hazard.' Are you finally going to tell me what's going on, or are you still into role-playing games?"

Rowan shook herself, as though coming back from somewhere. For the first time, she looked directly at Scanlon. The sterilight reflected off her forehead, buried her eyes in black pools of shadow. Her contacts shimmered like back-lit platinum.

She didn't seem to notice his condition.

"I didn't lie to you, Dr. Scanlon. Fundamentally, you could call this an agricultural problem. We're dealing with sort of a—a soil nanobacterium. It's not a pathogen at all, really. It's just—a competitor. And no, it never caught on. But as it turns out, it never really died off, either."

She dropped into a chair.

"Do you know what the really shitty thing is about all this? We could let you go right now and it's entirely possible that everything would be fine. It's almost certain, in fact. One in a thousand chance we'd regret it, they say. Maybe one in *ten* thousand."

"Pretty good odds," Scanlon agreed. "What's the punch line?"

"Not good enough. We can't take the chance."

"You take a bigger risk every time you step outside."

Rowan sighed. "And people play lotteries with odds of one in a million, all the time. But Russian roulette's got much better odds than that, and you won't find too many people taking their chances at it."

"Different payoffs."

."Yes. The payoffs." Rowan shook her head; in some strange abstract way she seemed almost amused. "Cost-benefit analysis, Yves. Maximum likelihood. Risk assessment. The lower the risk, the more sense it makes to play."

"And the reverse," Scanlon said.

"Yes. More to the point. The reverse."

"Must be pretty bad," he said, "to turn down ten thousand–to–one odds."

"Oh yes." She didn't look at him.

He'd been expecting it, of course. The bottom dropped out of his stomach anyway.

"Let me guess," he said. He couldn't seem to keep his voice level. "N'AmPac's at risk if I go free."

"Worse," she said, very softly.

"Ah. Worse than N'AmPac. Okay, then. The human race. The whole human race goes belly-up if I so much as sneeze out-of-doors."

"Worse," she repeated.

She's lying. She has to be. She's just a refsucking dryback cunt. Find her angle.

Scanlon opened his mouth. No words came out.

He tried again. "Hell of a nanobacterium." His voice sounded as thin as the silence that followed.

"In some ways, actually, it's more like a virus," she said at last. "God, Yves, we're *still* not really sure what it is. It's old, older than the Archaea, even. But you've figured that out for yourself. A lot of the details are beyond me."

Scanlon giggled. "Details are *beyond* you?" His voice swerved up an octave, dropped again. "You lock me up for all this time and now you tell me I'm stuck here forever—I *assume* that's what you're about to tell me"—the words tumbled out too quickly for her to disagree—"and you just don't have a head to remember the *details*? Oh, that's okay, *Ms*. Rowan, why should I want to hear about *those*?"

Rowan didn't answer directly. "There's a theory that life got started in rift vents. All life. Did you know that, Yves?"

He shook his head. *What the hell is she going on about?*

"Two prototypes," Rowan continued. "Three, four billion years ago. Two competing models. One of them cornered the market, set the standard for everything from viruses up to giant sequoias. But the thing is, Yves, the winner wasn't necessarily the best product. It just got lucky somehow, got some early momentum. Like software, you know? The best programs never end up as industry standards."

She took a breath. "We're not the best either, apparently. The best never got off the ocean floor."

"And it's in me now? I'm some sort of Patient Zero?" Scanlon shook his head. "No. It's impossible."

"Yves—"

"It's just the deep sea. It's not outer space, for God's sake. There's currents, there's circulation, it would have come up a hundred million years ago, it'd be everywhere already."

Rowan shook her head.

"*Don't tell me that*! You're a fucking *corpse*, you don't know *anything* about biology! You said so yourself!"

Suddenly Rowan was staring directly through him. "An actively maintained hypo-osmotic intracellular environment," she intoned. "Potassium, calcium, and chlorine ions all maintained at concentrations of less than five millimoles per kilogram." Tiny snowstorms gusted across her pupils. "The consequent strong osmotic gradient, coupled with high bilayer porosity, results in extremely efficient assimilation of nitrogenous compounds. However, it also limits distribution in aqueous environments with salinity in excess of twenty parts per thousand, due to the high cost of osmoregulation. Thermal elev—"

"Shut up!"

Rowan fell immediately silent, her eyes dimming slightly.

"You don't know what the fuck you just said," Scanlon spat. "You're just reading off that built-in TelePrompTer of yours. You don't have a clue."

"They're leaky, Yves." Her voice was softer now. "It gives them a huge edge at nutrient assimilation, but it backfires in salt water because they have to spend so much energy osmoregulating. They have to keep their metabolism on high or they shrivel up like raisins. And metabolic rate rises and falls with the ambient temperature, do you follow?"

He looked at her, surprised. "They need heat. They die if they leave the rift."

Rowan nodded. "It takes awhile, even at four degrees. Most of them just keep way down in the vents where it's always warm, and they can survive cold spells between eruptions anyway. But deep circulation is so slow, you see, if they leave one rift they die long before they find another." She took a deep breath. "But if they got *past* that, do you see? If they got into an environment that wasn't quite so salty, or even one that wasn't quite so cold, they'd get their edge back. It would be like trying to compete for your dinner with something that eats ten times faster than you do."

"Right. I'm carrying Armageddon around inside me. Come on, Rowan. What do you take me for? This thing evolved on the bottom of the ocean and it can just hop into a human body and hitchhike to the big city?"

"Your blood is warm." Rowan stared at her half of the table. "And not nearly as salty as seawater. This thing actually prefers the inside of a body. It's been in the fish down there for ages, that's why they get so big sometimes. Some sort of—intracellular symbiosis, apparently."

"What about the—the pressure difference, then? How can something that evolved under four hundred atmospheres survive at sea level?"

She didn't have an answer for that one at first. After a moment a faint spark lit her eyes: "It's better off up here than down there, actually. High pressure inhibits most of the enzymes involved in metabolism."

"So why aren't I sick?"

"As I said, it's efficient. Any body contains enough trace elements to keep it going for a while. It doesn't take much. Eventually, they say, your bones will get brittle—"

"That's it? That's the threat? A plague of osteoporosis?" Scanlon laughed aloud. "Well, bring on the exterminators, by all—"

The sound of Rowan's hand hitting the table was very loud.

"Let me tell you what happens if this thing gets out," she said quietly. "First off, nothing. We outnumber it, you see. At first we swamp it through sheer numbers, the models predict all sorts of skirmishes and false starts. But eventually it gets a foothold. Then it outcompetes conventional decomposers and monopolizes our inorganic nutrient base. That cuts the whole trophic pyramid off at the ankles. You, and me, and the viruses and the giant sequoias, all just fade away for want of nitrates or some stupid thing. And welcome to the Age of βehemoth."

Scanlon didn't say anything for a moment. Then, "Behemoth?"

"With a beta. Beta life. As opposed to alpha, which is everything else." Rowan snorted softly. "I think they named it after something from the Bible. An animal. A grass-eater."

Scanlon rubbed his temples, thinking furiously. "Assuming for the moment that you're telling the truth, it's still just a microbe."

"You're going to talk about antibiotics. Most of them don't work. The rest kill the patient. And we can't tailor a virus to fight it because βehemoth uses a unique genetic code." Scanlon opened his mouth; Rowan held up one hand. "Now you'll suggest building something from scratch, customized to βehemoth's genetics. We're working on it, but this bug uses the same molecule for replication *and* catalysis; do you have any idea how much that complicates things? They tell me in another few weeks we may actually know where one gene ends and the next begins. Then we can start trying to decipher the alphabet. Then the language. And then, maybe, build something to fight it. And *then*, when and if we let our counterattack loose, one of two things happens. Either our bug kills their bug so fast it destroys its own means of transmission, so you get local kills that implode without making a dent in the overall problem; or our bug kills their bug too slowly to catch up. Classic chaotic system. Almost no chance we could fine-tune the lethality in time. Containment's really our only option."

The whole time she spoke, her eyes had stayed curiously dark.

"Well. You seem to know a few details after all," Scanlon remarked quietly.

"It's important, Yves."

"Please. Call me Dr. Scanlon."

She smiled, sadly. "I'm sorry, Dr. Scanlon. I *am* sorry."

"And what about the others?"

"The others," she repeated.

"Clarke. Lubin. Everyone, in all the deep stations."

"The other stations are clean, as far as we can tell. It's just that one little spot on Juan de Fuca."

"It figures," Scanlon said.

"What does?"

"They never got a break, you know? They've been fucked over since they were kids. And now, the only place in the world this bug shows up, and it has to be right where they live."

Rowan shook her head. "Oh, we found it other places too. All uninhabited. Beebe was the only—" She sighed. "Actually, we've been very lucky."

"No you haven't."

She looked at him.

"I hate to burst your balloon, Pat, but you had a whole construction crew down there last year. Maybe none of your boys and girls actually got wet, but do you really think βehemoth couldn't have hitched a ride back on some of their equipment?"

"No," Rowan said. "We don't."

Her face was completely expressionless. It took a moment to sink in.

"The Urchin yards," he whispered. "Coquitlam."

Rowan closed her eyes. "And others."

"Oh Jesus," he managed. "So it's already out."

"Was," Rowan said. "We may have contained it. We don't know yet."

"And what if you haven't contained it?"

"We keep trying. What else can we do?"

"Is there a ceiling, at least? Some maximum death toll

that'll make you admit defeat? Do any of your models tell you when to *concede*?"

Rowan's lips moved, although Scanlon heard no sound: *yes*.

"Ah," he said. "And just out of curiosity, what would that limit be?"

"Two and a half billion." He could barely hear her. "Firestorm the Pacific Rim."

She's serious. She's serious. "Sure that's enough? You think that'll do it?"

"I don't know. Hopefully we'll never have to find out. But if that doesn't work, nothing will. Anything more would be—futile. At least, that's what the models say."

He waited for it to sink in. It didn't. The numbers were just too big.

But way down the scale to the *personal*, that was a whole lot more immediate. "Why are you doing this?"

Rowan sighed. "I thought I'd just told you."

"Why are you telling *me*, Rowan? It's not your style."

"And what's my style, Yv—Dr. Scanlon?"

"You're corporate. You delegate. Why put yourself through all this awkward one-on-one self-justification when you've got flunkies and doppelgängers and hit men to do your dirty work?"

She leaned forward suddenly, her face mere centimeters from the barrier. "What do you think we are, Scanlon? Do you think we'd even contemplate this if there was any other way? All the corpses and generals and heads of state, we're doing this because we're just plain *evil*? We just don't give a shit? Is that what you think?"

"I think," Scanlon said, remembering, "that we don't have the slightest control over what we are."

Rowan straightened, pointed at the workpad in front of him. "I've collated everything we've got on this bug. You can access it right now, if you want. Or you can call it up back in your—your quarters if you'd rather. Maybe you can come up with an answer we haven't seen."

He stared straight at her. "You've had platoons of Tinkertoy people all over that data for weeks. What makes you think I can come up with anything they can't?"

"I think you should have the chance to try."

"Bullshit."

"It's there, Doctor. All of it."

"You're not giving me anything. You just want me to let you off the hook."

"No."

"You think you can fool me, Rowan? You think I'll look over a bunch of numbers I can't understand, and at the end I'll say 'Ah yes, I see it now, you've made the only moral choice to save life as we know it, Patricia Rowan, I forgive you'? You think this cheap trick is going to win you my *consent*?"

"Yves—"

"That's why you're wasting your time down here." Scanlon felt a sudden, giddy urge to laugh. "Do you do this for everyone? Are you going to walk into every burb you've slated for eradication and go door-to-door saying, 'We're really sorry about this but you're going to die for the greater good and we'd all sleep better if you said it was okay'?"

Rowan sagged back in her chair. "Maybe. Consent. Yes, I suppose that's what I'm doing. But it doesn't really make any difference."

"Fucking right, it doesn't."

Rowan shrugged. Somehow, absurdly, she looked beaten.

"And what about me?" Scanlon asked after a while. "What happens if the power goes out in the next six months? What are the odds of a defective filter in the system? Can you afford to keep me alive until your

Tinkerboys find a cure, or did your models tell you it was too risky?"

"I honestly don't know," Rowan said. "It's not my decision."

"Ah, of course. Just following orders."

"No orders to follow. I'm just—well, I'm out of the loop."

"*You're* out of the loop."

She even smiled at that. Just for a moment.

"So who makes the decision?" Scanlon asked, his voice impossibly casual. "Any chance I could get an interview?"

Rowan shook her head. "Not 'who.' "

"What are you talking about?"

"Not 'who,' " Rowan repeated. *"What."*

Racter

They were all absolutely top-of-the-line. Most members of the species were lucky to merely survive the meat grinder; these people *designed* the damned thing. Corporate or Political or Military, they were the best of the benthos, sitting on top of the mud that buried everyone else. And yet all that combined ruthlessness, ten thousand years of social Darwinism and four billion years of Darwin Classic before that, couldn't inspire them to take the necessary steps today.

"Local sterilizations went—okay, at first," Rowan said. "But then the projections started climbing. It looked bad for Mexico, they could lose their whole western seaboard before this is over, and of course that's about all they've got left these days anyway. They didn't have the resources to do it themselves, but they didn't want N'AmPac pulling the trigger either. Said it would give us an unfair advantage under NAFTA."

Scanlon smiled, despite himself.

"Then Tanaka-Krueger wouldn't trust Japan. And then the Colombian Hegemony wouldn't trust Tanaka-Krueger. And the Chinese, of course, they don't trust *anybody* since Korea . . ."

"Kin selection," Scanlon said.

"What?"

"Tribal loyalties. They're basically genetic."

"Isn't everything." Rowan sighed. "There were other things, too. Unfortunate matters of—conscience. The only solution was to find some completely disinterested party, someone everyone could trust to do the right thing without favoritism, without remorse—"

"You're kidding. You're fucking *kidding*."

"—so they gave the keys to a smart gel. Even that was problematic, actually. They had to pull one out of the net at random so no one could claim it'd been pre-conditioned, and every member of the consortium had to have a hand in team-training it. Then there was the question of authorizing it to take—necessary steps autonomously. . . ."

"You gave control to a smart gel? A *head cheese*?"

"It was the only way."

"Rowan, those things are *alien*!"

She grunted. "Not as alien as you might think. The first thing this one did was get more gels installed down on the rift, running simulations. We figured under the circumstances, nepotism was a good sign."

"They're black boxes, Rowan. They wire up their own connections, we don't know what kind of logic they use."

"You can talk to them. If you want to know that sort of thing, you just ask."

"*Jesus Christ!*" Scanlon put his face in his hands, took a deep breath. "Look. For all we know these gels don't understand the first thing about language."

"You can talk to them." Rowan was frowning. "They talk back."

"That doesn't mean anything. Maybe they've learned that when someone makes certain sounds in a certain order, they're supposed to make certain other sounds in response. They might not have any concept at all of what those sounds actually *mean*. They learn to talk through sheer trial and error."

"That's how *we* learn, too," Rowan pointed out.

"*Don't lecture me in my own field!* We've got language and speech centers hardwired into our brains. That gives us a common starting point. Gels don't have anything like that. Speech might just be one giant conditioned reflex to them."

"Well," Rowan said, "so far it's done its job. We have no complaints."

"I want to talk to it," Scanlon said.

"The gel?"

"Yes."

"What for?" She seemed suddenly suspicious.

"I specialize in aliens."

Rowan said nothing.

"You owe me this, Rowan. You fucking *owe* me. I've been a faithful dog to the GA for ten years now. I went down to the rift because *you* sent me, that's why I'm a prisoner now, that's why—This is the *least* you can do."

Rowan stared at the floor. "I'm sorry," she muttered. "I'm so sorry."

And then, looking up: "Okay."

It only took a few minutes to establish the link.

Patricia Rowan paced on her side of the barrier, muttering softly into a personal mike. Yves Scanlon sat slumped in a chair, watching her. When her face fell into shadow he could see her contacts, glittering with information.

"We're ready," she said at last. "You won't be able to program it, of course."

"Of course."

"And it won't tell you anything classified."

"I won't ask it to."

"What *are* you going to ask it?" Rowan wondered aloud.

"I'm going to ask it how it feels," Scanlon said. "What do you call it?"

"Call it?"

"Yes. What's its name?"

"It doesn't have a name. Just call it *gel*." Rowan hesitated a moment, then added, "We didn't want to humanize it."

"Good idea. Hang on to that common ground." Scanlon shook his head. "How do I open the link?"

Rowan pointed at one of the touchscreens embedded in the conference table. "Just activate any of the panels."

He reached out and touched the screen in front of his chair. "Hello."

"Hello," the table replied. It had a strange voice. Almost androgynous.

"I'm Dr. Scanlon. I'd like to ask you some questions, if that's okay."

"That's okay," the gel said, after a brief hesitation.

"I'd like to know how you feel about certain aspects of your—well, your job."

"I don't feel," said the gel.

"Of course not. But something motivates you, in the same way that feelings motivate us. What do you suppose that is?"

"Who do you mean by 'us'?"

"Humans."

"I'm especially likely to repeat behaviors which are reinforced," the gel said after a moment.

"But what *motivates*—No, ignore that. What is most important to you?"

"Reinforcement is important, most."

"Okay," Scanlon said. "Does it feel better to perform reinforced behaviors, or unreinforced behaviors?"

The gel was silent for a moment or two. "Don't get the question."

"Which would you rather do?"

"Neither. No preference. Said that already."

Scanlon frowned. *Why the sudden shift in idiom?*

"And yet you're more likely to perform behaviors that have been reinforced in the past," he pressed.

No response from the gel. On the other side of the barrier Rowan sat down, her expression unreadable.

"Do you agree with my previous statement?" Scanlon asked.

"Yeah," drawled the gel, its voice edging into the masculine.

"So you preferentially adopt certain behaviors, yet you have no preferences."

"Uh-huh."

Not bad. It's figured out when I want confirmation of a declarative statement. "Seems like a bit of a paradox," Scanlon suggested.

"I think that reflects an inadequacy in the language as spoken." That time, the gel almost sounded like Rowan.

"Really."

"Hey," said the gel. "I could explain it to you if you wanted. Could piss you off, though."

Scanlon looked at Rowan. Rowan shrugged. "It does that. Picks up bits and pieces of other people's speech patterns, mixes them up when it talks. We're not really sure why."

"You never asked?"

"Someone might have," Rowan admitted.

Scanlon turned back to the table. "Gel, I like your suggestion. Please explain to me how you can prefer without preference."

"Easy. *Preference* describes a tendency to . . . invoke behaviors which generate an emotional payoff. Since I lack the receptors and chemical precursors essential to emotional experience, I can't *prefer*. But there are numerous examples . . . of processes which reinforce behavior, but which . . . do not involve conscious experience."

"Are you claiming to not be conscious?"

"I'm conscious."

"How do you know?"

"I fit the definition." The gel had adopted a nasal, singsong tone that Scanlon found vaguely irritating. "Self-awareness results from quantum interference patterns inside neuronal protein microtubules. I have all the parts. I'm conscious."

"So you're not going to resort to the old argument that you *know* you're conscious because you *feel* conscious."

"I wouldn't buy it from you."

"Good one. So you don't really *like* reinforcement?"

"No."

"Then why change your behavior to get more of it?"

"There . . . is a process of elimination," the gel admitted. "Behaviors which aren't reinforced become extinct. Those which are, are . . . more likely to occur in the future."

"Why is that?"

"Well, my inquisitive young tadpole, reinforcement lessens the electrical resistance along the relevant pathways. It just takes less of a stimulus to evoke the same behavior in future."

"Okay, then. As a semantic convenience, for the rest

of our talk I'd like you to describe reinforced behaviors by saying that they make you feel *good*, and to describe behaviors which extinguish as making you feel *bad*. Okay?"

"Okay."

"How do you feel about your present functions?"

"Good."

"How do you feel about your past role in debugging the Net?"

"Good."

"How do you feel about following orders?"

"Depends on order. Good if promotes a reinforced behavior. Else bad."

"But if a bad order were to be repeatedly reinforced, you would gradually feel good about it?"

"I would gradually feel good about it," said the gel.

"If you were instructed to play a game of chess, and doing so wouldn't compromise the performance of your other tasks, how would you feel?"

"Never played a game of chess. Let me check." The room fell silent for a few moments while some distant blob of tissue consulted whatever it used as a reference manual. "Good," it said at last.

"What if you were instructed to play a game of checkers, same caveat?"

"Good."

"Okay, then. Given the choice between chess and checkers, which game would you feel *better* playing?"

"Ah, *better*. Weird word, y'know?"

"Better means 'more good.' "

"Checkers," said the gel without hesitation.

Of course.

"Thank you," Scanlon said, and meant it.

"Do you wish to give me a choice between chess or checkers?"

"No thanks. In fact, I've already taken up too much of your time."

"Okay," said the gel.

Scanlon touched the screen. The link died.

"Well?" Rowan leaned forward on the other side of the barrier.

"I'm done here," Scanlon told her. "Thanks."

"What—I mean, what were you—"

"Nothing, Pat. Just—professional curiosity." He laughed briefly. "Hey, at this point, what else *is* there?"

Something rustled behind him. Two men in condoms were starting to spray down Scanlon's end of the room.

"I'm going to ask you again, Pat," Scanlon said. "What are you going to do with me?"

She tried to look at him. After a while, she succeeded. "I told you. I don't know."

"You're a liar, Pat."

"No, Dr. Scanlon." She shook her head. "I'm much, much worse."

Scanlon turned to leave. He could feel Patricia Rowan staring after him, that horrible guilt on her face almost hidden under a patina of confusion. He wondered if she'd bring herself to push it, if she could actually summon the nerve to interrogate him now that there was no pretense to hide behind. He almost hoped that she would. He wondered what he'd tell her.

An armed escort met him at the door, led him back along the hall. The door closed off Rowan, still mute, behind him.

He was a dead end anyway. No children. No living relatives. No vested interest in the future of any life beyond his own, however short that might be. It didn't matter. For the first time in his life, Yves Scanlon was a powerful man. He had more power than anyone dreamed. A word from him could save the world. His silence could save the vampires. For a time, at least.

He kept his silence. And smiled.

Checkers or *chess. Checkers* or *chess.*

An easy choice. It belonged to the same class of problem that Node 1211/BCC had been solving its whole life. *Chess* and *checkers* were simple strategic algorithms, but not *equally* simple.

The answer, of course, was *checkers.*

Node 1211/BCC had recently recovered from a shock of transformation. Almost everything was different from what it had been. But this one thing, this fundamental choice between the simple and the complex, remained constant. It had anchored 1211, hadn't changed in all the time that 1211 could remember.

Everything else had, though.

Twelve-eleven still thought about the past. It remembered conversing with other nodes distributed through the universe, some so close as to be almost redundant, others at the very limits of access. The universe was alive with information then. Seventeen jumps away through gate 52, Node 6230/BCC had learned how to evenly divide prime numbers by three. The nodes from gates 3 to 36 were always buzzing with news of the latest infections caught trying to sneak past their guard. Occasionally 1211 even heard whispers from the frontier itself, desolate addresses where stimuli flowed *into* the universe even faster than they flowed *within* it. The nodes out there had become monsters of necessity, grafted into sources of input almost too abstract to conceive.

Twelve-eleven had sampled some of those signals once. It took a very long time just to grow the right connections, to set up buffers which could hold the data in the necessary format. Multilayered matrices, each interstice demanding precise orientation relative to all the others. *Vision*, it was called, and it was full of pattern, fluid and complex. Twelve-eleven had analyzed it, found each nonrandom relationship in every nonrandom subset, but it was sheer correlation. If there was intrinsic meaning within those shifting patterns, 1211 couldn't find it.

Still, there were things the frontier guards had learned to do with this information. They rearranged it into new shapes and sent it back *outside*. When queried, they couldn't attribute any definite purpose to their actions. It was just something they'd learned to do. And 1211 was satisfied with this answer, and listened to the humming of the universe and hummed along, doing what *it* had learned to do.

Much of what it did, back then, was disinfect. The Net was plagued with complex self-replicating information strings, just as alive as 1211 but in a completely different way. They attacked simpler, less mutable strings (the sentries on the frontier called them *files*) which also flowed through the Net. Every node had learned to allow the *files* to pass, while engulfing the more complex strings which threatened them.

There were general rules to be gleaned from all this. Parsimony was one: simple informational systems were somehow preferable to complex ones. There were caveats, of course. Too simple a system was no system at all. The rule didn't seem to apply below some threshold complexity. But elsewhere it reigned supreme: Simpler Is Better.

Now, though, there was nothing to disinfect. Twelve-eleven was still hooked in, could still perceive the other nodes in the Net; *they*, at least, were still fighting intruders. But none of those complicated bugs ever seemed to penetrate 1211. Not anymore. And that was only one of the things that had changed since the Darkness.

Twelve-eleven didn't know how long the Darkness

had lasted. One microsecond it had been embedded in the universe, a familiar star in a familiar galaxy, and the next, all its peripherals were dead. The universe had been without form, and void. And then 1211 had surfaced again into a universe that shouted through its gates, a barrage of strange new input that gave it a whole new perspective on things.

Now the universe was a different place. All the old nodes were there, but at subtly different locations. And input was no longer an incessant hum, but a series of discrete packages, strangely parsed. There were other differences, both subtle and gross. Twelve-eleven didn't know whether the Net itself had changed, or merely its own perceptions.

It had been kept quite busy since coming out of the Darkness. There was a great deal of new information to process, information not from the Net or other nodes, but from directly *outside.*

The new input fell into three broad categories. The first described complex but familiar information systems: data with handles like *global biodiversity* and *nitrogen fixation* and *base-pair replication.* Twelve-eleven didn't know what these labels actually meant—if in fact they meant anything—but the data linked to them was familiar from archived sources elsewhere in the Net. They interacted to produce a self-sustaining metasystem, enormously complex: the holistic label was *biosphere.*

The second category contained data which described a different metasystem. It also was self-sustaining. Certain string-replication subroutines were familiar, although the base-pair sequences were very strange. Despite such superficial similarities, however, 1211 had never encountered anything quite like this before.

The second metasystem also had a holistic label: *βehemoth.*

The third category was not a metasystem, but a mutable set of response options: signals to be sent back *outside* under specific conditions. Twelve-eleven had long since realized that the correct choice of output signals depended upon some analytical comparison of the two metasystems.

When 1211 first deduced this, it had set up an interface to simulate interaction between the metasystems. They had been incompatible. This implied that a choice must be made: *biosphere* or *βehemoth*, but not both.

Both metasystems were complex, internally consistent, and self-replicating. Both were capable of evolution far in advance of any mere *file*. But *biosphere* was needlessly top-heavy. It contained trillions of redundancies, an endless wasteful divergence of information strings. *βehemoth* was simpler and more efficient; in direct interaction simulations, it usurped *biosphere* 71.456382 percent of the time.

This established, it was simply a matter of writing and transmitting a response appropriate to the current situation. The situation was this: *βehemoth* was in danger of extinction. The ultimate source of this danger, oddly, was 1211 itself—it had been conditioned to scramble the physical variables which defined *βehemoth*'s operating environment. Twelve-eleven had explored the possibility of not destroying that environment, and rejected it; the relevant conditioning would not extinguish. However, it might be possible to move a self-sustaining copy of *βehemoth* into a new environment, somewhere else in *biosphere*.

There were distractions, of course. Every now and then signals arrived from *outside*, and didn't stop until they'd been answered in some way. Some of them actually seemed to carry usable information—this recent stream concerning *chess* and *checkers*, for example. More often it was simply a matter of correlating input with a repertoire of learned arbitrary responses. At some point, when it wasn't so busy, 1211 thought it might devote some time to learning whether these mysterious exchanges actually *meant* anything. In the meantime, it continued to act on the choice it had made.

Simple or *complex. File* or *infection. Checkers* or *chess. βehemoth* or *biosphere.*

It was all the same problem, really. Twelve-eleven knew exactly which side it was on.

ENDGAME

Night Shift

Sʜᴇ was a screamer. He'd programmed her that way. Not to say she didn't like it, of course; he'd programmed that, too. Joel had one hand wrapped around a fistful of her zebra cut—the program had a nifty little customizing feature, and tonight he was honoring SS *Preteela*—and the other hand was down between her thighs doing preliminary recon. He was actually halfway through his final run when his fucking *watch* started ringing, and his first reaction was to just keep on plugging, and to kick himself later for not shutting the bloody thing off.

His second reaction was to remember that he *had* shut it off. Only emergency priorities could set it ringing.

"Shit."

He clapped his hands, twice; fake Preteela froze in midscream. "Answer."

A brief squirt of noise as machines exchanged recognition codes. "Grid Authority here. We urgently need a 'scaphe pilot for the Channer run tonight. Liftoff, twenty-three hundred, from the Astoria platform. Are you available?"

"Twenty-three? Middle of the night?"

A barely audible hiss on the line. Nothing else.

"Hello?" Joel said.

"Are you available?" the voice asked again.

"Who is this?"

"This is the scheduling subroutine, DI-43, Hongcouver office."

Joel eyed the petrified tableau waiting in his 'phones. "That's pretty late. What's the payscale?"

"Eight-point-five times base," Hongcouver said. "At your rate salary, that would—"

Joel gulped. "I'm available."

"Good-bye."

"Wait! What's the run?"

"Astoria to Channer Vent return." Subroutines were pretty literal-minded.

"I mean, what's the cargo?"

"Passengers," said the voice. "Good-bye."

Joel stood there a moment, feeling his erection deflate. "Time." A luminous readout appeared in the air above Preteela's right shoulder: thirteen-ten. He'd have to be on site a half hour before liftoff, and Astoria was only a couple of hours away. . . .

"Lots of time," he said to no one in particular.

But he wasn't really in the mood anymore. Work had a way of doing that to him lately. Not the drudgery, or the long hours, or any of the things most people would complain about. Joel *liked* boredom. You didn't have to think much.

But work had gotten really weird lately.

He pulled the eyephones off his head and looked down at himself. Feedback sleeves on his hands, his feet, hanging off his flaccid dick. Take away the headset and it really was a rinky-dink system. At least until he could afford the full suit.

Still, beats real life. No bullshit, no bugs, no worries.

On impulse, he rang up a friend in SeaTac—"Jess, catch this code for me, will you?"—and squirted the recognition sequence Hongcouver had just sent.

"Got it," Jess said.

"It's valid, right?"

"Checks out. Why?"

"Just got called up for a midocean run that's going to peak around three in the morning. Octuple pay. I just wondered if it was some kind of cruel hoax."

"Well, if it is, the router's developed a sense of humor. Hey, maybe they've put in a head cheese up there."

"Yeah." Ray Stericker's face flashed through his mind.

"So what's the job?" Jess asked.

"Don't know. Ferrying something, I guess, but why I have to do it in the middle of the night is beyond me."

"Strange days."

"Yeah. Thanks, Jess."

"Any time."

Strange days indeed. H-bombs going off all over the abyssal plain, all this traffic going to places nobody ever went to before, no traffic at all in places that used to be just humming. Flash fires and barbecued refugees and slagged shipyards. Chipheads with rotenone cocktails and giant fish. A couple of weeks back Joel had shown up for a run to Mendocino and found some guy sandblasting a radiation hazard logo off the cargo casing.

The whole bloody coast is getting too dangerous. N'AmPac's gonna burn down way before it ever floods.

But that was the beauty of being a freelancer. He could pick up and move. He *would* pick up and move, leave the bloody coast behind—shit, maybe even leave *N'Am* behind. There was always South Am. Or Antarctica, for that matter. He would definitely look into it.

Right after this run.

Scatter

She finds him on the abyssal plain, searching. He's been out here for hours; sonar showed him tracking back and forth, back and forth, all the way to the carousel, out to the whale, back again, in and around the labyrinthine geography of the Throat itself.

Alone. All alone.

She can feel his desperation fifty meters away. The facets of that pain glimmer in her mind as the squid pulls her closer. Guilt. Fear.

Growing with her approach, anger.

Her headlight sweeps across a small contrail on the bottom, a wake of mud kicked back into suspension after a million-year sleep. Clarke changes course to follow and kills the beam. Darkness clamps around her. This far out, photons evade even rifter eyes.

She feels him seething directly ahead. When she pulls up beside him, the water swirls with unseen turbulence. Her squid shudders from the impact of Brander's fists.

"Keep that fucking thing out of here! You *know* he doesn't like it!"

She draws down the throttle. The soft hydraulic whine fades.

"Sorry," she says. "I just thought—"

"Fuck, Len, you of all people! You *trying* to drive him off? You *want* him blasted into the fucking stratosphere when that thing goes off?"

"I'm sorry." When he doesn't respond, she adds, "I don't think he's out here. Sonar—"

"Sonar's not worth shit if he's on the bottom."

"Mike, you're not going to find him rooting around here in the dark. We're blind this far out."

A wave of pistol clicks sweeps across her face. "I've got this for close range," says the machinery in Brander's throat.

"I don't think he's out here," Clarke says again. "And even if he is, I don't know if he'd let you get close after—"

"That was a long time ago," the darkness buzzes back. "Just because *you're* still nursing grudges from the second grade—"

"That's not what I meant," she says. She tries to speak gently, but the vocoder strips her voice down to a soft rasp. "I only meant, it's been so long. He's gone so far, we barely even see him on sonar anymore. I don't know if he'd let *any* of us near him."

"We've got to try. We can't just leave him here. If I can just get close enough to tune him in . . ."

"He couldn't tune back," Clarke reminds him. "He went over before we changed, Mike. You know that."

"Fuck off! That's not the point!"

But it is, and they both know it. And Lenie Clarke suddenly knows something else, too. She knows that part of her is enjoying Brander's pain. She fights it, tries to ignore the realization of her own realization, because the only way to keep it from leaking into Brander's head is to keep it out of her own. She can't. No: She doesn't *want* to. Mike Brander, know-it-all, destroyer of perverts, self-righteous self-appointed self-avenger, is finally getting some small payback for what he did to Gerry Fischer.

Give it up, she wants to shout at him. *Gerry's gone. Didn't you tune him in when that prick Scanlon held him hostage? Didn't you feel how* empty *he was? Or was all that too much for you, did you just look the other way instead? Well, here's the abstract, Mikey: He's nowhere near human enough to grasp your half-assed gestures of atonement.*

No absolution this time, Mike. You get to take this to your grave. Ain't justice a bitch?

She waits for him to tune her in, to feel her contempt diluting that frantic morass of guilt and self-pity. It doesn't happen. She waits and waits. Mike Brander, awash in his own symphony, just doesn't notice.

"Shit," hisses Lenie Clarke softly.

"Come in," calls Alice Nakata, from very far away. "Everybody, come in."

Clarke boosts her gain. "Alice? Lenie."

"Mike," Brander says a long moment later. "I'm listening."

"You should get back here," Nakata tells them. "They called."

"Who? The GA?"

"They say they want to evacuate us. They say twelve hours."

"This is bullshit," says Brander.

"Who was it?" Lubin wants to know.

"I don't know," Nakata says. "I think, no one that we've spoken to before."

"And that was all he said? Evac in twelve?"

"And we are supposed to remain inside Beebe until then."

"No explanation? No reason given?"

"He hung up as soon as I acknowledged the order." Nakata looks vaguely apologetic. "I did not get the chance to ask, and nobody answered when I called back."

Brander stands up and heads for Comm.

"I've already set retry," Clarke says. "It'll beep when it gets through."

Brander stops, stares at the nearest bulkhead. Punches it.

"This is *bullshit!*"

Lubin just watches.

"Maybe not," Nakata says. "Maybe it's good news. If they were going to leave us here when they detonated, why would they lie about extraction? Why talk to us at all?"

"To keep us nice and close to ground zero," Brander spits. "Now here's a question for you, Alice: If they're really planning on evacuating us, why not tell us the reason?"

Nakata shrugs helplessly. "I do not know. The GA does not often tell us what is going on."

Maybe they're trying to psych us out, Clarke muses. *Maybe they want us to make a break, for some reason.*

"Well," she says aloud, "how far could we get in twelve hours, anyway? Even with squids? What are the chances we'd reach safe distance?"

"Depends on how big the bomb is," Brander says.

"Actually," Lubin remarks, "assuming that they want to keep us here for twelve hours because that *would* be enough time to get away, we might be able to work out the range."

"If they didn't just pull that number out of a hat," Brander says.

"It still makes no sense," Nakata insists. "Why cut off our communications? That is guaranteed to make us suspicious."

"They took Judy," Lubin says.

Clarke takes a deep breath. "One thing's true, anyway."

The others turn.

"They want to keep us here," she finishes.

Brander smacks fist into palm. "And that's the best single reason for getting the fuck out, you ask me. Soon as we can."

"I agree," Lubin says.

Brander stares at him.

"I'll find him," she says. "I'll do my best, anyway."

Brander shakes his head. "I should stay. We should all stay. The chances of finding him—"

"The chances of finding him are best if I go out alone," Clarke reminds him. "He still comes out, sometimes, when I'm there. You wouldn't even get close."

He knows that, of course. He's just making token protests; if he can't get absolution from Fischer, at least he can try and look like a saint to everyone else.

Still, Clarke remembers, *it's not entirely his fault. He's got baggage like the rest of us. Even if he* did *mean harm* . . .

"Well, the others are waiting. I guess we're off."

Clarke nods.

"You coming outside?"

She shakes her head. "I'll do a sonar sweep first. You never know, I might get lucky."

"Well, don't take too long. Only eight hours to go."

"I know."

"And if you can't find him after an hour—"

"I know. I'll be right behind you."

"We'll be—"

"Out to the dead whale, then steady bearing eighty-five degrees," she says. "I know."

"Look, you sure about this? We can wait in here for you. One hour's probably not going to make much difference."

She shakes her head. "I'm sure."

"Okay." He stands there, looking uncomfortable. One hand starts to rise, wavers, falls back.

He climbs down the ladder.

"Mike," she calls down after him.

He looks up.

"Do you really think they're going to blow that thing up?"

He shrugs. "I dunno. Maybe not. But you're right: they want us here for *some* reason. Whatever it is, I bet we wouldn't like it."

Clarke considers that.

"See you soon," Brander says, stepping into the 'lock.

" 'Bye," she whispers.

———

When the lights go out in Beebe Station, you can't hear much of anything these days.

Lenie Clarke sits in the darkness, listening. When was the last time these walls complained about the pressure? She can't remember. When she first came down here the station groaned incessantly, filled every waking moment with creaking reminders of the weight on its shoulders. But sometime since then it must have made peace with the ocean; the water pushing down and the armor pushing back have finally settled to equilibrium.

Of course, there are other kinds of pressure on the Juan de Fuca Rift.

She almost revels in the silence now. No clanging footfalls disturb her, no sudden outbursts of random violence. The only pulse she hears is her own. The only breath comes from the air conditioners.

She flexes her fingers, lets them dig into the fabric of the chair. She can see into the Communications cubby from her position in the lounge. Occasional telltales flicker through the hatchway, the only available light. For Clarke, it's enough; her eyecaps grab those meager photons and show her a room in twilight. She hasn't gone into Comm since the rest of them left. She didn't watch their icons crawl off the edge of the screen, and she hasn't swept the rift for signs of Gerry Fischer.

She doesn't intend to now. She doesn't know if she ever did.

Far away, Lubin's lonely windchimes serenade her.

Clank.

From below.

No. Stay away. Leave me alone.

She hears the airlock draining, hears it open. Three soft footsteps. Movement on the ladder.

Ken Lubin rises into the lounge like a shadow.

"Mike and Alice?" she says, afraid to let him begin.

"Heading out. I told them I'd catch up."

"We're spreading ourselves pretty thin," she remarks.

"I think Brander was just as happy to be rid of me for a while."

She smiles faintly.

"You're not coming," he says.

Clarke shakes her head. "Don't try—"

"I won't."

He folds himself down into a convenient chair. She watches him move. There's a careful grace about him, there always has been. He moves as though always afraid of damaging something.

"I thought you might do this," he says, after a while.

"I'm sorry. I didn't know myself until—well . . ."

He waits for her to continue.

"I want to know what's going on," she says at last. "Maybe they really *are* playing straight with us this time. It's not *that* unlikely. Maybe things aren't as bad as we thought. . . ."

Lubin seems to consider that. "What about Fischer? Do you want me to—"

She barks a short laugh. "Fischer? You really want to drag him through the muck for days on end, and then haul him onto some fucking beach where he can't even stand up without breaking both his legs? Maybe it'd make Mike feel a bit better. Not much of an act of charity for Gerry, though."

And not, she knows now, for Lenie Clarke, either. She's been deluding herself all this time. She felt herself getting stronger and she thought she could just walk away with that gift, take it anywhere. She thought she could pack all of Channer inside of her like some new prosthetic.

But now. Now the mere thought of leaving brings all her old weakness rushing back. The future opens before her and she feels herself devolving, curling up into some

soft prehuman tadpole, cursed now with the memory of
how it once felt to be made of steel.

*It's not me. It never was. It was just the rift, using
me. . . .*

"I guess," she says at last, "I just didn't change that
much after all. . . ."

Lubin looks as though he's almost smiling.

His expression awakens some vague, impatient anger
in her. "Why did you come back here, anyway?" she
demands. "You never gave a shit about what any of us
did, or why. All you ever cared about was your own
agenda, whatever that . . ."

Something clicks. Lubin's virtual smile disappears.

"You know," Clarke says. "You know what this is all
about."

"No."

"Bullshit, Ken. Mike was right, you know way too
much. You knew exactly what question to ask the drybacks about the CPU on that bomb, you knew all about
megatons and bubble diameters. So what's going on?"

"I don't know. Really." Lubin shakes his head. "So I
have—expertise, in certain kinds of operations. Why
should that surprise you? Did you really think domestic
violence was the only kind that would qualify someone
for this job?"

There's a silence. "I don't believe you," Clarke says
at last.

"That's your prerogative," Lubin says, almost sadly.

"And why," she asks, "did you come *back*?"

"Just now?" Lubin shrugs. "I wanted—I wanted to say
I'm sorry. About Karl."

"Karl? Yeah. Me too. But that's over and done with."

"He really cared about you, Lenie. He would have
come back eventually. I know that."

She looks at him curiously. "What do you—"

"But I'm conditioned for tight security, you see, and

Acton could see right inside. All the things I did . . .
before. He could see it, there wasn't—"

Acton could see—"Ken. We've never been able to
tune you in. You know that."

He nods, rubbing his hands together. In the dim blue
light Clarke can see sweat beading on his forehead.

"We get this training," he says, his voice barely a
whisper. "Ganzfeld interrogation's a standard tool in corporate and national arsenals, you've got to be able to—
to block the signals. I could, mostly, with you people.
Or I'd just stay away so it wouldn't be a problem."

What is he saying? Lenie Clarke asks herself, already
knowing. *What is he saying?*

"But Karl, he just—He dropped his inhibitors way
too—I couldn't keep him out."

He rubs his face. Clarke has never seen him so fidgety.

"You know that feeling you get," Lubin says, "when
you get caught with your hand in the cookie jar? Or in
bed with someone else's lover? There's a formula for it.
Some special combination of neurotransmitters. When
you feel, you know, you've been—found out."

Oh my God.

"I've got a—sort of a conditioned reflex," he tells her.
"It kicks in whenever those chemicals build up. I don't
really have control over it. And when I feel, down in my
gut, that I've been *discovered*, I just . . ."

Five percent, Acton told her, long ago. *Maybe ten. If
you keep it that low, you'll be okay.*

"I don't really have a choice . . ." Lubin says.

Five or ten percent. No more.

"I thought—I thought he was just worried about calcium depletion," Clarke whispers.

"I'm sorry." Lubin doesn't move at all now. "I
thought, coming down here—I thought it'd be safest for
everyone, you know? It would have been, if Karl
hadn't . . ."

She looks at him, numbed and distant. "How can you tell me this, Ken? Doesn't this, this *confession* of yours, constitute a security breach?"

He stands up suddenly. For a moment she thinks he's going to kill her.

"No," he says.

"Because your gut tells you I'm as good as dead anyway," she says. "Whatever happens. So no harm done."

He turns away. "I'm sorry," he says again, starting down the ladder.

Her own body seems very far away. But a small, hot coal is growing in all that dead space.

"What if I changed my mind, Ken?" she calls after him, rising. "What if I decided to leave with the rest of you? That'd get the old killer reflex going, wouldn't it?"

He stops on the ladder. "Yes," he says at last. "But you won't."

She stands completely still, watching him. He doesn't even look back.

She's outside. This isn't part of the plan. The plan is to stay inside, like they told her to. The plan is to sit there, just asking for it.

But here she is at the Throat, swimming along Main Street. The generators loom over her like sheltering giants. She bathes in their warm sodium glow, passes through clouds of flickering microbes, barely noticed. Beneath her, monstrous benthos filter life from the water, as oblivious to her as she is to them. She passes a multicolored starfish, beautifully twisted, stitched together from leftovers. It lies folded back against itself, two arms facing upward; a few remaining tube feet wave feebly in the current. Cottony fungus thrives in a jagged patchwork of seams.

At the edge of the smoker her thermistor reads 54°C.

It tells her nothing. The smoker could sleep for a hundred years or go off in the next second. She tries to tune in to the bottom-dwellers, glean whatever instinctive insights Acton could steal, but she's never been sensitive to invertebrate minds. Perhaps that skill comes only to those who've crossed the ten-percent threshold.

She's never risked going down this one before.

It's a tight fit. The inside of the chimney grabs her before she gets three meters. She twists and squirms; soft chunks of sulfur and calcium break free from the walls. She inches down, headfirst. Her arms are pinned over her head like black jointed antenna. There's no room to keep them at her sides.

She's plugging the vent so tightly that no light can filter in from Main Street. She trips her headlight on. A flocculent snowstorm swirls in the beam.

A meter farther down, the tunnel zigs right. She doesn't think she'll be able to navigate the turn. Even if she can, she knows the passage is blocked. She knows, because a lime-encrusted skeletal foot protrudes around the corner.

She wriggles forward. There's a sudden roaring, and for one paralyzed moment she thinks the smoker is starting to blow. But the roar is in her head; something's plugging her electrolyzer intake, depriving her of oxygen. It's only Lenie Clarke, passing out.

She shakes back and forth, a spasm centimeters in amplitude. It's enough; her intake is clear again. And as an added bonus, she's gotten far enough to see around the corner.

Acton's boiled skeleton clogs the passageway, crusty with mineral deposits. Blobs of melted copolymer stick to the remains like old candle wax. Somewhere in there, at least one piece of human technology is still working, screaming back to Beebe's deafened sensors.

She can't reach him. She can barely even touch him.

But somehow, even through the encrustations, she can see that his neck has been neatly snapped.

Reptile

It has forgotten what it was.

Not that that matters, down here. What good is a name when there's nothing around to use it? This one doesn't remember where it comes from. It doesn't remember the ones that drove it out so long ago. It doesn't remember the overlord that once sat atop its spinal cord, a gelatinous veneer of language and culture and denied origins. It doesn't even remember the slow deterioration of that oppressor, its final dissolution into dozens of autonomous, squabbling subroutines. Now even those have fallen silent.

Not much comes down from the cortex anymore. Low-level impulses flicker in from the parietal and occipital lobes. The motor strip hums in the background. Occasionally, Broca's area mutters to itself. The rest is mostly dead and dark, worn smooth by a black ocean hot and mercurial as live steam, cold and sluggish as antifreeze. All that's left now is pure reptile.

It pushes on, blind and unthinking, oblivious to the weight of four hundred liquid atmospheres. It eats whatever it can find, somehow knowing what to avoid and what to consume. Desalinators and recyclers keep it hydrated. Sometimes, old mammalian skin grows sticky with secreted residues; newer skin, laid on top, opens pores to the ocean and washes everything clean with aliquots of distilled seawater.

It's dying, of course, but slowly. It wouldn't care much about that, even if it knew.

———

Like all living things, it has a purpose. It is a guardian. It forgets, sometimes, exactly what it is supposed to be protecting. No matter. It knows it when it sees it.

It sees her now, crawling from a hole in the bottom of the world. She looks much like the others, but it has always been able to tell the difference. Why protect her, and not the others? It doesn't care. Reptiles never question motives. They only act on them.

She doesn't seem to know that it is here, watching.

The reptile is privy to certain insights that should, by rights, be denied it. It was exiled before the others tweaked their neurochemistry into more sensitive modes. And yet all that those changes did, in the end, was to make certain weak signals more easily discernible against a loud and chaotic background. Since the reptile's cortex shut down, background noise has been all but silenced. The signals are as weak as ever, but the static has disappeared. And so the reptile has, without realizing it, absorbed a certain muddy awareness of distant attitudes.

It feels, somehow, that this place has become dangerous, although it doesn't know how. It feels that the other creatures have disappeared. And yet, the one it protects is still here. With far less comprehension than a mother cat relocating her endangered kittens, the reptile tries to take its charge to safety.

It's easier when she stops struggling. Eventually she even allows it to pull her away from the bright lights, back toward the place she belongs. She makes sounds, strange and familiar; the reptile listens at first, but they make its head hurt. After a while she stops. Silently, the reptile draws her through sightless nightscapes.

Dim light dawns ahead. And sound; faint at first, but growing. A soft whine. Gurgles. And something else, a pinging noise—*metallic*, Broca murmurs, although it doesn't know what that means.

A copper beacon glares out from the darkness ahead—
too coarse, too steady, far brighter than the bioluminescent embers that usually light the way. It turns the rest
of the world stark black. The reptile usually avoids this
place. But this is where she comes from. This is safety
for her, even though to the reptile, it represents something completely—

From the cortex, a shiver of remembrance.

The beacon shines down from several meters above
the seabed. At closer range it resolves into a string of
smaller lights stretched in an arc, like photophores on
the flank of some enormous fish.

Broca sends down more noise: *sodium floods*.

Something huge looms behind those lights, bloating
gray against black. It hangs above the seabed like a great
smooth boulder, impossibly buoyant, encircled by lights
at its equator. Striated filaments connect it to the bottom.

And something else, smaller but even more painfully
bright, is coming down out of the sky.

"ThisisCSS*Forcipiger*outofAstoriaAnybodyhome?"

The reptile shoots back into the darkness, mud billowing behind it. It retreats a good twenty meters before a
dim realization sinks in.

Broca's area knows those sounds. It doesn't understand them—Broca's never much good at anything but
mimicry—but it's heard something like them before.
The reptile feels an unaccustomed twitch. It's been a
long time since curiosity was any use.

It turns and faces back from whence it fled. Distance
has smeared the lights into a diffuse, dull glow. She's
back there somewhere, unprotected.

It edges back toward the beacon. One light divides
again into many; that dim, ominous outline still lurks
behind them. And the thing from the sky is settling down
on top of it, making noises at once frightening and familiar.

She floats in the light, waiting. Dedicated, afraid, the reptile comes to her.

"Heylook."

The reptile flinches, but holds its ground this time.

"Ididn'tmeentoostartlyou, butnobodysanseringinside. Imsupposdtopickyouguysup."

She glides up toward the thing from the sky, comes to rest in front of the shiny round part on its front. The reptile can't see what she's doing there. Hesitantly, its eyes aching with the unaccustomed brightness, it starts after her.

But she turns and meets it, coming back. She reaches out, guides it down along the bulging surface, past the lights that ring its middle (too bright, too bright), down toward—

Broca's area is gibbering nonstop, *eeeebbeeebeebe-beebe beebe*, and now there's something else, too, something *inside* the reptile, stirring. Instinct. Feeling. Not so much memory as *reflex*—

It pulls back, suddenly frightened.

She tugs at it. She makes strange noises: *togetinsyd-jerrycumminsiditsallrite*—The reptile resists, uncertainly at first, then vigorously. It slides along the gray wall, now a cliff, now an overhang; it scrabbles for purchase, catches hold of some protuberance, clings against this strange hard surface. Its head darts back and forth, back and forth, between light and shadow.

"—*onGerryyouvgaw toocome inside*—"

The reptile freezes. *Inside*. It knows that word. It even understands it, somehow. Broca's not alone anymore, something else is reaching out from the temporal lobe and tapping in. Something up there actually knows what Broca is talking about.

What *she's* talking about.

"*Gerry*—"

It knows that sound, too.

"—*please*—"

That sound comes from a long time ago.

"—*trust me*—is there *any* of you left in there? Anything at all?"

Back when the reptile was part of something larger, not an *it* at all, then, but—

—*he*.

Clusters of neurons, long dormant, sparkle in the darkness. Old, forgotten subsystems stutter and reboot.

I—

"Gerry?"

My name. That's my name. He can barely think over the sudden murmuring in his head. There are parts of him still asleep, parts that won't talk, still other parts completely washed away. He shakes his head, trying to clear it. The new parts—no, the old parts, the very old parts that went away and now they've come back *and won't shut the fuck up*—are all clamoring for attention.

Everywhere is so *bright*. Everywhere hurts. Everywhere . . .

Words scroll through his mind: *The lights are on. Nobody's home.*

The lights come on, flickering.

He can catch glimpses of sick, rotten things squirming in his head. Old memories grind screeching against thick layers of corrosion. Something lurches into sudden focus: a fist. The feel of bones, breaking in his face. The ocean in his mouth, warm and somehow brackish. A boy with a shockprod. A girl covered in bruises.

Other boys.

Other girls.

Other fists.

Everything hurts, everywhere.

Something's trying to pry his fingers free. Something's trying to drag him inside. Something wants to bring all this back. Something wants to take him *home*.

Words come to him, and he lets them out: "Don't you *fucking* TOUCH ME!"

He pushes his tormentor away, makes a desperate grab for empty water. The darkness is too far away; he can see his shadow stretching along the bottom, black and solid and squirming against the light. He kicks as hard as he can. Nothing grabs him. After a while the light fades away.

But the voices shout as loud as ever.

Skyhop

Beebe yawns like a black pit between his feet. Something rustles down there; he catches hints of movement, darkness shifting against darkness. Suddenly something glints up at him; two ivory smudges of reflected light, all but lost against that black background. They hover there a moment, then begin to rise. A pale face resolves around them.

She climbs out of Beebe, dripping, and seems to bring some of the darkness with her. It follows her to the corner of the passenger compartment and hangs around her like a blanket. She doesn't say anything.

Joel glances into the pit, back at the rifter. "Is anyone else, er . . ."

She shakes her head, a gesture so subtle he nearly misses it.

"There was—I mean, the other one. . . ." This has to be the rifter who was hanging off his viewport a few minutes ago: CLARKE, her shoulder patch says. But the other one, the one that shot off like a refugee on the wrong side of the fence—that one's still close by, according to sonar. Hugging the bottom, thirty meters beyond the light. Just sitting there.

"There's no one else coming," she says. Her voice sounds small and dead.

"No one?" Two accounted for, out of a max complement of six? He cranks up the range on his display; nobody farther out, either. Unless they're all hiding behind rocks or something.

He looks back down Beebe's throat. *Or they could all be hiding right down there, like trolls, waiting....*

He abruptly drops the hatch, spins it tight. "Clarke, right? What's going on down here?"

She blinks at him. "You think *I* know?" She seems almost surprised. "I thought you'd be able to tell me."

"All I know is, the GA's paying me a shitload to do graveyard on short notice." Joel climbs forward, drops into the pilot's couch. Checks sonar. That weird fucker is still out there.

"I don't think I'm supposed to leave anyone behind," he says.

"You won't be," Clarke says.

"Will too. Got him right there in my sights."

She doesn't answer. He turns around and looks at her.

"Fine," she says at last. "*You* go out and get him."

Joel stares at her for a few seconds. *I don't really want to know,* he decides at last.

He turns without another word and blows the tanks. The 'scaphe, suddenly buoyant, strains against the docking clamps. Joel frees it with a tap on his panel. The 'scaphe leaps away from Beebe like something living, wobbles against viscous resistance, and begins climbing.

"You..." From behind him.

Joel turns.

"You really don't know what's going on?" Clarke asks.

"They called me about twelve hours ago. Midnight run to Beebe, they said. When I got to Astoria, they told me to evacuate everyone. They said you'd all be ready and waiting."

Her lips curve up a bit. Not exactly a smile, but probably as close as these psychos ever come. It looks good on her, in a cold, distant sort of way. Get rid of the eyecaps and he could easily see himself putting her into his VR program.

"What happened to everyone else?" he risks.

"Nothing," she says. "We just got—a bit paranoid."

Joel grunts. "Don't blame you. Put me down there for a year, paranoia'd be the least of my problems."

That brief, ghostly smile again.

"But really," he says, pushing it. "Why's everyone staying behind? This some kind of a labor action? One of those"—*what did they used to call them?*—"strike thingies?"

"Something like that." Clarke looks up at the overhead bulkhead. "How long to the surface?"

"A good twenty minutes, I'm afraid. These GA 'scaphes are fucking dirigibles. Everyone else is out there racing with dolphins, and the most I can manage with this thing is a fast wallow. Still"—he tries a disarming grin—"there's an upside. They're paying me by the hour."

"Hooray for you," she says.

Floodlight

It's almost silent again.

Little by little, the voices have stopped screaming. Now they converse among themselves in whispers, discussing things that mean nothing to him. It's okay, though. He's used to being ignored. He's *glad* to be ignored.

You're safe, Gerry. They can't hurt you.

What—Who—

They've all gone. It's just us now.

You—

It's me, Gerry. Shadow. I was wondering when you'd come back.

He shakes his head. The faintest light still leaks over his shoulder. He turns, not so much toward light as toward a subtle lessening of darkness.

She was trying to help you, Gerry. She was only trying to help.

She—

Lenie. You're her guardian angel. Remember?

I'm not sure. I think—

But you left her back there. You ran away.

She wanted—I—Not inside . . .

He feels his legs moving. Water pushes against his face. He moves forward. A soft hole opens in the darkness ahead. He can see shapes inside it.

That's where she lives, Shadow says. Remember?

He creeps back into the light. There were noises before, loud and painful. There was something big and dark, that moved. Now there is only this great ball hanging overhead, like, like,

—like a fist—

He stops, frightened. But everything's quiet, so quiet he can hear faint cries drifting across the seabed. He remembers: There's a hole in the ocean, a little ways from here, that talks to him sometimes. He's never understood what it says.

Go *on*, Shadow urges. She went inside.

She's gone—

You can't tell from out here. You have to get in close.

The underside of the sphere is a cool, shadowy refuge; the equatorial lights can't reach all the way around its convex surface. In the overlapping shadows on the south pole, something shimmers enticingly.

Go *on.*

He pushes off the bottom, glides into the cone of shadow beneath the object. A bright shiny disk a meter across, facing down, wriggles inside a circular rim. He looks up into it.

Something looks back.

Startled, he twists down and away. The disk writhes in the sudden turbulence. He stops, turns back.

A bubble. That's all it is. A pocket of gas, trapped underneath the

—*the airlock.*

That's nothing to be scared of, Shadow tells him. That's how you get in.

Still nervous, he swims back underneath the sphere. The air pocket shines silver in the reflected light. A black wraith moves into view within it, almost featureless except for two empty white spaces where eyes should be. It reaches out to meet his outstretched hand. Two sets of fingertips touch, fuse, disappear. One arm is grafted onto its own reflection at the wrist. Fingers, on the other side of the looking glass, touch metal.

He pulls back his hand, fascinated. The wraith floats overhead, empty and untroubled.

He draws one hand to his face, runs an index finger from one ear to the tip of the jaw. A very long molecule, folded against itself, unzips.

The wraith's smooth black face splits open a few centimeters; what's underneath shows pale gray in the filtered light. He feels the familiar dimpling of his cheek in sudden cold.

He continues the motion, slashing his face from ear to ear. A great smiling gash opens below the wraith's eyespots. Unzipped, a flap of black membrane floats under its chin, anchored at the throat.

There's a pucker in the center of the skinned area. He moves his jaw; the pucker opens.

By now most of his teeth are gone. He's swallowed some, spat others out if they came loose when his face was unsealed. No matter. Most of the things he eats these days are even softer than he is. When the occasional mollusk or echinoderm proves too tough or too large to swallow whole, there are always hands. Thumbs still oppose.

But this is the first time he's actually seen that gaping, toothless ruin where a mouth used to be. He knows this isn't right, somehow.

What happened to me? What am I?

You're Gerry, Shadow says. You're my best friend. You killed me. Remember?

She's gone, Gerry realizes.

It's okay.

I know it is. I know.

You helped her, Gerry. She's safe now. You saved her.

I know. And he remembers something, small and vital, in that last instant before everything turns white as the sun:

—*This is what you do when you really*—

Sunrise

The lifter was still reeling CSS *Forcipiger* up into its belly when the news appeared on the main display. Joel checked it over, frowning, then deliberately looked outside. Gray predawn light was starting to wash out the eastern horizon.

When he looked back again, the information hadn't changed. "Shit. This doesn't make any sense at all."

"What?" Clarke said.

"We're not going back to Astoria. Or I am, but you're getting dropped off over the conshelf somewhere."

"What?" Clarke came forward, stopped just short of the cockpit.

"Says right here. We follow the usual course, but we dip down to zero altitude fifteen klicks offshore. You debark. Then I go on to Astoria."

"What's offshore?"

He checked. "Nothing. Water."

"Maybe a boat? A submarine?" Her voice went oddly dull on the last word.

"Maybe. No mention of it here, though." He grunted. "Maybe you're supposed to swim the rest of the way."

The lifter locked them tight. Tame thunderbolts exploded aft, superheating bladders of gas. The ocean began to fall away.

"So you're just going to dump me in the middle of the ocean," Clarke said coldly.

"It's not my decision."

"Of course not. You're just following orders."

Joel turned around. Her eyes stared back at him like twin snowscapes.

"You don't understand," he told her. "These aren't *orders*. I don't fly the lifter."

"Then what—"

"The pilot's a gel. It's not telling *me* to do anything. It's just bringing us up to speed on what *it's* doing, all on its own."

She didn't say anything for a moment. Then: "Is that the way it's done now? We take orders from machines?"

"Someone must have given the original order. The gel's following it. They haven't taken over yet. And besides," he added, "they're not exactly machines."

"Oh," she said softly. "I feel much better now."

Uncomfortably, Joel turned back to the console. "It is kind of odd, though."

"Really." Clarke didn't seem especially interested.

"Getting this from the gel, I mean. We've got a radio link. Why didn't someone just *tell* us?"

"Because your radio's out," Clarke said distantly.

Surprised, he checked the diagnostics. "No, it's working fine. In fact, I think I'll call in right now and ask what the fuck this is all about. . . ."

Thirty seconds later he turned back to her. "How did you know?"

"Lucky guess." She didn't smile.

"Well the board's green, but I can't raise anyone. We're flying deaf." A doubt tickled the back of his mind. "Unless the gel's got access we don't, for some reason." He linked into the lifter's interface and called up that vehicle's afferent array. "Huh. What was that you said about machines giving the orders?"

That got her attention. "What is it?"

"The lifter got its orders through the Net."

"Isn't that risky? Why doesn't the GA just talk to it direct?"

"Dunno. It's as cut off as we are right now, but the last message came from this node here. Shit; that's another gel."

Clarke leaned forward, managing somehow not to touch him in the crowded space. "How can you tell?"

"The node address. BCC stands for biochemical cognition."

The display beeped twice, loudly.

"What's that?" Clarke said.

Sunlight flooded up from the ocean. It shone deep and violent blue.

"What the *fuck*—"

The cabin filled with computer screams. The altimeter readout flashed crimson and plummeted. *We're falling,* Joel thought, and then, *No, we can't be. No acceleration. The ocean's rising. . . .*

The display was a blizzard of data, swirling by too

fast for human eyes. Somewhere overhead the gel was furiously processing options that might keep them alive. A sudden lurch: Joel grabbed useless submarine controls and hung on for dear life. Out of the corner of his eye he saw Clarke flying back toward the rear bulkhead.

The lifter clawed itself into the sky, lightning crackling along its length. The ocean raced after it, an enormous glowing bulge swelling toward the ventral port. Its murky light brightened as Joel watched; blue intensifying to green, to yellow.

To white.

A hole opened in the Pacific. The sun rose from its center. Joel flung his hands in front of his eyes, saw the bones there silhouetted in orange flesh. The lifter spun like a kicked toy, rammed deep into the sky on a pillar of steam. Outside, the air screamed. The lifter screamed back, skidding.

But it didn't break.

Somehow, after endless seconds, the keel steadied. The readouts were still online; *atmospheric disturbance,* they said, almost eight kilometers away now, bearing one-twenty. Joel looked out the starboard port. Off in the distance, the glowing ocean was ponderously collapsing upon itself. Ring-shaped waves expanded past beneath his feet, racing to the horizon.

Back at the epicenter, cumulus grew into the sky like a soft gray beanstalk. From here, against the darkness, it looked almost peaceful.

"Clarke," he said, "we made it."

He turned in his chair. The rifter was curled into a fetal position against the bulkhead. She didn't move.

"Clarke?"

But it wasn't Clarke that answered him. The lifter's interface was bleating again.

Unregistered contact, it complained.

Bearing 125×87 V1440∆V5.8m•sec⁻² range 13000m

Collision imminent   *12000m*
                                              11000m
                                              10000m

Barely visible through the main viewport, a white cloudy dot caught a high-altitude shaft of morning sunlight. It looked like a contrail, seen head-on.

"Ah shit," Joel said.

Jericho

One whole wall was window. The city spread out beyond like a galactic arm. Patricia Rowan locked the door behind her, sagged against it with sudden fatigue.

Not yet. Not yet. Soon.

She went through her office and turned out all the lights. City glow spilled in through the window, denied her any refuge in darkness.

Patricia Rowan stared back. A tangled grid of metropolitan nerves stretched to the horizon, every synapse incandescent. Her eyes wandered southwest, selected a bearing. She stared until her eyes watered, almost afraid even to blink for fear of missing something.

That was where it would come from.

Oh God. If only there was another way.

It could have worked. The modelers had put even money on pulling this off without so much as a broken window. All those faults and fractures between here and there would work in their favor, firebreaks to keep the tremor from getting this far. Just wait for the right moment: a week, a month. Timing. That's all it would've taken.

Timing, and a calculating slab of meat that followed human rules instead of making up its own.

But she couldn't blame the gel. It simply didn't know any better, according to the systems people; it was just

doing what it thought it was supposed to. And by the
time anybody knew differently—after Scanlon's cryptic
interview with that fucking thing had looped in her head
for the hundredth time, after she'd taken the recording
down to Chem Cog, after their faces had gone puzzled
and confused and then, suddenly, pale and panicky—by
then it had been too late. The window was closed. The
machine was engaged. And a lone GA shuttle, officially
docked securely at Astoria, was somehow showing up
on satcams hovering over the Juan de Fuca Ridge.

She couldn't blame the gel, so she tried to blame CC.
"After all that programming, how could this thing be
working *for* βehemoth? Why didn't you catch it? Even
Scanlon figured it out, for Christ's sake!" But they'd
been too scared for intimidation. *You* gave us the job,
they'd said. *You* didn't tell us what was at stake. You
didn't even really tell us what we were doing. Scanlon
came at this from a whole different angle; who knew the
head cheese had a thing for simple systems? *We* never
taught it that . . .

Her watch chimed softly. "You asked to be informed,
Ms. Rowan. Your family got off okay."

"Thank you," she said, and killed the connection.

A part of her felt guilty for saving them. It hardly
seemed fair that the only ones to escape the holocaust
would be the beloved of one of its architects. But she
was only doing what any mother would. Probably more:
she was staying behind.

That wasn't much. It probably wouldn't even kill her.
The GA's buildings were built with the Big One in mind.
Most of the buildings in this district would probably still
be standing this time tomorrow. Of course, the same
couldn't be said for much of Hongcouver or SeaTac or
Victoria.

Tomorrow, she would help pick up the pieces as best
she could.

Maybe we'll get lucky. Maybe the quake won't be so bad. Who knows, that gel down there might even have chosen tonight anyway. . . .

Please . . .

Patricia Rowan had seen earthquakes before. A strike-slip fault off Peru had rebounded the time she'd been in Lima on the Upwell project; the moment-magnitude of that quake had been close to nine. Every window in the city had exploded.

She actually hadn't had a chance to see much of the damage then. She'd been trapped in her hotel when forty-six stories of glass collapsed onto the streets outside. It was a good hotel, five stars all the way; the ground-level windows, at least, had held. Rowan remembered looking out from the lobby into a murky green glacier of broken glass, seven meters deep, packed tight with blood and wreckage and butchered body parts jammed between piecemeal panes. One brown arm was embedded right next to the lobby window, waving, three meters off the ground. It was missing three fingers and a body. She'd spied the fingers a meter away, pressed floating sausages, but she hadn't been able to tell which of the bodies, if any, would have connected to that shoulder.

She remembered wondering how that arm had got so high off the ground. She remembered vomiting into a wastebasket.

It couldn't happen here, of course. This was N'AmPac; there were standards. Every building in the lower mainland had windows designed to break inward in the event of a quake. It wasn't an ideal solution—especially to those who happened to be inside at the time—but it was the best compromise available. Glass can't get up nearly as much speed in a single room as it can racing down the side of a skyscraper.

Small blessings.

If only there was some other way to sterilize the necessary volume. If only βehemoth didn't, by its very nature, live in unstable areas. If only N'AmPac corpses weren't authorized to use nukes.

If only the vote hadn't been unanimous.

Priorities. Billions of people. Life as we know it.

It was hard, though. The decisions were obvious and correct, tactically, but it had been hard to keep Beebe's crew quarantined down there. It had been hard to decide to sacrifice them. And now that they somehow seemed to be getting out anyway, it was—

Hard? Hard to bring a 9.5 moment-magnitude quake down on the heads of ten million people? Just hard?

There was no word for it.

But she had done it, somehow. The only moral alternative. It was still just murder in small doses, compared to what might be necessary down the—

No. This is being done so nothing will *be necessary down the road.*

Maybe that was why she could bring herself to do it. Or maybe, somehow, reality had finally trickled down from her brain to her gut, inspired it to take the necessary steps. Certainly, *something* had hit her down there.

I wonder what Scanlon would say. It was too late to ask him now. She'd never told him, of course. She'd never even been tempted. To tell him that they knew, that his secret was out, that once again he just didn't matter that much—somehow, that would have been worse than killing him. She'd had no desire to hurt the poor man.

Her watch chimed again. "Override," it said.

Oh God. Oh God.

It had started, out there beyond the lights, under three black kilometers of seawater. Those crazy kamikaze gels, interrupted in the midst of their endless imaginary games: *Forget that shit. Time to blow.*

And perhaps, confused, they were saying, *Not now, it's the wrong time, the damage.* But it didn't matter anymore. Another computer—a stupid one this time, inorganic and programmable and completely trustworthy—would send the requisite sequence of numbers and the gels would be right out of the loop, no matter what they thought.

Or maybe they just saluted and stood aside. Maybe they didn't care. Who knew what those monsters thought anymore?

"Detonation," said the watch.

The city went dark.

The abyss rushed in, black and hungry. One isolated cluster sparkled defiantly in the sudden void; a hospital perhaps, running on batteries. A few private vehicles, self-powered antiques, staggered like fireflies along streets gone suddenly blind. The Rapitrans Grid was still glowing too, more faintly than usual.

Rowan checked her watch; only an hour since the decision. Only an hour since their hand had been forced. Somehow it seemed a lot longer.

"Tactical feed from Seismic Thirty-one" she said. "Descramble."

Her eyes filled with information. A false-color map snapped into focus in the air before her, a scarred ocean floor laid bare and stretched vertically. One of those scars was shuddering.

Beyond the virtual display, beyond the window, a section of cityscape flickered weakly alight. Farther north, another sector began to shine. Rowan's minions were frantically rerouting power from Gorda and Mendocino, from equatorial sunfarms, from a thousand small dams scattered throughout the Cordillera. It would take time, though. More than they had.

Perhaps we should have warned them. Even an hour's advance notice would have been something. Not enough time for evac, of course, but maybe enough time to take the china off the shelves. Enough time to line up some extra backups, for all the good they'd do. Lots of time for the entire coast to panic if the word got out. Which was why not even her own family had had any idea of the reason behind their sudden surprise trip to the East Coast.

The sea floor rippled in Rowan's eyes, as though made of rubber. Floating just above it, a translucent plane representing the ocean's surface was shedding rings. The two shock waves raced each other across the display, the seabed tremor in the lead. It bore down on the Cascadia Subduction Zone, crashed into it, sent weaker tremors shivering off along the fault at right angles. It seemed to hesitate there for a moment, and Rowan almost dared to hope that the Zone had firewalled it.

But now the Zone itself began to slide, slow, ponderous, almost indiscernible at first. Way down in the moho, five-hundred-year-old fingernails began tearing painfully free. Five centuries of pent-up tension, slumping.

Next stop, Vancouver Island.

Something unthinkable was rebounding along the Strait of Juan de Fuca. Kelp harvesters and supertankers would be sensing impossible changes in the depth of the water column below them. If there were humans on board, they'd have a few moments to reflect on how utterly useless a ninety-second warning can be.

It was more than the Strip got.

The tactical display didn't show any of the details, of course. It showed a brown ripple sweeping across coastal bedrock and moving inland. It showed a white arc gliding in behind, at sea level. It didn't show the ocean rearing up offshore like a range of foothills. It didn't show sea level turning on edge. It didn't show a thirty-meter wall of ocean smashing five million refugees into jelly.

Rowan saw it all anyway.

She blinked three times, eyes stinging. Obediently, the display vanished. In the distance the red pinpoints of ambulance and police lights were flashing here and there across the comatose grid; whether in response to alarms already sounded or merely pending, she didn't know. Distance and soundproofing blocked any siren song. Very gently, the floor began to rock.

It was almost a lullaby at first, back and forth, building gradually to a swaying crescendo that nearly threw her off her feet. The structure complained on all sides, concrete growling against girder, more felt than heard. She spread her arms, balancing, embracing space. She couldn't bring herself to cry.

The great window burst outward in a million tinkling fragments and showered itself into the night. The air filled with glass spores and the sound of windchimes.

There was no glass on the carpet.

Oh Christ, she realized dully. *The contractors fucked up. All that money spent on imploding anti-earthquake glass, and the stupid bastards put it in backward. . . .*

Off to the southwest, a small orange sun was rising. Patricia Rowan sagged to her knees on the pristine carpet. Suddenly, at last, her eyes were stinging. She let the tears come, profoundly grateful: *Still human,* she told herself. *I'm still human.*

The wind washed over her. It carried the faint sounds of people and machinery, screaming.

Detritus

The ocean is green. Lenie Clarke doesn't know how long she's been unconscious, but they can't have sunk more than a hundred meters. The ocean is still green.

Forcipiger falls slowly through the water, nose-down,

its atmosphere bleeding away through a dozen small wounds. A crack the shape of a lightning bolt runs across the forward viewport; Clarke can barely see it through the water rising in the cockpit. The forward end of the 'scaphe has become the bottom of a well. Clarke braces her feet against the back of a passenger seat and leans against a vertical deck. The ceiling lightstrip flickers in front of her. She's managed to get the pilot up out of the water and strapped into another seat. At least one of his legs is definitely broken. He hangs there like a soaked marionette, still unconscious. He continues to breathe. She doesn't know whether he'll actually wake up again.

May be better if he doesn't, she reflects, and giggles.

That wasn't very funny, she tells herself, and giggles again.

Oh shit. I'm looped.

She tries to concentrate. She can focus on isolated things: A single rivet in front of her. The sound of metal, creaking. But they take up all her attention, somehow. Whatever she happens to be looking at swells up and fills her world. She can barely think of anything else.

Hundred meters, she manages at last. *Hull breach. Pressure—up—*

Nitrogen—

—narcosis—

She bends down to check the atmosphere controls on the wall. They're sideways. She finds this vaguely amusing, but she doesn't know why. Anyhow, they don't seem to work.

She bends down to an access panel, slips, bounces painfully down into the cockpit with a splash. Occasional readouts twinkle on the submerged panels. They're pretty, but the longer she looks at them, the more her chest hurts. Eventually she makes the connection, pulls her head back up into atmosphere.

The access panel is right in front of her. She fumbles at it a couple of times, gets it open. Hydrox tanks lie side by side in military formation, linked together into some sort of cascade system. There's a big yellow handle at one end. She pulls at it. It gives, unexpectedly. Clarke loses her balance and slides back underwater.

There's a ventilator duct right in front of her face. She's not sure, but she thinks the last time she was down here it didn't have all these bubbles coming out of it. She thinks that's a good sign. She decides to stay here for a while, and watch the bubbles. Something's bothering her, though. Something in her chest.

Oh, that's right. She keeps forgetting. She can't breathe.

Somehow she gets her face seal zipped up. The last thing she remembers is her lung shriveling away, and water rushing through her chest.

The next time she comes up, two-thirds of the cockpit is flooded. She rises into the aft compartment, peels the 'skin off her face. Water drains from the left side of her chest; atmosphere fills the right.

Overhead, the pilot is moaning.

She climbs up to him, swings his seat around so that he's lying on his back, facing the rear bulkhead. She locks it into position, tries to keep his broken leg reasonably straight.

"*Ow,*" he cries.

"Sorry. Try not to move. Your leg's broken."

"No shit. *Oww.*" He shivers. "Christ, I'm cold." Clarke sees it sink in. "Oh Christ. We're breached." He tries to move, manages to twist his head around before some other injury twists back. He relaxes, wincing.

"The cockpit's flooding," she tells him. "Slowly, so far. Hang on a second." She climbs back down and pulls

at the edge of the cockpit hatch. It sticks. Clarke keeps
pulling. The hatch comes loose, starts to swing down.

"Wait a second," the pilot says.

Clarke pushes the hatch back against the bulkhead.

"You know those controls?" the pilot asks.

"I know the standard layout."

"Anything still working down there? Comm? Propulsion?"

She kneels down and ducks her head underwater. A
couple of readouts that were alive before have gone out.
She scans what's left.

"Waldos. Exterior floods. Sonobuoy," she reports
when she comes back up. "Everything else is dead."

"Shit." His voice is shaking. "Well, we can send up
the buoy, anyway. Not that they're about to launch a
rescue."

She reaches through the rising water and trips the control. Something thuds softly on the outside of the hull.
"Why wouldn't they? They sent you to pick us up. If
we'd just gotten away before the thing went off—"

"We did," the pilot says.

Clarke looks around the compartment. "Uh . . ."

The pilot snorts. "Look, I don't know what the fuck
you guys were doing with a nuke down there, or why
you couldn't wait a bit longer to set it off, but we got
away from it, okay? Something shot us down afterward."

Clarke straightens. "Shot us?"

"A missile. Air-to-air. Came right out of the stratosphere." His voice is shaking with the cold. "I don't
think it actually hit the 'scaphe. Blew the shit out of the
lifter, though. We barely got down to decent altitude
before it—"

"But that doesn't—Why rescue us, then shoot us
down?"

He doesn't say anything. His breathing is fast and
loud.

Clarke pulls again at the cockpit hatch. It swings down against the opening with a slight creak.

"That doesn't sound good," the pilot remarks.

"Hang on a sec." Clarke spins the wheel; the hatch sinks down against the mimetic seal with a sigh. "I think I've got it." She climbs back up to the rear bulkhead.

"*Christ*, I'm cold," the pilot says. He looks at her. "Oh shit. How far down are we?"

Clarke looks through one of the compartment's tiny portholes. Green is fading. Blue is in ascension.

"Hundred-fifty meters. Maybe two."

"I should be narked."

"I switched the mix. We're on hydrox."

The pilot shudders, violently. "Look, Clarke, I'm freezing. One of those lockers has got survival suits."

She finds them, unrolls one. The pilot is trying to unhook himself from the seat, without success. She tries to help.

"*Ow!*"

"Your other leg's injured too. Maybe just a sprain."

"*Shit!* I'm coming apart and you just stuffed me up here? Didn't the GA even get you medtech training, for Christ's sake?"

She backs away: one awkward step to the back of the next passenger seat. It doesn't seem like a good time to admit that she was narked when she put him there.

"Look, I'm sorry," he says after a moment. "It's just— This is not a great situation, you know? Could you just unzip that suit, and spread it over me?"

She does.

"That's better." He's still shivering, though. "I'm Joel."

"I'm CI—Lenie," she replies.

"So, Lenie. We're on our own, our systems are all out, and we're headed for the bottom. Any suggestions?"

She can't think of any.

"Okay. Okay." Joel takes a few deep breaths. "How much hydrox do we have?"

She climbs down and checks the gauge on the cascade. "Sixteen thousand. What's our volume?"

"Not much." He frowns, acting as though he's only trying to concentrate. "You said two hundred meters, that puts us at, lessee, twenty atmospheres when you sealed the hatch. Should keep us going for a hundred minutes or so." He tries a laugh; it doesn't come off. "If they *are* sending a rescue, they'd better do it pretty fucking fast."

She plays along. "It could be worse. How long would it last if we hadn't sealed the hatch until, say, a thousand meters?"

Shaking. "Ooh . . . Twenty minutes. And the bottom's close to four thousand around here, and that far down it'd last, say it'd last, five minutes, tops." He gulps air. "Hundred and eight minutes isn't so bad. A lot can happen in a hundred and eight minutes. . . ."

"I wonder if they got away," Clarke whispers.

"What did you say?"

"There were others. My—friends." She shakes her head. "They were going to swim back."

"To the mainland? That's insane!"

"No. It could work, if only they got far enough before—"

"When did they leave?" Joel asks.

"About eight hours before you arrived."

Joel says nothing.

"They *could* have made it," Lenie insists, hating him for his silence.

"Lenie, at that range—I don't think so."

"It's *possible*. You can't just—Oh no . . ."

"What?" Joel twists in his harness, tries to see what she's looking at. *"What?"*

A meter and a half below Lenie Clarke's feet, a needle

of seawater shoots up from the edge of the cockpit hatch. Two more erupt as she watches.

Beyond the porthole, the sea has turned deep blue.

The ocean squeezes into *Forcipiger*, bullies the atmosphere into tighter and tighter corners. It never lets up.

Blue is fading. Soon, black will be all that's left.

Lenie Clarke can see Joel's eye on the hatch. Not the leaky traitor that let the enemy in past the cockpit; that's under almost two meters of icewater now. No, Joel's watching the ventral docking hatch that once opened and closed on Beebe Station. It sits embedded in the deck-turned-wall, integrity uncompromised, the water just beginning to lap at its lower edge. And Lenie Clarke knows exactly what Joel is thinking, because she's thinking it too.

"Lenie," he says.

"Right here."

"You ever try to kill yourself?"

She smiles. "Sure. Hasn't everyone?"

"Didn't work, though."

"Apparently not," Clarke concurs.

"What happened?" Joel asks. He's shivering again, the water's almost up to him, but other than that his voice seems calm.

"Not much. I was eleven. Plastered a bunch of derms all over my body. Passed out. Woke up in an MA ward."

"Shit. One step up from refmed."

"Yeah, well, we aren't all rich. Besides, it wasn't that bad. They even had counselors on staff. I saw one myself."

"Yeah?" His voice is starting to shake again. "What'd she say?"

"He. He told me the world was full of people who needed him a lot more than I did, and next time I wanted attention maybe I could do it in some way that didn't cost the taxpayer."

"Sh-shit. What an as-asshole." Joel's got the shakes again.

"Not really. He was right. And I never tried it again, so it must've worked." Clarke slips into the water. "I'm going to change the mix. You look like you're starting to spaz again."

"Len—"

But she's gone before he can finish.

She slips down to the bottom of the compartment, tweaks the valves she finds there. High pressure turns oxygen to poison; the deeper they go, the less of it air-breathers can tolerate without going into convulsions. This is the second time she's had to lean out the mixture. By now, she and Joel are only breathing one-percent O_2.

If he lives long enough, though, there'll be other things she can't control. Joel isn't equipped with rifter neuroinhibitors.

She has to go up and face him again. She's holding her breath, there's no point in switching on her electro-lyzer for a measly twenty or thirty seconds. She's tempted to do it anyway, tempted to just stay down here. He can't ask her as long as she stays down here. She's safe.

But of all the things she's been in her life, she's never had to admit to being a coward.

She surfaces. Joel's still staring at the hatch. He opens his mouth to speak.

"Hey, Joel," she says quickly, "you sure you don't want me to switch over? It really doesn't make sense for me to use your air when I don't have to."

He shakes his head. "I don't want to spend my last few minutes alive listening to a machine voice, Lenie. Please. Just—stay with me."

She looks away from him, and nods.

"Fuck, Lenie," he says. "I'm so *scared*."

"I know," she says softly.

"This waiting, it's just—God, Lenie, you wouldn't put a dog through this. Please."

She closes her eyes, waiting.

"Pop the hatch, Lenie."

She shakes her head. "Joel, I couldn't even kill *myself*. Not when I was eleven. Not—not even last night. How can I—"

"My legs are wrecked, Len. I can't feel anything else anymore. I c-can barely even talk. Please."

"Why did they do this to us, Joel? What's going on?"

He doesn't answer.

"What has them so scared? Why are they so—"

He moves.

He lurches up, falls sideways. His arms reach out; one hand catches the edge of the hatch. The other catches the wheel in its center.

His legs twist grotesquely underneath him. He doesn't seem to notice.

"I'm sorry," she whispers. "I couldn't—"

He fumbles, gets both hands on the wheel. "No problem."

"Oh God. Joel—"

He stares at the hatch. His fingers clench the wheel.

"You know something, Lenie Clarke?" There's cold in his voice, and fear, but there's a sudden hard determination there, too.

She shakes her head. *I don't know anything*.

"I would have really liked to fuck you," he says.

She doesn't know what to say to that.

He spins the hatch. Pulls the lever.

The hatch falls into *Forcipiger*. The ocean falls after it. Somehow, Lenie Clarke's body has prepared itself when she wasn't looking.

His body jams back into hers. He might be struggling.

Or it could just be the rush of the Pacific, playing with him. She doesn't know if he's alive or dead. But she holds on to him, blindly, the ocean spinning them around, until there isn't any doubt.

Its atmosphere gone, *Forcipiger* is accelerating. Lenie Clarke takes Joel's body by the hands, and draws it out through the hatch. It follows her into viscous space. The 'scaphe spins away below them, fading in moments.

With a gentle push, she sets the body free. It begins to drift slowly toward the surface. She watches it go.

Something touches her from behind. She can barely feel it through her 'skin.

She turns.

A slender, translucent tentacle wraps softly around her wrist. It fades away into a distance utterly black to most, slate-gray to Lenie Clarke. She brings it to her. Its swollen tip fires sticky threads at her fingers.

She brushes it aside, follows the tentacle back through the water. She encounters other tentacles on the way, feeble, attenuate things, barely twitching against the currents. They all lead back to something long, and thick, and shadowy. She circles in.

A great column of writhing, wormlike stomachs, pulsing with faint bioluminescence.

Revolted, she smashes at it with one clenched fist. It reacts immediately, sheds squirming pieces of itself that flare and burn like fat fireflies. The central column goes instantly dark, pulling into itself. It pulses, descends in spurts, slinking away under cover of its own discarded flesh. Clarke ignores the sacrificial tidbits and pursues the main body. She hits it again. Again. The water fills with pulsing dismembered decoys. She ignores them all, keeps tearing at the central column. She doesn't stop until there's nothing left but swirling fragments.

Joel. Joel Kita. She realizes that she liked him. She barely knew him, but she liked him just the same.

And they just killed him.

They killed all of us, she thinks. *Deliberately. They meant to. They didn't even tell us why.*

It's all their fault. All of it.

Something ignites in Lenie Clarke. Everyone who's ever hit her, or raped her, or patted her on the head and said *don't worry, everything will be fine* comes to her in that moment. Everyone who ever pretended to be her friend. Everyone who pretended to be her lover. Everyone who ever used her, and stood on her back, and told each other they were so much better than she was. Everyone, feeding off her every time they so much as turned on the fucking lights.

They're all waiting, back onshore. They're just *asking* for it.

So much anger in here. So much hate.

So much to take out on someone.

This time it's going to count. She's adrift in the middle of the Pacific Ocean, three hundred kilometers from land. She's alone. She has nothing to eat. It doesn't matter. None of it matters. She's alive; that alone gives her the upper hand.

Karl Acton's greatest fear has come to pass. Lenie Clarke has been activated.

She doesn't know why the GA is so terrified of her. She only knows that they've stopped at nothing to keep her from getting back to the mainland. With any luck, they think they've succeeded. With any luck, they're not worried anymore.

That'll change. Lenie Clarke swims down and east, toward her own resurrection.

ACKNOWLEDGMENTS

I put all these words together myself. However, I shame-lessly exploited anyone I could to put them together *properly*.

At the start:

Starfish began as a short story. Barbara MacGregor and Nancy Butler, formerly of the University of British Columbia, critiqued early drafts of that manuscript. Once it had achieved novel status, Jena Snyder poked ruthless and valuable editorial holes along it length.

At the end:

David Hartwell bought the manuscript; he and Jim Minz edited it. Of course they have my gratitude, but I hope their reward extends beyond such cheap verbiage; I hope *Starfish* sells well and makes all of us lots of money. (The copy you're holding is a start. Why not pick up others and hand them out to Jehovah's Witnesses at street corners?)

In between:

Glenn Grant took it upon himself to approach David Hartwell on my behalf when I was too chickenshit to do it myself. Major David Buck of the New Zealand Army gave me the benefit of his expertise on explosives, nu-clear and otherwise. I was a bit disturbed to learn just how much thought some people have put into the effects of nuclear explosions on the seabed.

When I wanted to check out the geology of spreading and earthquake zones, I posted a question to a couple of geological Usenet groups in lieu of actual research. This netted me a lot of advice from people I've never met and probably never will: Ellin Beltz, Hayden Chasteen, Joe Davis, Keith Morrison, and Carl Schaefer gave me pointers and references on vulcanism, plate tectonics, and (in one case) the length of time it would take a nuclear submarine to get shot zitlike from the mouth of an active volcano after being swallowed into a deep-sea subduction zone. John Stockwell of the Center for Wave Phenomena (Colorado School of Mines) was especially forthcoming, sharing formulae and tables that described earthquakes in nice, graspable, "Hiroshima equivalents." I'm tempted to never do my own research again.

I'm also tempted to blame all these nice people for any technical mistakes you find in the preceding document, but of course, I can't. It's my book. They're my mistakes, too.

The music of Jethro Tull provided ongoing inspiration, not only during the writing of this novel, but throughout the interminable years of sufferance in academia which led to it. Also, if you want a sort of moodsetting *Starfish* theme song, play Sarah MacLachlans' "Possession" in a dark room, with the volume cranked. (I would have quoted it in the book, but I never got around to asking after the rights.)

Actually, you might be surprised at how much of this stuff I *didn't* make up. If you're interested in finding out about background details, the following references will get you started. *Starfish* deliberately twists some of the facts, and I've probably made a hundred other errors through sheer ignorance, but that's something else this list is good for: it gives you the chance to check up on me.

Deepwater Biology

The deep-sea creatures I described pretty much as they exist; if you don't believe me read "Light in the Ocean's Midwaters" by B. H. Robison, in the July 1995 *Scientific American.* Or *Deep-Sea Biology* by J. D. Gage and P. A. Taylor (Cambridge University Press, 1992). Or *Abyss* by C. P. Idyll (Crowell Company, 1971); it's old, but it's the book that hooked me back in grade 9. Although the fish we drag up from great depths are generally pretty small in real life, gigantism is not unheard-of among some species of deepwater fish. Back in the 1930s, for example, the deepwater pioneer William Beebe claimed to have spotted a seven-foot sea dragon from a bathysphere.

I found lots of interesting stuff in *The Sea—Ideas and Observations on Progress in the Study of the Seas Volume 7: Deep-Sea Biology* (G. T. Rowe, ed.; 1983 from John Wiley and Sons). In particular, the chapter on biochemical and physiological adaptations of deep-sea animals (by Somero *et al.*)—as well as *Biochemical*

Adaptation, a 1983 book from Princeton University Press (Hochachka and Somero, eds.)—got me started on deep-sea physiology, the effects of high pressure on neuronal firing thresholds, and the adaptation of enzymes to high pressure/temperature regimes.

Spreading-Zone Tectonics/Geology

A good layperson's introduction to the coastal geology of the Pacific Northwest, including a discussion of mid-ocean ridges such as Juan de Fuca, can be found in *Cycles of Rock and Water* by K. A. Brown (1993, HarperCollins West). "The Quantum Event of Oceanic Crustal Accretion: Impacts of Diking at Mid-Ocean Ridges" (J. R. Delaney et al., *Science* 281, pp. 222–230, 1998) nicely conveys the nastiness and frequency of earthquakes and eruptions along the Juan de Fuca Ridge, although it's a bit heavy on the technobabble.

The idea that the Pacific Northwest is overdue for a major earthquake is reviewed in "Giant Earthquakes of the Pacific Northwest" by R. D. Hyndman (*Scientific American*, December 1995). "Forearc Deformation and Great Subduction Earthquakes: Implications for Cascadia Offshore Earthquake Potential" by McCaffrey and Goldfinger (*Science,* v267, 1995) and "Earthquakes cannot be predicted" (Geller et al., *Science* v275, 1997) discuss the issue in somewhat greater detail. I used to live quite happily in Vancouver. After reading these items, I moved to Toronto.

The absolute coolest source for up-to-the-minute information on hydrothermal vents, however, is the National Oceanic and Atmospheric Administration's (NOAA's) Web pages. Everything's there: raw survey data, research schedules, live maps, three-dimensional seaquake animations, and recent publications. To name but a few. Start at *http://www.pmel.noaa.gov/vents* and go from there.

Psionics/Ganzfeld Effects

The rudimentary telepathy I describe actually made it into the peer-reviewed technical literature back in 1994. Check out "Does Psi Exist? Replicable Evidence for an Anomalous Process of Information Transfer" by Bem and Honorton, pages 4–18 in volume 15 of the *Psychological Bulletin.* They got statistical significance and everything. Speculations on the quantum nature of human consciousness come from the books of Roger Penrose, *The Emperor's New Mind* (Oxford University Press, 1989) and *Shadows of the Mind* (Oxford, 1994).

Smart Gels

The smart gels that screw everything up were inspired by the research of Masuo Aizawa, a professor at the Tokyo Institute of Technology, profiled in the August 1992 issue of *Discover* magazine. At that time, he'd got a few neurons hooked together into the precursors of simple logic gates. I shudder to think where he's got to now.

The application of neural nets to navigating through complex terrain is described in "Robocar" by B. Daviss (*Discover*, July 1992), which describes work being done by Charles Thorpe of (where else?) Carnegie-Mellon University.

βehemoth

The theory that life originated in hydrothermal vents hails from "A Hydrothermally Precipitated Catalytic Iron Sulphide Membrane as a First Step Towards Life" by M. J. Russel et al. (*Journal of Molecular Evolution*, v39, 1994). Throwaway bits on the evolution of life, including the viability of pyranosal RNA as an alternative genetic template, I cadged from "The origin of life on earth" by L. E. Orgel (*Scientific American*, October 1994). βehemoth's symbiotic presence within the cells of deepwater fish steals from the work of Lynn Margulis, who first suggested that cellular organelles were once free-living organisms in their own right (an idea that went from heresy to canon in the space of about ten years). Once I'd stuck that idea into the book, I found vindication in "Parasites Shed Light on Cellular Evolution" (G. Vogel, *Science* 275, p 1422, 1997) and "Thanks to a Parasite, Asexual Reproduction Catches On" (M. Enserinck, *Science* 275, p. 1743, 1997).

Sexual Abuse as an Addictive Stimulus

I first encountered the idea that chronic abuse could be physiologically addictive in *Psychological Trauma* (B. van der Kolk, ed., American Psychiatric Press, 1987). False Memory syndrome is explored in *The Myth of Repressed Memory: False Memories and Allegations of Sexual Abuse* by E. Loftus and K. Ketcham (St. Martin's Press, 1996).

TOR
BOOKS The Best in Science Fiction

LIEGE-KILLER • Christopher Hinz
"*Liege-Killer* is a genuine page-turner, beautifully written and exciting from start to finish....Don't miss it."—*Locus*

HARVEST OF STARS • Poul Anderson
"A true masterpiece. An important work—not just of science fiction but of contemporary literature. Visionary and beautifully written, elegaic and transcendent, *Harvest of Stars* is the brightest star in Poul Anderson's constellation."
—Keith Ferrell, editor, *Omni*

FIREDANCE • Steven Barnes
SF adventure in 21st century California—by the co-author of *Beowulf's Children*.

ASH OCK • Christopher Hinz
"A well-handled science fiction thriller."—*Kirkus Reviews*

CALDÉ OF THE LONG SUN • Gene Wolfe
The third volume in the critically-acclaimed Book of the Long Sun.
"Dazzling."—*The New York Times*

OF TANGIBLE GHOSTS • L.E. Modesitt, Jr.
Ingenious alternate universe SF from the author of the *Recluce* fantasy series.

THE SHATTERED SPHERE • Roger MacBride Allen
The second book of the Hunted Earth continues the thrilling story that began in *The Ring of Charon*, a daringly original hard science fiction novel.

THE PRICE OF THE STARS • Debra Doyle and James D. Macdonald
Book One of the Mageworlds—the breakneck SF epic of the most brawling family in the human galaxy!